PRAISE FOR

Belladonna

"A deliciously deadly Gothic romance."

—Stephanie Garber, #1 *New York Times* bestselling author of *Once Upon a Broken Heart*

"Decadently atmospheric."

—Kerri Maniscalco, #1 *New York Times* bestselling author of the Kingdom of the Wicked series

"The kind of wicked fairy tale I've loved for most of my life. Grace's world is vivid and sexy."

—Renée Ahdieh, #1 *New York Times* bestselling author of *The Wrath & the Dawn*

"A perfect, addicting escape."

—Adrienne Young, *New York Times* bestselling author of *Fable*

"A Gothic-infused masterpiece sure to become YA's new obsession. Utterly original and completely addictive, *Belladonna* is a fantasy to die for."

—Rachel Griffin, *New York Times* bestselling author of *The Nature of Witches*

"This book is a true pleasure to read from beginning to end."

—Jennifer L. Armentrout, *New York Times* bestselling author of *From Blood & Ash*

"With... an absolutely spellbinding mix of mystery and romance, this is YA fantasy at its finest."

—Jessica Olson, author of *A Forgery of Roses*

"Equal parts sensuous and sinister."

—Astrid Scholte, author of *Four Dead Queens*

WIST

ERIA

ADALYN GRACE

LITTLE, BROWN AND COMPANY
New York Boston

Little, Brown and Company
Hachette Book Group
1290 Avenue of the Americas, New York, NY 10104
Visit us at LBYR.com

Originally published in hardcover and ebook by Little, Brown and Company in August 2024
First Trade Paperback Edition: July 2025

The Library of Congress has cataloged the hardcover edition as follows:
Names: Grace, Adalyn, author.
Title: Wisteria / Adalyn Grace.
Description: First edition. | New York : Little, Brown and Company, 2024. | Series: Belladonna ; 3 | Audience: Ages 14 and up. | Summary: "When headstrong Blythe Hawthorne finds herself bound to the insufferable deity Fate, she begins to uncover the truth about their connection and her own astonishing powers." —Provided by publisher.
Identifiers: LCCN 2024006440 | ISBN 9780316569385 (hardcover) | ISBN 9780316569415 (ebook)
Subjects: CYAC: Magic—Fiction. | Ability—Fiction. | Fate and fatalism—Fiction. | Fantasy. | LCGFT: Fantasy fiction. | Novels.
Classification: LCC PZ7.1.G6993 Wi 2024 | DDC [Fic]—dc23
LC record available at https://lccn.loc.gov/2024006440

ISBNs: 978-0-316-56939-2 (trade paperback), 978-0-316-56941-5 (ebook)

Printed in New Jersey, USA

CCR, 07/25

10 9 8 7 6 5 4 3

I started this book by the fireside on a rainy day with one of my best friends working beside me. This book is for her—for her friendship, her soup, and for being one of the best and kindest humans I'm lucky enough to know.

PROLOGUE

On the morning of her impending death, Life lounged beneath a wisteria tree.

Her magic had shaped the branches, twisting them into a canopy to shield her from the sun while she curled her feet in the grass, its dampness slick between her toes. Beside her, Fate was hunched over his latest work in progress. Life followed every twitch and pull of his deft fingers as they wove a lifetime into a tapestry. There was a glimmer in his eyes as he worked, one that Life wished to forever commit to memory.

Because soon Death would arrive to take all that she was. And once he came, there was no knowing what pieces of herself might be left. She could only hope to remember that Fate tended to bounce ever so slightly when he was particularly pleased with one of his creations, and that he had a dimple on his right cheek that looked as though someone had carved the tip of their fingernail into his flesh, forever marking him with a mischievous crescent moon. She hoped she remembered the way all the light in the world seemed to pool toward him at any given moment, and how he would bask in it. Whether it was midafternoon or an hour when only the crickets sang, her husband was radiant.

Life hoped that she would remember his hands, too. Not just how clever they were—as precise with an instrument or a paintbrush as they were with thread and needle—but how they melded against her body. She had no awareness of how she came to exist, and often wondered whether she'd been one of Fate's sculptures magicked to life, for it was his hands alone that knew her every contour. Every touch between them was familiar, instinctual.

"Enjoying the view?" Fate didn't need to peer behind him to know that Life was spying, no less struck by his beauty now than the day she'd first laid eyes on him. Fate was her summer sun—too intense for most to bear, while she tipped toward him like a flower, craving his touch.

Life shifted to her knees, wrapping her arms around Fate's neck as she looked over his shoulder at the tapestry.

Red. There was always so much red.

She'd known Fate long enough to understand why—red symbolized passion, and there was nothing he loved more. Fate's favorite stories were always rife with the color, telling tales of those who would give up their very soul to have whatever it was they most yearned for. He was never choosy with what that passion was. It could be art, literature, invention, romance, cooking, gardening.... If there was passion to be found, Fate would weave the most glorious stories out of it. For he, too, was a man of great passion.

Fate's hunger for the world and all its treasures was the very trait that Life loved most about him. Yet while there wasn't anything inherently *wrong* with passion, Life had long since found that people too frequently lost themselves within it. Fate was no exception; too many times she'd found him hunched like a wolf before its feast, a bloodied maw replaced by unblinking, ravenous eyes as he crafted his tales.

Passion made people forget themselves. It kept them from feeling the change of seasons upon their skin or curling their toes into the grass. Passion stole their health. It made both time and families slip away as people lost themselves to their pursuits.

If Life had her way, she'd weave more blue into those tapestries. Red might have made for the most entertaining stories, but it was the calm of blue that made the happiest ones. And so Life slid her hand down her husband's arm, savoring the warmth of his skin as she whispered, "I know it's hard for you, but do remember to be kind."

His hand stilled midstitch, and Fate sighed at the familiar argument as he set his work on the grass. He stared at it for a long while, fingers twitching as he fought the urge to pick the tapestry back up. It took him longer than it should have to turn toward Life, capturing her by the waist and drawing her into his lap. "I'm kind to you. Is that not enough?"

Life slipped her fingers through the silk of his golden hair, wishing it could be the two of them here forever, rooted beneath the wisteria. She would sustain herself on his lips and would make her home within his voice, never tiring of his touch.

"I am not the only one in this world who matters, my love."

Fate's fingers curled against her waist. "You are to me."

Even knowing that this argument was futile, she should have pressed harder. Instead, the tension in her body eased as Fate laid her upon the grass. His weight was the most comforting warmth as he lowered himself onto her. His lips drew a path from her jaw to her collarbone, and Life angled her head back, eyes fluttering shut as she lingered on each sensation. She wanted to wrap his love around her. To bury herself in it. But as quickly as Fate was atop her, he was off again when someone cleared their throat from the opposite side of the wisteria.

"You're fighting a losing battle," Death said, his shadows slipping around the tree's roots, stretching along them until he stood before her. "You know it's not in Fate's nature to be kind." His voice was laced with an edge of sorrow that raised the hair on her arms. Life sneaked a sideways glance at Fate, wondering if her husband noticed.

"The next time you visit, do me a favor and bring a bell that I may fasten upon your shawl" was all Fate grumbled as he smoothed a hand over his shirt to readjust himself.

The tension in Life's chest eased. Perhaps it was cruel of her, but she was glad that Fate didn't know this was to be their final night together. He would only argue, demanding his brother save her when all Life wished was for her final hours to be spent with the sun's warmth against her skin and Fate as her companion.

Just as it was not in his nature to be kind, it wasn't in Fate's nature to understand why she needed to die. He wouldn't understand that, although she spent each morning fighting the deep lines in her skin to appear as youthful as the day they'd met, her bones had grown weary. She no longer had the energy to journey with him to remote villages or bustling cities to check in on his favorite creations and sample their art. She could no longer travel the world just to taste the finest food or the richest wine, and though Fate had promised her that he was happy, she knew he yearned for everything she'd kept him from these past several years. Age had fatigued her, stripping away all pretenses and desires so that nothing in the world sounded nicer than feeling the pulse of the earth against her skin as she rested beneath her favorite tree with her favorite people.

Life had given up on fighting the inevitable. There could be no life without the experience of death, so what choice did she have but to let herself finally succumb?

Death presented his charges with three options once he claimed their life. The first was the least favorable: A soul could choose to remain on earth, stuck where they died until they were ready for the second option, which was to move into the Afterlife. The third choice he presented them with was reincarnation, which was Life's only option. Her soul would come back in a new vessel, and so long as she existed in some capacity, souls would continue to be made.

Life had long accepted a future where she would leave her body behind and come back anew. Though she'd never tell her husband, she was excited to discover what awaited her and to try out a new form as it journeyed through every stage of life. The only thing that frightened her was her memories, for while Death believed they could find a way for her to keep them, there was no guarantee.

"You know little of my nature these days," Fate told his brother.

"I've hardly seen you the past year. For all you know, I could be a changed man."

Life said nothing as the shadows melted from Death's skin, knowing full well the reason for his absence. Death could barely look at her without his emotion seeping through. Life had known she would die this year; she'd asked only that he wait until autumn so that she could enjoy the summer sun one last time. For who knew whether it would feel different in her next body? Perhaps the next one would prefer winter. Perhaps, in the future, she would hate to be warm.

"I'm glad to see you," Life whispered at last, standing to greet her brother by marriage.

"I wish you weren't." Death's whisper was a winter storm. "We don't have long. You need to tell him now, Mila, or I will."

Beside her, Fate went rigid. "Tell me what?"

Life turned to her husband, whose eyes dawned with an understanding that burned her soul. "I had hoped for one more night with you, my love, but it seems we do not have that luxury."

"No," he whispered, stepping forward to grab Life's hand. He wound his fingers through hers before she could peel back, his eyes twin flames that festered with a rage she could not turn from.

"No," Fate repeated, this time directed at his brother. "She's not going anywhere."

Only then did Death lift his eyes. "I have no say in where I am called, brother. As you cannot control your charges, neither can I." His whisper was as gentle as morning dew; never had Life heard him so quiet.

Her heart fractured when Fate's golden threads wound around her body, drawing her back so that he was positioned between her and Death. He held his hand before him as he spoke, as if to placate his brother. "There is no call." Life could not see then how Fate's expression softened. She could not see the eyes that pleaded with Death, nor his fragility. "She is my *wife*. You have taken from me everything that I've ever cherished, and I have never stood in your way. I have never asked you for anything. But I am asking you now, brother, to make an exception. You cannot take her from me."

Death's resolve splintered, and Life knew then that she would not be the one to come out ahead. There was nothing soft about his voice this time as he drew closer toward Fate, whose light dimmed before the reaper. "What, exactly, is her life worth to you?"

Life opened her mouth to speak, to argue, but Fate's golden threads wound around her tongue, holding it down as Fate promised, "She is worth everything."

Life jerked her head toward the reaper, pleading for eyes he would not show her. For a touch he would not provide. She fought Fate's restraints, reaching out a trembling hand, but Death turned his face into his cowl and drew away.

"For a life such as hers," he whispered, "*everything* may just be the cost."

Life clawed at the threads, wishing she could tell Fate that this was not their goodbye. That she wanted him to let her go in peace so that she could one day return to him. For in peace, Life hoped that she could remember all she'd left behind once she found her new body. But should the death be painful... should it be one that consumed her so thoroughly that she could think of nothing else... Death had warned her that retaining her memories might be a challenge, and Life knew without a doubt that should such a death happen, she would lose everything. She would lose *him*.

And yet the threads upon her tongue were soon shackles on her wrists, holding Life back as she felt a terrible fate carve its place within her.

And as her husband sealed his bargain with Death, he turned toward Life and promised, "I will not lose you."

But he already had.

PART ONE

CHAPTER ONE

IT'S SAID THAT THE WISTERIA VINE IS A SYMBOL OF IMMORTALITY.

Blythe Hawthorne had often admired the flower—as deadly as it was beautiful, and resilient enough to thrive for centuries even if left forgotten. Yet as she crushed a petal between her fingers and let its color bleed onto her skin, she pitied the wisteria for the fate that she and the flower shared. How tragic that they were to forever remain rooted in Aris's garden, their splendor wasted on the likes of him.

Blythe, at least, had one advantage over the wisteria—she had thorns. And when it came to Aris Dryden, she had every intention of using them.

Blythe trailed a look across the garden to where dozens of guests stood in wait. Sunlight cut through the wisteria canopied above them, bathing the courtyard in a golden haze of light that had people squinting as they chatted, their breath pluming the air.

Blythe envied their fine coats. Her skin was chilled from

autumn's dampness, and the gossamer sleeves of her gown did little to stave it off. November was an unusual time for a wedding, though with Aris, she supposed she should always expect the unusual. If the alleged prince decided he wanted to get married on an autumn morning at an hour when the sun hadn't yet dried the dew on the moss, who was society to question him?

Aris Dryden was a man who got what he wanted. This day just happened to be a rare exception, for he was being forced to marry a woman he could not stand.

And to be fair, the feeling was mutual.

"You don't have to do this." It was Blythe's father, Elijah Hawthorne, who spoke. "Say the word, and I'll get you out of here."

In any other world, Blythe would have taken him up on the offer to flee Wisteria Gardens. But to secure Elijah's safety after he was falsely accused of murder, Blythe Hawthorne had spilled her blood upon a golden tapestry and bound herself to Aris—to *Fate*—for the remainder of her years. She even had a glowing band of light on her ring finger to show for it, the golden hue so faint that it was nearly invisible to the eye.

"I'll be all right," she told her father. It was no use to try to sway him with sweet words about how much she loved Aris or how happy she was to be marrying the brute. As it was, she was shivering in the damp air and itchy from what felt like a hundred layers of taffeta, and she had to keep fighting off a sneeze every time her veil brushed near her nose. She had no patience left within her to lie, and Elijah was no fool; he knew that Blythe had never intended to marry.

"You'll make a beautiful princess," he whispered, and Blythe surely would have agreed, had Aris *actually* been royalty. "But I want you to remember that Thorn Grove will always be open to you. No matter the day or the hour, you can always return home."

"I know that," Blythe promised, for she understood that truth better than anything.

Only when Elijah seemed certain that there would be no talking her out of this wedding did he bend to kiss her head. He adjusted Blythe's veil to shroud her face as he eased away. She scrunched her nose, turning to the side to sneeze.

When the lilting pings of a harp began a sauntering melody, Elijah extended his arm. "Are you ready?"

Never. A million years would need to pass before Blythe could even consider being *ready*. But instead of the truth, she told her father, "I am," for if this was what it took to keep him from being hanged, it was more than worth the sacrifice.

As much as Blythe tried to focus, the world spun as she walked into the courtyard. The ground was a pathway of stepping stones with vibrant clovers that curved around each one; Elijah steadied her as she nearly slipped on them, her choice of shoe providing little grip.

Blythe's heart beat against her chest like a torrent, drowning out the pinging of the harp, which slowed its tune to match her careful footsteps. She looked to the crowd, to faces that blurred into sharpened slivers of too-white teeth and hungry eyes that devoured her with every step, as if readying to pluck the skin from her bones. Blythe held her chin sharp even as her hands fought to tremble, refusing to let anyone scent her fear.

It wasn't until she saw her bridesmaid, Signa, standing near the front of the crowd in a beautiful lace gown that the pressure in Blythe's chest deflated. Death loomed behind Signa, his shadows winding around her own fretting hands.

Tiny shocks pulsed up Blythe's spine at the sight of him touching her cousin. Everything in her body ached to flee from Death's presence, and yet... he was the one Signa had chosen. Blythe would never understand *why*, but if Signa was happy and Elijah was free, then all was well in the world.

As Blythe passed her cousin, the harp song faded, and her father drew to a halt. Blythe was left with no choice but to finally turn her attention to the golden-haired man who stood before them in a coat as richly hued as a sapphire. *Handsome*, she supposed others might think him, and yet all Blythe could see was the resentment that festered within Aris Dryden like a poison. He masked it with a cleaving smile, as if ready to join the fray of predators set to devour her.

Aris stepped forward, offering Blythe his hand. Had Elijah not tensed beneath her grip, reminding Blythe of his presence, she might not have taken it.

"Hello, love." Aris may have whispered the words, but his voice was a weapon that slipped through Blythe's skin and struck to the hilt. "I hoped you wouldn't make it."

She squeezed his hand, forcing her own smile onto a face she hoped looked half as vicious as his. "I wouldn't have missed this for the world, my darling. Though do feel free to divorce me tomorrow." The thread between their fingers shone bright, searing into their skin so intensely that Aris laughed to cover his grimace.

"And spare you a lifetime of misery? I think not. You have no idea how much I intend to—" He froze, having been speaking so quietly that their heads were bowed, nearly touching each other, when he demanded in a dangerous tone, "What on earth are you wearing?"

Blythe didn't need to follow his gaze down to her feet to know that he was referring to her green velvet slippers. Her favorite pair, in fact. She'd adjusted her dress just enough to allow him a glimpse. As buttoned-up as Aris was, Blythe hadn't had any doubts that he'd notice.

So, it seemed, had their guests. A quiet tittering sounded from the audience, and though Blythe paid it little mind, Aris's jaw tensed. He squeezed her hands, hissing words through a false smile. "You are not marrying me in *slippers*. Go and change."

Blythe curled her toes into the velvet. "And stop the wedding? I wouldn't dream of it."

If she weren't already so aware of Aris's power, she would have realized the full extent of it as his eyes flashed gold and the world fell still. Elijah's foot stopped midstep on his way back toward the guests, and Blythe reached out to stroke her finger along the belly of a hummingbird that had frozen beside her, its wings unmoving. Some of the guests had their mouths ajar, bodies bent in stilled whispers, and not a single eye blinked in awareness. Only Signa and Death continued to move, swathed in the shadows. Signa drew a step closer, though Aris halted her with a scowl that seared like a melting sun.

"Go and put on shoes." Aris bowed his head to Blythe's level, holding back none of his contempt now that their guests were frozen. "This is ridiculous. I refuse to play your games."

Blythe had earned every bit the reaction she'd hoped to from such a proud man, and the grin she sported said as much. "It seems you haven't noticed, my love, but you're already playing."

The millions of golden threads surrounding them glimmered. Several wound around her wrist, and as Aris made a motion as if to tug her forward, Blythe braced herself. Yet it was Aris who stumbled back, clutching his own wrist with a hiss of pain. He looked not at Blythe but to Signa, whose face was stony.

Had her cousin also struck a bargain with Fate? It seemed that he was unable to harm her, and Blythe's realization came in the form of a baleful laugh as she drew chest-to-chest with Aris. Or chest-to-stomach, really, given that he was a good head taller.

"I will wait out the rest of my life rooted in this spot if it means besting you," she told him, meaning each and every word. "Free the others from whatever spell you placed upon them and let's get on with this charade."

A long moment passed in which Aris did nothing. So long, in fact, that Death began to stir. Though she knew the reaper meant to help, Blythe tensed when his shadows inched closer. It was all she could do to keep her eyes on Aris, trying to ignore Death's presence by putting as much heat into her glare as she could summon. She couldn't say how long Aris matched that stare until, eventually, he gritted his teeth and grabbed hold of her skirts, tossing them over her slippers. Only then did Elijah's foot hit the ground with a slap and the quiet whispers resume. The hummingbird darted over Aris's head as the minister approached.

"Wilt thou have this woman to be thy wedded wife..." he began, and no sooner had the words left his mouth than Blythe's world swayed. She dug her heels into the earth, rooting deeper with each vow that passed his lips. "Wilt thou love her... forsaking all others... so long as you both shall live?" Though she missed most of what the minister said, her world came crashing to a halt with his last question. Blythe glanced sideways at Aris, who kept his head down and his jaw so tight that she thought his teeth might snap.

"For as long as she lives," he agreed, so curt that the minister flinched before turning his attention to Blythe.

"And wilt thou have this man to be thy wedded husband, to live together after God's ordinance in the holy estate of matrimony? Wilt thou obey him, serve him, love, honor, and keep him in sickness and in health; and, forsaking all others, keep thee only unto him, so long as you both shall live?"

Aris shot Blythe a dark look that halted her laughter before it could escape. She cleared it from her throat and said sincerely, "I will marry him, and I will love him even more when he is sick."

The minister brought forward a golden ring designed to resemble a snake, set with eyes of jade. "Repeat after me. With this ring I thee wed, with my body I thee worship..."

Each word was poison on Blythe's lips, the ring burning as Aris shoved it down her finger while reciting the vows. Blythe bit her tongue as he pressed it so deeply toward her knuckle that she'd have to oil the blasted thing to get it off. Which she certainly would be doing the moment they were out of the public eye.

"Hello, *wife*," Aris spat, voice too low for anyone else's ears.

Blythe smiled through the pain, curling her hands around his so that she could dig her nails into his palms. "Hello, husband."

Neither looked away as the minister motioned them to their knees for the ceremonial prayer, and the rest of his words fell away as Blythe's ring finger seared beneath her golden band.

It was not a ring but a shackle. One, it seemed, that neither she nor Aris would be escaping any time soon.

CHAPTER TWO

Most days, Blythe found solace in the act of slipping into her favorite ball gown. Yet on the day of her wedding she couldn't stop fidgeting, claustrophobic in the mountains of taffeta that'd been piled upon her. Her feet, too, were positively freezing, the morning dew sinking into the fabric and dampening the velvet soles. Had she not fought so hard to aggravate Aris, she would have long since changed into something warmer.

She reminded herself how sweet that small victory had tasted as the slippers squished beneath her toes and a perpetual chill settled into her bones. Yet all the while she kept a grin plastered to her lips as she stood beneath a wisteria awning, stuck beside Aris as they were forced to greet their guests. Surrounding her was a blur of faces she'd known all her life. Too many of them, in fact. This was no small ceremony, but a celebration worthy of a prince, where delicate chocolates and miniature cakes decorated with golden leaves were ceremoniously displayed on gilded trays and everyone's wrists and throats glittered with their finest jewels.

Charlotte and Everett Wakefield greeted the newlyweds with smiles and words of encouragement. The duke and duchess leaned into each other, a sparkle in their eyes that had Blythe wondering what it must feel like to be so in love. She likely would never know.

There were faces in the crowd that Blythe didn't recognize, too. Arrogant ones that waltzed about the reception as if in constant assessment. As Blythe scrutinized them more closely, however, she noticed their eyes were glassy and that they never uttered a word to anyone but one another. They must have been Aris's guests, as it would have drawn attention if he didn't have any in attendance.

The townsfolk never let these new guests stray far from sight. From the corner of her eye, Blythe watched as Diana Blackwater slid closer to one of Aris's enchanted puppets—a man who could be no older than thirty, who claimed a pretentious air and was neatly styled in imported fabrics. Diana positioned herself in an effort to capture his attention, though the man could spare her no notice even if he wanted to as he looped slow circles around the garden, inspecting the decor. After several moments of following after him, Diana gave up with a hiss, fanning herself in a fluster. The moment she noticed Blythe watching, her spine stiffened. Ever so slowly—as if doing so physically pained her—Diana curtsied.

It was then, as satisfaction warmed her from head to foot, that Blythe realized how irredeemable her own soul truly was. That curtsy alone almost made her soggy slippers worth it.

Almost.

"Can you not simply magic this day to its end?" Blythe asked after she and Aris were congratulated by a woman who ran a modest apothecary shop in town. Blythe had never properly met her before, yet she smiled and accepted the woman's profuse congratulations all the same. "Must we see this charade through in its entirety?"

"You're the one who insisted on a proper wedding," Aris reminded her. "I wouldn't dream of taking such an experience away from a blushing bride."

Blythe swallowed the foul words that threatened to sear holes in her tongue. It wasn't worth getting into another bickering match with him. Especially not when her father stood in the near distance, observing the newlyweds with a cautious eye.

It wasn't that Blythe had wanted a *wedding*, exactly. Rather, she'd hoped to delay her inevitable fate for as long as possible, and had wanted something that Elijah could bear witness to. She'd wanted her father to see that she was well and that he needn't worry, which was why she now smiled so wide that her cheeks were beginning to ache. She even wound herself around Aris's arm when she wished for nothing more than to recoil. His hand snaked around her waist, gripping so tight that pinpricks shot along her skin and all she could think was how she would have to burn this gown and scrub his touch from her body the second she had an opportunity.

It wasn't until Signa approached that Aris eased his hold, his steely demeanor cracking. If Signa noticed—and Blythe assumed she would have, given that Signa tended to notice most things—she said nothing. Instead, Signa took Blythe's hands in her own. "You are the finest bride I have ever seen," she told her, and Blythe smiled despite knowing she was one of the *only* brides Signa had ever seen. Blythe couldn't believe that only a few short months ago she'd been uncertain whether she'd ever speak to her cousin again, just as she couldn't believe that she'd only known Signa for the span of a single year. After all they'd survived, it felt as though they'd shared a lifetime together.

Signa looked to Aris next, whose jaw ticked. Only Blythe could feel how greatly he deflated in Signa's presence, and while she did not favor Aris, she did pity him. Aris believed Signa to be the reincarnation of the woman he'd spent centuries searching for; he believed her to be Life, the only person Aris had ever loved. And Signa would never be his.

"Miss Farrow," Aris greeted coolly, though every part of him turned predatory as Death's shadows loomed closer. *"Brother."*

"A shame that my invitation was lost in the mail." Death's voice was the shock of an eclipse, or the danger of seawater filling one's throat. It suffocated Blythe, so different from Fate's rich exuberance that she at once felt ensnared in an icy current and at a loss for breath.

"Have you plans for the honeymoon?" Signa asked. Despite the fact that the honeymoon was meant to be a surprise to the bride, that hadn't stopped half the people who'd greeted them from asking about it. Still, from Signa the question was odd, for surely she could not be hopeful about this sham of a marriage. She was the only one who knew just how preposterous it truly was, though Blythe suspected that Elijah was also leery. And yet the warmth in Signa's eyes was so genuine that Blythe's stomach curled. Leave it to the girl in love with Death to be optimistic about Blythe being bound to Fate.

Signa, in part, had always reminded Blythe of an owl. Her eyes were unnervingly large, and whenever she was lost in her thoughts she often forgot to blink. Blythe had long since made up a game in which she would count how long it took Signa to remember, and Blythe played it then as her cousin stared Fate down with a pinch between the brows. It had been thirty seconds so far, and still Signa had not blinked. It was no wonder so many people found the girl odd; it was a wonder, too, that she never complained of dry eyes. Signa only stirred when Death steadied a gloved hand on her shoulder, and Blythe wondered whether he, too, counted the seconds. Or perhaps the couple filled their evenings staring into each other's eyes and seeing who could be the most unnerving and go the longest without blinking.

"Why do you want to know, Miss Farrow?" Aris asked, the timbre of his voice earning the reaper's attention. "Would you like to join me, instead?"

Death, to his credit, did not take the bait. Though his eyes were dark, fathomless things, Blythe got the distinct impression that the reaper was watching *her*. Every inch of her skin crawled, and the hair upon the back of her neck stood alert. As Blythe smoothed it back down, Signa chided, "This situation is only as bad as the two of you make it. If you're stuck with each other from here on out, I'd hope that at the very least you stop trying to kill each other."

Blythe bit back her scoff. How easy that was for Signa to say. She wasn't the one who had to spend the rest of her living years with this beast.

"I *can't* kill her," Fate corrected in a flat monotone. "You saw to that when you made me vow not to hurt her. It's no matter, though, as her pathetic human life will soon pass and one day I shall build my bed atop her bones and sleep soundly for the rest of eternity."

As silly as the imagery was, it sparked a fire in Blythe's chest. "Don't sound so eager, husband. I plan to live at least a century more, if only to spite you."

Signa pressed her lips together, and Blythe knew her cousin well enough to recognize there was something on her mind as she took hold of Blythe's gloved hands. "Let me know the moment you've returned home," Signa whispered, an urgency in her tone. "There's something I really must tell you."

Blythe wanted to tell her that whatever it was, it needn't wait. And yet Signa was already being pushed forward by the never-ending line of guests eager to congratulate the new couple on a happy marriage. The next time Aris decided to throw a soiree, they would need to discuss the list of attendees beforehand.

Quickly, Blythe promised, "I will, of course," before Signa and Death were swept away.

Blythe hadn't the faintest awareness of how long she stood there, lips frozen into a false smile and her tongue thick from repeating her thanks. It was a relief when the line ended and she was finally able to get her hands on a glass of champagne.

She watched as the others drank, then waited for Aris to try a sip before she cautiously took the flute from his hand and drank that.

She ignored his scowl and waited five minutes to ensure nothing happened before taking another sip.

Across from her, a striking woman with deeply suntanned skin and a pompous man of fair complexion greeted fawning guests. They wore outfits adorned with gold, and the woman's hair was nearly a perfect match. They had the glassy eyes of the other marionettes, though these two at least spoke to those around them with pleasant smiles.

"Who are they?" Blythe asked, squinting at the golden haze around the couple to distinguish the thousands of threads woven around their bodies.

Aris polished off his champagne. "They believe themselves to be my parents," he said, as simply as if he was telling her that the month was November.

It was not the response she'd anticipated, and Blythe cleared her throat before she could choke on her drink. "What do you mean they *believe* themselves?"

Aris's eyes shone for the briefest moment as one of the staff passed by. Blythe watched as his threads ensnared the maid, altering her path so that he could pluck two more flutes from her serving tray. Blythe reached out, expecting that one of them was for her until Aris made fists around both stems. "Someone had to play the part. It wasn't as though a prince would be allowed to marry without his own family in attendance. Besides, they'll forget everything that's happened once their purpose has been fulfilled."

"It's not fair to turn these people into your puppets, Aris. You shouldn't twist someone's mind just to fit your agenda."

"Why not?" He twirled a finger lazily along the rim of the crystal flutes. "I've done it to you thrice."

It was fortunate that she'd not yet eaten, for Blythe's stomach flipped. Vaguely, she remembered one of the times, back when Aris had tried to extract information about Signa and why she'd been banished to Foxglove. Blythe had a feeling that the second time had to do with the gap in her memory from her first night meeting Aris and visiting Wisteria Gardens. But as for the third . . . she hadn't the faintest clue, which was all the more terrifying.

Trying to fight back the shakiness from her voice, Blythe told him, "You will never again use such powers on me." She wasn't sure what leverage she had or what she could offer to make such an agreement worth his while. Regardless, she spoke the words plainly, and with every ounce of fire that raged within her.

"Dear God, do you always screech when you talk?" He rubbed at his temples with a groan. "Your cousin already saw to it that I can bring you no harm." Though Blythe had guessed something of the sort based on their earlier conversation with Signa, she was surprised by how easily Aris admitted to it. For someone as dangerous and as aggravating as he was, the man was certainly forthcoming.

Still, Blythe pressed, "Even if it's not to hurt me, you must promise that you'll never make me into one of your puppets. I will not live in a home with someone who manipulates me."

She tipped her chin, defiant despite having no leg to stand on in this argument. Still, to her surprise, Aris did not taunt her. He only drank deeply from his champagne and said, "That was never my intention."

The squeeze of her chest loosened. "I'm relieved to see that you can be reasonable."

"Reasonable?" So bleak was his laugh that Blythe was immediately on edge. "It's not worth the effort to manipulate you when I have no desire to even look at you for any longer than necessary. Though I do advise that you get comfortable with my powers, love. If you insist on keeping up our guise, know that there is a cost."

Blythe set down her flute with such force that she had to double-check she hadn't shattered the glass. "If you hadn't pretended to be a prince in the first place, there would be no guise to keep up with."

Aris shrugged. "Perhaps. But with a face like mine, what other role do you expect I might play?"

She couldn't tell whether he was joking, but Blythe laughed at the ridiculousness all the same. She was about to inform Aris just how much of a fool he was when Blythe caught sight of her father. Though he'd been in conversation with Signa, it seemed that Blythe's laughter had drawn his attention. Her spine snapped straight as Elijah descended on them. Quickly, she leaned toward her husband and commanded, "Pretend that I am the most brilliant person on this earth, or I will make every second of your life absolute misery."

"Do you mean to say that you're not already doing that?" Aris scrunched away from her, though there was no time for him to ask questions before Elijah stood across from them. Aris straightened. Powerful though he was, it seemed even a deity could become nervous in the presence of a father-in-law.

"Mr. Hawthorne," Aris acknowledged with a dip of his blond head.

"Your Highness." There was an iciness to Elijah as he greeted the prince, though it melted as his attention turned toward his daughter and he held out his hand. "Dance with me."

There was no universe in which Blythe would ever refuse. Letting her hold on Aris slip, she took her father's hand and wordlessly allowed him to lead her to the dance floor. Given Elijah's distaste of society, Blythe had nearly forgotten just how refined her father could be, his chin high and his shoulders confident as he swept her into a waltz, each of his steps utterly precise. Even more surprising, however, were his words.

"I put a knife in your travel chest." Elijah spoke easily, and Blythe was grateful for the swell of the music that swept his voice away from the other dancers. She gaped up at him, though there wasn't so much as a furrow between Elijah's brows.

"An unusual gift for a new bride," Blythe admonished. "Do remember that I chose this, Father. Aris isn't forcing me into anything—"

"Oh, come off it." Though his words were blunt, they were not unkind. "I was set to *hang*. I have been in this world long enough to know not to look for coincidence where none can be found. You may bat your eyes at that man all you'd like, but do not take me for a fool."

Blythe ground her teeth, knowing there was no choice but to choose her next words carefully. "Marriages of convenience happen every year."

"They do," he agreed, cutting cleaving glances in Aris's direction. "But that was never meant to happen for my daughter. I would sooner have died a thousand deaths than have put that on you."

"You've put nothing on me," she whispered, breathing a little easier now that some truth of her and Aris's arrangement was out in the open. "Perhaps you were ready to die, but should we have a million more lifetimes, I still would not be ready to let you go." Blythe had lost too many people she loved in the past two years, and she'd be damned before she let anything happen to her father. Something in her expression must have made him understand as much, for his hold on her softened.

"Very well," Elijah whispered. "But know that you are my world, Blythe. You are my proudest accomplishment, my heart and my soul. Should anything happen to you—"

"It won't," she promised. "It's marriage, Father, not murder." Though she tried to say it jokingly, Elijah's eyes held storm clouds.

"I put a knife in your travel chest," he repeated, and it was an effort for Blythe to not roll her eyes. As perceptive as her father was, there was no way for him to ever know that a mere knife would never be enough to kill Aris. Still, if it made him feel better, she'd accept it.

"I'm glad you told me before I accidentally stabbed myself," she said. "I'll accept it, though I'll have no need to use it."

Elijah continued without pause. "I want you to write to me every week, at least for the first few months. End every letter with a random fact so I know it was written by your hand. And should something ever happen—should you need me, or if you're hurt—mention your mother by name and I'll know to come at once."

"It's not as if I'm going far," Blythe said. "Wisteria Gardens is but a carriage ride away."

"No doubt Aris will want to return to Verena," Elijah challenged, and Blythe wished with everything in her that she could tell her father such a place was not even real. She'd tried to look for it on a map once, just to see, though every time she searched her vision would swim and her mind would grow hazy until she eventually forgot what she'd been searching for. Aris was nothing if not thorough.

"We'll remain here in town once we return from our honeymoon." Neither she nor Aris had actually spoken of their plans. In fact, they'd hardly spoken at all since the day she spilled her blood onto his tapestry. She hadn't given thought to where they might live, for the answer seemed obvious—there was no Verena. Surely they would remain at Wisteria Gardens. And yet her father's eyelids drooped, and while he made no further argument, he seemed saddened by Blythe's confidence.

"A letter," he repeated, holding her tighter as the music quieted, the song coming to its end. "Every week, no matter where you are in this world. Promise me that."

It seemed there would be no getting around it. "If I cannot take a carriage ride here myself, then fine, I will send you a letter. And you will send me one as well, so that I know neither you nor Thorn Grove has crumbled without me holding everything together." She punctuated her jesting with a smile, though it wavered at the corners. Most young girls assumed they would one day leave their home to start a new phase of life, but Blythe had never seen the appeal. She loved Thorn Grove, just as she loved her family. The idea of leaving them behind—especially when her father had overcome so much these past years—was something Blythe never thought she'd have to face.

Blythe held tighter as the waltz came to an end. It was Elijah who slowly released hold of his daughter, though he waited a beat too long to do so.

"It is my hope that I'm only becoming more paranoid in my old age," he told her softly. "It is also my hope that Aris is a good husband, and that you will one day share the kind of love that your mother and I once had. But if not—if anything should ever happen—there's always the knife."

Even Elijah cracked a smile when Blythe laughed, though it was short-lived as guests began to file toward the courtyard where four gray horses waited with an ivory carriage.

Gently, Elijah squeezed her hand. "Do not make yourself small. Do not change yourself to suit him. Teach him how to treat you, and remember that you deserve everything this life has to offer."

Heat prickled Blythe's eyes, and she looked away before her father could see the tears fall. She turned her face ahead, to where Aris waited, and nodded. "I will."

Before she could change her mind, Blythe released her hold on her father and stepped toward Aris and into her new life, feeling her heart shatter with every step.

CHAPTER THREE

Blythe wondered if there was a world in which she might have enjoyed having a wedding. Was it possible that she'd have gotten misty eyed as she looked upon the faces of loved ones waving her off? Could she have laughed with her beloved as they ran hand in hand toward a gilded carriage, dodging rice and flowers thrown by cheering guests?

She wondered, too, how quickly her thoughts might have wandered to the honeymoon. Customary though it was for a bride not to know what her new husband had in store, Blythe imagined she would have spent weeks sleuthing for answers, determined to uncover where they were traveling and how to best pack.

She supposed she should have been glad to have never wanted to get married, for she had no preconceived notions or idealistic fantasies as to what she should expect as Aris pushed her into the carriage and slumped in after her. He wore his smile until the very moment the door shut and he drew the velvet curtains closed. Only then, as their carriage took off down the hill, did Aris throw himself into the seat across from Blythe, drawing his legs close to avoid having to touch her. God forbid.

She scoffed, choosing to listen to the vengeful little voice in her head that told her to stretch her legs and take up as much space as physically possible in the confines of this carriage. She propped her feet onto the leather seat beside him and bent to touch her toes.

"What's wrong, love?" she teased as he shifted away. "Afraid I'll ruin you?" They were the same cloying words that Aris had thrown at her the day she'd barged into Wisteria Gardens and demanded his help saving her father, and they made his lips twist. If he wanted to scowl and bemoan their situation, Blythe had no problem letting him. But the carriage was much too small and oppressive for her to do the same. She swept fallen strands of hair off her neck, mulling over ways to make this trip at least moderately tolerable.

All the while, Aris rubbed the band of light around his finger as if trying to pry the thing off, glaring at the drawn curtains as though they were the source of his immense dissatisfaction. Blythe barely spared him a glance, aware of how futile the effort was. She'd tried removing it herself too many times to count.

When the toe of her slipper brushed his thigh, Aris looked half ready to burst from his skin. "You are a filthy, deplorable abomination—" He paused, brows pressing toward the sky. "What on earth are you doing?"

Blythe was bent forward at the waist, hands behind her as she stretched her fingers back to try to tug the fastenings of her corset. "Surely you don't expect me to sit here for hours, hardly able to breathe. Your temper is making this carriage so unbearably hot that

I will perish if I cannot cool myself. Besides, we're married now. You should be the one tearing me out of this infernal thing." She sighed her relief as one of the laces finally came loose, giving her enough room to wiggle an inch or two in the corset. She'd have pried more free if she could reach them, but for now this would have to do.

All the while, Aris observed her straining with flattened lips and brewing annoyance, but that was nothing new. "Why would I expect you to sit in here for hours?"

Blythe made a gesture to all that surrounded them. "We took off in a carriage after our wedding reception. What else am I to assume but a honeymoon?"

Aris's bitter laughter slithered over her, making Blythe's loosened fastenings feel like snakes gliding across her skin.

"I would sooner drive a stake through my chest than travel anywhere with you. *Honeymoon.*" He scoffed, eyes flashing a dangerous molten gold. "You have lost your mind. We'll be returning to Wisteria once our guests have dispersed."

In the blink of an eye, golden threads shone from every direction. No longer did they seem like distant gossamer things, but slick as metal and so sharp that a single touch threatened to break skin. Blythe pushed to the edge of her seat and threw open the curtains, craning her neck to see that, in the distance, guests were filing out of Wisteria Gardens. One after the other they shuffled forward, silent as they ducked into their carriages.

Aris was controlling them. Of *course* he was controlling them, because why wouldn't he be?

"You have all the power in the world and this is how you choose to behave?" She leaned back before she caught a glimpse of her father or Signa, tempering herself. It wasn't worth making a fuss; that would only encourage him. "The least you could have done was take me to the sea. I wouldn't have said no to a safari, either."

"I would rather chew off my own arm" was his only reply.

"People will ask questions if they know we're still here," Blythe argued. Ten minutes in the carriage and already the horses were circling back to Wisteria Gardens.

"No one will ask questions if they can't find us," he said. "I've had enough of your friends pestering me. We'll leave town for the length of a honeymoon, return when the timing is appropriate, and then we'll say our goodbyes—"

"To each other?" Blythe perked up.

"To this *town*, you cretin."

At first, Blythe thought he must have been joking. She waited for him to laugh or for those smug lips of his to twist into a smile that would confirm he was only trying to rile her. Yet Aris kept all composure as the palace came back into view.

Blythe stared at it, her mouth dry as she thought of her father's warning. "Excuse me?"

"This entire town believes me to be a prince," he said with a flourish of his hand. "Surely you did not expect that we would remain here." Though he wasn't asking, Blythe made it a point to answer him.

"And whose fault is it that they believe such nonsense? If you hadn't felt the need to inflate your already monstrous ego, we wouldn't have this problem."

Aris's knuckles whitened as he clenched his hands against the seat. "If you hadn't ruined my bargain with Miss Farrow, then we wouldn't have *this* problem, either."

She folded her arms, ready to rip the stifling lace sleeves from her gown. They were only feet away from Aris's palace now, and every inch that the carriage crawled forward had Blythe pushing back in her seat, trying to create distance between herself and Wisteria Gardens.

She'd always known that she'd made a rash decision in taking Signa's place. It hadn't ever been one that she'd regretted, though. At least not until that moment, when the prospect of building a life away from her father loomed before her.

"I'm not leaving." Blythe kept her voice void of the emotion that threatened to make her sick.

"Of course you are. Everyone expects that I'm taking you to Verena—"

"Verena isn't a real place!" she hissed. "It doesn't matter what they expect. You have the power to placate their minds, should anyone question me staying."

The courtyard they approached was a ghost of what it'd been less than twenty minutes prior, all signs of the wedding eradicated as though it had never happened. If only she could be so lucky.

"I may have that power," Aris said, "but that doesn't mean I intend to use it for *you*. My home was made to move; I will not remain here a second longer than necessary."

Blythe's mother had died, and it hadn't taken long for her brother, Percy, to follow. Byron Hawthorne, too, had gone away with his new bride so that she could give birth to Blythe's nephew without anyone analyzing the timing of their union.

That left Elijah without a familiar soul, and after all he'd been through, the thought of him wandering alone through Thorn Grove was too much to bear.

The carriage rolled to a stop on the pristine path of the courtyard, and while Aris hurried out, Blythe remained seated.

"I won't leave." Though the words were a whisper, the ferocity within each one was unrivaled. "Should you try to take me, I will tear my nails across your eyes and crawl back here if I must. I will tie myself to the forest trees and bite every hand that tries to drag me away."

"You are a demon in human flesh." Aris tugged a hand through his hair, turning his dissatisfaction toward the sky before he blew out a breath. "Where do you even come up with this nonsense?"

Blythe braced herself against the carriage, both heels pressed against either side of its door as if pushing herself deeper inside. She clutched the seat, fingers curling into the leather. "I will not leave this carriage until you agree that we are staying."

Aris looked plainly upon her defiance, hands held behind his back as he studied her. "Is that so? Very well, then, let's see if you mean it." Without missing a beat, he slammed the carriage door shut so hard that Blythe had to draw her feet back at the last moment so they wouldn't be caught. She fell to the carriage floor, clawing her way back up in time to see through the window that Aris had given one of the horses a slap on the rump. Whoever their driver was, they were clearly magicked and not in their right mind, for the carriage once again took off down the hill.

Blythe's mouth hung ajar as she tried to find the words to convey her rage as she watched Aris's figure shrink in the distance. He waved as she journeyed onward, and the last thing she saw of him was the infuriating, satisfied smile etched across his lips.

Blythe hadn't the faintest clue where the carriage was destined for, nor did she care. She'd spent the past hour cursing her wretched husband with every foul word she'd ever overheard, still in her bridal gown with half of her corset laces loosened and her hair strewn about. She was too lost in her own thoughts—concocting plans on how she might commandeer the carriage and run away to Foxglove to spend the winter with Signa—to notice when they stopped moving.

She froze at the sound of a horse's weary huff, only then pulled from the happenings of her own mind.

"Why have you stopped?" Blythe called to the driver, the hairs on her neck standing. She was met with no reply.

Peeling apart her fretting hands, she bent to peer out the window.

To anyone else, the trees that surrounded her might have looked the same as any other forest. But Blythe had spent her entire childhood among these trees and recognized with a single glance precisely where the carriage had taken her—to the woods behind Thorn Grove.

To the woods that housed her mother's garden.

All at once, the tension left her body. She stepped out of the carriage, heedless of the threads of fate that wound around her, guiding her through windswept trees that bowed as if to greet their forgotten ruler. Their beauty came with great greed as they swallowed up every ounce of warmth and sunlight, leaving nothing but darkness and a bitter chill that bit through her slippers. Blythe braced herself against the cold, wondering with each step forward why Aris would bring her here of all places. It took several minutes before she stopped looking for him behind every tree, half convinced that he intended to jump out and surprise her only to laugh at his own cruel joke. But the deeper into the woods she traveled, the more Blythe realized that Aris was nowhere to be found.

She hadn't visited her mother's garden since before Lillian fell ill. Blythe had been too sick to argue when her father made the choice to seal it off and hadn't felt prepared to face it once she'd healed from her poisoning. Then there'd been the fire, of course, and Blythe couldn't bear seeing her mother's favorite place reduced to ashes.

Even in a bitter winter, her mother's garden had always been a spectacle. Lillian had donned her thickest coat and walked there every afternoon to ensure the resilient hellebore and pansies that took their turn in the spotlight were tended to. Elijah had once asked why Lillian wouldn't let him send one of the servants in her place; she hadn't believed any of them could properly care for the garden. Not like she could.

For the majority of her youth, Blythe had gone with her mother, enjoying her time watching the tiniest sprouts bud into spectacular flowers. As she got older, though, Blythe's visits became less frequent, for she was distracted with tea and lessons or with books that seemed so much cozier to read inside by the hearth.

Footsteps soft so as to not disturb the garden's silence, she made her way around its edges, tiptoeing over char and toward where her mother's grave sat at the edge of the pond. It'd been cleaned recently, though even a scrubbing could not conceal the havoc the fire had wrought. The headstone was a fragile thing, one corner cracked and crumbling and another section discolored, making the words upon it difficult to read. The earth was overtaking it, too, moss from the pond's edge climbing its way up the stone. But that was only nature, and Blythe didn't think her mother would have minded. She probably would have enjoyed the idea of having her body taken by the earth she so loved.

Blythe pressed her hand against the stone, feeling the sting of heat behind her eyelids as she curled her fingers into Lillian's engraved name.

"Hello." Blythe's voice was little more than a breath as she sank beside the headstone. "I'm sorry that it's taken me until now to visit, but I bet you never believed that I'd get married, did you?" Blythe's smile was small as she leaned her head against the stone, listening for a response that would never come.

What she would have given to go back. To have set aside whatever it was that had felt so important at the time and joined her mother on her journeys to the garden. Even if Blythe could have gone just once more—even if she could have made a single new memory with Lillian—she would have bent the world to make it so.

She pressed a kiss to the stone, chest aching. It was a feeling she knew would never go away—one that dulled with time, perhaps, but also one that spawned from the absence of something that could never be returned. As if someone had reached within her to pluck out a piece of her very soul, and had left her fumbling as she learned to live without it.

How cruel Aris was to bring her to this place. Every day she felt her mother's absence like a knife between her ribs, and on the day of her wedding it was worse than ever.

But Lillian wasn't the only one who had taken their last breath in this garden.

Blythe rose from the headstone, not bothering to lift the hem of her dress as it dragged through ash she wished would have disappeared by now. She hated wondering whether it belonged to the flowers that once filled this garden, or to her brother's corpse.

Percy had never loved the garden as she and her mother had. He'd accompanied them numerous times over the years, though mostly so that he and Blythe could chase each other through the trees. She could still hear his laughter in the wind and her mother's gentle chiding in the birdsong that slipped down her skin and made her shiver.

Percy had changed over the years, but never would she have suspected him capable of harming their family. The pain of his betrayal was worse than any poison, and she understood why Signa had kept the secret from her for so long. It was the same reason she wished to keep the truth from Elijah.

Never, not in a million years, would Blythe have hurt Percy the way that he had hurt her. Not even now, knowing all that she did.

"I wish that things had worked out differently." Standing atop the bare soil of all that once was, Blythe stooped to her knees. "I wish you would have told me all that you were dealing with. We could have figured it out together." She kissed her hand, then pressed it to the ground. Burnt twigs littered the earth where Blythe used to spend days smelling rows of hyacinth. She waited every year for the wolfsbane to bloom in the spring, and for the frogs to come out of hiding and perch themselves atop the lily pads.

Now it was quiet. There were no frogs. No wolfsbane or hyacinth, or even the most resilient of hellebore. The fire had ravaged the garden that she so loved, and Blythe doubted that it would ever regain the splendor it once had. Every scorched tree was a reminder of all that had changed over the past two years, and all that Blythe had lost.

But there was no going back. The pain of that knowledge and the ache of her loss drew a tear from her eyes, and as it slipped down her cheek and onto the earth, Blythe forced herself back to her feet.

It was then that she saw it—a tiny crimson petal beneath where she'd been crouched. Certain that her eyes were betraying her, Blythe bent to inspect it. But before she could get any closer, she cried out as her ring finger burned with such a sharpness that her vision swam. The world tipped beneath her as a hot current beat against her skin. She stumbled in search of the nearest tree, but it winked out of sight before she could grab hold of it. One blink, and her vision went black.

Another blink, and Blythe's entire being felt as though it was being swallowed whole. As if someone was breathing through a reed and had sucked her up into it.

She clamped her eyes shut to fend off her sickening stomach, and the next time she opened them she was back at Wisteria Gardens, on her knees in the empty courtyard and in the precise spot where she and Aris had separated hours prior.

CHAPTER FOUR

Blythe stood at the front door of Wisteria Gardens clad in only her ruined wedding dress. She had no coat to protect her from autumn's chill as the sky darkened—she'd left it in the carriage with the rest of her belongings. Once, months ago, she'd stood in this very spot of her own accord, readying herself to propose marriage to the man she truly believed was a prince who'd be able to help solve all her problems.

She supposed there was some dark humor to be found as she pounded on the door—this time with his ring on her finger—though Blythe was having trouble unmasking it.

It took Aris far too long to throw open the door, his eyes twin blades that sliced across her. He'd changed attire since the wedding, the collar of his white button-down looser and his waistcoat disappeared. "I thought I sent you away."

Oh, what grand illusions she had of one day pummeling this

man's thick head into the snow that would soon shroud this entire mountaintop. "That was a cruel trick, Aris." She shivered as her breath made plumes in the air. "Why would you bring me to the garden of all places?"

"What *garden*?" he scoffed. "You were meant to go to the train station, you prat. I'd hoped to get at least a month free from your whining."

"I never made it to any *station*. If it wasn't you who brought me back, then who did? Am I to believe the driver magicked me here?"

Blythe noticed that Aris was rubbing absently at his left hand, near the spot where hers still burned. He stepped outside, scanning behind her for what she presumed was any sign of the carriage. He could look all he liked, but neither it nor her belongings were anywhere nearby. It was as though the sky had swallowed her up and spit her out on his doorstep.

Behind Aris, Blythe caught a glimpse of a glowing hearth and tried to duck beneath his arm and step inside. The moment her foot crossed the threshold, however, a great pressure seized Blythe's chest and she was tossed back onto the lawn. She hissed with pain not from the blow of falling onto her backside, but from the ring of light that flared as bright as starlight upon her finger. She clutched it to her chest as the skin beneath it burned.

Aris, blast him, tossed his golden head back with a riot of laughter that made her wish for a pair of shears. She'd cut that pretty hair right off his head the moment she had the chance.

"Shall I fetch you a blanket?" he asked, smug. "If the house doesn't want you in it, then perhaps you can make a space for yourself in the stables. A beastly little rat like you should feel at home there." He turned to go back inside. Like Blythe, however, Aris was at once tossed backward as he tried to reenter Wisteria Gardens. His own ring flared gold, and he clutched at it with his opposite hand, trying to tear it off. "Blast it, you infernal—"

"Aris." Blythe was barely breathing. Her focus was trained on the space between their hands, where a golden thread shone bright. She moved her hand toward him and the thread shrank. Then she jerked it back, but rather than snap, the thread tugged at Aris's band as well.

"Careful," he grunted, but Blythe wasn't listening. She stood, once again testing a step closer to her new groom. The heat on her finger lessened.

"Together," she whispered, making a face as she glared at the wretched thing. "I think it wants us to stay together."

"To enter my home?"

"*Our* home," Blythe corrected as Aris rose to his feet, dusting dirt from his pants. "I think the ring is what brought me back here." Saying the words aloud felt ridiculous, but how else could she explain that searing burn upon her finger?

Aris ran a hand through his hair, pulling too tightly at the strands. "Do you ever listen to yourself when you speak? If a magical ring wanted you back at Wisteria, then why would it stop you from coming inside?"

Blythe hated to give him credit, but Aris had a point. There had to be more to it, a piece that she was still missing. She took Aris by the shoulder, trying to pull him to her side.

He jerked back, shrinking away like her touch alone would soil him. "Get your hands off of me, you boorish—"

"I'm not sure whether you've noticed, but it's getting dark," Blythe snapped. "As cold as I am now, it'll be worse in a few hours. So unless you feel like building us a fire and sleeping beneath the stars, I suggest you cooperate."

"*You* may be wild enough to sleep on the dirt, but I will do no such thing." Aris stepped toward the door again, only to scowl at the manor as it halted him at the threshold. "I have *magic*, you foolish girl."

"Go on and use it, then," she challenged. "Use your silly enchantments and get us inside." If she had to spend another minute stuffed in her suffocating gown, she would lose her mind.

"Enchantments? You've been reading too many fairy tales." After another unsuccessful attempt at ramming his way into the manor, his eyes flashed a burnished gold. Enraged, Aris began to roll up his sleeves as if to better his concentration. Once, Blythe had to focus all her attention into seeing the golden threads that wound around him. Now, she only had to squint to see the full scene as Aris winked out of view only to reappear seconds later, the threads unraveling at his feet. Given the heaviness of his breathing, Blythe guessed that whatever he'd tried had not gone according to plan. He punched the door only to be tossed once more onto his backside, clutching his left hand.

Blythe watched his ridiculousness with her arms folded, preserving her warmth.

"*Now* can we try my way?" she pressed, unflinching when Aris stalked forward to stand before her, his hair disheveled.

"And what, exactly, is *your* way?"

Blythe didn't subject herself to looking at Aris, but instead directed her attention to her left hand. Aris was right that Blythe had read many fairy tales, enough to understand that all stories had some truth, no matter how fantastical. And the truth was that it could be no coincidence that this bond between her and Aris had taken the form of a wedding band.

Quietly, she told him, "I think you should try to carry me over the threshold," and as silly as the words felt upon her tongue, Blythe could hear the truth in them and knew in her bones that she was right. The rings were a reminder of their bond—of their *marriage*—and both she and Aris had a role to play.

"*Carry* you? You have the world's most luxurious slippers. Use them."

It was a struggle for Blythe to maintain her temper, though she tried her hardest as she motioned toward the thread binding their rings. "It's tradition, Aris. I am your wife, and when a husband brings his wife home for the first time, he's to carry her over the threshold."

"It's also tradition to consummate the wedding night, but you're not in your right mind if you think—"

"Dear God, just carry me!" Perhaps it was her confidence, or perhaps it was that Aris could somehow sense that she was minutes away from prying the clothes off his body so that she might find extra warmth, but either way Aris's mouth snapped shut. He looked none too happy to be standing so close to her, and literally grimaced—yes, grimaced, as though he was touching rubbish with his bare hands—as he gripped her by the waist. He was a breath from tossing her over his shoulder like some barbarian before Blythe grabbed hold of his wrist and instead placed it on the small of her back.

"Hold me properly, you brute!" she gasped. "Not like I'm some prize from a hunt!"

"A prize you are not." His frown was so deep that she wouldn't have been surprised if it grew roots and made a permanent home on his face, though Aris sighed only once before hoisting Blythe bridal-style into his arms. "I despise you."

"I loathe you, too, darling. Now get walking." Blythe held her breath as he started for the door, squeezing her eyes shut when Aris took a step over the threshold. The next time she opened them, they were inside the palace.

Even Aris had the decency to look shocked before his expression quickly soured. Blythe, however, was practically bursting with joy, for her skin was already pricking with the warmth of the hearth.

"Wonderful," she said. "Now if you could put me down—"

Aris didn't wait for the end of that sentence. Nor did he wait until they were nearer to a chair. Without a lick of remorse, he dropped Blythe straight onto the hardwood floor. She hit it rump-first and turned to bare her teeth at the man as she rubbed the pain from the small of her back. But Aris was already gone, his blond head disappearing down the hall as he twisted his ring finger.

Blythe didn't bother following him and turned her attention instead to her new home.

Wisteria Gardens was nothing like the regal palace that Blythe had visited before. Gone were the ivory paneling and the gilded flourishes, the walls nothing but bare slate stone. The statues and art that had once been proudly displayed, too, had given way to dust and cobwebs. Blythe thought back to the stories she'd read, thinking of fairy-tale homes with their many curses and secrets. Wisteria Gardens felt very much the same. Even the hearth, which had felt like the greatest reprieve only moments ago, now seemed sad and wearied. Its flames flickered, shrinking as she sidled up to it. The poor thing groaned from the exertion of keeping itself alive, pluming dark gray smoke with low crackles that seemed like it was coughing.

"I see you've redecorated," Blythe whispered, though she knew no one was there to listen. "In case you were wondering, I much preferred how it looked before." She kicked her slippers off and set them beside the woeful flames to dry. While she would have given her own arm to be able to bathe and tear herself free from her wedding gown, Blythe hadn't the faintest clue whether the rest of her belongings had been sent over from Thorn Grove yet. And considering everything else had been with her in the carriage...

She dragged a hand down her face. Had Aris been more accommodating, she might have asked to borrow something. As it was, she pulled the lace fabric away from where it bunched into her armpits before setting off, deciding that if the rest of her luggage was here, she wasn't going to find it by sitting in the parlor.

It was time, she supposed, to settle into her new home.

Blythe had a distinct memory of walking into Wisteria Gardens—or simply Wisteria, as Aris called it—for the first time and believing that any person would be lucky to live among such splendor. She even recalled believing that she herself would have been happy to exist in such a space.

What a fool she'd been to have ever put that idea into the universe.

Blythe had expected that Wisteria would have dozens of rooms to choose from and maintain, and yet as she made her way up one of the creaking double staircases and passed walls made of chipped stone that looked a hair's breadth away from crushing her beneath its rubble, she found that there was but a single door situated at the end of the narrow, unadorned hallway. So unnerving was the sight of that door that Blythe thought to turn heel and instead search other floors of the manor for a library. Or perhaps there was a dining room to investigate.

Wisteria, however, had other plans.

The moment Blythe tried to turn from the withered mahogany door, a strange pressure set her back on the path toward it, twisting her feet and pushing her forward as if the manor itself was goading her down the hall. She tried once more to turn back toward the staircase, not caring for the way the edges of her mind grew fuzzy whenever she glanced away from the door. It was undoubtedly Aris's doing, and for that reason Blythe fought against it. Yet as soon as she managed to turn away, it was as if the hall stretched endlessly forward, only stone as far as the eye could see. It reminded her of the prison where her father had been detained, desolate and decaying. So empty was the stretch of space that it was disorienting.

Blythe took one step from the door, then another five. No matter how much she walked, however, she never seemed to get anywhere. With a fire in her belly she turned to glare at the space behind her, heart skipping a beat upon realizing that it was still within arm's reach. Beneath her breath, she cursed Aris's name. It seemed there was no getting around his games for the time being, and she was left with little choice but to grasp the knob and throw the door open, seized by a rush of cold air that set her teeth chattering.

This was her room?

Every window had been left open, and thanks to the surrounding stone that hoarded every ounce of the bitter cold, it was more unbearable inside Wisteria than it'd been in the courtyard. Blythe hugged herself, wishing all the while that she had something other than lace to cover herself with. Fortunately, there was a hearth inside her drawing room, a cramped and dingy space that looked as though someone had taken it by the corners and pinched the room together. Unfortunately, the hearth wasn't lit and Blythe hadn't the faintest idea how to use the tinderbox that had been tossed haphazardly beside it. She clutched it to her chest regardless—for surely it could not be so difficult to start a fire—and continued into what was evidently to be her suite.

The room was positively uninhabitable. Apart from the tinderbox, Aris had not made the slightest effort to make Wisteria accommodating. The walls and floors were not made of wood, but of the same gray stone as the rest of the manor, so frigid against her bare feet that her toes numbed. There was but a single piece of furniture in the drawing room—a simple oak writing desk. Inside the drawer was a crooked pen and an ancient jar of congealed ink. The parchment, though, was of fine quality. Probably, Blythe guessed, because Aris had overheard her conversation with her father and was mocking their meager attempts at subterfuge.

So ridiculous was this beast of a man that she scoffed and shoved the items back into the drawer.

Blythe abandoned any hope that her bedroom would be more hospitable as she stepped inside, for there was no bed, but in its place a flat slab of raised stone to lie upon. Blythe pondered the shape of the stone, for it looked very much like some sort of strange sacrificial altar that an evil witch might use.

Like the drawing room, there was no rug nor so much as a vase. No wallpaper, or even curtains to cover the windows she slammed shut. There was, at least, her honeymoon luggage, which had somehow made its return to Wisteria. How fortunate it was that the almighty Aris had deemed her worthy enough to have her belongings, for the swath of fabric on her "bed" was more a rag than a blanket, and was hardly proper protection from this dreadfully frigid hovel. She'd need to bundle up if she was to stand a chance in this place. There was nowhere to *hang* said clothing, however, nor did it seem that Aris had any hired staff to help with the washing.

To her name, Blythe had only her packed and ready travel chests, and she understood at once how easy Aris was making it for her to leave. For her to call off their marriage and put an end to the oath she'd made to protect Signa. He was all but pushing her out the door, and were she any less stubborn, she might have had the mind to go.

"You'd certainly like that, wouldn't you?" she seethed at the room, whose walls groaned a weary response.

Aris would need to try harder if he believed that a bit of cold and discomfort was all it would take for her to break.

Blythe flung open the lid of her packing chest and rifled through it to procure the warmest items she owned—a hodgepodge assortment of wool dresses and coats, of which she pulled out multiple. They'd be a thousand times more practical and infinitely warmer, but first she'd need to get into them.

Blythe drew a breath before she leaned over her desk, one side of her cheek pressed against the wood as she reached for the laces of her corset, stretching the tips of her fingers in a desperate attempt to free herself from the ridiculous sham of a bridal gown. It took at least twenty minutes of straining from multiple angles before she managed to loosen the remaining ties, sighing her relief as she shimmied out of the taffeta, kicked it to the side, and hurried into a wool wrapper, a coat heavier than she was, mittens, and a fresh pair of dry slippers. Only then was she able to quell her brewing tension, her focus shifting to the fact that at least her room didn't seem to be situated anywhere near *his*.

Aris probably had the warmest room in the palace, decorated with gilded wallpaper, rugs so plush they thawed the toes, and a dozen mirrors and paintings of his own likeness. It probably had perfect sun-blocking curtains and a bed that felt like clouds, too. That bastard.

Blythe moved to the hearth next and spent a solid half hour with the tinderbox, prying her gloves off and then stuffing them back on whenever her fingers became too numb to properly grasp the tools. She tried to recall every time she had ever watched her previous lady's maid, Elaine, make the fire. Blythe went through every motion she could remember, striking steel against flint until she frightened herself with the sparks and had to try again. Upon realizing that she had no idea what to do after those sparks were made, however, Blythe eventually recognized that it was a useless endeavor and decided it was time to try her luck elsewhere, for she wasn't only cold but also hungry.

She cracked the door into the hallway open and poked her head out. She blinked once, then twice, and when she was certain that the walls weren't morphing or stretching around her, she stepped through.

"Aris?" Blythe set a hand against the right wall, having once heard it was a certain way to escape any maze, which was precisely what Wisteria felt like. "I'm not sure how it works for you, but I require sustenance to maintain my existence and I'm certain that one could hear my stomach all the way across town."

Silence rang through the palace, and Blythe's skin crawled as she made her way down the hall. New doors paved her path, each of them identical with the exception of their handles. One was brass, another iron. Some were in the shape of birds, and another a small fox head. Hers, she noticed as she looked back, was wooden and carved with a rather hideous head of a wild boar that hadn't been there earlier. It seemed almost sentient when she stared into its eerie brass eyes and at the tusks she'd have to reach into to grasp the handle. They looked ready to bite her at any moment; the only consolation Blythe felt was that she at least would never have trouble remembering which room was hers.

She continued farther down the hall with a hand pressed to her stomach. She hadn't been exaggerating when she'd told Aris that it was in severe protest; its rumbling was loud enough to rouse someone from sleep. In her stress, Blythe hadn't been able to eat the prior night and hardly had any opportunity for a bite during the reception. She was famished, which was perhaps her least favorite thing in the world.

Apart from Aris.

She intended to head downstairs and find the kitchen, but before she took hold of the railing Blythe noticed that the dimmed candlelight above her head was flickering. Not just one candle, but all of them. It was as though something had stolen their light, for they did not cast a typical glow upon the floor. Their flames instead pulled toward the staircase that stretched up toward the ballroom. Though vastly different from when she'd first visited, Blythe recognized the space; up the stairs and down the hall was where she'd met Aris for the first time. And as the light pooled ahead, illuminating her path, she got the sense that she was meant to follow it.

Blythe hurried upward, passing the flat iron doors of a once-gilded ballroom bathed in amber. She chased after a light that glowed brighter as it led her to a familiar portrait—the only one she'd seen so far, and frankly one of the lone sources of color left in Wisteria.

Life's portrait remained untouched, exactly as it'd been the day Blythe had first seen it. And yet looking at it felt like an entirely new experience, for Blythe recognized the woman for who she was now—her husband's first wife. The one whom he'd actually loved, and had fought so hard to get back.

Blythe hesitated beneath the towering portrait. It was a strange thing—beautiful, certainly, but unnerving. The woman stood in a haze of water, surrounded by foxes that peered out among ferns with eyes that glowed gold from the light that drenched the portrait. Life's eyes, however, had been cut off.

Blythe drew a step closer, searching the curve of Life's cheek, the tenderness of slender fingers wound around the handle of a chalice. She searched every piece of this woman for any sign that she could be Signa, but Blythe found no similarity. Squinting, she noticed that the canvas had a long seam down the center that was barely visible to the naked eye. She followed its path to discover that it wasn't a seam at all, but the edge of a door. One that she immediately stepped toward, grasping a small handle that was hidden among the ferns. Before she could turn it, however, the door swung open.

Blythe staggered back, scarcely avoiding having her face struck by the wood. Aris's dour presence filled the hall as he stood at the threshold with folded arms and a seemingly permanent scowl curling his lips. Though his body concealed most of the room, Blythe managed to catch a glimpse of a brilliantly bold tapestry above his head. It seemed there were more, too. Giant, colorful creations that traveled on lines stretching across the ceiling. She stared past Aris, trying to get a better vantage, but he stepped outside and shut the door behind him.

"Is that where you work?" She moved closer. "What is it that you do in there?" A deep curiosity festered within her, though if the haughty set of his jaw was any indicator, Aris was not inclined to share details.

"This room is off limits" came his answer, as chilled as ice. "You have a suite of your own. Go to it."

Blythe puffed the full extent of her sigh from somewhere deep in her lungs, sparing him none of her resentment. "You are primeval if you think that where you put me could ever be called a suite. It feels as though I've been trapped on an expedition to the arctic north. Which is not how I would ever choose to spend my honeymoon, in case you were wondering."

"I wasn't." He didn't lean back against the portrait but instead held his spine so rigid that for perhaps the first time, Blythe found that he looked more inhuman than not. "It's not my fault that you can't start a fire."

She made a fist around the skirts of her gown. "It *is* your fault that I have need for one."

"What do you suppose I'm to do about—" He stilled, forehead crinkled as Blythe's stomach chose that precise moment to scream its dissatisfaction over the fact that she still was not eating. She only stared back, refusing to let herself feel any embarrassment, for it was Aris who should feel bad for putting her in such a state.

When he only continued to stare, however, looking entirely disgusted, Blythe pressed, "Why don't we say that this is a problem to be solved at a later time? Perhaps after supper. You do eat, don't you?"

The light drew away from the portrait, following Aris as he stepped toward her. "Of course I eat, you miserable girl."

Such brilliant news was this that Blythe clapped, ignoring the jab. All his names for her practically felt like terms of endearment at this point. It seemed they were to have a lifetime of exchanging them, and she wondered what else he might one day come up with. "Wonderful. What are we having?"

"We?" It seemed there was some sort of silent war raging within him. Whatever he was brooding over, Blythe didn't care. She waited, arms crossed, for him to eventually hiss through his teeth, "There's nothing prepared."

"Nothing prepared?" Surely she had misheard him, for how could that be true? "You told me months ago that you employ a cook and a butler." Though she was fully aware of how foolish she sounded, Blythe's aching stomach refused to give up hope. Desperately, she asked, "Then what on earth were you planning to eat?"

There was little warning for what came next as Aris gripped her by the shoulder, fingers curling into her skin. And suddenly, the walls of Wisteria were melting around her once more.

CHAPTER FIVE

THE SPACE BETWEEN BLYTHE AND ARIS MORPHED INTO AN IMPOSSIBILITY, encompassing them in a wonderscape crafted from the depths of Aris's imagination. There was a midnight lake filled with water that shone silver, and a sky so inky black that the smattering of the stars upon it looked like a lie, as if someone had taken a paintbrush and flicked them onto a blank canvas.

Even more impossible was the water itself, for they stood upon it as a banquet table took shape between them. Blythe slid free from her slippers, and though she was able to feel the water rippling beneath her toes, they did not get wet.

On the table were two place settings and ornate flatware with a black base and a golden handle that shimmered as she held it. Even the chairs were fabulously odd creations, for the back of each one had been carved into an intricate design—one of them like the head of a deer, with antlers that spiraled high over the back of the seat, tall enough to make whoever was sitting there appear to wear them like a crown. The second was carved like an owl, its wings stretching to the sides of whoever was to sit there.

"What is this place?" Blythe made no effort to conceal her wonder. Though Aris kept his face flat as he took the seat with the antlers—somehow managing to look powerful as they adorned the back of his head—she could tell by the slight lessening of his severity that he was glad she asked.

"It's tonight's dining room."

Wherever they were, it was certainly no room. There wasn't a single wall as far as the eye could see. Blythe had no doubt that Aris was trying to show off, wanting her to better understand the magnitude of his power. Unfortunately for him, it didn't unnerve her as he might have hoped. Blythe certainly was beginning to understand just how much power this man she'd bound herself to had. As alarming as it was, it was also fascinating. If she had powers, turning her dining room into a starscape was precisely the sort of ridiculous thing she might do. How wonderfully dramatic Aris was.

She touched the back of the owl's wing before taking a seat in the chair. It was sturdy beneath her, not just an illusion. "Where did this come from?"

"From the most brilliant minds all across the world. Most of them horrendously underappreciated."

She mulled over that comment, confused. "Couldn't you change their fate if you find them so undervalued?"

"I could," Aris answered, "but I won't. The unfortunate truth is that the world doesn't work that way. Not every genius will be appreciated, and too many amateurs will get the attention that others deserve."

She noticed then that there was a chandelier above their heads, one made of iron branches and elongated black candlesticks that seemed to float in the air. What any of it hung from, Blythe couldn't say. She tipped her head back to stare at the marvel, feeling as though she'd entered another world.

And she had, she supposed, for she was now married to Fate. Married to a man who, without batting an eye, could give her a dining room made of midnights. A man who looked entirely unimpressed by his own creation, one who, Blythe realized, must have spent a hundred thousand nights just like this one, alone beneath an impossible sky.

As much as Blythe enjoyed spending time on her own, it seemed a shame not to have someone to share a space like this with. Already she was thinking of how to word such an experience into the letters she'd write to Signa. She glanced at Aris, wondering how many times he'd brought his late wife to a space like this, and how it might have felt to come here alone after he'd lost her. Blythe thought of nearly twenty years of dinners spent with her family. With her mother chatting with everyone about their day while Percy either asked after their father on the nights Elijah had stayed late at the office, or busied himself with trying to look impressive when Elijah was there, stoic and always focused on work. In her mind's eye she even saw Warwick standing at the side of the room, trying to pretend like he wasn't eavesdropping on every conversation as he waited to be of service.

She may have never dined upon an iridescent lake with a sky of stars that pressed so close it felt like she could reach out and snatch one, but she'd had a dining room that had always been noisy with tinkling silverware and chatter. Exquisite as it was, the space around them was too quiet. Too empty. It reminded her of the months she'd spent sick and alone in her room without a soul for company. She curled her toes against the lake, dread lodged in her chest.

Never again would she let herself feel that way. Which was why she tested her weight once more upon the water before dragging her seat closer to Aris, closing some of the wide berth between them.

"I much prefer this place to Wisteria," she told him simply. "I hate how you've redecorated since your soiree. If stagnant spaces bore you, you ought to revisit the palace's design."

"This *is* Wisteria. And everything in it is designed exactly as I intend." So cutting was his tone that the stars winked out just long enough for Blythe to see that beyond them lay the same flat gray stone of the palace. This dining room was an illusion, then, at least in part. The table and chairs seemed real, but everything else was of Fate's creation, making her see whatever he intended. As remarkable as it was, the realization of such a power was so unnerving that she picked up her knife just to have something solid in her grasp.

"What do you want to eat?" Fate asked, stiffer now that Blythe was nearer.

She leaned in. "What are my options?"

"The better question is what isn't."

She chose not to be surprised by this and answered without hesitation, "A hot pie with stew and mulled wine." There was little that sounded better on a cold night.

No sooner had she requested it than the food arrived on the table in a shimmer of gold. Steam wafted from the lid of the stew's tureen, its onion and thyme so fragrant that Blythe salivated. The pie had the most perfect golden crust and smelled like heaven on a plate. The wine came in a silver chalice, so rich a color that it was more a cherry hue than it was purple, which was fortunate as Blythe still had difficulty with anything the shade of belladonna.

And then there was the cake. Blythe didn't have nearly the same palate for sweets as her cousin, but she couldn't deny wanting a taste of the gorgeous wedding cake that manifested at the head of the table. It was at least two feet tall, with ivory icing and white lilies that cascaded down the sides, simple in its elegance and nothing at all like the fantastical wonderland in which they sat. Blythe wasted no time as she loaded her plate, already warmer simply from looking at the piping hot feast laid before her.

Though Aris said nothing, Blythe could feel his eyes on her, watching as she took a spoonful of stew and nearly cried when it hit her tongue. Never had she tasted lamb so rich and tender that she barely had need to chew. She took a bite of the pie next, warm and buttery as it slid down her throat. Blythe slumped in her chair, letting it heat her from the inside out. Was that melted goat cheese inside? Heavens, it was divine. Even the wine did not taste of any fruit that she knew, but of starlight soaked in the finest ambrosia.

The meal was, in every sense of the word, impeccable. After all their bickering and being given a room with no bed, Blythe couldn't believe Aris had even allowed her to taste it. She could only hope he wouldn't take it away from her once she got used to such finery, for if this was how Aris ate, then at least there was one part of this new life that she could look forward to. "It's incredible," she whispered as she took another spoonful. "Where did it come from?"

Aris had stopped watching her, looking mildly more satisfied as he cut into his venison. "All over the world, same as everything else."

Blythe's hand stilled midway to her lips. She didn't need to ask to understand what he meant—looking around the table, it was clearer by the second that every bit of this meal had been stolen. She looked immediately toward the wedding cake and, with great effort, set her fork down.

"Please tell me you didn't take this from someone else."

"Shall we start our marriage on a bed of lies? This is what you requested." He twirled his wineglass before taking a swig.

It was frustrating how much Blythe craved to pick her spoon up and take another bite. Instead, she resisted the urge to throw her fork at him. "I never asked for you to steal a *wedding* cake, Aris. We didn't even eat the one at our own wedding!"

"Do give me some credit. I don't despise marriage, Miss Hawthorne—" Aris froze with a quick hiss of breath, rubbing the band of light on his finger, which seared brighter at the use of her maiden name. When he could, Aris continued, "I despise *our* marriage. The wedding in question was called off once the groom realized that his betrothed had been scrumping his brother. I did everyone a favor by taking this cake off their hands."

That, at least, made Blythe feel less guilty about the severity in which she craved a slice. "What about the rest of it?"

"If you'd prefer not to eat, then we can be done." When Aris started to push from the table, however, Blythe grabbed hold of her fork and stuck it straight into the warm pie.

She couldn't say where any of the food came from, and she didn't understand Aris well enough to know whether he'd ever steal from anyone who needed it. Sometimes, like when he'd rescued a young kit during the Wakefields' fox hunt several months prior, it seemed there might be an honorable man beneath that rigid demeanor. And yet she couldn't forget how he'd tried to manipulate her, or how easily he was able to coerce a person's mind into believing whatever he desired.

Aris was dangerous, but Blythe needed to eat. And so she resigned herself to the fact that she, too, was likely doomed to become a horrible person now that she'd married this brute, and dug back into the pie.

"Just so I know for our very long and arduous future, is stealing from the unsuspecting something that you do every night?" She stuffed another bite into her mouth, having to make a concentrated effort not to look *too* thrilled by the taste of it.

To her surprise, she noticed that Aris was no longer scowling, though his frown was still carved deep. It didn't seem that her question annoyed him; rather, everything Blythe asked seemed to deplete him, as if Aris were a rag wrung dry. "You ask too many questions."

Perhaps, but Blythe only flourished her fork and asked, "How else am I to get to know my husband?"

His jaw clenched at the word, and Blythe made a mental note to use it more often.

"If you must know, I spend most dinners outside of my home. I travel to get whatever I desire from where I know it'll taste the best. The rest of my meals I'll either make myself, or take from those who have no use for them."

Blythe had many questions about this, and yet the one she gave voice to was, "You can cook?" Aris didn't seem the sort who would do anything to dirty his own hands. "Are you any good at it?"

"If you had centuries to practice something, don't you imagine you might become rather skilled? I've had the best instructors in the world."

She thought back to the art that had been displayed throughout the manor during the first night she'd seen Wisteria and how offended Aris had been when she'd commented that some of it seemed rather pretentious. If she had to guess, she'd say that Aris had been the one to create those sculptures. For what else was a person to do when they lived alone for an eternity?

"You've done a lot of traveling, then?" she asked, for as much as she despised Aris, Blythe had always wanted to travel. She'd spent hours holed up in Elijah's study with maps, and in the library reading tales of far-off countries and distant cities over and over again until she knew the details by heart. When she closed her eyes, she'd envision herself visiting those many places, tearing her way through a jungle with a machete or holding a parasol as she strolled beside a cerulean sea, the spray of salt upon her skin and wind gusting her hair.

"I rarely remain in one place for long." Aris's tone was suggestive enough to prickle Blythe's skin. Other than for her father and Thorn Grove, Blythe had no attachments to this town and would have loved to explore the world. But for Elijah's sake, she couldn't leave.

"Then it sounds like staying here will be a good change of pace for you," she told him as she took a heaping spoonful of wedding cake. She wondered where it had come from, for it tasted nothing like any cake she'd ever tried but of honey and ripe plums.

"We are not staying." Far behind Aris roused a great storm. Lightning cracked over his stag horns, and she followed its tail down to the golden burn of Aris's eyes.

"Well *I* am not going."

"I could always make you." He whispered the words as soft as a lover. It was clear when Aris was trying to rile her, but this he spoke plainly, as they both knew it was the truth.

"Should you try, I will tie myself to the trees," she promised him. "And every time you leave, our rings will ensure that you end up right back with me again."

Aris must have anticipated such an argument, for he didn't seem as bothered as Blythe had hoped. He only stood, the plates and flatware clearing themselves before Blythe had finished her meal. She barely managed to scavenge herself another bite of cake before it disappeared. "I wasn't finished!"

"But I am." He smoothed down his shirt. Each of his gilded buttons was straight and precise, and there wasn't so much as a crease in the white fabric. Aris looked so straitlaced that Blythe itched to reach out and make his collar crooked.

"The decision is yours," he said, "but know that if you refuse, then you cannot leave this palace any earlier than in a month's time. Your father and all your acquaintances believe that we are off on some extravagant honeymoon, and I do not care to deal with their questions or your frustrations when you get caught up in your own lies. Should you agree to leave with me, however, I will take you on that honeymoon and you will see parts of the world that you've never imagined."

It was no tiny inkling of curiosity that stirred within Blythe but an awful, colossal desire. She was disgusted with herself for even allowing the idea purchase in her mind, yet Blythe couldn't control it as she thought of all the places she'd imagined visiting, now within her reach without any of the hassle of travel. And she couldn't deny that escaping the dungeon that was Wisteria wouldn't be the worst fate.

"If I were to agree to such terms," she asked, "would we ever return to Celadon?"

It was Aris's easy answer that damned him. "Eventually, perhaps for a visit."

It wasn't good enough. Not nearly. Every vision of travel faded at once from her mind's eye, for Blythe refused to leave her father without some guarantee of when they'd be back.

"I'm not leaving," she told Aris. "I'll remain here, and in a month's time I will have my freedom." As dreary as Wisteria was, surely it was possible to survive it for a month.

Given Aris's smug expression, however, it seemed he held a different belief.

"Very well," he mused, too unbothered for Blythe's taste. "Do let me know when you change your mind."

And just like that, the night sky winked out of existence and the lake of silver slipped away to stone, stone, and more gray stone as far as the eye could see. Blythe once again stood in the hall, alone, as the fireplace rasped behind her.

CHAPTER SIX

One day at Wisteria, and Blythe already knew she'd made a grave mistake.

It was as though the manor had decided to punish her for staying by plummeting the temperature overnight. Cold as a corpse, she'd hardly managed a wink of sleep, having woken up coughing several times before she eventually rifled through her travel chest. She threw on some of her thicker wool dresses, layering them in an attempt to soothe her dry throat and chilled body so that she might find some modicum of rest.

If the temperature wasn't enough to keep her awake, the noise surely was. She was used to gusting storms and branches scraping at her windows. What she wasn't used to was a home that moaned and quivered with every breeze. At one point Blythe could have sworn that pieces of the ceiling crumbled to the floor, though they were gone by the time the sun rose. And she could tell, precisely, when the sun rose because she had no curtains to guard her against it. When she finally had managed to fall asleep, she woke what felt like minutes later to the burn of light behind her eyelids.

Fists curling, she promised to find a way to make Aris pay for this ridiculous behavior as she pushed from the bed. Out of habit she made to ready herself, only to think better of it before she took a brush to her disheveled hair. Who did she have to impress? Certainly not Aris. And if he wasn't going to allow her a good night's rest, then why should Blythe bother to make herself presentable for him?

She did not dress, clean her teeth, or do so much as pinch color into her cheeks before she slammed her feet into her slippers. She grabbed a robe out of sheer desperation for warmth, then pounded her way down the stairs.

To her surprise, the first sign of life was not Aris himself but the small black fox that they had rescued several months prior. It had been a kit at the time, though the creature was now fully grown as it slept curled on the stairs. The fox alerted at the sound of Blythe's stomping, and the moment she reached down to stroke its head, the foul thing hissed and lunged for her hand. She barely managed to yank her fingers back before the blasted creature could bite her.

With a chittering that sounded as if the beast was scolding her, the fox scurried down the stairs and out of view as if offended by Blythe's existence.

"I helped save you, you ungrateful beast!" she called after it, sharper than she meant to. She supposed she had the lack of sleep to blame for that.

As she continued down into the parlor, Aris was nowhere to be found. She hadn't seen him since the past night's dinner and looked toward the window in an unsuccessful attempt at finding some sign of his general direction from the slant of light. Her brows furrowed. How strange it was to search for magic and find none after being so entrenched in it.

The hearth was as glum as ever as Blythe took a seat to warm her hands. Though she knew the fire was not sentient, she couldn't help but pity the flames and hoped that by sitting there she might somehow inspire it to burn brighter. It didn't work in that present moment, though she intended to continue her efforts.

Blythe remained seated awhile longer, silent and listening for signs of Aris. He didn't seem to be anywhere in Wisteria, and though she should have been annoyed that he was able to somehow leave while she was pulled back any time she so much as thought of abandoning the palace, Blythe was surprised to find that she didn't mind. She'd never before been in a home entirely by herself. There had always been maids or a governess. Cooks, and men tending to the stable. Such a quiet was unfamiliar, and for a long moment Blythe remained motionless by the fire, unsure what to do other than listen to the crackle of the flames and the fox's claws scratching against the floors. When she could take no more of it she stood, deciding there was no better time to investigate Wisteria than with Aris gone.

She gave no thought to her first stop, for it had been on her mind since the prior night and throughout her few minutes of dreaming. She hurried up the stairs, skirts in hand—which were quite heavy when one had multiple layers of them to hold—and all the way to the highest floor where the ballroom and Life's looming portrait awaited her. As mysterious as her husband was, this was her chance to learn more about him and his magic. And so she reached for the door woven into Life's portrait, biting back a yelp when the knob stung her palm.

She reeled back, and upon further investigation saw that a thousand golden threads covered the door, barring it from entry.

So much for that plan.

A soft chittering sounded behind her, and Blythe glanced down to find the fox sitting several feet from her heels. She glared at the foul creature as it swished its black tail like a broom. The beast sounded as though it was laughing.

"Is everyone who lives here a monster?" Blythe asked.

The fox's glowing eyes observed her for a second longer before it jumped to all fours, head swiveling to look behind it. Blythe followed its gaze, choking on her breath when she saw a faint haze of what was most definitely white hair disappearing down a hall that Blythe was certain hadn't been there moments before.

Her body remained frozen even as the fox hurried after the figure.

"Aris?" Blythe hissed his name under her breath, arms winding around herself to quell her body's shivering. "If that's you, then stop this foolishness. This isn't funny."

It wasn't her husband who responded but a feminine laugh that should have made every hair on Blythe's body stand on end. Yet the sound was reminiscent of a summer breeze, soothing Blythe's fussing nerves and loosening her locked limbs.

Perhaps it was a hallucination. It wouldn't be the first time Blythe had had one, though it'd been months since she'd been plagued by that symptom of the belladonna poisoning. Still, how else was she to explain the hallway that emerged seemingly from nowhere, or the flashes of light in the corner of her vision that guided her path as she hurried forward?

The deeper she traveled, the more the palace began to shift from a drab Wisteria into the unfamiliar. Gray walls gave way to ivory paneling. Stone floors turned not to any wood or material she knew, but to patches of grass and clover that ensnared her ankles. It wasn't like wandering through a palace at all, but into a forest glade.

Whether this was real or happening within the confines of her own mind, Blythe knew she should be terrified. And yet she couldn't stop herself, one foot following after the other until she came upon a single door at the edge of a long, narrow hall. Behind it pulsed a warmth so grand that Blythe's longing flared to life.

Door was a loose term for what she saw, for it wasn't so much a door as an opening that appeared to be carved into the bark of a tree. It had a handle not of brass or iron but of wood carved into a spectacular design of a wisteria vine. Again Blythe heard the trill of butter-soft laughter, this time from behind the door.

"Do you hear her, too?" Blythe whispered to the fox, who wove between her ankles to scratch at the door. "Perhaps it's a trap. Aris might have my head if we go inside."

The fox did not care one bit about Blythe or her head. In the midst of her hesitation, it scratched harder and hissed its dissatisfaction. Blythe hissed back, and she'd have likely bopped the beast's rump with her toe had its teeth not looked so sharp.

"Fine," she told it. "But I'm opening it for *you*, not for me."

Against her better judgment, Blythe took hold of the handle and cracked the door open. Immediately, the fox slipped inside.

Blythe looked at once for the source of the laughter, though there was no one apart from herself and the fox inside this summer glade. It was so warm that Blythe could have stripped down to her bare skin. Though it was very much a room with its four-poster bed that was somehow carved into the base of a tree, it was also an impossibility. Another one of Fate's wonderscapes.

She tipped her head to the tree that towered over her. Once upon a time it might have been a wisteria, though now it was a husk that littered dried petals across a bed with sheets that had yellowed with age. Blythe circled the tree several times, believing it had to somehow be a wooden carving since there were no roots to be seen. Given the rotted wood that flaked against her palms, however, it couldn't be anything but real.

There were other oddities, too, like a vanity made of withered vines that were one touch away from snapping into dust. There was a mirror of chased silver and several portraits toward the back of the room painted in a vintage style one might find in a museum. In them, a man smiled as he danced with a woman whose hair shone as pale as moonlight. They wore nothing of the current fashion, but ancient clothing from a time long passed.

There was another portrait, too, of the same golden-haired man seated beneath the shade of a towering wisteria tree, his head leaning against the trunk as serene eyes looked back at the painter. It took Blythe a long moment to recognize that the man was Aris, as it was the first time she'd ever seen him wear such a placid expression. It took even longer to recognize that the woman in the first portrait was the one Blythe had been chasing down the hall only moments ago. She should have recognized who it was the moment she saw the white hair—Life.

The realization had Blythe backing into the wall, unconvinced that what she was seeing was more than a figment of her imagination. But the wall was firm against her back, and the trees chalky beneath her fingertips.

Which meant that, somehow, this place was real.

"What do you want with me?" she whispered to a room that met her only with silence. "If you're angry with me about Aris, you by all means can keep him. I lay no claim."

The heat of the room pressed against her again, firmer this time, and Blythe's head began to spin as a bead of sweat trailed down the back of her neck.

Blythe turned to the portraits, frowning at the man within them. At one point Aris had been an entirely different person, and the longer that Blythe stared and her vision swam, blurring the edges, the more she felt as if she were there before him. She could feel the painted moss against her bare soles and the pulse of the autumn forest that surrounded the two lovers against her skin. Heat from a waning sun bore down on her as fallen leaves crunched beneath her heels. There was music, too. Music that Blythe swayed to as she shut her eyes and let the story play out in her mind's eye. She watched as Aris smiled and drew her into his chest, able to feel the firmness of his body. The heat of his touch as he pulled her close, and—

Blythe nearly lost her footing when the fox scurried over her slippers, jarring her back into the long-forgotten suite and away from the handsome man she'd been dancing with in the middle of the woods. It took a moment to ground herself and remember that it hadn't been a handsome man at all, but *Aris*. And it hadn't been her, either.

This wasn't the first time such intrusive thoughts had entered her mind. Since around the time of Charlotte and Everett's wedding, Blythe had been plagued with visions of a faceless man whose laughter could ignite an inferno within her and whose touch she burned for. Never had such a person existed, and yet it always felt so real. Like the ghost of someone Blythe had spent her entire life waiting to meet.

At first she'd wondered whether it had anything to do with why she could see Death. If something within her had fundamentally shifted after the many times she'd been meant to die, only to be brought back from the precipice. Now, she wondered if it was Life, angry and toying with her for taking up this role in Aris's life.

Blythe held on to the wall for a good while as her mind swam with slivers of smiles and flashes of skin. Echoes of laughter and music. Always the same lilting music.

The longer she stood in the room, the more it felt like its walls were pressing against her, the weight so suffocating she thought she might fold into the floor. As odd as Thorn Grove was, there had been a charm to its eeriness. Her childhood home had embraced the rumors and leaned in to its quirks. But this once-thriving suite was merely a shell of something that had once been extraordinary. Something that was digging its claws beneath her skin and begging not to be forgotten.

Blythe picked up her skirts, ready to flee when she caught sight of a hand mirror lying among the vines on the vanity. It was of considerable age with a handle inlaid with gold filigree. Trembling, Blythe picked it up, surprised by how familiar it felt in her grasp.

It was then that the lights flickered, blurring until they simultaneously slanted to the door. The fox perked its ears, and as it sprinted to greet its returned master, Blythe clutched the mirror to her chest. She knew she should return it to the vanity. Knew that she should flee and leave this place behind. Yet her fingers refused to unfasten from its handle, her thumb stroking up and down the filigree.

Perhaps it was to prove to herself that this was real, or perhaps it was another reason entirely that drove Blythe to tuck the relic into the folds of her dress. It was only a mirror after all, pretty but trivial. Yet there was no time to ponder it as pale light spilled through the doorway and flooded the floorboard as Aris grew nearer. She tossed the door open before he could find her and sprinted through Wisteria with the nimblest steps she could manage.

Blythe did not stop until she'd made it back to her room, the memory of Life's laughter still ringing in her head.

Dearest Father,

Do forgive my delay in correspondence and the briefness of my letter; I'm writing to you from the frosted wonderland that is the city of Verena.

Though it is barely winter, Aris's home is Christmas incarnate, full of quaint shops and streets blanketed with snow so powdery that special shoes are sometimes required to avoid sinking into it. Though Verena is not necessarily how I envisioned spending a honeymoon, I am glad to see where my husband comes from. I do wish I had packed a few more coats, though Aris is having several made for me as we speak.

While we had hoped to make it to the countryside to visit Byron and Eliza, I'm afraid that foul weather has cut our bridal tour short. It seems that we will be spending the next several weeks here in Verena. I do so wish that you could come, as I'm certain you would love it.

Do not worry for me. The city is splendid, and I will undoubtedly find countless ways to entertain myself. Also, I would be remiss not to mention the food, as the palace chefs are the finest I have ever known. I do not say this so that you might think I've moved on from life at Thorn Grove, however, for nothing could be further from the truth.

How are you faring? I eagerly await stories of all the adventures I hope you've been having, and assurance that everyone at Thorn Grove is doing well. I miss you dearly, and I will see you as soon as I'm able.

And before I forget—Aris keeps a fox for a pet. Isn't that a delightful and purely random fact?

Yours always,
Blythe

My Wonderfully Strange Cousin,

I begin this letter by expressing to you, with full sincerity, that I am well. Aris has yet to murder me in my sleep, though every so often I admit to catching a gleam in his eyes that convinces me he's considering it.

Fear not, as if either of us are to perish from the other's hand, I assure you that I will not be the first to die. Perhaps that is dramatic, but fret not, dearest cousin. I do not regret the deal I made with Aris. In fact, this war between us has become rather like a game, and I do so love to win.

I hope that you are warm and well at Foxglove, and that the estate is treating you well. I say warm because Aris has turned Wisteria Gardens into an everlasting and uninhabitable winter, much like the kind you read about in fairy tales. I fear how much worse it may become once it truly does begin to snow, though I have some time before then to plan my next move. It'll have to be a memorable one, as Aris has forbidden me from leaving Wisteria for at least one month's time so that no one will question the validity of our honeymoon. What kind of honeymoon anyone might have believed we'd have in mid-November is beyond rationale. I told my father I was in Verena, and think that perhaps I have a career in fiction-writing. As I cannot sleep, I've made up the entire town in my mind's eye. It's so maddeningly thorough that I'm almost disappointed it's not a real place. How fun it would be to rule a land of winter!

Though a month is a small amount of time in the grand scheme, I know in my heart that I will perish should I wait that long to see your face. Which brings me to why I am writing you today—not to lament Aris (although do be assured that I find great pleasure in such a task), but to tell you that every morning for the past week he has left me to fend for myself in Wisteria as he does God knows what. I find myself with plenty of time alone and admit that after months of being stuck dying in Thorn Grove, I find that solitude is not to my taste. You mentioned at the wedding that you had something to tell me, and I'd like to know what it is. Boredom has made me impatient.

While I will readily admit that I do not fully understand your abilities, I hope that when you receive this letter you will become one with the shadows and slither through the darkness to come and fetch me. I do hope that you find a way, as I'm looking forward to seeing you very soon. For the sake of my sanity, do make haste.

Eagerly awaiting your visit,
Blythe

CHAPTER SEVEN

Blythe hunched toward the waning candlelight, reading over the still-damp ink three times before sealing the letters with wax. The one she'd written to her father wasn't her greatest work, but she was anxious to hear from him and prayed that her words would offer enough of the truth to quell his worries. Elijah was a clever man, though, and she worried over how little information she had available to share with him. It wasn't as though anything of interest was happening within the dreary walls of Wisteria. Blythe was tired of being perpetually cold and eternally bored. In fact, her greatest thrill from the past several days as a married woman was prying at the edges of her imagination to write the letter to her father, and being as dramatic as she craved while writing Signa's.

She was glad, at least, that Verena wasn't a real place, for her father would never be able to look it up on a map and learn of her deceit.

Blythe stretched from her seat, fingers curled around the

crinkled envelopes. It was an hour meant for slumber, yet one would never know that from the moonlight that spilled in from her window. She'd tried to sleep, though the hovel that was her suite kept her coughing at all hours. When she wasn't consumed by a spell, her mind was too thick with visions of the faceless man whose presence made her chest ache. And when she did not think of him, she thought instead of Life's chambers. Of the forest glade and the vanity at which Life would have sat, brushing her silver hair.

She never should have taken the mirror off that vanity. The thing was so ancient that it was one too-tight grip away from snapping in half, so she'd swaddled it in satin and enclosed it within the safety of a drawer she hoped Aris would never have any reason to search.

She kept the sealed letters clutched to her chest with one hand as she took hold of her candle with the other. If sleep was useless, then she might as well figure out how to send her messages. Aris would likely try to read them, yet he was her only option. While she'd heard signs of his presence every now and then, he'd kept his distance. She'd checked her serpentine ring several times to ensure that the band of light was still beneath it, for the blasted thing had not burned once despite how he'd spent the past several days gallivanting off to God knows where. He was gone whenever she'd searched for him, returning in time to leave dinner at her door and disappear before she could open it.

Blythe had tried not to give this habit of his any thought, for it angered her to know that he was off doing whatever it was that people with mystical powers did while she was forced to spend her days with a hearth that wheezed as much as she did, and a maniacal fox who had soiled one of her favorite gowns and kept stealing her stockings like it was a game. At this rate, she had half a mind to skin the beast and use it as a blanket, which she told the fox every time she had the opportunity. It was a shame the beast was so cute.

It was impossible *not* to wonder about Aris, though. Especially when Blythe had nothing better to do than spend her waking hours puzzling over the mystery that was her husband. He'd looked like an entirely different person in the portraits—so much softer and kinder as he danced atop moss and burnished leaves with a silver-haired beauty.

And it was even more impossible not to think about him when he'd left a pastry at her door several hours prior—a sticky, honey-flavored mound of perfectly cooked dough that wasn't too sweet. It was still warm by the time she bit into it, and while Blythe was initially startled by Aris's random display of kindness, she quickly realized that he wasn't being *kind* at all. Rather, he wanted to make it abundantly clear that he was off somewhere magical while she was stuck in a stone dungeon, hoping that he would take pity on her and bring her his crumbs.

Though it seemed unlikely that Aris was home, she planned to leave the letters somewhere he could find them. If she didn't get one sent to her father soon, she had no doubt that Elijah would hunt her down himself, even all the way to the imaginary kingdom of Verena. As much as she'd like to see him, the idea of Aris and her father mingling formed a knot in her stomach.

She was grateful for the glow of the candlelight to guide her through the stony halls as she wandered down the steps and toward the parlor where Aris often took his tea by the forever-burning hearth. While she planned to leave the letters for him on the tea table, she was surprised to find that Aris was not off gallivanting at all. Rather, he sat in one of the high-backed leather seats, a half-empty glass of bourbon beside him. The sight stuttered Blythe's heart. She blew out her candle, lungs squeezing as she leaned around the corner to spy on him.

Perhaps it was the hour that had Aris so disheveled. He looked every bit like a man who'd tossed around in bed, his head bent in exhaustion. All the same, if she looked at him in precisely the right light, Aris reminded her of a fairy-tale prince, with fitted pants and a loose white tunic that was unbuttoned at the collar and rolled up his forearms. His hair was mussed, and the veins in his forearms were pronounced as he took a swig from his glass. His chair was positioned close enough to the hearth that he'd kicked up his boots to warm himself.

Upon his lap was a tapestry. It was similar to the golden one that Blythe had spilled her blood onto all those months ago, but far larger and decorated with an impossibility of colors she'd never seen. Between Aris's fingers glinted a silver needle that moved with such swiftness Blythe wouldn't have been able to see it if not for the way it shone in the fire's glow.

It was wrong to say that Aris looked relaxed—his movements were manic and precise—but he did look peaceful, if inhuman. His chest hardly rose or fell, every part of him still with the exception of his sewing arm. One could not look at him and see anything but the paranormal as he wove colors across his canvas, each stitch like the strike of a blade.

What began as a standard tapestry soon waterfalled down his lap, pouring over his knees and piling onto the wood floor, lengthening until the threads turned black and Aris stilled. Only then did his lips part with the first softened breath he'd taken in minutes. Blythe very much wished to be able to see his eyes as he roused, for it seemed that his mind had been somewhere else entirely. Silence stretched as she contemplated her escape, feeling as though she was intruding on something private, before Aris's whisper came as quiet as snowfall, "Why aren't you sleeping?"

His voice was dazed and hollow, as if she'd awakened him from a dream.

"It's too cold to sleep." It was a strange thing, to match his softness. Never had they spoken so simply to each other. "I fear that if I do, I may never wake up."

Aris made a strange sound in the back of his throat. A laugh, possibly? "Perhaps that was by design."

"I have no doubt that it was." Blythe's nightgown trailed behind her as she tried to get a better look at the tapestry Aris held in a white-knuckled grip. "What is it that you're working on?"

He loosened his hold, eyes bleary as he ran a hand down the length of his jaw. "What do you think it is?"

Blythe didn't need to *think*. Despite her question, she knew exactly what Aris wove. Still, it felt like too much of an impossibility to acknowledge aloud. Rather than answer, she asked, "Do the colors mean something?"

Aris peered down at the tapestry as if seeing it for the first time, his thumb skimming the threads. Tension knitted his brows; whether he'd found something in the design that he was unsatisfied with or whether he was debating the merits of answering her was impossible to say. At first, it seemed he was keen to ignore her. But just as Blythe drew a step back and contemplated returning to her suite he said, "Each color is an emotion. Together they tell a story, because that's all that a life really is—a series of feelings and emotions that draw a person toward action or inaction."

What a horribly clinical definition.

"And what emotions do these represent?" She took a seat on the arm of his chair, peering down at butter-soft yellows and greens as bright as moss that transitioned into what reminded Blythe of a sunset—rich pinks and plums that darkened into a shade she had no name for, but that looked the color of a summer sky before a storm.

While the tightness between Aris's brows remained, he must have been able to sense that Blythe's curiosity was genuine, for he did not shoo her away and instead angled the tapestry to allow her a better view.

"Every emotion under the sun," he said. "The possibilities are limitless, and though there is an endless variety of colors, each hue represents something particular to some degree. But as no two people will ever feel anything the exact same, no two tapestries will ever look identical."

Blythe bent to inspect his work, scanning it for any patterns. Though Aris drew away from her nearness, she could still see that the stitching was flawless, not a single thread frayed.

"There's a lot of blue," she noted, admiring the many variants—from a shade as pale as dawn to one as dark as ripened berries.

"There is." Aris's fingers once again curled around the cloth. "The man this tapestry belongs to will lead a content life. Nothing special, though he'll live well into his years and will die at peace."

By the monotone of Aris's voice, one might think that he was telling her this man would suffer a great curse and die in a tragic accident.

"You speak as though that isn't an admirable achievement in itself," Blythe said. "Is it so wrong to have a simple life that makes you happy?"

Having been drawn in by the tapestry, Blythe hadn't realized how close she was to Aris until she turned to face him, seeing that his head was against the back of the seat, eyes hardened as they scrutinized her. "I never said there was anything wrong with it."

"You didn't," she agreed, fully aware of how his breath grazed her cheek and of how her nightgown was tangled around her ankles. "You just said it like you were delivering bad news and couldn't possibly look more uninterested if you tried."

His golden eyes were as searing as the sun. Though Blythe hadn't intended to, it seemed she'd struck a nerve and couldn't help but pry at its edges.

"Do you even remember the name of the person whose fate you just crafted?" she pressed, despite knowing that she was more than toeing her way into tumultuous waters.

"It's ridiculous to expect me to remember such a thing. I've woven more tapestries than you could fathom."

"Ridiculous to remember a name?" Blythe laughed, pleased when he continued to lean away. "You foretold his fate only minutes ago, and already you've forgotten him." She kept a close look on Aris's face, ensuring that he looked sufficiently annoyed—but not so much so that he'd turn her away—before continuing. "Admit it, you were bored by that man's life."

"Of course I was." Every inch that Aris sat up was an inch Blythe leaned back. "Human lives are inherently boring. People are born, they learn, they love, and then they die, always. I should not be condemned for wishing something would break the monotony of a story I've read infinite times before."

There was a crinkle of annoyance at the corners of his eyes that Blythe found somehow familiar. This entire conversation was.

"I understand wanting something that excites you," she told Aris, thinking of her father's maps and the many places she'd hoped to one day venture. "But that doesn't mean you shouldn't respect the other stories, too. Building a life that makes you happy is nothing to dismiss."

Aris ignored her as he melted back in his seat, becoming one with the chair. Though Blythe knew the safest thing to do would be to ease away from the conversation and leave him be, she could not stop the question that poured from her. "May I watch you weave another?"

"Are you going to have opinions about that one, too?"

"It's likely." She smoothed out her skirts, brushing the hem away from her bare feet. "I have an opinion about most things."

"Yes, I'm beginning to understand that." Though it took a long moment for him to rouse, eventually the tapestry on Aris's lap disappeared in a slant of light and a fresh cloth took its place. The moment his fingers skimmed its edges, shadows sharpened the hard planes of his face. Needle between his fingers, he hesitated before his canvas. His eyes flickered toward her, then back to the tapestry, and with a soft breath he struck the needle down. Instantaneously, the colors began to pour.

Blythe dropped to her knees beside him, leaning over the arm of the chair for a closer vantage. She was hypnotized by the dance of his needle, by the flashes of silver that poured color faster than she could keep up with. Watching Aris was like watching the most extraordinary performance, and Blythe hung on every deft twist of his fingers. It took her a long while to notice that this tapestry was nowhere near as bright as the previous, woven primarily in shades of gray and deep plums that faded into black. Whereas the former tapestry had stretched onto the floor, this one barely reached Aris's lap.

Blythe understood the bleakness that made his face gaunt. Understood his hesitation as he trailed a gentle finger down the final black stitch.

She set a hand atop his shoulder. "Can you not change it?" While she'd tried to keep anything that resembled accusation from her voice, Aris's shoulders tensed all the same. He clenched the needle tighter.

"*Can I* isn't the question. It's a matter of *should I*." Blythe drew her hand away at the bite of his words. "Not everyone gets to grow old. Not everyone gets to love or be loved in return. Sometimes the world is cruel."

"But they *should* get those things. And if it's as simple as a few threads on a tapestry, then why not?"

"Just as Death does not choose when people die, I do not choose how they live," Aris argued. "I write their story as it's shown to me, and that is the way of things. It matters not if someone is cruel or kind. It makes no difference whether they deserve the life that they get. Once a soul tells me its story, I do not alter it. I do not embellish. I give it the fate I foresee, nothing more, nothing less."

"And that fate can never change from how it was foretold?" she asked. "Are you saying there's nothing a person could ever do to make a difference in their tapestry?"

For a long while Aris answered with only his glare, for they both knew the truth of it—Blythe had changed her own fate not once, but several times. Whatever story he'd woven for her, she had defied.

"You are an anomaly, aided by Death's hand." Though there was much more that Blythe wanted to ask, the shadows across Aris's face had moved to hollow out his eyes. "Other lives were taken so that yours could continue."

Cold sweats raked over her as Blythe thought of Percy. She wrapped her hands around herself, so deep in her haze of thoughts that she barely realized the hearth was no longer struggling. It fed off of Aris's intensity, drawing sweat upon her brow. She leaned back, fearful of breaking whatever strange spell was allowing them to have a relatively civil night.

Aris scrutinized her as if waiting for Blythe to stand and see herself out. Instead, a question brewed, and though it seemed most comfortable concealed in the depths of her mind, she forced it out before the opportunity was lost. "What does my tapestry look like?"

Aris disappeared the second tapestry from his lap, elbows propped on his knees as he leaned down to her level.

"Your tapestry," he began, the words soft at first, though each one grew progressively more biting, "is one of the most hideous abominations I have ever seen."

Though they were no strangers to finding ways to get under each other's skin, Blythe got the distinct impression that Aris's answer was honest, and she felt a certain pride at his utter distaste for the thing. If he hated it, then it was undoubtedly spectacular.

She tried to laugh, but managed hardly a sound before a fit of coughing overtook her.

Aris's frown cleaved deep into his face as he recoiled. "Cover your mouth, you mongrel."

"I *am* covering my mouth," she snapped. "What do you want me to do, magically cure a cold? It's the fault of you and your dusty, arctic torture chamber"—Blythe broke off to cough again, then continued sharply—"that I'm falling ill in the first place!"

He drummed his fingers along the side of his chair, and as if deciding that he had nothing more to say on the matter, Aris dropped his attention to the letters that Blythe had forgotten she was carrying.

"What are those?" he asked.

Blythe clutched them to her chest, thumb pressing down on one of the wax seals. "They're letters."

"I can see that. Why are there two of them?"

She fought the urge to chew her lip, not wanting to draw suspicion to the fact that one of her letters practically begged Signa to come and break her free from this place. "One for my father, and another for Signa. Surely I'm not forbidden from speaking to my cousin?"

Just the mention of Signa's name seemed to settle an infinite amount of weight upon Aris. "I hope that you've told her to come to her senses and trade places with you?" He held his hand out, and though it took a great deal of nerve, Blythe dropped the letters into his waiting palm. She half expected him to tear the envelopes open. Instead, the parchment winked out of sight the moment it touched his hand.

Her surprise must have shown, for Aris cast a tired frown. "I have more self-respect than to degrade myself by reading your private letters. As curious as I am about what you have to say on the topic of our extravagant honeymoon and all the fun we're having, I'll use my imagination like any civil person would."

Were she in his position, Blythe had to admit that she would have allowed her nosiness to get the best of her. She supposed she should be grateful that Aris had more tact, as infuriating as that truth was.

"They'll receive your letters in this afternoon's post." He pushed from his seat, unrolling his sleeves as he turned his back to Blythe and made his way down the hall. "Go and take your disease-ridden self to bed."

It took everything in Blythe's power to bite her tongue as Aris strolled away. She used the hearth to relight her candle, silently cursing the brute as she made the trek back to her room. After a cursory scowl at her ridiculous boar handle, she threw the door open.

Only this time, the room was not bathed in silver light. It was shrouded in such darkness that Blythe wouldn't have been able to see so much as a foot ahead of her if not for the candle. And was it her imagination, or was the room warmer, too?

Blythe stretched the candle before her, spotting the source of the darkness at once.

Curtains. Finally, the brute had given her curtains.

CHAPTER EIGHT

Blythe tried to return Life's mirror the next morning only to find that the hall leading to the woman's suite was once again obscured. For an hour she looped the upper floor, squinting in the hopes that the light would shift and reveal a path, and always ending right back where she started—beneath the forever-looming portrait of a woman long deceased.

Only when she reached it this time, Blythe took a seat, mirror in hand. Its surface was not of glass, but one of polished obsidian, obscuring her reflection in darkness and a thick haze. Still, she had trouble looking away from it. Not because of how ridiculous she looked in her several layers of dresses and coats, but because the longer she stared at its inky surface, the more the haze began to move. Her finger skimmed the length of the carved handle as she squinted, drawing her reflection closer.

Rubbing her eyes did not clear the darkness that swirled not *within* the mirror but outside it. Behind her. Every muscle in Blythe's body tensed, for she knew in her bones that this was no trick of her vision.

"So this is the state in which my brother has kept you." It was Death who emerged from the shadows brewing behind her. Blythe knew it was him from the timbre of his voice and the darkness that swathed him, but as he moved to stand before her, he took a form that she'd not seen before. Not one of a reaper, but of a broad-shouldered man with fair skin, gray eyes, and hair the color of bone. As human as he appeared, there was an unnatural stillness that made him even eerier in this form, for his chest didn't rise or fall with the steadiness of breath and, like Signa, he did not blink nearly as much as he ought to. What an unnerving couple they made.

"Your brother is not known for his kindness." She turned toward Death, lowering the mirror to her lap. Her eyes skimmed to the writhing shadows at his feet, where the traitorous fox looped circles around his ankles. "Have I finally frozen to death? Is that why you're here?" Blythe's lips pressed tight as Death stooped to the fox's level, running a gloved hand down the length of its spine. The blasted thing practically purred.

"Fate may want you to give up," Death said, "but he won't go as far as to kill you." He straightened, and in his hand was a letter. *Her* letter, Blythe realized. The one she'd written to Signa.

"That wasn't meant for you!" Blythe knew that Death had tried to help her, that he'd broken rules to keep her alive. Even so, she couldn't help the anger that flared in his presence.

"She gave it to me. Signa doesn't have the power to transport other people," he told her. "I, on the other hand, can slither through the shadows, as you so eloquently put it, and bring you to Foxglove."

Blythe's throat was thick with dread, for all she could think about was how he'd have to step closer. How he'd have to touch her. She scanned down the length of his arms, fixated on his leather gloves. They weren't the only things that covered his body; in fact, all skin apart from Death's face was covered. He was finely dressed in a coat of black, with a cravat tightened against his throat and matching trousers and boots of great making. In this form, Blythe supposed he could be considered handsome. Still, how Signa had fallen in love with the literal embodiment of Death was entirely lost on her.

Blythe couldn't breathe in his presence. It was as though her throat was full of gravel, every inhale a rasp. But Death was her ticket to Foxglove. He alone could get her out of Wisteria and to civil company before boredom had her chewing off her own arm.

When Death's eyes fell to the mirror, she curled it quickly into her skirts. "Will it hurt?" she asked, seized with dread when Death's expression pinched.

"No, but it will feel strange." Slowly, he pulled his focus back up to her face. "I swear on everything that I am that I will never again hurt you. And I will speak to my brother, too, about getting you better accommodations."

Death watched her with such intensity that Blythe flinched, uncertain what to do with the vow. It was strange how adamantly he spoke it, though if that vow was what kept her alive, then she'd gladly accept it.

"You will do no such thing." Though Death was too close for

comfort, Blythe stood to look him firmly in those strange, unblinking eyes. "I have this handled. If Aris thinks I've spoken with you, his temper will only worsen. The last thing I need is for him to believe that we're conspiring against him."

She took a step forward before Death could argue and demanded, "Do you swear on your life that this will not kill me?"

With a quiet puff of air that might have been a laugh, he answered, "I swear it."

"Then what about Signa's life?" she pressed, for his answer was not enough to quell her worries. "Do you swear on hers, as well?"

Death's jaw tensed. "I do not care for this question, though my answer is the same. Going with me will not kill you." He stretched a hand toward hers, though he didn't touch it just yet, leaving it up to Blythe to close the distance between them.

Even through his gloves, touching Death felt like falling beneath a frozen lake. Every part of her body seized with a shock so great that she forgot to breathe, remembering to do so only when her vision flickered to black. It felt like she was swimming, like the ground beneath her gave way to water that she slipped straight through. It was similar to what she'd felt days ago in her mother's garden, but different. Colder, but calmer. All the more terrifying, and yet not painful in the slightest.

Time was a construct, for she had vanished from Wisteria and arrived at Foxglove within the span of a single blink, though it somehow felt like ages had passed. She swayed on her feet, adjusting to the wood beneath her and squinting her eyes against the light until she could see the room Death had brought her to.

It looked like a study, though it was in far worse shape than her father's had ever been. There were papers littered about and journals spread open on the desk and floor. Through the window was a thrashing sea, and though the skies were gray, the manor was brightly lit. It was warm, too. So warm that Blythe shuddered as her temperature rose. She clenched and unclenched her fists, working feeling back in her limbs only to realize that Life's mirror was gone.

Good. Better that Death had it than she.

He'd moved to stand behind Signa, who sat cross-legged on the floor several feet away, sporting a genuine smile despite the shadows beneath her eyes and the disarray of her hair. The stains on her dress, too, had Blythe wondering when she'd last changed.

Though it was Blythe who ought to have posed the question, it was Signa who asked, "What on earth are you wearing?"

Blythe glanced down at her slippers and the layers of dresses she wore beneath her wool coat. She'd been so eager to leave that she hadn't even considered the need to get ready. "It seems I'm wearing my pajamas."

"That's what you sleep in?" Signa blinked those strange, too-wide eyes of hers before whipping her head toward the reaper. "And you didn't let her change?"

Death eased into a chair beside her, stroking the head of his massive hound, Gundry, as he tipped back in his seat. "She didn't ask to." In that moment, the brotherly resemblance between him and Aris was unmistakable. Blythe didn't appreciate the squint of Death's eyes or the way his head tilted to observe her, as though she were a puzzle in need of solving. Especially when the only puzzle here was what Signa was up to.

"What is all this?" Blythe asked, taking her skirts in hand as she stepped over one of the journals, crouching to observe its messy scrawl.

Though Signa was still side-eyeing Blythe's many layers, she brightened at the question. "It turns out that my mother kept journals. We found dozens of them beneath a false bottom in one of her chests. I'm hoping to use them to figure out who killed my parents."

She should have known Signa would piece together another mystery for herself if left to her own devices. Blythe moved to investigate the journal that Signa was perched nearest to, trailing a finger down one of its yellowed pages. Though her touch was gentle, Signa frowned and shifted the journal away when she thought Blythe wasn't looking. It was no wonder the shadows beneath Signa's eyes were so severe. She looked like a dragon within the depths of its lair, hoarding treasures from all who dared approach.

Death stirred as he watched her, a small frown curling his lips. If Signa's behavior was unnerving to even him, that seemed like the most dangerous sign of any as to her cousin's mental state. Blythe was glad she'd sent Signa a letter, even if it had been for her own benefit.

She was about to close one of the journals and say something of the sort when Signa's attention flew to the door behind her. Her face at once went tart as she stepped before Blythe, as if to block her. Behind her, Gundry growled low in his throat.

"Shut your eyes if the light bothers you," her cousin hissed, glaring daggers toward an empty doorway. Then softer, she added, "And no, Liam, we have everything we need. Thank you." Blythe leaned around Signa, trying to get a better look. No matter how much she squinted, she was certain that no one was there.

It took a few more moments before Signa relaxed, telling her, "Don't worry, it was only the spirits." It was not lost on Blythe how dismissive the words were. Like talking to spirits was a casual, everyday occurrence. "Pay them no mind. They're mostly harmless."

"Mostly?" Blythe echoed, her pulse in her throat.

Signa lifted one of the journals from the floor, marking its page with a rose petal she plucked from a vase. "Even if they act out, you'll be fine."

As curious as Blythe was to learn what, exactly, a spirit could do, being harassed by one was the last thing in the world she ever wanted to experience. She glanced around the room—at Signa's state—and kept a false smile plastered to her lips as she asked, "I'm surprised by how quiet it is. Where has all your staff gone?"

"Most fled after the ball." Signa stepped gingerly around two more journals and sketches that lay open across the floor. "They couldn't stomach being in a place that lived up to its rumors of being haunted. I do have Liam now, though, and you'd be surprised how handy a ghost butler can be. Oh, and Elaine is still here. She's in charge, though there's not much of anyone for her to manage considering she can't see Liam. Which is a good thing, as he believes himself in charge. We have to come up with tasks for him, otherwise he starts shattering the windows. Anyway, I'd have Elaine bring up some tea so you could see her if it wouldn't raise a thousand questions about your arrival."

Blythe nodded for show only, once again sliding Death a look as she digested this information. This time he looked back, the shadows beneath his eyes acknowledging her concern about Signa's disarray.

At least Death had his wits about him. Though Signa seemed well and happy, it was clear she was spending far too much time with only the dead for company. Even her latest mystery was so entrenched in death that Blythe scrunched her nose. She understood Signa wanting to solve her parents' murder, truly, but there was no ticking timer or any reason for her to hole up inside Foxglove and become as inhuman as the rest of the company she kept.

Gently, Blythe took Signa's hand and gave it a good squeeze. "It sounds like we have much to catch up on, cousin. But I, for one, would like to enjoy the sun on my skin. What do you say to us getting dressed and taking this conversation outside?"

Though Signa cast one last look at a journal behind her, she squeezed back. "That's an excellent plan. Just as soon as I finish this last page."

CHAPTER NINE

When Blythe pictured the bustling seaside town in which her cousin lived, she'd imagined crisp blue skies and an ever-present warmth from the sun beaming down on them.

Fiore, however, had none of those things.

Blythe supposed it was her own fault for expecting warmth in the winter, though she never anticipated that a town by the water could be so abrasive. Yes, strolling down a vibrant green hill pocked with wildflowers was lovely if one could ignore the deadly cliffsides and the voracious sea that thrashed beneath them, but Blythe found that to be a difficult challenge. She hugged her coat against herself, trying to block all lethal drops from view as she trudged after her cousin in borrowed boots two sizes too large, walking lopsided and huffing for breath.

"Are you well?" Signa asked as they neared the bottom of the cliff. At first Blythe believed Signa was asking because of Blythe's gasps for air and the way her skin was probably turning pink from windchill and exertion, until Signa clarified, "At Wisteria, I mean. Is Aris treating you well?"

"Wisteria is in ruins," Blythe said by way of answer, careful with her words. She wanted to be honest with her cousin but also didn't want Signa to feel guilty for Blythe having taken her place in this marriage. "There isn't a single person employed to help me care for it, or at the very least help *warm* it. As for Aris..." Blythe trailed off. No curtains or heat in her room would ever make up for all that he'd put her through, but Blythe supposed he no longer warranted being called the devil incarnate. A "menace upon society" could still work, but Blythe held her tongue. "Aris is hurting. Whatever transpired between the two of you has left him wounded, and I believe he's acting out."

Signa's voice adopted a hardened edge. "Nothing *transpired* between him and I. Not in this lifetime, nor in any other."

To this, Blythe gave no response. Though she would have loved to believe that Signa was not the reincarnation of Life, how else could Blythe explain watching Signa raise a horse from the dead? Not to mention that Aris wouldn't have done half the things he did while trying to win Signa's heart if there wasn't irrevocable proof that Signa was the woman he'd been searching for.

As they approached the town center, Signa carved a path that had them weaving around an occasional passerby—none of whom stopped to converse with her, though some cast quick glances of acknowledgment that spoke of their familiarity. It didn't escape Blythe's notice how many others ducked their chins into their coats or scarves and hastened their steps when Signa strolled by.

If someone handed Blythe a blank canvas and instructed her to build a town befitting Signa Farrow, Fiore would be precisely what she'd design. The place had all the makings of charm but little of the execution. Quaint cobblestone streets gave way to vicious gales of salted wind that grated the storefronts. A man struggled to repaint the chipped and faded white exterior of his shop, paying close mind to any windblown drips.

The buildings, too, were deceptive. Though they were painted in light hues befitting the seaside, the town was built upon the bones of Gothic architecture. Twisting spires stretched atop shops that took great care to appear quaint despite the fanged gargoyles that loomed over empty streets. Strange a town as it was, Blythe's cousin looked perfectly at ease among its dreary skies, content as the wind swept her dark tresses back and the sea thrashed behind her. Shadows embraced Signa with every step, clinging to her skin and expanding around her as they journeyed deeper into town.

"Haven't you ever wondered what kind of person Life must have been?" Signa asked eventually, keeping her voice low so anyone who passed might think they were having a perfectly innocuous conversation.

"How could I not?" Too often Blythe pictured the woman whose bedroom suite she'd stumbled into. The one whose picture lorded over Wisteria—a constant reminder of her absence as well as her ever-looming presence.

Since her time spent in Life's old suite, Blythe could almost feel Life's presence seeping through Wisteria. Could almost see her strolling the halls with a paintbrush in hand or hear the echo of laughter as warm and soft as the rising sun. Wisteria was a tomb to Life's memory. A home where her ghost roamed free.

Blythe felt silly admitting any of this aloud, though the intensity of Signa's stare made it clear that her cousin was expecting more. And so she told her, "I have a hard time believing Aris was ever capable of love," just to fill the void. The lie seared her tongue the moment she'd said it, for the truth was that she knew no one as romantic as Aris. The man was more than capable of love; he was fueled by it. Who else would remain in search of his wife for so many centuries?

"Come now, he's not so bad as that." There was an inquisitive lilt in Signa's voice that had Blythe feeling like her cousin meant more than she was saying. "I believe Aris to be a man who would do anything for the person he loves, no matter the cost. Truth be told, I have admired him for it. There's no excusing what he's done, but I know that if I were him, I would do whatever needed to be done to get Death back." Signa inclined her head toward the sea, her last few words a breath on the wind.

Goose bumps flared along Blythe's arms, and she was glad that Signa was turned away and unable to see the nervousness that ate at her. Until she was given reason to, Blythe often failed to remember that Signa, too, was not entirely human. That she had killed so Blythe might live.

Blythe had never believed in the paranormal, but in the past year, she had come to accept that Death was real, her cousin was a reaper, and her husband the embodiment of fate itself. How quickly she had adapted to such a bizarre life.

"There's something I must tell you," Signa began after a brief silence, ignoring the shadows roiling at her heels. "Part of me believed I should stay out of it and let nature take its course, but it's about Aris and—" There was no warning for the pain that flared on Blythe's ring finger. She doubled over, clasping her hand with a cry as Signa's words cut off with a sharp gasp. Her lips pressed shut, as if tied by invisible strings.

Death emerged before her as if spun from the gales themselves. Darkness swathed his body as he took Signa by the shoulders, trying to steady her. While Blythe very much wanted to ask why he hadn't simply walked beside them like a civilized man, her cousin was unfazed by Death's arrival. And because Signa was unfazed, *Blythe* was somehow left feeling like the odd one in this situation, even though it was he who had just appeared from the shadows at her feet.

"You know it's no use," he whispered, though Signa shook his warning off with a hiss.

"Aris," Signa repeated, seething his name through clenched teeth. It seemed that each syllable pained her to speak. "It's not me that he's—" Again the band of light on Blythe's finger burned with such an intensity that she wondered if it might melt through her skin. Meanwhile, Signa looked ready to claw her nails into something when she couldn't get the words past her lips.

"That's enough about Aris!" Though anger made her chest tense, Blythe exhaled some relief as the light around her finger dimmed and the pain ebbed. "Whatever terrible thing you're trying to warn me about, I don't care to know. Not when this bloody ring doesn't want me to."

She kept her gaze lowered, not caring for the concern she'd seen on Death's face.

"Your parents," Blythe demanded, needing a distraction. "Tell me about your parents. Have you learned anything about what happened the night of their death?"

They began to walk again, Signa's heeled boots clomping slowly across the pavement. She seemed to be chewing on her words, testing whether they would make it through her lips this time. "I've been trying to read the journals in order," she said eventually, relaxing when her voice came freely, "but there are so many. My mother wrote in them nearly every night, beginning a year or so prior to her starting finishing school at a place called Hellebore House. She is . . . different than I expected. I always knew from stories that she had a hunger for the world, but I never quite realized the extent of it. She's seventeen in the journal I'm reading now and has not yet mentioned my father once."

"She's still young," Blythe offered, softening at her cousin's obvious distress. "Who knows who she might become over the next few journals." While she kept her voice light, Blythe's thoughts strayed toward thoughts that Rima was not the only Farrow who was different than expected.

Though the woman Blythe had seen in the portrait and the one whose room she'd visited neither felt nor looked like the Signa that she knew, there was no denying that she was the one Aris was searching for. Signa surely must have realized it, too. But instead, she'd fallen in love with Death and had left Blythe to fill her absence in Fate's life.

Blythe supposed this was why, as much as she'd loved fairy stories, she'd never believed in true love. Aris believed he'd found his soul mate, but in another life, that person had fallen in love with a different man.

That was the problem with love—there were too many variables. Too many things that could go wrong for anyone who dipped their toes into its tumultuous waters. Perhaps it was fortunate that Blythe had ended up in a loveless marriage. At least this way neither of them would ever be hurt.

Blythe flexed her left hand before her, staring at her ring as she so often found herself doing.

"Death," she called, sparing him a hesitant glance. "Have you ever seen a ring like mine before?"

"You may call me Sylas," he offered, which Blythe casually ignored. "And no, I cannot say that I have."

She wrung her wedding ring—her true one that resembled a snake—around her finger. She'd hoped that if he rifled through his memory for long enough, Death might come up with *something* to explain what was happening between her and Aris.

"Is it bothersome?" he asked, and all Blythe could think was that it wasn't nearly so bothersome as his voice—a sound that made every ounce of darkness more apparent.

"Of course it is. I can never figure out its rules. The blasted thing seems to always want us together. It usually burns when Aris and I are apart, but look." She waved her hand before him. "No burning. And he's been coming and going as he pleases while I'm left stuck in Wisteria."

If Death noticed the way she curled back when he drew nearer or inspected her too closely, he said nothing of it. A chill bit into her shoulders as she leaned against the stone entrance of a weatherworn tea shop, trying to keep a sufficient distance from him. It was fortunate that so few people were out today; how must she have looked, talking to someone that only she and Signa could see.

"Are you certain of that?" Death asked with such an intensity that Blythe felt the urge to settle her hands into her pockets and pull her coat tight. "You say that the ring wants you together; I doubt that even my brother could outwit whatever magic is brewing. You and Aris share an inseparable bond; focus on it. You may be surprised by what you discover."

If Death didn't sound so challenging, Blythe might have ignored him. But *because* he was challenging her, Blythe took that to mean he believed she might not be able to do it, which was enough reason to shut her eyes and prove him wrong.

She focused on the bite of metal around her finger, then the ring of light beneath it. On the bond that tethered her and Aris—slack and so loose that she felt as if she could grab it and pull. Mentally, that's exactly what she did. She pulled on the bond, testing it, and it grew taut beneath her hold.

Blythe's eyes flew open as the blood drained from her face. "He's here." Blythe couldn't say whether she was glad or all the more angry to learn of Aris's deceit. "You're telling me that he's been *lying*? That all this time he's been stuck at Wisteria like me?"

"Not stuck at Wisteria necessarily, but stuck with *you*." It was odd to see Death shrug, for he looked too human. "It's only a guess, though that ring binds him as much as it does you. It must be that when he felt you disappear—"

"He followed me," Blythe finished for him, a bitter laugh cleaving through her throat. The light that bound her to Aris burned brightly in her mind's eyes, casting an unsettling warmth across her skin. She prodded at it, watching the gold brighten as she drew one step, then two, following it.

A pressure in her chest acted as her unseen guide, urging her over loose cobblestone to sandy hills. Everything became warmer. Brighter, too, until she saw Aris standing on the windswept shore, just as she'd somehow known he'd be.

Aris wore a coat in so rich a navy that it conjured memories of a summer tempest. His golden hair was tousled by the wind and curling around his ears, touched by the sea salt. His face hardened as he glanced first to Signa, then to Death, before settling on Blythe.

"You simple, foolish man!" Despite herself, Blythe's body shook with laughter. "It's true, isn't it? Just as I cannot escape you, you cannot escape me." Sand made her steps slow as she closed the space between them. "Are you so prideful that you would have yourself suffer just so I could be kept miserable? If we cannot escape each other, then where on earth have you been spending your days?"

Aris looked as though he'd rather be anywhere else in the world as he returned his glower toward the sea. "Quit laughing, you ridiculous girl. Just because I can't leave for long doesn't mean I cannot leave at all."

"*I'm* the ridiculous one? You disappear just long enough to fetch me a pastry so that you can pretend you're off gallivanting around the world!" How delighted she was by the idea. So much so that, to Aris's dismay, Blythe began to laugh even harder. "I don't believe I've ever known someone as preposterous as you."

As severe as Aris tried to look, his efforts were futile given that the wind was whipping his hair into his mouth. "I came to fetch you," he told her. "You have no business being here."

Blythe filled with such disdain that her good humor sobered at once. She gnashed her teeth. "You do not control what I do or who I see. If I want to visit my cousin, then I shall visit my cousin."

"Not when it's my brother who's your chauffeur." With each word his ferocity raged like the sea at his back.

"I have no intention of harming her." Death's voice was the press of wind, somehow still firm even while wisping through the air with such a gentleness that Blythe found herself questioning whether he'd truly spoken at all.

Aris slipped his hands into his coat pockets. "What do I care? Take the life of this devilish girl if you'd like. The sooner you do, the sooner I'll be unburdened by the plague of her existence."

Blythe had never known someone better suited for tea with the ton. Aris was more dramatic than anyone she'd ever met.

She wondered whether Signa noticed how Aris's focus kept rolling back to her. Wondered if she noticed his wounded pride, or whether any part of Signa even cared.

Blythe may have bound herself to Aris—she may have taken away any power he had to threaten Signa—but that didn't mean Aris was over her cousin. Blythe could see his hopelessness even now and knew that some small part of him still believed that Signa would regain her memories and all would be well in the world.

But there was no denying the tenderness in Signa's touch as she reached behind her to curl her fingers around Death's. She rested her head against him, squeezing tighter whenever Blythe's or Aris's temper surged. Perhaps she remembered everything. Perhaps she knew exactly who Aris had been to her in another life, but was choosing to spend the rest of her years with another and didn't want to break Aris's heart twice by admitting the truth.

"It's tradition for newlyweds to visit their family." Every word out of Signa's mouth darkened the sky. "I'm the one who asked Death to bring Blythe here. I wanted to ensure that she was well."

Aris opened his mouth to speak, only for his words to be halted by a crack of lightning that turned the sky silver. A storm was inevitable, and though the darkness swarmed to Signa, it was Blythe who felt like the eye of the storm as Aris grabbed hold of her hand.

"It doesn't matter," he told her. "Come, we're returning to Wisteria."

She wanted to fight. To throw his hand off her. But warmth spread through her veins like a poison as Aris wrapped his fingers around her wrist, and the world tilted and winked out before she could open her mouth to argue. Blythe hadn't any chance to bid her cousin farewell before Aris reached for the air as if grasping for a door, pulled open an invisible handle, and tossed her across the threshold to let Wisteria imprison her once more.

CHAPTER TEN

"I despise you," Blythe spat, ripping off her gloves and tossing them at Aris's chest before she hiked up her dress and stomped to take a seat beside the fire. Though the skies had been clear when she'd left, all of Wisteria trembled from roars of thunder. How strange it was that the storm mirrored the one brewing in Fiore so perfectly.

"Get in line." She hadn't heard Aris sit down, but suddenly he was beside her, his voice low as he asked, "Did he touch you?"

Blythe knew at once who he referred to. She was grateful for the flames against her back, for goose bumps slithered down her spine at the memory of Death's touch. "I'd be dead if he had."

The firelight cast severe lines across Aris's face, sharpening the planes of his scowl. "You were a fool to let Death so close."

"Don't pretend you're worried for me." It was impossible to tell how cross Aris was, for Blythe made a pointed effort not to meet his eye. All she could see was that he'd swung one leg over the other and that his foot tapped a silent rhythm in the air as the stillness between them stretched on. Eventually, as the storm died down and Death's lingering chill finally seeped from her bones, Aris asked, "Did you have a good time at Foxglove?"

It was such a ridiculous question that she laughed. "Of course I did. I was glad for the company and to spend my day staring at more than hideous gray stone because you're angry that I stopped your attempts to manipulate my cousin."

"Manipulate? She was my *wife*. It's Death who's manipulating—"

"*Signa* was never your wife. *Life* may have been, once upon a time, but not Signa. My cousin is free to spend her years with whomever she wants, and it isn't going to be you."

The lights flickered as Aris reached out, taking her chin in a deft hand to demand her stare. "And you know that for a fact?"

Blythe wasn't so foolish as to cower. It wasn't as though he could hurt her, so what was the worst he could do? Send her to sleep in the stables? That, at least, would be more comfortable than her stone slab of a bed.

Aris didn't want Blythe to believe that she had any power in this situation. But if there was one thing that Blythe was growing more certain of by the day, it was that she had so much more than he'd planned for. And she'd proved it today when she'd left for Foxglove.

When Aris bent so that his forehead was pressed against hers, she kept her gaze level.

"It's your fault she doesn't remember," he spat. "I could have brought her here. I could have shown her the life we used to have!"

"And what life are you referring to, exactly? One that existed literal centuries ago? Whatever caveman life you had back in the prehistoric age is gone. Continue to waste your years pining, or do everyone a favor and move on."

He was so bright that Blythe's eyes burned to look at him. She nearly pinched them shut but didn't want to give him the satisfaction. Something about Aris's anger and the burn in her belly felt familiar. Almost... expected. So much so that she did not lose her voice but told him sternly, "Burn as brightly as the sun if you wish, Aris, but I will not look away."

To her surprise, the light flickered out as quickly as a snuffed candle. Blythe hardly had the chance to blink clarity back into her eyes before she saw that Aris once again stood before her. Not angry this time, but with his lips pressed tight and a crease between his brows.

"What did you say?"

Blythe thought over her words—a little forthcoming, perhaps, but not so aggressive as to warrant his reaction. She gave Aris no response as he drew back to lean against a settee, perhaps plotting his next move. He looked not to Blythe, but at his hands. Then, to her surprise, he laughed.

Blythe wondered if perhaps she should hide, though she couldn't convince a single one of her limbs to budge. She was too enamored by the sound, for this laugh was not like his others. This laugh was the first light of dawn, warm and pleasant as it shuddered across her. It was a sound that lasted only a second, but in that second Aris became another person entirely. One she did not recognize, but found herself unnervingly curious to know.

"Life once said that very thing to me," he told her eventually, which was fortunate given that Blythe had lost her voice. "It was during our first true argument, so long ago that I'd nearly forgotten."

Despite everything, Blythe found herself softening. "She meant a lot to you," she whispered. Aris gave no response, for none was necessary. Only a fool would doubt Aris's love for this woman. "Would you tell me about her?"

So much of Blythe's past two days had been spent pondering the woman from the portrait, and whether it was truly Life who Blythe had seen wandering the halls. She yearned to peel back the layers of time and unearth the secrets shrouding this woman, to know what kind of person could look upon Fate and find him worth a shared existence.

Aris's expression bore the weight of complex memories, a mixture of softness smoothing his edges while anguish pinched the corners of his eyes. In a tone as delicate as a secret unveiled to the night, he asked, "What do you want to know?"

Everything. It was strange, this insatiable curiosity that had taken root, a growing obsession with the woman whose life Blythe felt as though she'd stepped into. "Did she have a name?"

While she'd thought it would be one of the simpler questions for him to answer, the veins in his hand pulsed as he clenched his hand against the armrest.

"We all have an alias," he finally said. "She called herself Mila when I first met her, though I've not spoken that name in ages." Aris kept two fingers pressed against his lips as if savoring the taste of it. "It was important to her that she felt close to humans. To ensure that the souls she brought into this world were as happy and as thriving as she could make them."

It was curious how someone who seemed so kind could end up with someone as rigid as Aris. Had he always been the way he was now, or just how hardened had he become since losing his first wife?

"How did you and Mila meet?" The fire was warm against her skin, and Blythe leaned toward it, ready to cozy up and fall into the story as Aris ran a hand down the length of his jaw and rubbed away the hint of a smile that had come with the memory.

"She sought me out." There was a fondness to his words. "At first, she despised me. My job and hers were not so well aligned. She thought I should be kinder, for the life of a human is a short and fragile thing."

As if the story was waiting there behind her eyelids each time she blinked, Blythe could nearly picture it. "And what did you think?" she asked. "Did you become any kinder?"

Aris lifted his eyes, and for a moment Blythe wondered whether she had shattered their tentative peace and if the conversation was over. But then he said, "I will tell you the same thing I told her, which is that when a soul unveils its future, I weave the path it has chosen and set it into motion. Sometimes things happen beyond anyone's control, but I am never cruel by choice. Every soul is different. Each one is circumstantial. I was as kind to the souls she gave me as I could be."

Blythe thought on those words as she slipped from her boots. She detested the very thought of her future being some rigid, predetermined story that could never be changed. Yet at the same time, she could acknowledge that at least a portion of her anger was unjust. Aris had not asked for the burden of this job, which was why she folded her hands into her lap and told him with bated breath, "I am tired of fighting with you, Aris."

"And I am tired of listening to you fight."

Blythe bit back a smile, refusing to let him see just how amusing she found his stubbornness. "Then what do you suppose we do about it?"

His eyes were strange in the haze of the firelight. Darker, and somehow so piercing that if Blythe didn't know better, she'd think he was looking through her.

"We form a truce, I suppose. Stop pestering me, and I will in turn at least attempt civility." He reached into his pocket, fishing around. "I'll start by giving you this." He handed her a letter with her father's handwriting on the front.

"You thief!" Blythe snatched the envelope from his hands, thumb running over the wax seal and relaxing only when she found that it was still intact.

"Civility, remember?" Aris sighed as he kicked his feet up, spun sideways in his chair. "You can't be angry when we've only just formed a truce."

"Civility my ass." She pried the envelope open. Perhaps it would have been better to wait until she was alone, but she'd never had much patience and there was nothing she wanted more than assurance that her father was well. And so Blythe unfolded the paper and read over the letter hastily.

Several lines in, however, her blood ran cold. She must have made an involuntary sound, too, for Aris rose and crossed the floor toward her within a second, his brows cast low.

"What is it?" he pressed. If Blythe had the wherewithal, she might have thought to pay more attention to Aris's tone and decipher whether it was worry or curiosity that drove him closer. Perhaps he *was* every bit as nosy as she was. He tried to peer over Blythe's shoulder but she was clutching the parchment too close, reading over the words again and again in the hope that something in them would change.

"Read it out loud," he urged, trying to snatch the letter from her. "If you won't, then hand it over so I can read it myself."

Blythe curled her fingers against the page, and though every word was lodged in her throat, she forced herself to read what her father had written.

" 'My Dearest Daughter,' " she began, " 'I hope this letter makes it to you safely. I must admit that in all my travels I have not yet had the pleasure of visiting Verena. Until your letter, I was unconvinced that it was a true place at all, as I have not been able to find it on any map. Prior to writing this, I found myself wandering my study in search of it, yet I have been unsuccessful in my attempts.' "

Aris made a low noise of impatience in the back of his throat, urging her to go on.

" 'Since your departure, I have been increasingly interested in this kingdom you are to rule. I believe it's only fitting that I pay it a visit, which is why I was ecstatic to receive your . . .' " She trailed off, daring a sideways look at Aris.

"Your *what?*" he demanded, jaw tight. "What was he so ecstatic to receive?"

Blythe wished in the moment that she could flip her body inside out so that she might crawl into her own skin. She shut her eyes as she read the next part, for there was no forgetting what the last line read. " 'Your invitation.' "

Never had Blythe thought it possible for Aris to look as cold as Death.

"You *invited* him?" His voice swelled like the tempestuous storm, mirroring the hearth's fiery display. "To where, you buffoon? The land of make-believe?"

"You cannot be angry with me," Blythe bit back. "We have a *truce*! Besides, this is *your* fault. I'm not the one who felt the need to pretend I was the prince of an imaginary kingdom, and it's not like I actually *invited* him! All I said was that I wished he were here."

Aris raked his fingers through his hair, tugging at the ends. "There's no choice but to wipe his mind. I'll have to use my magic—"

"Touch him and I swear I'll find a way to kill you in your sleep." Never had Blythe felt more lethal than she did then, each word striking with the force of a bullet. If there was one thing that she would make certain of, it was this. Elijah had been through more than enough for a lifetime. "My father is no plaything and you will not turn him into one of your puppets."

"Oh? Then what do you suppose we do, love? Tell him the truth and pray for the best?"

That certainly wasn't an option. As wonderful as it might have been to be able to tell her father the truth, every time she imagined doing so she thought only of the alcohol he'd once relied on to quell his woes and how grief had altered him into a stranger she didn't care to know.

She worried for her father more than anyone. So no, she wouldn't tell Elijah the truth. Not when he was only just beginning to return to his old self.

"We'll have to come up with something else," she decided, clenching the parchment. "He says that he'll be waiting for your driver to pick him up on Friday morning. We've no choice, Aris. We have to bring him here."

"And then what? I transport Wisteria to some magical spring forest that I pretend to rule?"

"Somewhere in the snow, actually," Blythe admitted with a wince. "I might have told him that Verena was basically an arctic tundra. Though I did say it was beautiful."

Aris shot her a bleak look. Blythe, to her credit, had only wanted to tell her father how she was faring and stop him from worrying. She'd never thought that he'd want to come *see* her. At least not immediately.

"There's no other choice," Blythe decided when Aris still had not spoken. "You said yourself that Wisteria can move. We'll have to find a place that matches the description I gave and bring him there."

"Oh, yes. A simple task." With his back to the hearth, dark shadows cut across Aris's face. "What of the *people*? The staff? Your father believes you are a princess."

"Then make me a princess. You are *Fate*, are you not?" On Blythe's tongue, it was more an accusation than a question. "You have the power to control people. How they behave, what they perceive... If what I'm asking for is beyond your ability, then you are weaker than I was led to believe."

"Beyond my *ability*?" Such words hit their mark, striking Aris as fiercely as if she'd slapped him across the face. "There is nothing that's beyond my ability, you petulant girl."

Frustrating though it could sometimes be, Blythe appreciated Aris's pride, for it was the greatest source of leverage to use against him.

"Prove it," she demanded. "My father is a clever man. Your party tricks will not be enough to fool him."

"Party tricks? My *party tricks*?" Under his breath Aris repeated those words quietly, spitting more venom into them each time. He opened his mouth—likely to curse her, Blythe guessed—but she held up a hand to stop him.

"Prove. It." Her words were slower this time, brimming with challenge. And to her delight, Aris could not avoid the bait. He stepped forward, his glare smoldering.

"And what, pray tell, is in it for me?"

Blythe had expected this much, which is why the offer rolled smoothly from her tongue. "If you can manage to fool my father and make him believe that Verena is a real place, then I will put up no fight to traveling with you. Not so long as you promise to take me to see my father whenever I'd like."

"Twice a year," he argued, but Blythe held firm.

"Whenever I'd like," she repeated. "Within reason, but no more than once a week unless it's agreed by both parties."

Tension knitted Aris's brows, and Blythe was relieved by the cluck of his tongue and the way he threw his shoulders back, trying to fill the room with his presence. God, did she love a good ego. Especially when it had his lips thinning and his face twisting with a displeasure that told Blythe everything she needed to know—she had won this round.

"Fine, you wretch. But should you have me do this, know that in Elijah's place, I will have no choice but to manipulate the minds of dozens of others if this farce is to work."

Blythe shrugged. "Do whatever you must. So long as my father's mind isn't touched, I don't care." And she truly didn't. As uneasy as Aris's manipulation often made her, in this moment she wouldn't have it any other way. Elijah was no easy man to placate. Unlike so many, Blythe's father didn't view her as an exchange of property or a way to bolster his own name. He did not care remotely that Aris was a "prince." He cared only to see Blythe well and happy, and so, for his sake, that was the life she intended to show him.

Around Aris, the glow of the firelight burned brighter. He drew a step closer, taking her chin in his hand once again. "If so much as one complaint of my magic passes your lips, I will end the charade then and there and claim victory over our little wager," he whispered, tilting her head so that she couldn't turn away. "I shall do this my way. Am I clear?"

She didn't draw back, nor allow a single ounce of hesitation to pass over her features as she locked eyes with him and said, in a voice as bright as a spring day, "Perfectly."

PART TWO

CHAPTER ELEVEN

"My way," Aris soon came to learn, meant "his way with Blythe's non-negotiable input."

"I think Verena needs a national flower," she said by way of greeting the next morning, the legs of her chair screeching against the stone as she dragged it from the parlor and into the foyer where Aris was rolling up his sleeves. She'd listened, ear pressed to the door, for him to tiptoe through the hall and down the stairs that morning. If his groan was any indicator, Aris had been hoping to do this work himself while Blythe slept. But Blythe was no fool; she wasn't going to miss the opportunity to watch his magic in action.

"I've no need for your advice." His voice was a flat monotone. "Now if you could leave—"

"What about hellebore?" she asked, sitting sideways in her seat and swinging her legs over the arm. "They're sometimes called winter jewels, you know. They're hearty against the cold."

"The *cold*," he hissed. "Had you left the imagining to me, Verena could have been a tropical paradise that we'd be enjoying presently."

He had a point, though it was too late now. Blythe sat on the room's right side, angling herself so that she could watch Aris work. He looked different today. The collar of his white button-up wasn't as tight as usual, and she found herself staring at the skin beneath the sleeves he'd rolled over his biceps. His golden hair, too, looked soft and untamed. She wouldn't say it was *wild* by any means, as even then Aris's posture gave him an air of rigidity that made him more formal than most. But Blythe found it difficult to look away from this man before her, searching for slivers of the relaxed boy she'd seen in Life's portraits. If anything, he looked eager to work, and perhaps even a little nervous, if the sideways glances he kept giving Blythe meant anything.

"Hellebore," he murmured as he smoothed his fingers through his hair and surveyed the room. "Very well."

All at once his threads were before him—thousands of them, gleaming a brilliant gold and weaving intricate lies in patterns too fast for Blythe to follow. The front pieces of Aris's hair stirred as he worked, more threads joining the others by the second until even his shirt began to billow as if roused by an invisible wind that gusted as his magic took form. Beneath him, the stone floor of Wisteria morphed to an iridescent blue that stretched through the length of the room, shaping itself into something similar to the wintertime lake Blythe had played upon as a child. But the floor held steady when Blythe pressed her boots against it, as solid as stone. She sucked in a breath, fingers winding around the arm of her chair.

Blythe had always known that Aris was talented. She'd seen the proof of it through his various wonderscapes and in the ease with which he used his magic, as if it was an extension of his very soul. But watching him create something of this level felt wholly new.

Aris was an artist at his very core. The universe was a canvas he molded like clay between his palms, shaping it to his will. Imagination was given life as golden-framed portraits that spanned an entire lineage filled endless halls, and banisters twisted to mirror the crystalline floor. At the base of those banisters sprouted delicate hellebore sculpted from ice, their edges as smooth as if they'd been real. The flower was woven around the staircase balusters, too, its petals flourishing the higher the staircase rose.

Rather than his signature gold, a silvery sheen was cast over the foyer, making Wisteria look as though someone had taken a chisel to the moon and carved out this home. It was a palace spirited straight from the pages of a fairy tale, kissed by the stars themselves.

Blythe's heart forgot how to beat as she rose, drawing tentative steps toward the banister, as if one wrong move would cause the world to crumble beneath her. She trailed a trembling finger down its length, then let out a startled breath—*warm*. Somehow the ice was warm.

Aris must have heard her. Everything from the gleam in his eyes to the delight that sharpened his lips turned wild.

"Impressed?" he taunted, surely expecting a cutting response and the banter they'd grown so accustomed to.

Instead, Blythe whispered, "Yes," as she smoothed her thumb around the edge of a sculpted hellebore. Beautiful. It was all so delightfully beautiful. "Aris, this is outstanding."

His face twisted as if waiting for her to laugh or mock him for believing it. But as he watched Blythe's skirts drag across the floor as she circled the banister, captivated by the smallest details, the tension in his shoulders loosened.

What must it be like, Blythe wondered, to be able to weave an entire world from one's fingertips? What must it feel like to let one's imagination run rampant, knowing that every impossibility was within reach?

It was wondrous. And for a sliver of a moment, as the barest hint of a smile crossed his lips—not a smirk nor any hint of smugness, but a true and proper smile—so was Aris.

But Blythe didn't care for that thought and was eager to rid it from her mind. "One room is simple enough, but surely you cannot manage the same grandeur throughout an entire palace?"

"Grandeur?" Still mollified by her earlier admittance, Aris smirked and rolled his sleeves up farther. "You haven't seen anything yet. Have a seat, love. We're just getting started."

Blythe had known that fooling her father would be a feat, and yet still she'd underestimated even the early stages of the work involved. Aris's magic worked as quickly as his imagination. Six hours later, however, Blythe learned that it was not his magic that consumed the majority of their time, but the forethought needed to craft a believable lie.

He'd refused to give her paints and an easel, but Blythe had convinced Aris to magic her a sketchbook to draw her ideas, wanting to participate. "We'll need people," she reminded him as she sketched a crude city full of figures, exhausted from the arduous role she'd assigned herself as the director of this project. Aris hadn't agreed to giving her that role, of course, but when she'd persisted through the first few hours of his scowling, he'd eventually given up and allowed Blythe to dictate. Or at least she had *tried* to—Aris had not listened to so much as half of her grand ideas, often scowling about how she needed to practice her drawing strokes.

"Of course we'll need people," Aris huffed as he eyed her work. The pair sat across from each other on the crystalline floor, Blythe cross-legged, bowed over like a prawn with the sketchbook in her lap, while Aris sat with one knee drawn to his chest and his elbow propped upon it. Tea and sandwiches had been served on magicked plates between them. Blythe was on her third helping. As was expected with the food Aris gave her, it was one of the best things she'd ever tasted. Who would have thought that a chicken sandwich coated with toasted almonds could be so delicious? Aris, too, had eaten several and had silently replenished the plates when they'd gotten low.

"And we'll need a town," she said, speaking between a mouthful and wagging her sketchbook at him.

Aris frowned, but Blythe made no correction in her manners. "I already have one in mind." He turned his face from her, quieter than usual, his vitriol waning from exhaustion.

They—because Blythe had decided that she, too, would be sharing in some of the credit for this masterpiece—had made superb work in mere hours. Around them, what was once the palace of Wisteria had given way to their new temporary quarters, Verena. It was twice the size that Wisteria had been, and more than once Blythe found herself wondering how such magic could be possible. In the end, she knew it wasn't worth her musings. No matter how hard she tried or how many years they'd have together, Blythe doubted that she'd ever come to understand Aris's magic.

Not everything he'd created was ice, of course. The suite her father would be staying in was filled with dazzling stained-glass windows and vaulted ceilings adorned with white-and-silver crown molding. Fantastical figures of griffins and unicorns had been carved into it, so well embellished that it would take weeks of scrutinizing before someone would be able to spot each design.

There were ornate rugs and gold-leaf chandeliers with candles that sprouted from flowerlike buds. Every gilded portrait frame was over-the-top, and several of the rooms on the lower level displayed grand paintings on the ceilings. She couldn't tell for certain what all of them were—some looked like angels, some of them were floral, and others were of strange and mythical monsters that had Blythe wondering just what went on in Aris's mind. There were statues, too. Busts of men with wings that covered their eyes, and a giant bronzed stag head. There was even a curious bust of a boar that held an uncanny resemblance to the one on her doorknob, and though she wondered whether Aris was baiting her with its existence, Blythe said nothing. She didn't need to.

The palace that Aris—and she—had constructed felt lived in. Like a real place that had stood for centuries, collecting bobbles and expanding its royal splendor. Verena was a wonderland she wanted to get lost in. One where she could spend a week investigating a single wing of the palace and still not be convinced that she'd seen everything.

Aris had planned his creation down to the finest sliver of a detail, and it was a masterpiece. Watching him pluck away at his threads—crafting and then recrafting a painted ceiling several times until he got it right—taught Blythe more about Aris than the couple of weeks she had spent with him.

Whether it came to food, painting, music, or even sculpting, Aris expected the finest. At first, Blythe believed that he was just particular about what he consumed, but given the looks he'd sneaked her way or how his chest had swelled whenever something he did earned Blythe's delight, she soon realized that it wasn't only himself that Aris was concerned with.

Perhaps that was why he shared his meals and kept the dining room so impressive even when the rest of Wisteria had been left to ruin. Yes, Aris wanted to impress her with his magic and to maybe even scare her a little. But if Blythe didn't know any better, she would have guessed that what Aris really wanted was someone to share it all with. Someone who would delight in the art and the splendor, and who would revel in all the grand things that he reveled in.

Blythe had peeled back one thin layer, perhaps, but there was still so much more to Aris that she'd yet to uncover. He was particular and precise, and as she inspected the smallest detail of dust between two of the frozen hellebores, she was fascinated.

"Do you love your magic?" Blythe couldn't say what drew the

question out of her. Perhaps it was how struck she was by all she'd seen or the fact that they'd gone several hours without arguing. There had been some bickering over his choice of paint color, but overall they'd been doing remarkably well.

The sandwich he'd been about to bite into stilled at his lips. His reaction was so subtle that Blythe almost wondered if she was imagining it—a sudden stiffness of the shoulders and the ever-so-slight straightening of his spine that took Aris from relaxed to once again looking like his typical buttoned-up self.

"Are you trying to imply something?" His words held a defensiveness that hadn't been there minutes prior.

Blythe flicked her gaze from Aris and stole another sandwich for herself. She took her time answering, pretending that her curiosity wasn't urgent and pressing or that she wasn't dying to peel him like an apple and bite into his innermost layer.

"I'm not implying anything, Aris," she promised. "It's just that, for once, you looked truly happy."

Aris wasn't quick enough at concealing the shadow that slipped across his face. "I find great joy in creating," he said at last, though his brows pulled close to his nose. "I've never known anything but my magic. Using it is just a part of what I am."

"Don't you mean *who* you are?" Blythe corrected. "*What* you are is Fate, certainly, but you're more than what you do."

He exhaled a quiet, splintered laugh. "I'm afraid not everyone feels that way. People fear what they do not understand, and few understand their fate. You cannot fathom how close to their lives I get each and every day. And yet, despite that, you humans resent me.

Not that it matters. Even if you didn't, my brother will one day pluck you all from this world regardless."

For the first time since Aris had created it, the palace was every bit as cold as it looked. The chill lasted only seconds before Aris turned his face to the floor, and Blythe saw him then—a hint of that man from the portrait, so much younger and boyish despite his years.

Looking at him, Blythe knew she'd been right. Aris didn't want to be alone; he wanted to share his life with someone. Perhaps that was why Wisteria remained so bare—so that he would not be reminded of the world's splendor when he hadn't a soul to share it with.

"Well," Blythe told him as she licked the almond crumbs from her fingers, "I think your powers are amazing. I wish that I had them myself—not the work that comes with them, of course, but the rest of it."

It was astonishing how much Aris's shoulders eased. He looked curiously toward Blythe, welcoming those words as if she was the first breeze on a weary summer day.

"If that's true, then you're one of the few."

There was no saying why Blythe reached forward to set her hand atop his, trying to console the emotion he tried so hard to hide. It was instinctual, and so impulsive that she didn't realize she was touching him until a flame ignited within her chest. The breath that Aris drew was sharp, but before Blythe could pull away she tore her focus from their hands long enough to look up. Past Aris and his scrutiny. Past the iridescent banisters and deep into the foyer, to where a flash of white hair skimmed the edge of her vision.

"Blythe?" Aris's voice was distant, muddled through the sound of laughter and the same lilting tune that had plagued her mind. She felt as if she were spinning, her vision swimming as an ache blossomed across her temples. With each passing second the music swelled until it pounded against her skull, and in the corner of her gaze she watched as Life picked up the hem of her ivory dress and twirled.

"Blythe." Aris yanked away from her, and all at once the world steadied. No more music. No more apparitions of a woman in white dancing.

"Dear God, what's gotten into you?" Aris was on his knee, face bent to inspect hers.

Realizing just how close he was, Blythe waved him off. "I'm fine. You need to work on your bedside manner," she grumbled, trying to avoid his prying eyes.

Aris grabbed her by the shoulders, holding her still. "If you're *fine*, then do you care to explain why your eyes were rolling back into your skull?"

She didn't. Especially not when she thought they'd been open, staring down the foyer at the ghost of his dead lover.

Blythe sucked her bottom lip between her teeth and bit down on the skin, combing her mind for answers. She was hallucinating, surely. But why?

Realizing she had nothing to say and likely growing tired of trying to pin down her gaze, Aris released her with a weary sigh. "I can finish the rest of Verena on my own."

"You'll need my help," she argued despite how weak those words felt upon her lips. Aris must have felt similar.

“I have it handled,” he told her. “Come tomorrow, you will fall at my feet in tears over how amazing I am.”

“It’s a wonder how you manage to stay on the ground with that inflated ego,” she spat. “I’m *fine,* Aris. Only a little tired—”

He wasn’t hearing it. Golden threads wound around her wrists before Blythe could argue further, tugging her toward the staircase. Blythe swatted at them, hissing names for Aris so foul that at one point—when she’d tripped backward up the first flight of stairs—he turned to her with folded arms and scrutiny pinching his face. It was impossible to say whether he was offended or impressed.

“Where do you *learn* these things?”

“Books,” she seethed, met with only a grunt of acknowledgment before a thousand more threads wound around her waist and ankles. They dragged a protesting Blythe up the stairs, down the hall, and to her room, sealing the door shut behind her. And though Blythe’s tongue burned to tell Aris that she hadn’t even gotten started on the list of names she had for him, she didn’t once try to test the locks.

Because either Mila’s ghost had taken to haunting Wisteria, or Blythe was losing her mind.

CHAPTER TWELVE

Elijah was due to arrive at any moment, and Blythe was still far from convinced that she and Aris were going to pull this off.

All night her thoughts wandered to every way Elijah might realize their deceit, and what he would do once he did.

Would he try to bring Blythe back to Thorn Grove? Would Aris protest by using his magic against her father, manipulating Elijah's mind?

She felt ill at the thought.

Having been banished to sleep well before either her room or the surrounding town had been consumed by Aris's magic, Blythe had roused not on her slab of stone, but in a proper four-poster bed canopied by cream linen. The sheets were plush and pleasant, made of earthy shades of green and amber.

When she peeled back the canopy, it was to a gloriously rich room with dark mahogany flooring and a thick Persian rug that promised warmth for her bare toes. Her walls held the loveliest wallpaper with delicate imagery of thin golden branches adorned with perched birds. Her headboard was a deep autumnal green, embroidered with hellebore. It was a stately room, and delicately feminine in a way she found quite lovely.

The best part, though, was that she was not seized with cold as she drew herself from the sheets, despite the brightness of the snow that glimmered through a gap in the curtains. She hurried to pull them aside and take in a lawn covered with powder so thick that Blythe could see nothing but whiteness and the shine of Aris's golden threads woven as far as the eye could see.

Wherever Aris had taken them was a far cry from her hometown.

When a knock sounded at her door, Blythe drew on her robe. "Come in!"

The young woman who entered wasn't at all who Blythe expected. Her black hair was sleek and polished, and she carried the scent of freesia upon her skin. She had a sharp jaw and held herself with the grace of a noble in a fitted gown of emerald. She smiled at Blythe before curtsying.

"Good morning, Your Highness," said the woman. "Shall I help ready you for the day?"

Blythe grabbed on to her bedpost, faint when she realized this was no random woman. She was a lady-in-waiting.

For a long while Blythe could only stare, her tongue numb and useless. She and Aris had discussed the need for people, yes, but Blythe hadn't expected she'd ever have the privilege of a lady's maid, let alone a lady-in-waiting. How nice it would be to dress without struggling with every testy button and frivolous ribbon.

"You absolutely may," Blythe practically sang, beginning to disrobe in haste. Perhaps she was too hasty, however, for the woman's large brown eyes blinked in surprise as Blythe pulled on her stockings. "May I have your name?"

The woman smiled as she helped Blythe into a fresh chemise. "It's Olivia Wheaton, Your Highness." She had a low, graceful voice thick with an accent Blythe didn't recognize.

Blythe repeated her name aloud, beyond pleased to have not only one of the most remarkable bedrooms she'd ever seen, but also to have another woman to share the space with. What Blythe liked best, though, was that Olivia did not feel as though she was deeply influenced by Aris's magic. Her eyes were warm and kind rather than hollowed out like his usual puppets. While he'd undoubtedly cast some sort of glamour on Olivia's mind, Blythe wondered what the extent of that was and whether Aris was decent enough to actually hire staff.

Olivia put her into a thick wool dress lined with white fur and gloves as blue as sapphires, and Blythe wondered whether Elijah would see a healthy, thriving princess when he looked upon her. Or would he see someone who had just spent their first night in a proper bed after two full weeks of marriage? In the end, Blythe decided it didn't at all matter what she wore, for the true test would be proving to her father that she had a proper relationship with Aris. That they were truly husband and wife, working together to rule a kingdom as a united front.

The very thought had anxious laughter brewing within her. Her stomach knotted, yet there was no choice but to swallow those nerves as Olivia finished pinning her hair into mesmerizing plaits unlike any Blythe had ever seen. She wondered what country they were in and could only hope that Aris would have picked somewhere remote enough for her father not to recognize.

"His Highness has asked that you join him for breakfast," Olivia said in her gentle brogue, waiting for Blythe to join her before she paved the way down the hall. It was fortunate that Olivia knew where she was going, for more of the palace's layout had changed overnight. Blythe skimmed her fingers along the frosted railings as they wound their way down the stairs.

How odd a place this was. Odd but mesmerizing and every bit as exuberant as she might expect from a palace that had birthed a prince with Aris's insufferable ego.

Blythe kept quiet as Olivia steered her toward the dining room, where a giant table of frosted glass waited for her. Her husband stood on the opposite side in a coat of deep crimson and gloves trimmed with gold, and he wasn't alone.

A familiar couple sat at the table beside Aris, both of them donning warm smiles. It took Blythe a moment to place them as the pair who'd pretended to be Aris's parents at the wedding.

Their smiles made her skin itch. Blythe hated that she hadn't the faintest clue where they were from, just as she hated that she and Aris were once again using them for their own benefit.

Still, they seemed happy enough, and Aris had made it perfectly clear that should she voice even a hint of discontentment, this charade would be over. So she forced her own smile when the woman who played Aris's mother looked at her fondly, as though she and

Blythe had spent a great deal of time together. The woman patted the seat beside her, and Blythe flashed Aris an anxious look before taking it.

"Are you going to be able to play along?" he asked between sips of his coffee. "Or do you require my hand to control you, too?"

"Touch me with your magic and I will burn down all of Wisteria with you in it," Blythe said sweetly as three servants appeared with a strange assortment of food—cold fish and boiled eggs that were too small to be from a chicken. There were plump gooseberries, and warm potatoes mashed with vegetables. It wasn't like any breakfast she was used to, though given that Aris was eating it, she didn't doubt its quality.

She allowed the servants to set the food before her, and sure enough, Blythe nearly melted into a puddle of satisfaction at her first taste. What a blessing it was that she hadn't told her father that the food in Verena was foul.

"Don't worry about me," she said as she helped herself to a heaping of gooseberries. "I'll manage just fine."

He waited for whipped honey to arrive before spreading it onto steaming sourdough. "I'm glad to hear it, because your father's here."

There came a knock on the silver double doors not even a second after Aris had spoken. A portly gentleman who reminded Blythe vaguely of Warwick stepped inside, bowed, and announced, "Mr. Elijah Hawthorne has arrived."

Sure enough, her father strolled in, his luggage and coat abandoned. He looked every bit like a man who had spent several days traveling by train and coach, haggard and with a shadow of blond stubble along his jaw. His eyes, however, were alight with twin flames as they flicked to Blythe. She was on her feet before her body even registered the movement, crossing the floor to throw her arms around him.

Her body sagged with relief as Elijah laughed, embracing her with a tight squeeze before gently easing away to inspect her. His gaze narrowed at the meticulous plaited coif of her hair, skimming down to her cheeks before finally settling on her eyes.

"I'm glad to see you," he whispered, clasping her once on the shoulder before turning his attention to the royals behind her. "And thank you all for having me. I've only seen it through the carriage window, but already Verena seems to be quite the spectacle, as is your beautiful home."

There was an edge of ruefulness to his words that Blythe couldn't help but smirk at. She wondered what jokes Elijah would crack about the grandeur of the palace once the two of them were alone. Not that he had much room to talk, given the oddness of Thorn Grove's architecture.

"It's our pleasure to have you," said the woman at the table. The queen, Blythe supposed. Blythe might have thought to better introduce her, though she hadn't the faintest idea what the woman's name was. As if able to see the struggle on her face, Aris pushed from the table with a quiet creak.

"I know you met briefly at the wedding, but allow me to reintroduce my mother, Queen Marie Dryden. And my father, King Charles Dryden." It was a wonder how much Aris was able to manipulate the minds of these people, for the king only bobbed his head. He looked a touch put off by Elijah's presence, eager to return to his feast. Blythe wondered what the man might be like without the facade that Aris had cast on his mind. Would he be as disinterested as Aris portrayed him, or might he be a kind man, always attentive? She supposed she'd never know.

"We're glad to have you, Mr. Hawthorne," Aris continued, drawing Blythe's interest with his pleasantries. Was it in her mind, or was he somehow standing even taller than usual? He was making a ghastly amount of eye contact with her father, too, all charm and poise as he offered Elijah a seat.

Her father took it at once, scooping a fork into his hand. "I have eaten nothing but trolley cart food for days," he said. "Blythe tells me that the meals here are spectacular."

There was an edge to Elijah's voice when he said it, almost like an accusation. While Aris smiled, she was certain from the glint in his eyes that he'd noticed it. "Please, help yourself."

Elijah accepted that offer liberally. He took food from every dish laid out on the table, sitting comfortably in his chair as if *he* were the king of this establishment. Had such gall not been so impressive—and had these people not all been under a spell that would wipe their memory the moment Blythe and Aris no longer required them—Blythe might have been embarrassed. She could tell from the way Elijah pressed the cold fish to his tongue that he was disappointed. Even the fish was every bit as delicious as she'd promised him in her letter.

He sampled several more bites between fielding questions about what he'd been up to—enjoying retirement—and if he had any exciting upcoming plans—"Catching up on years' worth of sleep and hobbies"—before wiping his lips with his handkerchief and leaning back in his chair. "The food is wonderful, though I fear that my body is wearier than I realized."

"I could have someone show you to your room," Aris offered, though Elijah cut him off with a swift wave.

"That won't be necessary. I was thinking a stroll around Verena might be enough to wake me up." Elijah gave his leg a tap. "These old bones haven't seen nearly enough use in days."

Blythe slid Aris a sideways glance. While he may have managed to make the palace spectacular, she had no idea the limits of his illusions or how entrenched in his magic this town was. But if Aris was worried, he showed no hint of it. Adjusting his gloves, Aris matched Elijah's smile and stood. "I would be happy to accompany you. My dear wife is still learning how to navigate the town."

Not one to be left out, Blythe stood. Apparently too fast, however, as her heart was beating so furiously that she saw stars and had to take a moment to grip the edge of the table. "I will join as well," she told them, not about to leave Aris alone with her father.

As Aris excused himself from the table, he went to Blythe's side to offer his arm. Only when he gave a quiet clearing of his throat did she realize that she was meant to take it. She nearly pounced on him then, looping her arm through his with such fervor that his lips thinned.

"I'm doing my part," he whispered, the words soft as a breath against her ear. "Now gather your wits and do yours."

"Forgive me if I'm alarmed by your behavior. I didn't know you were capable of being a gentleman," she hissed as they made their way through the palace, flocked by attentive servants. Blythe was assaulted by a sharp gust of wind as two of them pulled open the ornate double doors onto the front lawn. The wind carried the scent of fresh pine and baking dough, and Blythe breathed deeply before she glanced up to glistening hills of snow and the bustling city that awaited them.

Verena was a town plucked from the pages of a storybook.

At first Blythe wondered if it was one of Aris's illusions, for surely no place could be so charming. But the deeper they traveled into a city built atop a giant canal and witnessed its rosy-faced denizens strolling the streets bundled in thick furs, the more she realized that this place was no illusion.

Meticulously maintained boats traversed through channels of the canal, carrying people who seemed unbothered by the plunging temperature. They bustled about as normal despite the iciness that wound its fingers around Blythe's throat and squeezed tight. Each person who caught sight of her and Aris either bowed or dipped into a low curtsy while Aris pressed onward, flashing friendly smiles and nods. He looked every bit like a poised and dignified prince admired by his subjects—a role, Blythe couldn't help but think, that Aris embodied with great pleasure.

Blythe and Elijah followed close behind him, the latter scrutinizing everything from the streets to the faces of those who passed by. Blythe left him be, too distracted by Verena's beauty to be responsible for reining in her father's skepticism. She doubted that he'd find anything; Verena was far too real, and far too breathtaking. If not for the millions of gossamer threads that wove throughout the town and around every person they passed, Blythe might have truly believed that Aris was a prince and that she was the future queen of the most magical land, where the buildings were made of cheerfully colored stone and sharpened with twisting spires. The melodic tune of an accordion floated through the streets, and all of it was so wondrous that Blythe would have squealed if not for the fact that she had to pretend she was already familiar with such a mystical place.

She sneaked a glance at Elijah, satisfied by his flattened expression as he took in the sights. Considering that he was not scowling, Blythe knew he was impressed.

"Are you up for a tour of the city?" Aris posed the question to Elijah. It hadn't escaped Blythe's notice that he was dressed finer than she had ever seen, or that he was cognizant of Elijah's every step, searching for anything her father might need before he could voice it. Seconds after Elijah squinted at the glaring sun, a cloud passed over it, shading his face.

It was a subtle action, one that Blythe was certain Aris would never assume she'd notice. But she *did* notice and was quick to smother her smile, worried it might embarrass her husband. She more than welcomed the change from Aris's typical behavior; before the eyes of her father, he was the perfect gentleman.

He helped Elijah into a small wooden boat, then extended his hand for Blythe. She took it gingerly, forever surprised by the warmth of his touch and the heat that shuddered through her as her fingers folded around his and she allowed herself to be pulled in. There was barely enough room for the three of them to squeeze in tight behind a gondolier who wore a uniform different from the others Blythe had seen rowing by—a white coat with a golden insignia of a fox surrounded by hellebore. A palace gondolier, then.

She nearly laughed, impressed by Aris's thoroughness.

Wedged between him and her father, Blythe watched the kingdom stretch before them—gabled buildings with snowcapped roofs lined the canal, where tiny dustings of snowflakes glittered before melting into the water. Massive horses with thick tufts pulled immaculate carriages through plowed cobblestone streets, the melody of their huffing blending with the accordion and easing something in her chest.

This city was alive in a way that filled Blythe with a longing that burned to her very core. She watched as people flocked to a street vendor who poured cups of chocolate so thick and dark that Blythe's mouth at once began to water. She must have been staring, for the tendrils of her father's breath slipped into the air as he laughed.

"Is it good?" he asked, but it was Aris who answered, already waving for the gondolier to glide them over.

"Blythe hasn't tried it yet, but that man makes the best chocolate in the country." Aris had the same eager gleam in his eyes as he'd had when he'd begun crafting Verena the night prior. Such a raw expression could not only be for her father's benefit, and Blythe felt her cheeks warm as she watched Aris bolt to his feet before the boat had come to a stop.

"Wait here," he told them, swaying a little before he leapt onto the streets. The boat tipped, and Blythe clutched the edge as Aris hurried to the vendor. One look at him and all others bowed their heads, quick to greet him with friendly words that the alleged prince matched.

The vendor was a frail, older man with deep wrinkles set around kind eyes that brightened when Aris approached. His hands trembled as they poured three cups of the steaming chocolate, though he grinned from ear to ear and shook Aris's hands with great excitement. He tried to send Aris away without charge, but Blythe was glad to see the golden coin that glinted in the vendor's palm when Aris pulled away from shaking the man's hand.

Chocolate was a small thing to share with someone, and yet Aris had never looked more radiant. It seemed he was far more drawn to humans than he'd ever admit, especially those who were skilled or clever, or turned their passion into a finely honed craft. Blythe drew her hands back from the edge of the boat, wiping away the dampness on her gloves as she mulled that thought over. She wasn't quite certain what to do with the knowledge, let alone the pattering of her heart.

Aris carried three overflowing cups back to the boat, careful not to spill a drop as he handed the first to Blythe, then one to Elijah. He took his seat, but rather than immediately take a sip of his own, he cast Blythe and her father a sideways stare. Blythe pretended not to notice how eager he was for them to taste it.

She, for one, didn't need any encouragement. Blythe lifted the cup to her lips and let herself melt as the chocolate poured down her tongue, thick and richer than she'd ever tasted. Its heat spread through her belly, filling her with a pleasant warmth. Elijah must have been pleased as well, for while he chose not to admit it aloud, his chocolate was already halfway gone by the time Blythe turned to him.

"This place is not at all like I envisioned," Elijah said eventually, interrupting the comfortable quiet that had blossomed between the three of them. It was likely as close to a compliment as Aris would get from him.

"Nor is it what I envisioned," Blythe admitted. "It's so much better." Perhaps it was more than just the chocolate that had her so warm, more content on this cramped boat in an unfamiliar town than she'd felt in ages. The gondolier steered them farther down the canal and beneath a bridge so low that Blythe reached up to brush her palm against its worn stone, filled with such joy that her eyes grew hot.

How was it that a place like this existed in the world without her ever knowing? And how many more places like this were there, just waiting for her to discover?

Blythe held her cup close, hoping to always remember the joy she felt in that moment. The way her world had become so much grander that day, and how eager she was to explore it.

"Thank you," she whispered, smiling to herself when Aris's spine stiffened. His eyes darted away from her, and when he spoke it was with his lips an inch away from his drink, its steam against his face.

"It's only chocolate," he said before sipping. She might have specified that it was much, much more than that, but Blythe got the feeling he already knew.

"It's certainly beautiful," Elijah acknowledged. "But what are the neighboring countries like? How are your relations?"

Blythe nearly swatted her father on the arm. God forbid she truly *had* married a prince. Surely one would have believed her father a menace cut from poor cloth. Fortunately, Aris maintained his good-natured attitude with a laugh.

"I assure you that Verena is at peace and its people are happy. Your daughter is safe, Mr. Hawthorne. She'll always be well taken care of."

When the corners of Elijah's eyes creased, Blythe almost felt guilty. It was clear that he wanted to believe there was more to this story than he was being told, but there wasn't a way for him to prove anything. Aris was being as kind as he was poised. Verena was thriving, and at every turn its adoring denizens threw hellebore into the canal as they passed. The food was delicious, and Blythe... well, frankly Blythe wasn't certain that her eyes hadn't turned starry. She wanted to see what this place looked like at night, with hazy golden lights glowing from the windows of snowy streets. She wanted to see it in the spring, when the flowers were blooming, and in the heat of the summer when a splash of the canal's water against her skin would be a welcome delight. Aris had taken her to a place with magic in its bones, and she never wanted to leave.

Elijah, it seemed, could sense this. He set one hand on Blythe's shoulder as he used the other to lift his cup so he could polish off the remaining dregs of his hot chocolate. "She does seem happy," he admitted with words so soft they were meant only for her.

A smile cracked Blythe's lips as she leaned her shoulder against his. "You don't have to worry for me," she told him, though it didn't stop Elijah from snorting as he took her gloved hand in his and patted it softly.

"I will always worry for you," he said. "How are you faring in this weather? Are you staying healthy?"

While the question might have been silly to someone else, Blythe understood what he was truly asking. Less than a year had passed since she'd been on her deathbed. As improved as she was, it was no secret that Blythe was smaller than she ought to have been, still slowly putting weight back on. Her muscles, too, had atrophied during her illness but had shown much improvement over the months thanks to routine walks and horseback rides on Mitra.

Still, she was tired. The stone bed and Wisteria's cold had been doing her no favors, and while her coughing had been a little better the past few days, she'd awoken weak and with her nose stuffy. And then there were the visions....

Aris tried to steal a glance at her, likely thinking of her spell from the night prior. Blythe looked purposefully at her father.

"I'm well, and that's how I intend to stay for a very long time," she told Elijah, speaking each word with such finality that they had no choice but to be the truth. Blythe rested her head against his shoulder, watching as Verena faded behind them and the glistening silver of the palace came back into view. Bodies were strange and sometimes frustrating things, but her slow recovery would not be enough to soil her spirits. Not today.

"And how are you?" she asked when she couldn't spare another second considering all the oddities she'd been seeing. "How are things back at Thorn Grove?"

She hadn't missed how Elijah had ignored this question in his last letter, nor how his face tightened even then. "All will be well, Blythe. It always is."

It was far from a favorable answer. Her heart spiked, though Elijah's avoidance of her eyes told her not to press. At least not yet. She'd have time to pry the information from him before he left.

Blythe hadn't noticed that the boat had been slowing until they came to a stop. She could have traveled through the canals for endless hours if it was up to her. But the gondolier's chest was rising and falling with heavy breaths as he wiped sweat from his brow, and the temperature was dropping to a level they would soon be unprepared for.

"Here." Aris shrugged out of his coat and draped it over Blythe's shoulders at her first shiver. She stilled, uncertain how she was meant to react until she noticed that Elijah was watching and forced herself to smile and pull the coat tighter.

"Thank you," she whispered, unable to shake the nerves from her throat.

Aris offered only a curt nod before he stepped out of the boat with one foot and used the other to brace it, closing the gap from the dock to the water. He helped Elijah out, and then with his lips pressed in a thin line, extended a hand to Blythe. Her eyes flicked down to it, skeptical.

"My hand isn't going to bite you, love," he said with a flattened tone that Blythe had since realized meant he was attempting politeness. He flexed his fingers, nodding her along. But before Blythe could take hold, Elijah stepped beside Aris and clasped him on the shoulder.

"The two of you don't have to come in on my account," he said. "If I try to sit through dinner, I will fall asleep on my plate. I can see the two of you off, though. Surely there must be something around here that you do for fun?"

Blythe slid Aris a sideways glance, unnerved by his easy smile. To his credit, he didn't appear at all unprepared.

"A brilliant idea, Mr. Hawthorne," Aris said as he took Blythe's hand and hauled her off the boat. "I know just the thing."

CHAPTER THIRTEEN

Eight dogs stood panting in the snow outside the palace gates. They were as large as wolves but thicker, their coats a fluffy white beneath the heavy leather harnesses that strapped them not only to one another but to a strange iron contraption.

"Is that a sled?" Blythe's voice was breathy as she approached it. A few of the dogs snuffed at her legs, and she gave one a gentle pat on a head that was larger than her hand, before it resumed its panting.

"It's the same idea as a carriage," Aris answered, taking Blythe's wrist and steering her inside. "Only this one is pulled by dogs bred to withstand the snow. I've been meaning to bring you, though we never had the right excuse."

"I've never seen such a thing," said Elijah as he circled the contraption, inspecting it while Aris observed with an easy slant to his shoulders.

"My family has been practicing the sport for ages," Aris told them both. "We'll be perfectly safe."

Blythe hardly cared for such assurances. Even if he told her that there was an accident on this sled just yesterday, that wouldn't have quelled the excitement buzzing through her. She gripped the sled's edges, wondering how to control these hounds—and where Aris's sled was—when she felt the press of his body behind her. She startled as she felt each and every line of him against her. The hardness of his chest. The steadiness of his thighs against her hips, bracing her.

Good God, why couldn't she breathe? She tossed her head to steal a sideways glance at him, wishing at once that she could stomp on his foot when she saw the upward slope of his lips.

"Relax," he whispered as several servants checked the sled over, taking great precaution as they strapped the two into one tiny, hopelessly cramped sled that had them pressed even closer by the time the servants were done. Blythe wasn't sure how that was physically possible, but even breathing felt scandalous.

"You could at least act like my touch doesn't repulse you," Aris whispered against her ear, raising gooseflesh across her skin. "We're married. There isn't a single person here who doesn't believe that you and I have been significantly closer than this."

Oh, how she wished she could curse the blasted stuttering of her heart. She managed to grit a sharp "Is this necessary?" between her teeth, whispering so that her father would not overhear.

"Only if you care to have your father see that I am an exceptionally caring husband who shows his daughter a delightful time." He curled his fingers around her hips, so close that Blythe felt each of his words hot against her skin. "Do not sabotage our agreement. Act like you like me, or you'll ruin everything."

Was it her imagination, or was his voice huskier than normal? Probably it *was* her imagination, for her mind was in another place entirely when she felt the press of his fingertips against her hips, stirring particular . . . *feelings* inside her. She swallowed the lump in her throat, certain that she was flushed from head to toe as she offered her father a quick wave.

"Are you certain you wouldn't like to join us?" she asked out of desperation, biting back a groan when her father nodded, that curious glint still in his eyes.

"I'm certain that it's time for me to retire," Elijah told her. "But I'll be eager to hear about it over breakfast."

This time when her father walked into the palace, he looked so much more at ease than when they'd left it earlier that day. Aris sent the attendants with him, which left just the two of them and a choir of panting dogs beneath the glow of a rising moon.

When they were alone, Aris reached around Blythe to simultaneously grab the reins and toss a thick blanket around their shoulders. Then he pulled out two pairs of the most absurd goggles and ignored her protests as he forced a pair onto her eyes before slipping on his own.

"You look ridiculous." She scowled, readjusting the eyewear.

"Be quiet and hold on to the blanket," he commanded, and Blythe barely had the chance to grab hold while hissing at him not to tell her what to do before he gave the reins a snap.

The dogs shot to attention, tongues lolling and their excitement close to bursting as they took off at a sprint. Blythe slid back from the jolt of it, though given how cramped the space was, there was nowhere for her to go but against Aris's chest.

Icy wind whipped across her cheeks and stung her skin, and though they obscured her vision, she was grateful for the goggles. She was grateful, too, for the warmth of Aris's body as she found herself leaning into him. Delighted laughter bubbled in her throat as the hounds twisted around the palace, headed toward the thicket of evergreens that towered behind it. Aris didn't echo the sound, but his grip on her tightened as they picked up pace, expertly gliding over the snowy trail as if the hounds had traversed them a hundred times before.

She opened her mouth to speak, only to end up choking as some foul insect hit the wall of her throat.

"I told you to be quiet." Aris did laugh then, the low timbre rumbling against her back. She hissed a few choice words at him, though the sound of his laughter had warmed her skin in a way she didn't care to acknowledge. A way that made her vision tunnel, the snow slipping away as her mind stirred up a strange image.

She saw a flash of the same daydream that had been plaguing her for the past several months, ever since the night that Signa had saved Eliza. It was a glimpse of a man from the neck down. His skin was bare and hot, and the world around them was hazy as he laughed. It wasn't a delighted sound like Aris's, but a dark, pleased sound before the man pulled her into his lap, tucking her body around his. His lips were on hers as he hiked her up by the hips, and there was nothing soft about him or his touch.

Blythe knew what happened next from too many late nights spent lingering indulgently on the memory, and nearly sputtered as she forced the imagery away before things progressed. She gripped on to the steel bars of the sled, telling her treacherous mind to behave itself.

She hadn't the faintest clue why her brain had taken to producing such dreams, but they came at least once a week and never failed to leave her tossing in her sheets, flushed and wanting and exploratory since she could not rip the thoughts from her mind.

She was roused into awareness when the world slowed and Aris yelled something behind her in a murky voice that sounded as though she was underwater. The dogs were coming to a halt beside a blanket that had been laid out beneath the bend of a tree. A lantern hung from one of its branches and Blythe stared at it, then at Aris as she removed her goggles. He was already undoing the sled's fastenings, slipping out, and offering her a hand.

It was so dark that the woods were nearly black, their tree lit only by the lantern and a rising moon whose light filtered in through the occasional thicket of branches. Still, even if Blythe couldn't see a thing, the dogs were relaxed enough for her to know that there were no servants around. No Verena residents. And certainly not her father. There was no one to impress, and yet Aris led her to the blanket with a tightness in his jaw.

"Why are we here?" It wasn't an accusation, but genuine curiosity that had Blythe asking. "We could just turn around and sneak back into Verena. My father would be none the wiser."

"A grand idea, if I believed he was actually sleeping."

She took a seat when he did, noticing with delight that there was a basket atop the blanket. She'd never been on a late-night picnic before, let alone one in the snow.

Blythe pulled the blanket around her shoulders closer as Aris fetched a jug of hot chocolate from the basket. Magically, it was still steaming. He divided it into two cups and then retrieved a bottle of something that smelled distinctly like liquor and poured some into each. Then he handed one to her, flipping over the basket lid to show a plethora of other delights: jams, cookies, meats, cheeses.

Blythe held her cup close as he doled it onto plates, taking a deep swig and sighing as the chocolate warmed her from the inside out.

"Your father is a deeply suspicious man." Aris leaned back on one hand and drank deeply from his own cup.

"He has every right to be," Blythe said simply. "Please continue to be kind to him, Aris. I know you've got it in you."

He grunted as he turned toward the trees, the angles of his face softened by the lamplight's dim glow. "I don't understand why you care so much about what he thinks. Children marry and leave their nests all the time. It's nature."

"Perhaps that wouldn't have been so awful, had I not been leaving him entirely on his own." Blythe stared into her mug, breathing so deeply that she blew steam upon her face. "I think something has happened back at home, and my father won't tell me what it is. Were it anything serious, I worry no one would help him. Society is full of vultures who pick you apart and would sooner peel your skin from their teeth than raise a hand to assist you. They judge and they ridicule, and my marrying you certainly did not help with that."

Aris retracted his neck with a look of disbelief. "What's wrong with marrying me? If anything, your *society* should treat him better knowing that he's connected to royalty."

"*Royalty*," she scoffed. "You strutting about like a peacock has not helped me. It's only opened my family up to more criticism. Whether you and I show up to gatherings, or how much you smile when I dance with you, it will all be ridiculed. If I visit home alone, or whether you come with me... they watch everything. It's taxing enough when you have someone to share the burden with. But my father has no one. All I want is for him to live in peace."

Aris frowned and took another swig of his drink. Clearly, he hadn't considered this nearly as much as Blythe. "I will give them no reason to fault your father," he said at last, the words as soft as a promise. "I have no quarrel with him. Elijah will be spared any burdens of our arrangement, you have my word."

It was a good word. One that took Blythe by surprise, and that she was immediately grateful for. But as she opened her mouth to tell Aris as much, she was struck by a sudden sneeze. She barely had time to turn her head away, taken by a small fit of them. By the time they stopped her eyes were red and bleary, and she sniffed.

Aris's bottom lip curled under. "You're repulsive."

"I'm afraid I might be getting a cold," she told him, admittedly happy to realize as much. If she was getting sick, then perhaps that explained the prior night's strange hallucinations. "I'm sure the snow isn't helping me any."

Aris did not look half as pleased by this realization as Blythe did. "You should have told me when you first noticed you were ill.

Neither of us may ever like it, but we're bonded now. We can spend our years bickering and being miserable. We can keep secrets and argue and never leave Wisteria because we hate each other. Or I can travel freely and live the life that I want to live while allowing you to leech onto it like a warm and healthy parasite. That, to me, is the best answer."

She forced back a scoff because Aris was right about one thing—if they were to spend the rest of their lives together, it would be a hell of a lot better not to do it as enemies. That didn't mean they had to *like* each other, necessarily. He could still call her whatever foul name he wanted; she rather enjoyed his creativity. But if a tolerance between them meant that she could travel—if it meant that her days would be spent touring marvelous cities and her nights eating delicious food in a wintry forest without a single care or worry in the world—then who was she to pass up such a grand opportunity?

"If I feel like keeling over, you'll be the first to know." She leaned forward to fetch a plate and silverware from the basket, wiping her nose on her sleeve. "As much as I've begun to enjoy our bickering, I agree with you. So long as you give me a proper bed and fix up Wisteria for whenever we *are* at the manor—and so long as you do not go back on your word about allowing me access to Thorn Grove—then I will... attempt civility. At the very least, I promise not to plot your murder while you sleep."

"It sounds like I'm getting quite the bargain." His smile truly was a wondrous thing, a beauty wasted on the likes of him. "Very well. I agree to those terms."

"Then we have ourselves a deal." Satisfied, Blythe turned her attention to the food and took hold of a biscuit as her vessel for the most vibrant orange marmalade. As she spread it on the biscuit, however, she moved too quickly in the darkness and cut clean through to her palm.

Blythe dropped the knife as she yelled profanities that would put a sailor to shame. She clutched her hand tight as the blood welled, nausea rolling in her stomach.

Aris was crouched before her in an instant, grabbing hold of her wrist. Though Blythe's instinct was to keep her hand tucked close and wallow in her pain, there was enough authority in his body language that she couldn't refuse him.

"I'm going to need a doctor," she said pathetically. "It'll need stitches, probably dozens of them."

"My needlework is better than any doctor's." Aris pried her fingers one by one from where they pressed protectively over her wound. "Now let me see—" He stilled, staring at her open palm. Blythe practically withered into the ground.

"What is it?" she moaned. "Is it horrible? Will I lose the hand?"

Aris's brow furrowed as he tossed her wrist to the side. "You devilish girl. Are you always this dramatic?"

"Have some delicacy, I'm wounded!" She brought her hand back to her lap, nursing it. "Sometimes I wonder whether you walked straight off the pages of a fairy tale."

"Because of my princely charm, I'm aware." Aris rose to his feet.

"No, because you're as beastly as a troll." Blythe unclenched her hand, expecting that he was undermining the severity of her wounds. What she didn't expect was for her palm to be perfectly smooth, not even a line of pink to show for the injury. There was no blood. No cut. Only a pulse of phantom pain, and a few remnants of orange marmalade that Aris brushed away before licking his finger.

Surely she couldn't have been imagining such gut-wrenching pain. She skimmed her thumb down the length of her palm, searching the blanket and the nearby snow for any sign of blood. And yet when she looked around, she saw only the tiniest bit of green grass at the base of a nearby tree, so bright in its color as it poked upward through the snow.

Fresh grass in December. Such a peculiar sight that she wondered if perhaps she was once again seeing things. Dizziness plagued her, and Blythe's vision became fuzzy from the quickness of her breathing.

"Perhaps I am being dramatic," Blythe whispered at last, though she didn't believe those words. Not when it was one more item on her list of oddities, like when she'd seen her previous maid's haunted reflection in the mirror months ago, or had seen Eliza Wakefield lying in her bed with sunken flesh and protruding bones like the dead reawakened.

And now there was pain with no injuries. Visions of a man and the echoes of music at all hours of the day. A white-haired woman roaming Wisteria's halls, always lingering just out of view.

Her body grew cold, an inescapable chill permeating her bones.

Blythe curled her hand into her chest, making a fist. She felt like a child's used doll, fraying open at the seams. Her mind was a foreign place these days, stuffed full of oddities and unfamiliar memories.

She took hold of her drink, downing the rest in a single gulp in an effort to ease her disquieted mind and the pulse of pain that still thrummed in her palm. Aris observed all the while, spine drawing straight when she finished.

"Are you well?" he asked, and Blythe could hardly bite back her laugh, for she found that she had no answer to his question.

Was she well? It was impossible to say.

The blanket did little to assuage the bout of shivers coursing through her. She tried to stand. Tried to get her mind straight, but the moment she rose to her feet, her head pounded with such severity that it felt as though the ground gave way beneath her.

Aris caught her before she fell, and Blythe had just enough awareness to realize that his arms were around her, drawing her into his chest as he stood.

"Don't you dare fall asleep," he told her, an edge in his voice that roused her enough to squint up at him. "This isn't one of your fairy tales, and I have no desire to rescue a damsel in distress." In her blurring vision Aris did not have one face but three, and all of them scowled with expert finesse.

She tried to speak, though it took a moment before she managed. "The trolls are never the ones who save the damsels." At least that's what she thought she said. Admittedly the words came out garbled.

Aris blew out a sigh. "You are a thorn in my side." Sharp as his words were, the tension in his body relaxed. "Where's the pain?"

"There isn't any," she told him, ignoring the sear of her palm. "It's a dizzy spell. They happen occasionally, ever since the belladonna. Now put me down."

Aris ignored her, and though she scowled at him, in truth Blythe was quite grateful. For if he had set her down, she likely would have fallen again.

Aris tucked her back into the sled, doing up the fastenings and pressing so close against her that she was undeniably secured. This time, she didn't resist his touch. Instead, she relaxed against his body as Aris gave the reins a gentle snap and had them on their way back to the palace.

CHAPTER FOURTEEN

THE PALACE WAS SILENT WHEN THEY ARRIVED, AND BLYTHE GUESSED Aris was to thank for that.

He did not return Blythe to her room, but instead carried her through an ornately carved door down the hall from her own. Had it always been there, or had he magicked it into existence for the sake of convenience?

"Where are you taking me?" she demanded, blinking eyes that had long since lost their bleariness. By this point, Aris was just being stubborn to not put her down.

"To my room, where I can keep an eye on you. The last thing I need is the hassle of your death while your father's down the hall."

He gave her no time to argue as he opened the door not into a dusky purple sky pocked with starlight or an enchanting forest glade, but into a plain suite with a plain sitting area and an unadorned bedchamber similar in layout to the one she'd woken up in that morning.

"*This* is your room?" Aris must have registered her surprise, for he gave the space a single glance before shaking his head.

"Of course not. For the length of your father's visit, this is *our* room. We're happy newlyweds, remember?"

"Our room." She chewed at her bottom lip, sucking it between her teeth. "Right." The suite was larger than hers, though far less grand, with walls of a rich forest green and all the basic furniture. There was no sign of originality. No sign of *Aris*.

Though she could see the hardwood floors against her soles, she kept expecting them to split open and force her to step around bushels of lavender or sage that spread like wildflowers. How jarring it was to be surrounded by magic and wonder, only to suddenly not find any of it. It seemed Blythe was getting spoiled, so accustomed to Aris's magic that reality felt dull.

Aris strolled inside, loosening his cravat. She noticed then how slowly he moved, his footsteps a shuffle and his head drooped as if pulled down by an invisible weight. He worked at his cuff links, fumbling over them for so long that Blythe could no longer stand it and eventually stepped forward to take hold of his wrists.

"You are not yourself," she said as she undid her gloves to get a better grip. "Why is it that we're surrounded by plain walls and your shoulders are bowed just so?"

He stiffened at her touch, rigid as her fingers brushed against the smooth skin of his inner wrist.

"Magic of this level is not easy to maintain, even for me." Blythe felt his eyes on her as she worked off the first link, then started on the second. "Right now, everyone is asleep in their homes. My control over them can drop for as long as they remain that way, and it should be enough for me to maintain this ruse for a few days more. But this magic doesn't come freely."

That much was certainly clear. He'd seemed far more energized early in the day. But as the hours passed, the magic had taken its toll. Even his voice was haggard, words a slow drawl as exhaustion clung to him.

She hurried to undo the second link, guilt thickening her throat. He was the one who had put them in this situation, but her father was the reason that Aris had to go to such extravagant lengths, and seeing the toll it took on him had Blythe pausing before she drew her hands away.

"I appreciate what you've done," she told him. "You've gone beyond your means to put my father at ease. And I appreciate your bringing me to whatever town we're in, because it's the most enchanting place that I have ever seen."

So still was Aris that she could not feel the pulse of his wrist beneath her.

"I'm glad that you enjoyed it," he said. Though the words were no more than a whisper, they rang loudly against the silence. "Despite what some may think, I do not find delight in being cruel. I know how important Elijah is to you, and I know what he's gone through these past few years. I would not wish to bring him more pain by letting him believe that his daughter is suffering."

Blythe appreciated that more than words would ever convey.

Slowly, she peeled her hands away from him. "I've always wanted to travel. It's why I never planned to marry. I never wanted anyone to tell me where I could or couldn't go."

Aris looked to the floor as he admitted, "I know. I wove your tapestry, just like all the others. One does not easily forget such a blazing soul."

Of course he had. Yet while she'd always known this in the back of her mind, she'd never considered the implications of it. The knowledge stilled her, for if he knew that . . . "Is that why you kept me locked away in Wisteria?" she asked. "Because you knew how much I would hate you for it?"

His laugh was the softest puff of breath, warming her cheeks. This time when he answered, his eyes found hers. "We went to war with each other the moment you spilled your blood onto my tapestry. Do not be angry that my arsenal is better equipped than yours."

Perhaps she should have felt vexed from his statement, but Aris was right. She'd called for war, and if she'd had the advantages that Fate did, Blythe would have used them, too.

"So you know everything, then," she mused, trying to sound more rueful than she felt. "You likely even know how long you'll have to put up with me, don't you?"

Aris must have recognized the lie of her cheerfulness, for he stepped but a hair's breadth from her and spoke in a voice softer than she knew him capable. "Your tapestry became a mystery to me the moment your life was spared. I don't know when you'll die, if that's what you're asking. I don't know what you'll do, or the person you'll become. Not anymore. I wove your fate as I once knew it, which had you dying by your brother's hand. But you've changed your fate several times over. You are a mystery to me. A sweetbrier, full of thorns in my side."

Blythe could not make sense of the things his voice did to her. Days ago, all she could focus on was the hope that she and Aris could get through her father's visit without tearing out each other's throats. Now her mind was in disarray, flustered ever since being plagued by that vision of the man who had hiked her hips against his. Her heart pounded against her ribs like a caged beast as her body betrayed her, and Blythe peered behind Aris, to the single curtained bed. She swallowed.

Aris followed her gaze. "I don't have it in me to manifest another," he told her, sounding apologetic enough that she believed him. "Truth be told, your suite no longer exists. But do not delude yourself into thinking that I intend to seduce you. I'll sleep on the floor."

That would be the better option, and yet it was clear that what they both needed was a good night's rest. She told herself it was guilt and the fact that she needed him in his best shape to entertain her father that had her shaking her head. For she despised Aris.

Even if she couldn't pull her eyes away from his bare throat, visible now from his lack of cravat. Even if she was enamored by his body, so warm and inviting that she yearned to press herself against it.

"*I* will take the floor," she told him, forcing the words out. "I'm used to sleeping on a hard surface."

Aris winced. "I might have gotten carried away with that one, I admit. But you're sick, and this bed has more than enough space for us both . . . if you would like to share it."

He was right. The bed likely had enough room for four people to sleep comfortably. She wouldn't even be close to touching Aris if she agreed, and yet that didn't make it feel any less intimate.

Rather than answer, Blythe smoothed her hands down the length of her bodice and turned from him. "I'll need Olivia. Unless I'm to suffocate overnight, I'll need assistance getting out of this corset."

Silence stretched between them for a long moment until Aris admitted, "Olivia is asleep. Everyone is."

Well. That wouldn't do at all. It seemed she'd have to see to the matter herself.

"Turn off the lights," she told him, waiting until Aris obliged. "And draw the curtains, too." He sighed but did as instructed. Blythe waited until all traces of light were gone before she took a steadying breath, kicked off her boots, and then stretched her hands behind her in an effort to reach the laces. While she'd been growing accustomed to her routine when it was just her and Aris at Wisteria, Olivia had outfitted her properly for a woman of high society. Unfortunately, that meant that her clothing was nearly impossible to get off on her own.

But blast it all if she wasn't going to try.

Blythe bent at the waist, breath catching in her lungs as desperate fingers clutched for the laces, to no avail. She must have been trying for at least five minutes, attempting to quiet her huffing and gasps of air as Aris readied himself for bed in the dark. With every rustle of his clothing as he undressed, she huffed louder, trying not to think about whatever was happening behind her. Eventually she became so distracted by her efforts that she didn't notice him approach from behind. He set his hands on her waist and drew her upright so that Blythe was against the hardness of his chest, pressing one hand to her mouth and hoping that he couldn't feel the frenzy of her heart.

"I would very much prefer sleep over listening to you wrestle your gown." The night fought to steal his whisper, the sound hardly audible against her ear. "Be still, Sweetbrier."

He didn't need to tell her twice. Aris skimmed his hands down her back, having to use touch to guide his way in the absence of light. When Blythe's spine tried to arch, she silently cursed her traitorous body and forced herself rigid. She shut her eyes as his fingers hooked under the satin ribbons. He was slow, pausing every time that Blythe twitched or caught her breath. While his fingers were deft with tapestries, Aris worked at the laces at a glacial place, fumbling in the darkness.

Almost... almost as if this sort of thing were new to him.

"Aris." Blythe's voice was no louder than the slip of silk. "Have you done this before?" She knew it was one of those intrusive thoughts better left unasked, yet behind the shield of darkness she could not help but give voice to it.

Aris went taut. "Dresses have changed over the years. I swear they get more complicated with every century."

"Century?" she echoed, disbelieving. "Has it been that long since... well, since you..."

"Since I was with a woman?"

Blythe wasn't sure whether she should be thankful or embarrassed that he'd finished the sentence for her. She held her bodice tightly against her as he undid another lace. "Perhaps that's not something you're interested in."

His breath grazed her neck as he leaned in. "I am interested in all of life's pleasures, Sweetbrier, those of the body included. I do not limit who I find those with, though nothing has felt the same since my wife's death. Not that it's any of your concern, but I *have* tried to move on. Quite extensively, for a period. Sometimes I still do, though no matter how interested my body may be, my mind has found intimacy meaningless. Without my wife, the pleasure has been lost."

Good.

That was good. Because Blythe felt nothing, too. Obviously.

She hoped that he could not feel the heat radiating or the clamminess of her skin as his fingers brushed her back and the corset finally slipped down her body. Aris took her hand, helping her step out of the gown. She was left in only a thin slip of a chemise that was to act as a nightgown and was grateful for the darkness, overly aware of how some of her bones still protruded, persistent reminders of her months spent ill.

She was also pathetically aware of what his words had done to her. Aris had said nothing overt, and yet her mind had stretched itself, imagining fantastically ridiculous things that she had no business imagining. She wondered what Aris would be like as a lover—not that she had much to compare to. She'd read enough stories to know things that none but her mother ever thought important to teach her. Lillian, at least, had sat her down years ago and told her everything society expected of a woman. She told her to be safe and to be wise with her heart, but beyond that, she had left Blythe to her own devices.

Blythe was by no means an expert, though she'd had her fair share of trysts. Curious kisses that led to even more curious touches in the woods behind Thorn Grove. Sometimes with men, and twice with Lady Asherby, the daughter of a marquess who frequented her father's gentleman's club whenever he visited the country. She and Blythe had made a fast pair, though it had only ever been in fun. As far as emotions went, Blythe had never found herself serious about anyone. No matter how much she enjoyed a person's company, it had always felt like something was missing. Like there was something she was waiting for but hadn't yet discovered.

Still, Blythe had enjoyed her past experiences and had always expected that there would one day be more. It had been some time since she'd had a rendezvous, which likely explained why she was having such potent feelings in that moment. Aris was not at all someone she'd ever thought of in that way, but a brush of his finger against her back was all it took to send her mind spiraling. Would he be a passionate lover? Would his hands be gentle as they caressed her skin, or would he seize her by the shoulders with a commanding touch and pin her beneath him?

Until that moment, Blythe hadn't realized that this would be its own challenge in marriage. Would she and Aris both be free to take lovers if they wished? She could see him being too prideful for that, even if they were wed only in name. But Blythe was young and curious, and she had no desire to live through the remainder of her life without knowing physical intimacy with another.

She supposed Aris himself could be an option…

No.

Good God, what was she thinking? So much had happened today, and she wasn't in her right mind. She and Aris were only sharing a bed. They were married, and they were sharing a bed.

…Not that she'd ever shared a bed with a man before. Maybe it would be nice. Maybe she wouldn't be so cold, or better yet, it *would* be cold and then they'd have to—no. No, no, no. She needed to stop while she was ahead.

Blythe really ought to have been a writer. She might not have had much experience, but with as much as she read, she certainly had the imagination. And right then, that imagination was hopelessly explicit. She tucked herself under the sheets, grateful for the valley of space between them. The last thing she needed was any more accidental brushing of skin.

"Do you think you'll ever want to be with someone else?" she asked, wishing for the foresight to bite her tongue and end this conversation. "Would you ever be open to courting, I mean."

"I've had a long while to consider it." Blythe was surprised by the tenderness in his words. His voice was close, as if he was facing her. So she turned on her side as well, even if it was too dark to see him. "I spent ages hoping that time would lessen the loss, but I've never been able to get over the hurdle of knowing that she's still out there somewhere."

Blythe thought at once of Signa, and of Death's tender embrace the last time she'd seen her cousin. The way he held her without any signs of letting go, and the way she'd been so content to let him.

Blythe knew she was wading into dangerous waters, but still she asked, "And what if you do find her and she no longer feels the same? What if she doesn't remember you, or has fallen in love with someone else?"

Aris needed no time to ponder this. "Then I will hope that her next life will be one that favors me."

Blythe leaned into her pillow. It saddened her to think that someone would waste so much time pining when they could find someone else to be happy with. And yet she also wondered what it must be like to love someone or to be loved so profoundly. Blythe couldn't think of a single other person who would be so willing to wait even half as long as Aris had. If it was true that Life had loved him—and Blythe believed that she had—then she was a fool to have given up someone like him. Someone who would wait for her. Search for her. Bend the world for her.

It was so admirable that, for once, Blythe thought she might like to experience something akin to that love at least once in her life.

"I never asked whether you had someone?" Aris said, posing it as a question while Blythe fought off a yawn.

"Never anyone serious. Though it's like you said earlier—you already knew that."

He was quiet for a moment before he laughed, caught. "You're right. I asked in the hope that it would get me to what I really wanted to know, which is *why* you don't have someone. I may *see* a person's fate, but that doesn't mean I personally understand each of their decisions. I want to know why you were so content to be alone."

Blythe wasn't sure what to make of this fragile spell that had been cast between them. It seemed that this was one of those evenings that worked like magic, the darkness bleeding away inhibitions as the night snatched secrets from their tongues.

"I have never found someone who's held my interest," she admitted. It was an answer she didn't often give aloud, for friends had laughed at her, believing that she was joking or vain or something in between. But that was the truth, and to her surprise, Aris acknowledged it without so much as a hint of mockery. Curiosity, perhaps, but no mockery.

"I don't love compromise," she admitted when he said nothing in response, feeling a need to explain herself. "And I've always hated the rules and nonsense that we adhere to just to avoid being a social pariah. Why is it that we're expected to sit and accept flowers or ridiculous poetry from men who have determined us valuable from our pedigree or our faces, without ever truly getting to know us? Why is it that we are given a season to graze the surface of who someone is, and then are expected to make a match? And God forbid if it takes us more than one or two seasons to find someone in our tiny social pond. Not that it's any better if you *do* find someone, as everything the two of you do will forever be watched. Will you have children? *When* will you have children? If a woman is out without her husband, then certainly she must be up to no good. Maybe he's tired of her. Maybe she's not performing her womanly duties up to snuff, because heaven knows it can't possibly be him that's the problem, or that maybe she simply wants a night to herself."

She sighed, having grown more awake and heated with each word. So heated, in fact, that she bristled when Aris hummed his amusement.

"You've given this a lot of thought," he said, to which she snorted.

"How could I not, when so many people believe that this is all I amount to? I hear the gossip when a married woman shows up to a dance alone, or when someone is on their third season and has yet to make a match. Even if *I* know that it's all ridiculous, having enough people mock or ridicule you still takes its toll."

"The process leaves much to be desired," Aris agreed. "There is nothing that makes spring a better time to find love than winter. And no one should ever be expected to sit and listen to something as awful as poetry as a profession of love. I can see how that alone would sour the idea of marriage."

It was Blythe's turn to laugh. "I'd forgotten how much you detest poetry. It's really not so bad."

Aris's displeasure came from somewhere deep in his throat. It was a low, gravelly sound that had Blythe tucking her legs closer to her chest, more aroused than she had any right to be.

Fortunately, Aris didn't appear to notice. "There is nothing in this world that is more pretentious."

Blythe wanted to argue that *he,* in fact, was far more pretentious than poetry, thus disputing his claims. But for now she let it slide.

"Poetry and process aside, there are many joys to be found in partnership. There is friendship and trust. A joy of knowing that there is a person in the world who knows you truly, to the depths of your soul."

"Certainly, if you're one of the lucky ones," Blythe said.

"If you're one of the lucky ones," Aris echoed, his voice growing distant as he shifted to face the ceiling. "Though I don't suppose either of us will ever be."

"No." Blythe matched him as she, too, rolled to her back. "I don't suppose that we will."

CHAPTER FIFTEEN

Blythe had never roused from a bed faster than she did the next morning. When she blinked past the dregs of sleep and remembered where she was—and more importantly who she was next to—she pressed her eyes shut in a desperate attempt at teleporting herself to anywhere but the bed, then rolled herself off the mattress. She did so inch by inch, contorting herself in a desperate attempt to silently escape the room without waking Aris. And yet with her rolling came a throbbing head, and Blythe had to stifle her tired groan as she tried to re-center the world. Her efforts, however, were in vain.

"That was quite the performance." Aris was seated in an armchair behind her, a newspaper in one hand and a steaming cup of tea in the other. "I had no idea you were such an acrobat." The fox at his feet chittered quietly before curling into a tighter ball. Aris reached down, patting the top of the beast's head. Of course one monster behaved for another.

“I was trying to be mindful,” Blythe snapped, hoping that her cheeks weren’t as flushed as she felt. “Why are you awake so early?”

“It’s not early,” he said first, nodding to where sunlight filtered in through a gap in the curtains. “Also, I don’t require sleep in the same way that you do. I only needed a bit of rest with my magic so depleted.”

Blythe wished she’d never asked. Because now she had to reconcile not only the fact that she’d spent the night in the same bed as Aris, but that he hadn’t even been sleeping for all of it.

“It turns out I’m not the only troll in this relationship.” His eyes skimmed over the edge of the paper, observing her. “Did you know that you snore in your sleep?”

She didn’t know whether she wanted to stay and burn Aris alive, or whether she should flee the room and hope that she never saw him again. Both, unfortunately, were wishful thinking.

Blythe stepped closer to the curtains, ignoring his jab as she poked her head through. The town outside the palace walls was covered in fresh snow that whipped in the air as the beginnings of a blizzard stirred.

“It’s going to be foul weather today,” she commented, pulling the curtains open wider. “How are we meant to go outside in this?”

“We’re not.” Aris plucked a cube of sugar from a bowl and dropped it into his tea, followed by another. “There are fewer people I’ll have to manage if we stay inside for the day. It’s a better idea anyway, if you’re sick. You can have some tea and stay by the fire. You might want to put some clothes on, though. You’ll catch a chill dressed as you are.”

Clothes.

Blythe gaped down at the flimsy chemise that stopped an inch below her knee. It was thin and sheer, the edges of her body toeing the line of visibility. She could practically see the bones of her hips pressing through the fabric, too sharp. Too frail. Blythe hugged her arms tightly around herself as she hurried back to the safety of the sheets.

"You brute! Don't look at me," she spat, letting anger burn away her embarrassment.

"You're assuming that I'd want to." Aris licked the tip of his finger and skimmed to another page without turning to her. "There's a dress for you in the wardrobe."

Blythe spared a glance at the wardrobe in question, but she didn't move. After several long seconds of her stillness, Aris's sigh broke the silence as the legs of his chair scraped across the wood.

"A thorn," he whispered under his breath as he crossed to the wardrobe, "right in my side." He threw it open and tossed the dress at Blythe, who caught it as though it were a piece of gold.

It was an exquisite piece, the bodice a gentle cream color with embroidered hellebore that stretched down the length of her skirts, where threads of gold mixed with the green of vines. The top, however, was still a corset.

It had been one thing to allow Aris's help last night beneath the cover of darkness. Here, in the light of day, she refused to acknowledge anything they'd discussed or the people they had been the night prior.

"I can't—" She paused when a knock sounded. Blythe held the

sheets tighter as Aris moved toward the door with his lips pressed thin, opening it for Olivia. He let the woman inside, then grabbed his tea and stalked past her.

"Get dressed, you infernal creature," he told Blythe. "I'll see you at breakfast."

The king and queen were not in attendance when Olivia escorted Blythe to the dining room an hour later.

"You'll have to forgive their absence," Aris was telling Elijah as she walked in. "I'm afraid they've been summoned by their royal duties."

Now that Blythe was no longer avoiding his stare, she could see that while Aris smiled, the skin beneath his eyes had darkened overnight. She doubted he'd admit to it aloud, but it seemed that he needed more than "a bit of rest" to replenish himself.

Blythe would have loved to throw on a coat and further explore the brilliant town that surrounded them, but for his sake as well as her own need to heal, perhaps it was better to spend the day indoors. There were a few things she wanted to discuss with her father, anyway, and it was likely she'd have a better chance at getting her answers if Elijah had nowhere to run off to.

Blythe had barely sat before she homed in on her father, not bothering with niceties as she began filling her plate for breakfast.

"What's going on at Thorn Grove?" she asked plainly, unable to bear another second of not knowing.

Elijah sighed into the mug of coffee that had only just been poured. "Nothing is going on, Blythe." Beside him, Aris turned his attention to the herbed butter he was scraping across a scone as if trying to stay out of the cross fire.

"Of course something is going on." She gripped her fork tight, trying her best to remain civil. "You've avoided answering me three times now, which does not equate to nothing. So do us both a favor before I either pester you to death or spontaneously combust from my own stress of not knowing."

"So she's always been like this, then?" Aris cast Elijah a pitying look.

"As if you're not just as dramatic," Blythe spat before her father had the chance to answer.

Elijah looked between the pair as he finally drew his first sip, a pull between his brows that Blythe couldn't decipher—amusement? Curiosity?

"She is as bad as a bloodhound stuck on a scent," Elijah began. "But this matter doesn't concern either of you. Thorn Grove is well enough, but there's been a break-in at Grey's. It's only a bit of vandalism, nothing that can't be fixed."

Grey's. Blythe bit back her scoff at the word. God, how she hated that place. Hated who it turned the men of her family into and the suffering it had brought the entire Hawthorne family.

"Oh good, does that mean it's time to finally burn the place?" A sharp sound grated across her plate as she scraped her fork into some eggs.

"Perhaps," Elijah acknowledged. "Though Grey's is a blight with no cure. No matter how many times I try to rid myself of it, the blasted place never stays gone for good."

That much was undeniable. Her father had tried to run the gentleman's club into the ground after Lillian's death. Then, after refusing to let Percy or Byron Hawthorne take over the business, Elijah had tried to sell it to Lord Wakefield only for the man to drop dead.

Unfortunately, despite how little time Elijah tried to spend there, the club had once again risen to popularity ever since Blythe's engagement to Aris.

"Nearly half of its patrons have offered to help clean the place up. Probably they all think it'll curry my favor. Or yours." Elijah nodded to Aris, then took another sip. "I'm on the hunt to find someone new to sell it to. I'll keep a small percent to satisfy Byron and then wash my hands of the place once and for all."

Blythe stabbed her fork into a gooseberry. "Let's hope the next person who buys it doesn't drop dead."

While Aris tensed at this, arching a brow, her father only laughed. "Indeed." As content as he sounded, it didn't escape Blythe's notice that his smile didn't quite reach his eyes.

"Perhaps I should pay Thorn Grove a visit," she tested, searching her father's face for whatever information he might have been withholding. He lifted his chin as Blythe did, matching her glare.

"I look forward to the day that you do. I imagine running a kingdom keeps you both busy, but you should consider visiting Thorn Grove for the Christmas ball."

Blythe didn't have the heart to remind her father just how well Thorn Grove's past several soirees had gone. Parties were Elijah's way of getting his mind off things. He'd spent nearly a full year mourning her mother by throwing ridiculously lavish parties at Thorn Grove. If his mind was already fixating on the next, Blythe worried about the extent of the vandalism and all that Elijah wasn't saying.

"Perhaps I should return with you," she argued, "just to ensure that all is well."

At this, Elijah laughed. Blythe's eyes prickled at the sound; God, how she'd missed it. After they'd lost her mother and Blythe had fallen ill, she hadn't been sure she'd ever hear it again.

"It's better this way," he told her. "The two of you are meant to be on your honeymoon, which I've already infiltrated. I do apologize for that, Aris,"

"It's not a bother," Aris answered automatically. To anyone else's eye, he likely looked well and put together. But Blythe had seen him enough over the past month to realize just how haggard he was as he slumped over what was at least his third cup of tea. "Believe me when I say that I could use the help. I was in over my head marrying this one." He wagged his knife at Blythe, though there was no cruelty.

A joke. He was attempting to make a joke on her behalf. Her father slid her a sideways glance, intrigued by the banter.

Blythe rolled her eyes, arms folding as she leaned back in her chair. "I can hear you, you know. I'm sitting right here."

"And here is where you'll stay," Elijah told her. "At least until I'm certain that things are safe."

Safe. How tired she was of people always trying to decide things for her in the name of keeping her safe. Her father's words lit a fire in her chest, and it flared brighter when Elijah turned to Aris with that same pull of his brows and a look that Blythe couldn't decipher.

"I miss my daughter very much," he said, "but I don't want her involved in whatever is happening back at Thorn Grove."

Blythe's fists clenched in her skirts. Her anger was so palpable that she could barely breathe around it. Her father had told her that she was welcome back at Thorn Grove anytime, and now what? He was conspiring with Aris to keep her away even longer?

She opened her mouth, not about to spare him any of her rage, when Aris set down his tea and looked firmly at Elijah.

"I understand that is your opinion," he said. "I just don't agree with it or understand why it has anything to do with me."

The breath loosened from her chest.

"I understand her history, Elijah, but Blythe is not fragile, nor is she unwise. You're not protecting her by keeping her ignorant. She can make her own decisions." He said it so simply, as though it was the most obvious thing in the world, and all at once that fire that had been burning so intensely within Blythe was extinguished.

Throughout her entire life people had treated Blythe like some delicate heirloom. Something pretty to keep upon the shelf and far from harm's way. Of all people, Aris was the last one Blythe expected might protest this, and she didn't know what to do with the realization. She couldn't for the life of her stop staring at him, nor could her father.

"I see." Elijah whispered the words, though they didn't sound angry. If anything, he sounded almost pleased. He turned to Blythe, and with a small bow of his head offered, "Should anything else happen, I will keep you informed. But for now, there is nothing for you to help with. We'll reconvene on the matter when you come for the ball."

"We'll be there," Aris said, surprising Blythe yet again. Her lips refused to move how she wanted them to as her father pushed his plate aside and rose from the table.

"Excellent news. Now, I'd like to get to know my son-in-law better, and I have an idea that not even the foul weather can stop." Elijah's eyes were practically dancing. "How about we play a game?"

CHAPTER SIXTEEN

"I HAVE LIED FOR YOU," ARIS WHISPERED. "I HAVE SPUN A KINGDOM out of thin air. I have fed you and tolerated you, and have put up with all of your nonsense. But this is where I draw the line."

They were ducked into a corner of the foyer, Olivia and Elijah making small talk as they waited for the newlyweds in the parlor.

"Come now, Aris. It's only a game." It took everything in Blythe not to let on how entertained she was by his loathing. "What else are we to do during a blizzard?"

"Literally anything." Every word sounded as if it were being forcefully pulled from the depths of his gut. He hissed a long breath, smoothing a hand through his hair.

No longer able to contain herself, this time Blythe did laugh. "Why on earth do you look as though you're preparing for war?"

"Because I might as well be, you monstrous girl."

How ridiculous Aris was, brought to such turmoil by the

prospect of a silly game. The fact that he'd ever dared to call *her* dramatic was insulting. "It's *charades,* Aris. It isn't going to kill you."

His huff was a withering, pathetic thing. "Oh, but I wish it would."

"Wish all you want, but you're playing. Now put on a brave face so that we may join the others." Blythe took him by the wrist, content as hatred oozed from her husband's every pore.

"I detest you and your entire lineage," he spat.

Blythe patted his arm. "That's the spirit! Be sure to put all that fire into your gameplay."

As they entered the parlor, Blythe was glad to find that her lady-in-waiting had taken it upon herself to have the game prepared. Olivia held out an upside-down top hat, several slips of parchment folded inside.

"There's quite an assortment of things." She spoke coyly as she set the hat onto a small side table. "But I kept them simple enough to get the game started."

"Thank you, Olivia." Blythe beamed.

"Yes, *thank you,* Olivia," Aris grumbled, likely regretting his decision to give the woman free rein to act as a lady-in-waiting. Blythe didn't let his glumness get to her; it'd been far too long since she'd played a game. Before her mother died, the Hawthorne family had spent many nights just like this one, tucked away laughing by the hearth while Warwick filled a hat with countless papers of ridiculous things for them to act out. As Percy had gotten older and as Elijah's nights at Grey's grew longer, game nights had fallen to the wayside. But when Blythe thought of her family, those memories were some of her fondest.

If Elijah was wanting to play, then perhaps he, too, was feeling reminiscent.

"I'll go first," Blythe volunteered, standing before her husband and father to pluck a paper from the hat. It read: *modiste.*

Elijah and Aris sat side by side on a long leather sofa, the latter with his elbows propped upon his bouncing knees. His steepled fingers were pressed over his mouth, masking what was undoubtedly a most unfavorable grimace.

"The first one to guess correctly gets a point," Blythe reminded. Not one to let Aris's sourness deter her, she pulled up a chair and took her seat, mirroring the motions of sewing. She pushed invisible spectacles up the bridge of her nose, then paused to fuss with an imaginary measuring tape.

Aris's eyes locked on her imaginary needle, narrowing. "Are you mocking me?"

"What are you on about?" Elijah mused. "Clearly she's . . . sewing?"

Blythe tried not to roll her eyes as she flashed him the invisible measuring tape, making a show of taking measurements and pressing pins into fabric that wasn't there.

"Ah!" Elijah snapped his fingers. "The modiste!"

"Yes!" Blythe threw her arms up with a victorious laugh. God, she was so good at this. "That's one point for my father," she told Olivia, who sat near the hearth keeping a tally. "Aris, you're next."

He stood as if he'd just been told that his childhood pet had died.

Shoulders slumped and refusing to meet anyone's eye, Aris stalked across the rug to see what fate awaited him on those slips of papers. He unfolded one, taking a single glance before the entire world fell still around them. Elijah was caught midblink, and Oliva was stilled while scribbling down a tally next to his name. Only Blythe, Aris, and the fire remained moving.

Aris swiveled to face Blythe. "No." His voice was as hollow as his eyes. "Absolutely not. I'm not doing this."

Blythe had just taken a seat in Aris's former spot when she felt the magic slip across the room and jumped back to her feet. "What on earth are you doing? Unfreeze them this instant!"

He clenched the paper tighter. "Not until you tell me that I'm exempt from this ridiculous game."

"You most certainly are not exempt!" Oh, what she wouldn't give to clobber this ridiculous man. "Whether you like it or not, you are part of my family now, and in my family we play *games*. So cease your ridiculous magic before you lose our bargain, and get on with your turn!" Blythe matched the venom of his scowl with her own and waited, unwavering, for Aris to groan. Seconds later the magic unraveled around him, the other two falling into motion once again as Aris tossed his slip of paper into the bin.

Grinding his jaw, he lifted both hands into the air, elbows in toward his chest and his fingers pointed down. For a long while no one said anything, waiting to see what else he might do, but he never moved.

Elijah cocked his head to one side, scratching absently at his neck scruff. "Is that how you pray in this kingdom of yours?"

Though Blythe had already guessed what Aris might be attempting, she told him sweetly, "You're going to need to give us a bit more than that, darling."

The murder in his eyes was palpable.

With the longest sigh Blythe had ever heard anyone draw in their life, Aris lowered himself onto his knees. He kept his hands up like he was begging, looked her dead in the eye, and said in a low voice, "Woof."

It took everything within Blythe and her dark soul not to fall into a fit of hysteria. She covered her mouth, muffling the amusement that threatened to overtake her.

"No sound effects!" Olivia scolded, which was all it took for Blythe to fully lose herself and double over in laughter.

"I've no idea, Aris," she cackled. "Could you perhaps be a dog?"

Her laughter, in turn, got Elijah laughing.

"It's not the worst thing I've been called," Aris muttered as Blythe wiped at her watering eyes. She did feel a smidge guilty, but good God did she love watching this man make a fool of himself.

"Since you cheated, you have to go again," Blythe told him. She didn't know whether that rule was real, but it was today. "No sound effects this time. Just have fun with it. Pretend you're in a performance."

"A performance?" Aris looked to be having thoughts of skewering her upon a spit, but Blythe smiled all the while, pressing her fingers against her lips as Aris drew another slip of parchment from the hat. If possible, he looked even less enthused by this one than the previous. This time, though, Aris made no argument as he played along, extending one arm out and putting the other into a half circle before him, as if he were holding someone.

"Dancing!" Blythe shouted, unable to contain herself. Aris bobbed his head, signaling she was close but not quite there. He stepped up, to the right, back down, to the left, and began to hum.

Blythe was about to scold him again for the sound effects, but the words caught in her throat at his hummed melody. Her vision tunneled, swaying until it felt as though she were the one dancing in someone's arms, her body moving to the familiar rhythm. A melody that she knew deep in her bones, as if she'd danced to it a thousand times before.

Yet such a thing could not be possible. She had never danced to this song, nor had she danced with a faceless man who consumed her thoughts, every breath—every heartbeat—belonging to him. For months Blythe had pondered the song, mulling it over and over in her brain. Could it have been Aris that she'd heard it from?

Her heart thundered so loudly that Blythe wondered whether Olivia could hear it across the room. She pressed a hand to her chest, where the skin was clammy and likely flushed as she watched Aris dance, everything moving as though it were in slow motion.

"A waltz," her father said at last, his voice cracking something within her. Making time move again.

Aris stopped his dancing the second he was able. "Bravo, Elijah," he told her father. He might have said something else, too, but Blythe didn't hear it. Her mind was still playing the song forward and backward as she lowered her fretting hands to her lap, tearing at the skin around her cuticles.

She didn't want to ask in case she was wrong. Didn't want to worry her father in case she was hearing things, but Blythe couldn't stop herself. "What was that song?" She had to pause three times before speaking to ensure that her voice didn't quake. "I thought I heard you humming."

"Was I?" His brows pinched as he took a seat beside her. "It's a song I learned long ago. You don't hear it much these days, but it's always been a favorite."

She didn't need him to fill in the gaps. She knew who he had pictured dancing with just now as his eyes turned cloudy and unfocused. It was Life. Everything with Aris always circled back to *Life.*

But that song...

There was no doubt about it—she must have heard it from Aris. She must have held on to it subconsciously for all these months, not remembering where it came from. That, or Life truly was in her head, toying with her even now.

Blythe wound her arms around herself, squeezing to ensure she was solid. That she was there beside her father and Aris and that all was well.

But she couldn't shake the feeling that something was wrong. Her skin itched and her eyes grew bleary, temples pulsing with a blossoming headache that threatened to consume her.

Her father had gotten up to take his turn, but Blythe could hardly pay attention as he shuffled about, Aris calling out his guesses. He seemed to have loosened up, to be watching Blythe and Elijah closely and having a good time. But she couldn't focus.

"Blythe?" he whispered after a moment, trying not to draw Elijah's attention. "Are you well?"

"Just a little worn down is all," she lied. "I'll be all right."

She shifted her focus to her father, who was clearly acting out the role of a stable hand. Blythe thought that Aris must have known it, too, but was stretching it out for her enjoyment.

She appreciated it, truly. And yet she could barely look at Elijah, because all Blythe could focus on was the sound of the music swelling in her head, and the faint memory of two people dancing on a bed of autumn leaves.

CHAPTER SEVENTEEN

Blythe did not see Life's image the rest of that week, nor did she hear any traces of the song Aris had been humming.

The rest of their time with Elijah passed in a flurry of meals and outings. Spectacular gowns, gatherings, performances, and the constant buzz of movement and chatter around the palace. Blythe had grown accustomed to it over the days, several times catching herself forgetting that Verena was a world of make-believe and feeling the sting of its loss worse each time.

She was sad to see her father go, of course. But there would be a chance to see him again soon. The loss of Verena, however, was insurmountable. Blythe had come to appreciate mornings when she could throw her windows open to the tune of an accordion and afternoons spent strolling down cobblestone streets with hot chocolate in hand. She'd even come to appreciate her dinners with Aris and Elijah, chewing on whatever delectable Aris had magicked for them while he skillfully maneuvered around Elijah's questioning.

Or, rather, Elijah's antagonism on many of the nights, for her father seemed keenly aware that there was something off about their charade. That, and he seemed to be growing fond of Aris.

Aris had been a surprisingly good sport despite how much of a toll maintaining their lie cost him. Day by day she watched as his shoulders bowed and his frame withered. After a week of maintaining such a grand facade, Blythe had no doubt that he was desperate for a respite. Still, she would have given anything for one more night in Verena. Her despair must have been evident in her very bones, for Elijah squeezed her tight as they said their goodbyes.

"It's no Thorn Grove," he whispered with a tenderness reserved only for her, "but I suppose it's a close second. I'm glad to see that you're happy."

And to Blythe's surprise, she *was* happy. Happier than she'd been in ages, though all of it was to be torn from her the moment his carriage departed.

"Aris," Elijah acknowledged with a nod, glancing to where her husband stood behind her right shoulder. "Don't be a stranger."

"We'll return to Celadon soon," Blythe promised. "Next week, for the Christmas ball." While Elijah smiled, sadness lurked behind his eyes. He never seemed to believe her, though looking around Verena she could understand why.

"I'll see you then," he told them. "And I'll let you know what becomes of Grey's." Before they could linger on the topic, Elijah hauled himself into the carriage. Blythe gave him a final wave before the door was shut, her heart aching as the driver snapped the reins and the carriage started down the path.

With every clack of the wheels against cobblestone, Blythe's heart dropped deeper into her stomach. Already the glinting threads throughout Verena were unwinding, loosening their hold. Soon all the servants would return to their houses, forgetting that Blythe or Aris were ever there. Olivia would be out of her life, and Blythe would be back in Wisteria, alone. There would be no sign of her left in Verena. No mark that she had ever set foot in such an incredible place. She and Aris, too, would once again drift apart, and Blythe despised how much that thought unsettled her.

She couldn't look at Aris when he called for her, for she didn't wish to let him see how seized by emotion she'd become. Yet she couldn't ignore when he took her by the shoulders from behind, close enough to whisper his next words into her ear.

"Come here, Sweetbrier. There's something I want to show you."

She sniffed, grateful to the cold for freezing the tears before they could fall. "I'm not in the mood for games, Aris. You won our bargain, I concede." She tried to shake him off, but Aris held tight.

"Must you always fight me?" He gave her a gentle nudge toward Wisteria, and Blythe all but dug her heels into the ground. There were still threads as far as the eye could see, which meant that she still had precious moments before it all disappeared. Moments that she intended to spend right here, memorizing every detail of Verena.

When she refused to budge after another push, Aris sighed, rolled up his sleeves, and took her by the waist. Blythe gasped as he tossed her over his shoulder and made for the door.

"You brute!" she screamed, smacking at his back. "Put me down!"

"A troll, a brute... I really am so many things to you, aren't I?"

If Aris felt any of her protests—which Blythe was certain he must have, given her lack of restraint—he showed no sign of it as he hauled her inside. The moment she was dropped to her feet, Blythe swung around to face Aris, seething through her teeth.

"You're the devil is what you are. You couldn't let me have just five more minutes?" Given the pallor of his skin, she knew it wasn't a fair ask. Still, she wanted it all the same. "You boast about how magnificent and powerful you are, yet you couldn't last just a while longer?"

Aris was unflinching, looking down at Blythe with only a mild quirk of his brow. "Magnificent? If that's what you think of me—"

"It most certainly is not." What a relief it was that there were no longer servants bustling about, for they'd witness quite the spectacle as Blythe pressed close to argue. "You are a proper barbarian. You showed me the most glorious place in the world, then expect me to return to Wisteria with its hideous gray walls, and a sacrificial altar for a bed—"

"I told you to keep your new bed," Aris corrected. "And it was never an altar, you ridiculous girl. What is happening in that brain of yours to think these things up?"

"I am not ridiculous." She jabbed her finger into the center of his chest. "I am in *love*. And all I wanted was five more minutes to say goodbye."

To his credit, Aris had far more patience than she deserved. He kept his hands folded, only an occasional twitch in his jaw to give away what could have either been humor or immense dissatisfaction. Probably the latter.

"Are you quite done?" he asked with a softness that threw her off-balance. Blythe peeled back, drawing her finger from his chest and smoothing out the glove.

"If I must be."

"Glad to hear it." He dropped his hands, strolling past her and toward the door they'd just come through. Blythe was immediately on his heels, not about to let him leave without her. He stopped when he reached the door, making a fist around the knob. "There is no reason for me to give you another five minutes here. Should you be quiet long enough for me to speak, I would tell you that Verena may be a land of make-believe, as you so eloquently put it, but Brude is a city that's as real as could be. And I will not promise you five more minutes here, because that's not the only time that you'll have."

He opened the door then, and it was not snow and cobblestone that waited beyond it, but a desert of red sand with a glowing golden sunset beaming down. Before Blythe could take a step, Aris shut the door once more, then opened it again to an ocean, so unlike the one at Foxglove. One where the sky was warm and the sand pink. One where it was still morning, and the water shimmered as if filled with millions of crystal shards.

Aris pulled the door shut a second time, only to reopen it to the snowy streets of the place he called Brude once more. "We can go anywhere we want, Sweetbrier. Wisteria was made to travel."

Words were inadequate for the way she felt. Her mouth was so dry that she gave up trying to respond as she stared out at the brightly colored houses and let the music of the accordion sweep over her. She stepped beside Aris, sliding her hand over his and around the knob.

"How does it work?" she finally managed, a gloved finger skimming the iron.

Aris peeled his hand away. "It's my will. The house is a very part of my magic and soul. It does as I wish and will take me anywhere."

She thought of the cracking stone walls that had filled the majority of the palace for so long. If Wisteria was an extension of Aris's very soul, then what did that mean for the state of it?

"May I use it?" Blythe asked as she eased the door shut. Holding the knob felt like holding a key to the universe. Infinite possibilities awaited her; all she had to do was seize them. And yet when she went to open the door again, hoping to find Thorn Grove on the other side, Aris pressed his palm against the frame to still it.

"You are not a part of my soul." As gentle as the words were, they felt like a slap. "But, if you'll let me, I can take you wherever you wish to go."

Longing clawed at her. She couldn't remember a time when she'd felt such a bone-deep hunger, ravenous for the world that Aris was offering, a world that people could only dream of.

All her life she had wanted to travel. To be bound to no one and wander wherever it was that she most desired. Yet in the back of her mind, her family had always been by her side. She supposed that Aris was right to some extent, and that it was the nature of things to one day leave the nest. To mature and start a life of one's own, separate from the familial ties she had grown up with. Even animals did it, raising their young only to one day set them free.

Blythe had always known that day would come, but no one had told her that moving forward felt like a goodbye she wasn't prepared for. Even staring at the door and the limitless possibilities that awaited, Blythe's thoughts turned to Elijah, alone as he wandered the halls of Thorn Grove. Was it fair to leave him behind? To selfishly enjoy the spoils of Aris's magic while she abandoned him just as everyone else had?

"We can visit Thorn Grove as often as you'd like." Aris spoke at his most tender. Though he may not have known *what* was wrong, Blythe's poker face needed enough work that he must have guessed something was bothering her. "As impressive as Brude is, it's but a small part of where we'll go. I am not trying to take you away from your family, Sweetbrier. I am not trying to pull you from the life that you know. All I'm trying to do is show you a world that you deserve to see."

He reached his left hand out, where the faintest shimmer of light shone from his ring finger. Had he asked her a week ago, Blythe might have laughed in the man's face or perhaps spit on his boots, depending on how much sleep she'd gotten the night prior. It was a wonder how a few days could change everything.

She'd trusted Fate and had been burned once before. Yet this time when he held out his hand, she took it and kept close when he smiled and opened the door to birdsong and pale sunlight that glinted through a forest glade. There was not a snowflake in sight but a gentle gale that stole leaves from vibrant trees and sent them away with the wind. As Aris drew her out, Blythe shivered from the summer warmth that slipped up her skin. She let her furs and cloak drip from her shoulders and fall somewhere behind her, then did the same with her boots, tossing them aside as she followed Aris across softened soil.

"It's hard to believe this place was but a door away." The only noise in the glade came from the gentle call of robins and the soft gurgle of water from somewhere in the distance. There was no bustling. No rosy-cheeked denizens sipping mugs of hot chocolate as horses clopped along the cobblestone. Blythe doubted there was even a single home for miles. Unfamiliar trees sprouted tiny red-and-white-speckled mushrooms, and the forest floor showed no path or any signs of human touch.

It held a rare sense of wonder—one that made Blythe want not to stand and explore but to settle herself in the thickest tuft of grass she could find and lay her head against the earth to soak in the stillness of this thriving land.

She wanted to ask where they were, but such a question felt sinful. Like if Aris spoke its name aloud, time would somehow remember this place and it would forever cease to exist. And so she did not ask, but allowed the tension in her chest to settle as she took a seat in a patch of sun. Aris removed his gloves as he sat beside her, setting them neatly aside as he leaned back on his hands.

The quiet between them stretched for a long while—not fraught, but peaceful, neither of them feeling the need to fill the space with words. Eventually, though, she drew her stockinged feet beneath her and turned toward Aris.

"Why did you bring me here?" It was similar to the question she'd asked the night he'd taken her sledding. This time, however, he had a different answer.

"Because I knew you would like it."

Blythe wasn't sure what to make of how much those words

pleased her, or of the desire that pulsed in her low belly. She sat straighter, sucking her bottom lip between her teeth.

"I believe it's time that we discussed our arrangement in greater depth, Aris." Since making the bond, they'd never discussed the logistics of their marriage in detail. If they were to build a life between them—no matter how unconventional—Blythe wanted to have a better idea of what she might expect. The seriousness in which she asked the question roused Aris's interest. He leaned up, observing Blythe as though he were an astronomer scrutinizing the stars.

"What about it?" he asked, and at once Blythe felt as if she'd been transported several months prior, back to when she'd sat on the chaise across from him and had exposed herself so fully while offering herself as his bride. Aris had laughed then, and as Blythe chewed on her words, she wondered whether he would do the same now.

Slowly, hesitating with each word, she said, "I'd like to know what... rules we might have. About navigating the roles of a marriage."

Aris's face twisted as he tried to piece together her words and why her cheeks were beginning to flare pink. He certainly was not making this any easier. "I don't expect you to clean or anything of that sort. Even without servants there are no duties. Magic takes care of that."

Blythe drew in a breath, anchoring herself. "There are some things, Aris, that magic cannot take care of." She waited for the confusion to lift from his face. For his eyes to widen before he could right himself, and for him to clear his throat before she repeated, "What are our *rules*? Do we believe in the sanctity of marriage, or are we free to divert certain attentions elsewhere?"

He opened his mouth, only to snap it shut, fully at a loss for words. It was as stumped as she'd ever seen him, and Blythe found the nervous knots in her stomach untangling as she observed his struggle. Though she'd wanted to find a hole to crawl into only seconds ago, now she found that she wanted to laugh, caught off guard by how surprised he was and more entertained than she ought to have been by the idea of teasing him.

"You do know what couples often do after marriage, right?" she pressed, a sly tone in her voice that Aris homed in on.

"Of course I do, you insufferable girl," he grumbled. "But you are aware that for me there is no obligation of preserving a bloodline, aren't you? Or that I cannot bear children?"

She expected as much. "That's all very well because I have never intended to have children."

This caused the space between Aris's brows to pinch, which Blythe was quite used to. People always reacted so strangely when she told them her preferences, so she'd eventually stopped saying anything. She preferred for her time to stay wholly hers and not to lose it to childrearing she'd never been interested in.

"Then why are you asking?"

"You cannot presume that I would only be interested in such relations for the purpose of a *child*? I am but one and twenty years of age, Aris, with what I hope is a very long life ahead of me, filled with pleasures of the body as much as the mind. I am not asking anything of you. We can live together with this bond between us, and that will be the extent of it. I can find others to connect with for any additional purposes."

"And how will you do that," he asked, holding up his left hand, "when you and I cannot be separated?"

A blade of grass had slipped between the fabric of her stockings. Blythe stared as it scratched at her legs, refusing to look at him as she whispered, "I hadn't gotten that far just yet." Admittedly because a significant part of her was hoping for the first option, if only to get it out of her system.

As it was, over the past month there had been several thoughts that she'd not been able to shake from her mind. First was the night she'd seen him by the hearth, his shirt loose and hair astray. As uptight as Aris was, it had left more of an impression than she'd realized to see him so undone. More prominently, however, was the memory of him months ago, back at the Wakefield estate. Before she'd known the truth about who he was, she had let Aris help her overcome her fear of a tea she worried might have been poisoning Eliza. She'd let him sip from the tea when she couldn't, then he'd taken her face in his hands and pressed his mouth to hers. She recalled—in exorbitant detail—how it had felt when his tongue had slid against hers. How her heart had raced and her body had urged her forward, craving more. It wasn't a *kiss*, exactly. He'd been helping her test the drink for poison. But semantics aside, there was no denying that her mind had been forever soiled with desire despite how much she'd tried to stifle it.

She'd thought of that moment on more occasions than she cared to count, and as she leaned back against the grass, propped up on only her elbows to watch Aris, Blythe wondered whether he ever thought of it, too. Given that his eyes were on her legs, skimming up the length of her calves and thighs, she guessed he just might have. She kept quiet, pointing a toe and slowly extending one leg to give him a better view. All the while her eyes remained on his face, watching as his expression hardened, eyes flashing with a dark curiosity.

"Are you soliciting me, Sweetbrier?"

"I'm not *not* soliciting you." If she was going to be daring, then she might as well not hold back. "We can leave emotion out of it."

Though a battle warred on his face, Aris drew closer. "I am not who you want, love. Remember that you despise me."

"Oh, I remember." She brushed his leg with the tips of her toes. "But that doesn't mean I'm not curious." *Vastly* curious. So curious that she thought she might explode. She was married now, after all. If ever there was a time for her to explore such desires, this was it.

He, too, must have felt at least some curiosity, for there was no mistaking the hunger darkening his eyes. Blythe skimmed her foot along Aris's thigh, then up to his chest, waiting to see what he might do. To her surprise, he grabbed hold of her ankles, pulling her closer to curl his fingers into the bare skin just above her stockings.

His eyes found hers, full of challenge. He was testing her. Making sure she didn't have second thoughts. But Blythe had never met a challenge she didn't like.

If he was in, then so was she.

Aris was upon her a second later, taking Blythe by both thighs and hiking her down so that he could come on top of her. One knee settled between hers, and then his mouth was on hers a second later. Though she was certain that this was a very bad idea that both of them would soon regret, she didn't stop herself. Throwing inhibitions to the wind, Blythe leaned in to the wants of her body, winding her legs around his waist and threading her fingers through his hair, gasping against his lips as he took her bottom one between his teeth. His fingers curled against her thigh, gripping on to her like she was something to devour.

He smelled of wisteria and tasted like honeyed scotch as she drank him in. His touch was rougher than she'd expected, and his body harder as she arched against it, wanting more. So much more.

His hand slipped farther up her inner thigh, and she wished at once that she'd never let Olivia put her into a bloody corset that morning. She ached to rid herself of it, her breaths too sharp and her body far too confined.

When Aris's hand stilled, she tipped her head back to seek his stare.

"You don't have to stop." God, she sounded like she was panting. "I don't want you to stop." With one hand draped around his neck, she pulled him down to capture his lips again, ready to lose herself in the taste. His fingers stroked a mere inch from where she most wanted him and she drew in a sharp breath. But Aris stiffened as if something had pulled him taut, straightening his spine and snapping him from her. He tore away from Blythe, fingers combing desperately through his hair as he stumbled back. There was a wild look about him that had Blythe sitting up, her chest rising and falling too fast for her corset. The world blurred at its edges, her vision hazy.

"What is it?" she whispered, smoothing out her stockings. "Aris, what's wrong?"

He was on his feet before she'd even finished asking. "This was a mistake." He was already gathering her discarded boots and coat. He circled back only for her hand, the world winking away from them the moment he took hold of it.

They were back at Wisteria in a flash of light, no longer near the front door but in Blythe's room. She fell onto her bed, her back and the soles of her feet still damp from the grass.

"I'm sorry," Aris said as he set her boots by the door, refusing to look her in the eye. "That should have never happened."

"There's nothing to apologize for," Blythe promised. "I'm fine, Aris. Are you?"

With her coat still strung over his arm, he hurried to her armoire to put it away. "Yes," he said too quickly. "My apologies. We can discuss our arrangement another time—"

He went deathly still as the armoire swung open. Blythe sat up, her chest thundering as she saw the flash of gold inside.

Life's mirror. Death had been the last one to touch it and had not returned it to the vanity where she'd kept it tucked safely away.

There was no stopping Aris as he yanked the mirror out, trembling.

"Where did you get this?" She'd never heard his voice quite so soft. Quite so scared.

Blythe pushed to her feet, taking two strides to close the space between them but pausing before she got too close. This wasn't the man whose lips had been on her only a minute prior. This was someone new. Someone wild and fevered.

Blythe held her hands before her, placating. "I can explain."

He pressed his other hand against the mirror, cradling it against him with the tenderness of a newborn. It took a long while before his eyes flicked up to her, burning with their intensity. "Then explain."

Every thought fell from her mind at once, for what could she possibly say to him that didn't sound so hopelessly useless?

"Not long after we came to Wisteria, I saw a hall that I swore hadn't been there before. The blasted fox ran through it, so I did, too," she tried, though the words felt ridiculous. "I followed the path and we came across this room—"

She cut off the second his grip around the handle tightened, the veins in his forearm pulsing. "You went into her room." As softly as he spoke, the malice in his accusation sank into her gut and twisted there. "You had no right. You had no right to take her things, or to—" He cut off with a quiet choke, palming the wall as he swayed on his feet. "I wasn't even sure it still existed. I can't believe it showed itself. And to you, of all people . . ."

Blythe said nothing, knowing her words were unwanted. The sharpness in Aris's eyes had glazed over, and she had the distinct impression as he nearly crumpled in on himself that he'd forgotten she was here at all. She held her hands close, scratching at her cuticles as she debated reaching out to him. Debated telling him to take a seat and breathe. But before she could make up her mind, Aris heaved a shaking breath and he snapped his head toward her.

"Stay away from me." His grip tightened around the mirror, and those were the last words Aris spoke before he disappeared in a flash of light.

CHAPTER EIGHTEEN

Blythe's meals began to show up on a burnished tray outside her door the following day. For three days she consumed porridge for breakfast, cold meat and plain bread for lunch, and shepherd's pie for dinner. Nothing extravagant. Nothing varied. And none of it with any of the flourish she'd grown to expect from Aris.

She hadn't seen him since he'd found the mirror, though this wasn't like the last time he'd disappeared, when she'd had no clue where he'd run off to. All the lights in Wisteria slanted up toward his study. She'd not seen a single sign of his existence, or heard so much as a shuffle of footsteps to prove that he was alive. There was no opening of doors or clattering of a teacup on a saucer. No clinking of a fork against a plate.

And there was certainly no discussion of anything that had happened that night in the glade. Blythe, for her part, had not been able to get their kiss and all they'd nearly done from her mind. She cringed every time she thought of how she'd run her foot up his chest and how she'd urged him on, wanting so much more.

It was probably good that Aris had disappeared. How was she ever meant to face him again?

At least, that's what she'd thought the first day into his hiding. By the second, Blythe found herself wandering the halls just so she could listen for him to open his door. And by the third, she felt like she was losing her mind when he still hadn't. It didn't help that the weather had fouled into a flurry of a snowstorm that kept her trapped indoors with only a pesky fox that could do without her existence. There were a few times a day where the beast might deem her worthy enough for a visit, but it would scurry off into the shadows as soon as she made any effort to befriend it. Perhaps if she knew its name it might be more decent, but for that she'd have to ask Aris.

She'd tried, once. She'd stood outside his study calling for him and demanding he tell her the name of the beast, but he'd never answered. Not even to yell at her to go away or to force her back into her room with magic.

Whatever they'd built between them during their days in Verena was gone. One more day of solitude and Blythe feared that she might lose her mind.

Her discontent was bolstered by the fact that, despite Christmas being mere days away and the storm that was raging outside their door, Wisteria was no longer cold. It instead simmered with a heat so oppressive that Blythe took her fan with her as she paced the halls, opening the windows to cool herself only to have to shut them moments later when snow flurried inside.

She needed to get out of Wisteria. Needed to leave before she shriveled into a husk and fell dead, only to probably end up as a spirit forced to wander the halls of this place and torment Aris for all eternity. But this time there was no sending a letter to Signa to come rescue her. And it wasn't as though there were any horses for her to take to Thorn Grove even if the weather had been cooperative.

She pounded her way down the stairs, catching sight of the small fox curled up on an armchair, looking perfectly at ease in the warmth.

"Enjoying this, are you?" she asked, only for the fox to slit one eye to inspect her before returning to its slumber. Blythe sighed as she passed it, doing her routine check of the windows to see whether the storm had let up.

It hadn't, of course, and she threw the curtains over the panes with a stream of choice words to detail precisely how she felt about that. It wasn't until she stomped past the front door that she froze in place, a glimmer of a gilded knob catching her eye. She turned toward it, her throat thickening.

It wasn't possible. A thousand golden threads wound protectively around the door, and even Aris himself had told her that she'd never be able to use it when Wisteria was a very part of his soul. Still, desperation drove her toward it. She cast one look behind her, half expecting Aris to storm down the steps and laugh at her for even considering such an idea. But the halls remained silent.

Blythe turned back to the door, leaning into its frame as she whispered, "I need you to get me out of here." She dropped her head against the wood, gritting her teeth at the jolt that struck through her ring finger as she skimmed her fingers over the handle.

"Take me to Foxglove." She whispered the words like a spell, filling them with all her hope. But when she opened the door there was only an icy blast of snow to greet her. She shut it again and clenched the handle tighter. "Take me to Thorn Grove."

Again, another blast of snow smacked her face when she threw the door open. She slammed it back shut, fuming.

"To Brude!" This time she couldn't even twist the handle, for her ring burned with such ferocity that she clenched it into her skirts.

"Fine!" Blythe smacked her hand against the frame, then bit back her wince from the pain. "Fine, then, you wretched thing. Take me to wherever it is that you want me to go, so long as it's away from here!" All at once, her ring fell cold. Blythe stilled, not daring to breathe as the golden threads surrounding the door snapped in half. They did not fall but vanished before her eyes in a glimmer of light, leaving the handle bare. This time when Blythe curled her fingers around the knob and eased the door open, it was not a snowstorm that greeted her. This time, Wisteria opened into the last place she ever expected.

Her mother's garden was unrecognizable from what it had been a month prior.

One side of the gate hung open and was swaying in the wind, its tinny creaking the only sound aside from Blythe's own footsteps crunching against the snow as she stepped outside.

Grey's, it seemed, had not been the only place to be vandalized.

The fire's destruction was now but one small fragment of the garden's disarray. Parts of the ground had been completely uprooted, piles of dirt tossed haphazardly as though someone had been digging.

The snow cut into Blythe's bare soles, but she couldn't feel the sting of it. She couldn't feel anything but the rage that burned in her belly as she glanced past the empty pond to her mother's headstone, now decimated. Step-by-step, Blythe made her way toward it, falling to her knees beside the place where the grave had once lain. With trembling, frostbitten hands, she dug up broken pieces of the stone that lay half-buried beneath the snow.

She couldn't breathe. Couldn't believe that anyone could find it in themselves to ruin such a sacred place. Once upon a time, Blythe had hoped the garden would overcome its past year of suffering and would one day flourish. She'd hoped that flora would overtake her mother's grave, and that this place would forever thrive in secret deep in the woods behind Thorn Grove.

Blythe stared around the garden, at the dried twigs and scorched ground where she used to spend days smelling rows of hyacinth. She waited each spring for the wolfsbane to bloom and for the frogs to come out of their hiding and perch themselves atop the lily pads.

Now it was quiet. There were no frogs. No wolfsbane or hyacinth. There was only a broken gate, a shattered headstone, and a memory of a place Blythe would never be able to return to. The longer she stared, the more the loss festered within her, hastening her breaths.

She wanted it back. Wanted the overgrown flowers and the hum of insects buzzing in her ear. Wanted the croaking frogs she'd spent too many hours of her life trying to capture as they leaped from bank to bank. Blythe shut her teary eyes, ridding her mind of what this garden looked like now and instead satiating herself with memories of how it had looked in full spring bloom. She thought of the lavender that had grown taller than she was and the jasmine bushes that had never failed to make her sneeze. She filled her mind with the garden's image until it felt real enough to touch.

And when she opened her eyes, it was.

Ivy crawled across the ground, covering her heels and any signs of snow and ash. Wolfsbane ensnared her ankle, clawing up her thigh with such vigor that Blythe had to throw herself back lest she become part of the garden herself. She had to be dreaming, or perhaps she was still in Wisteria, overheated and passed out in a puddle of her own sweat.

No sooner had she let herself believe this than she gasped, having backed straight into a growing bush of plump white roses full of thorns that scraped her skin. One drew a bead of blood, which Blythe watched trickle down her elbow and fall onto the soil. Hellebore in the most peculiar shade of silver blossomed in the exact spot where it landed, and when Blythe inspected the injury, she found nothing. No trace of blood. No open wound. Just a tiny crescent scar that was nearly the same shade as her skin. Beneath it, she could still feel the ghost of the thorn's sting.

It was like what had happened during the picnic with Aris. Only this time, she was certain she'd seen the blood. This time, she was certain it was real.

Blythe stumbled backward, trembling as she fought to keep on her feet. The ivy at her heels kept growing, stretching toward her. It reminded her of the incident back in her father's study, where flora had blossomed out of nowhere and taken over everything in its path.

The snow that had blanketed the ground only moments prior had been absorbed into the earth, and in its place flowers blossomed. Clover spread beneath her bare feet while moss tore its way up what remained of her mother's grave and toward Blythe's hand. All the flora was reaching toward her, crooked stems bent as if craning their necks in search of her.

As if... as if they were a part of her.

Blythe's eyes fell to the hellebore, born of her blood, and the garden swayed. Her skin was clammy as her mind worked to process what she was witnessing. No trick of her imagination. Not a dream, but a flourishing spring garden in the midst of winter. Wounds that healed as fast as they were made.

Sickness churned her stomach, threatening its way out, but Blythe wound an arm around herself and held tight. She had to know the truth of it. Had to confirm. And so she bent to press a palm atop a bare bit of soil beside the growing clover and pictured a flower she had never before seen in her mother's garden. The first one that came to her mind—wisteria. She pictured a tree as strong and sturdy as the one at the palace, blooming over her mother's grave. And as she pictured it, she could feel the tree's roots spread through the earth. The base of a trunk grew, stretching into branches that filled with petals as white as snow.

Blythe lost her footing, sliding down to sit on the soil just as a frog leaped beside her, croaking as it dove into the melted pond. Was it her imagination, or was that blood slickening its back?

She turned only to find herself staring at a tree whose bark had been marred with crimson and at the bones of several frogs that lay at the base of it. One by one she watched as their bones stitched together, then their flesh. Soon, plump frogs hit the ground with a croak, blinking in confusion before they leapt toward the pond as well.

This time, Blythe could not hold down her sickness. She barely managed to make it five feet before she lost her stomach in the lilies.

For months she had believed that such oddities were Signa's doing. Back in her father's study she'd been devastated at the idea of losing Percy, and had hoped desperately that she'd been seeing things. Then with the horse, and with Eliza and the child... it was Signa who had acted as though she was the one helping them, but... hadn't Blythe wanted them healed just as much as her cousin? Was it not Blythe who had demanded that the horse be brought back to life and that Eliza be healed no matter the price? Hadn't her hands, too, been laid upon them?

She had seen Elaine sick in the mirror only for the woman to be healed after Blythe touched her.

She had made the door of Wisteria—a part of Aris's very soul—obey her command.

For months she had been plagued by visions that felt more like memories than dreams.

And now, as Blythe stared up at the wisteria tree, she understood why. It was not her cousin who Aris had been searching for all this time....

It was Blythe.

The realization was a weight that threatened to bury her. It was a tightness in her lungs that had her gripping her throat, fingers digging into her flesh, for she could not breathe.

She was the one who Aris was searching for, not Signa.

She was Life.

CHAPTER NINETEEN

Blythe knew there would be no returning to Wisteria that night, no matter what her blasted ring thought.

It was a wonder that she managed to make it out of the garden at all, let alone through the snow-drenched woods. Had traversing them not been second nature to her, she may never have found her way, for she was in no state to be traveling, let alone in waning daylight. She grabbed on to each tree she passed, bracing herself from the swaying world.

Moss sprouted beneath her fingers, infecting everything she touched. It grew beneath her bare soles, melting the snow with each step she took toward Thorn Grove. She had to rest when she reached the mouth of the forest, breathless with a sheen of sweat across her skin. She couldn't tell whether it was her clothing or moss that clung to her, for all her senses were too heightened to focus.

She could feel the buzz of the earth beneath her feet. The flora that slumbered in the peacefulness of winter, awaiting its rise with the warmth of spring. She could feel the roots of barren trees drawing life from the soil. There were animals, too. Birds flitting through the branches. Wolves prowling in the depths of the woods and rabbits hungry for their next meal. It was as if even the ants that crawled along fallen leaves were a part of her, each of their steps a tickle across her skin.

Her blood burned hot, thrumming with this new world she had never seen. A world where every breath, every particle, was hers to control.

Still, even through all that overwhelmed her, Blythe had enough sense to know she couldn't remain in the snow. Besides freezing to death, the flora would likely soon overtake her and she'd end up a tree herself, forever rooted in the woods.

With the manor in sight, she plucked twigs from her hair and tried to smooth out her pale gown with trembling hands that were now webbed in moss. As for her lack of shoes . . . there was nothing to be done. There would be questions when she reached Thorn Grove regardless of her state, but she tried her best to measure her breaths and wait for her clammy skin to dry. For her senses to dull and her skin to stop sprouting flora beneath its every touch. And when it did, she hurried down the snowy hills toward the manor.

Blythe kept out of view as much as she could, grateful that what few staff were left at Thorn Grove were busy preparing for the Christmas ball. The manor smelled of pine as maids strung garlands and mistletoe, and she inhaled deeply as she slipped through the door, hoping the scent of the holidays might ease her nerves.

For once Blythe wished that she had Signa's powers of dissolving into the shadows or whatever it was that she did, so she could slip into her old suite without being seen. She needed someplace that was quiet. Somewhere warm, where she might steady her thoughts and the memories that were pouring into her. Memories of music. Of Aris. Even of Death, seated in the shade of a towering wisteria. They were coming so fast that she couldn't make sense of them, struggling to differentiate one life from another.

A maid hurried down the stairs with armfuls of holly, and Blythe had only a moment to escape from view. She ducked into the parlor, peeking through a crack in the door and waiting for the woman to pass. The maids were not the only ones to worry about, however, for a voice behind Blythe demanded, "What on earth are you doing here?"

Blythe spun to find Warwick's eyes growing large behind his glasses. He looked paler than normal, and faint. As if he'd seen a ghost. One glance down at her numb toes and the dirt and debris caked onto her feet, and Blythe realized she must have looked like one.

"What's *happened* to you?" Warwick pressed, looking only at her feet. "Blythe, are you—"

"Hush! Are you trying to rouse the dead?" Blythe drew the door into the parlor fully shut before spinning toward him. "I need you to be very quiet. The others cannot know that I'm here."

"But your *feet*—"

"They're fine," she lied. "In need of a washing and a fire, but otherwise fine. I insisted on being dropped off near the woods to pay a visit to my mother's garden, and my boots were ruined on the way back—"

"You went out in this weather?" he demanded, behaving well above his station, certainly, though Warwick had always been more of a familial figure to her, given that he'd been working closely with Elijah since before Blythe's birth. "Without any chaperone? Where is your husband?"

"He's seeing to business." Blythe quieted with each word in the hope that it would encourage Warwick to do the same. "He doesn't know that I'm here."

She should have chosen her words better, for his eyes narrowed. "Has he hurt you?"

She had to bite back her laugh, for it would have come out as a sob as memory after memory of Aris played in her mind. Memories of him laughing. Of them arguing. Of time spent in silence in each other's company. With every blink she saw another flash of him, incomplete memories working to sew themselves together anew. "My husband couldn't hurt me if he wanted to."

Warwick was less than reassured as he took a gentle hold of Blythe's shoulder. "You're going to catch your death if you continue like this. If your father saw you—"

"He cannot!" Blythe said with the utmost urgency. "I realize how this must look, but I swear to you that I am well. I just need to get to my room without him seeing me in this state."

Though the pale press of his lips said that Warwick didn't at all care for her plan, he sighed. "Your father is out replacing a pair of boots he lost last week. But should any of the other staff see you, I cannot think what they might say to him."

Blythe knew a blessing when she saw one, and she had every

intention of seizing it before Elijah returned. "Then let's try our best to stay out of their way, shall we?" As used to her shenanigans as Warwick was, his severity did not put her at ease. As he led the way out of the parlor, he looked primed to speak with her father the moment he returned. Blythe would have to worry about that later. For now, she tossed her hair back, squared her shoulders, and did everything in her power to look positively proper so as to not give anyone reason to glance at her feet. Warwick barked out a command when a few of the maids started to turn their way, stepping in front of Blythe to block her from view as she hurried up the stairs.

Only at the edge of the long mahogany hall, her toes curled into the ornate crimson rug, did Blythe pause to fill her lungs with Thorn Grove's familiar musk. Gnarled trees bowed toward the windows, their ravenous branches grinding against the glass in a woeful symphony that Blythe had long grown accustomed to.

With every step she drew forward, curious eyes from the portraits of Hawthornes long deceased trailed her. Their prying itched at her skin, and yet each time she turned to catch them in the act, she found only blank faces staring ahead into nothingness. Just as she had since she was a young girl.

The manor was every bit the same as she'd left it, yet somehow unfamiliar in a way she couldn't place. Like a dream magicked to life: squint too close and the details became fuzzy.

"You have one hour to right yourself," Warwick told her as they reached the door to her suite. "I'll send up a maid, but see to that mud first. You've already arrived without a husband; you needn't give them more reasons to talk."

She despised that truth even while knowing he was right. Blythe's skin felt like a flimsy thing, and she was on the verge of bursting from it at any moment. Yet as much as she needed time to herself, it was a relief to know that she had an upcoming distraction. Because Blythe's room was no longer the sanctuary she'd built up in her mind. The moment the door shut behind Warwick, and Blythe was alone, all she could focus on was the pressure of the suite she was trapped in as she waited for her ring to burn. For the magic to summon her back to Wisteria.

But it never came.

Blythe stared around the reading room, with its wallpaper of soft blues and silver. At the fresh lilies sprouting from a vase atop the ivory mantel of a fireplace she'd so often relied on the past year. And then to her bedroom across from it, the door half-open. A glance at the canopied bed was all it took for repressed memories to shudder through her. She slammed the door shut, casting any thoughts of poisoning or death to the back of her mind as best she could.

A maid arrived not long after Warwick left, drawing a bath for Blythe that smelled of honey and lavender. She melted into it, and any time her mind strayed to thoughts of the blooming garden and the power she'd drawn from the earth with her bare hands, she'd scrub harder at the dirt. Even clean, Blythe could feel the memory of the moss lingering on her skin, forcing its way into her body and sticking to her ribs.

In the few spare seconds when she did not fret about her body becoming one with nature, her mind instead strayed to thoughts of Aris—to the memory of his hands against her, to a vision of her giggling as they danced to music she didn't recognize. Blythe sank deeper into the water, eventually letting it cover her entirely as she tried to drown out the sound.

She bathed until the water was too cold to bear, then until more was fetched and that too became like ice against her skin. Only when she was pruned and halfway to wilting did Blythe allow the maid to help her into a pretty blue muslin dress with matching embroidered slippers. Her pale hair was dried and done up as quickly as they could manage, and Blythe was grateful for the maid's silence all the while, too lost in her haze of thoughts to be any good at conversation.

It seemed Warwick must have bought her some time, for it was over an hour before a stern knock sounded at the door. The maid was quick to answer, sidestepping her father as Elijah let himself in.

"Thank you for your help, Angelica. You're dismissed," he told the woman, eyes never once straying from Blythe despite how she dared not meet them. Only when the door shut did he stride forward, taking a knee before her.

"What's wrong?" Elijah made to grab her hand, but Blythe tore it away in horror at the thought of somehow infecting him with moss. Or what if she did something worse, like make his skin sprout vines or something else utterly ridiculous and impossible?

Or at least it *should* have been impossible. Now she had no doubt that such absurdities were within reach and shook the violent thoughts from her mind so they would not become her reality.

"I'm fine," Blythe hurried to say, though she hardly sounded convincing.

"Blythe, if Aris has done something—"

"He hasn't."

Her forcefulness behind the declaration silenced him. The corners of Elijah's eyes narrowed for the briefest moment before he blinked the look away, his sigh deep.

"I told you not to come here until the ball. Warwick said that your husband doesn't know, and that you hadn't any *shoes*."

Blythe was too numb for retorts. She couldn't be *angry* with Warwick, though it certainly would have been nice if he'd chosen to leave that detail out.

"You said before that I could return at any time," she said by way of answer. "I'm not hurt. Aris didn't do anything to me. I was just... worried about you."

This, at least, was something that Elijah could believe. He forced his attention away, loosening a long breath from somewhere deep in his chest. "Very well, then I'll write to Aris to let him know that you're spending a few days here. Shall I have dinner brought up to you, or would you like to join me in the dining room?"

"Brought up, please," she said. As grateful for the distraction as she'd been, Blythe very much wanted a moment to herself to reflect on the situation. Her father, however, looked unnerved enough to spend the entire night with her. If not for her insistence that she needed rest, he just might have.

Not five minutes after he left, Blythe locked her door and took a seat at her writing desk. She was tired of her wandering mind. Tired of questions when she needed answers. She didn't allow herself time for thought as she pressed her palms against the surface of the wood and considered what it had once been. Not always a desk, but at some point a beautiful oak tree. Blythe allowed the image a home in her mind, and the longer she thought on it, the more the wood warped around her fingertips. It grew rigid beneath her palms, a splinter biting into the tip of her forefinger as she dragged her hand along its new shape. No longer flat, but curving into the shape of a log.

No, not a log—for logs did not grow branches or sprout leaves and twigs—but a *tree.*

Blythe snatched her hands away, clutching them to her chest as her palms pulsed with a heat that had no business feeling so pleasant. Breathless, she leaned back, still able to picture the tree in her mind's eye. Her body ached to bring it to fruition. To take what was dead and give it back to the earth anew.

To give it *life.*

How positively absurd.

Blythe smothered a bark of laughter. It was real, then. She had powers just like the others, but not the faintest idea of the extent of them. In her twenty-one years, never could she remember waking up one morning and just . . . *sprouting* things. And as far as she could remember, she'd always been able to bleed, too. Whatever had happened to change that, it had to have started around the same time that other paranormal elements had invaded her life.

Around the same time that she had nearly died.

Certainly it was all related, though she couldn't determine how. Aris might have answers, but the idea of talking to him—let alone announcing that she was the wife he'd been looking for all along—made her mouth feel as thick as if it was sprouting more moss.

There was, however, someone else that she could talk to. Someone who likely knew a lot more than they'd been letting on.

To My Dearest Cousin,

There is no chance on God's green earth that you can miss this year's Christmas ball. If you do not want me to turn into a tree that remains forever rooted into the earth, you must come to Thorn Grove at once.

Ever since I was bonded with Aris, whatever ridiculous magic makes up our rings has been paving our paths. It has informed all that I can and cannot do, and now in the moment when I need its guidance the most, it has fallen still and I fear that I know why. I fear that I know who I am and what you were trying to tell me that day in Fiore.

Tell me that you know something about this. Tell me that you know a way out, in which I may free myself from this mess looming before me. Tell me that I am hallucinating.

I need you, Signa. Please, make haste.

Your Cousin,
Blythe

CHAPTER TWENTY

To her dismay, Blythe's abilities did not work the same way as her counterparts'. Where Fate and Death were able to disappear in the blink of an eye and teleport themselves to wherever they fancied, Blythe, it seemed, still had to rely on letters to relay her desperation.

If she was going to have magic, she would have much preferred that it at least behaved as she wanted it to.

After slipping the letter to Signa into the post the morning after her arrival like some magicless peasant, Blythe found her stomach churning at the thought of returning to her suite in Thorn Grove and instead took to wandering the courtyard. The moors were covered in a fine layer of powder, only the most resilient thatches of grass peeking through. The staff flitted in and out of the manor, some of them hanging lavish adornments while others plowed the snow, creating a path for the carriages that would arrive the night of the ball.

Elijah had taken to overseeing the preparations, plucking

stubborn petals from mostly barren trees so they would all be uniform and restringing the boughs of holly that hadn't been hung to his satisfaction. His precision worried Blythe, for she knew her father well enough to understand that he was distracting himself. Likely from whatever was happening with Grey's.

She knew there would be no prying information from her father, who had preemptively banned all staff from allowing her a horse or taking her into town. Not that that would stop her from trying, considering she had absolutely nothing better to do. That, and the fact that she was in desperate need of a distraction from the way her palms itched to use a magic Blythe didn't know the first thing about.

She knew it was her magic that had brought the garden back to life, just as it was her magic responsible for making a mess of Elijah's office all those months ago. But she didn't have the faintest understanding of how it worked or all its possibilities.

Squeezing and unsqueezing her palms in an effort to quell the itch, Blythe double-checked that no one was looking before she cut a path to the stables. There'd been a knot in her chest since her arrival to Thorn Grove, but it eased its hold the moment she stepped over the threshold.

"Mr. Crepsley?" she called, searching for the young stable hand she'd made friends with several months prior. He would likely say that *friend* was a strong word considering she'd practically blackmailed him into helping her before. But that was semantics.

It didn't seem that the man was there, however, as only a choir of hoofbeats and gentle huffing greeted her. The sounds were like a warm blanket pulled tight around her shoulders, lulling her into comfort. Her mother's horse, Mitra, was one of the first that Blythe greeted, peeling off her gloves to brush a hand down the length of the mare's gorgeous golden mane. The unruly Balwin was farther inside, and the rotten creature snatched the gloves from Blythe's hands when she passed. She had to bop the pesky beast on the nose to get them back.

"William Crepsley, are you in here?" If Blythe could con anyone into allowing her a horse, it'd be him. But even the back of the stable was eerie in its silence, empty aside from a single horse that was smaller than the rest. Blythe's breath caught in her throat at the sight of the creature.

It was the foal. The one she'd believed Signa resurrected all those months ago. It was bigger now, with no lingering signs of the death it had once succumbed to. Instead, there was a glow to its body, a silver sheen so bright and divine that her eyes stung. Blythe stretched her hand forward, her palms itching so intensely it felt like they were burning.

"Hello." Blythe's words were no louder than a breath, but still the horse's ears twitched back, curious. Its large brown eyes blinked at her, and though Blythe couldn't be certain, it felt as if the young horse recognized her. It stepped forward, dipping its head to the level of her palm as it closed the space between them.

Blythe's hand rested on the soft space between its eyes before skimming down the length of its neck to where its skin warmed and she could feel its heartbeat beneath her fingers. She leaned in, pressing her forehead against the horse's.

She was the reason it was standing. She could feel that truth in the thrum of the horse's blood and by the sheen on its skin. It was resplendent, and it was *hers*.

"You should have known better than to bring it back."

The voice that sounded from behind her was decidedly not William's, nor was it any that Blythe recognized. She'd never heard a voice that inspired such terror.

Ten words, and with them Blythe felt her skin peeling from her bones. Tendrils of foreboding snaked down her neck as a cold sharper than even Death's seized her, plaguing her body with a dread worse than any poison she'd consumed. Bile rose to her throat, and it took everything within her for Blythe to choke it down and turn to seek out the face of a young woman who sat perched atop a hay bale, lounging back on one hand.

She had hair unlike any Blythe had ever seen, an unnatural shade that was as red as the devil himself. Her eye color, too, was inhuman, like dancing twin flames that never strayed from Blythe as she dangled her feet. She wore no apron, nor anything that could have placed her as one of Thorn Grove's staff. Instead, the cut of her scarlet bodice was scandalously low, the bust adorned with a silk bow as if she herself were a present to all the world. The ivory frills of her long sleeves matched her skirt's pleated ruffles, cut shorter than any dress Blythe had ever known. It ended well above her ankles, showing a daring slice of her slender leg and a full view of her short black boots.

Blythe found herself voiceless as she stared at the woman. Her skin was youthful, fair with a golden undertone. She didn't *look* much older than Blythe, yet there was something ancient in her blazing eyes, shaped like the most delicate teardrops. Something that reminded Blythe immediately of Aris and his brother.

Only this woman felt far more dangerous than either of those two. Her presence was like a fingernail scraping down the length of Blythe's spine. Like venom slipping through her skin and damning her blood. The hairs along Blythe's arms stood on end, her body trembling uncontrollably as she tried to move. Tried to *run*. But she couldn't take so much as a step.

"E-excuse me?"

The woman considered Blythe's confusion with a pout. "Well, that's no fun if you don't recognize me. I would have thought you'd have your memories back by now." Her singsong voice was coy and teasing as she stood up from the hay and onto her feet. As the woman drew closer, the horse bucked its legs, whinnying as it pushed itself against the back wall.

"I'm Solanine," said the woman, paying the horse no mind. "But you can call me Sol." She snatched Blythe's hand without waiting for her to close the gap, and it took only a single brush of her skin for Blythe to feel the seams of her world slice open. She saw the collapse of buildings to fire. Heard cries and the gunshots of war and smelled blood and charred bodies rotting the air. She blinked and Elijah was on the floor of Thorn Grove's ballroom, his throat slit open as rivulets of blood painted the marble scarlet. Signa was slumped beside him, her eyes hollow and her head bowed. Belladonna berries stained her lips, a handful of them rolling from her limp hand.

Blythe stared at them, her breaths coming faster until she could no longer pull air through her lungs. She clenched her throat with both hands, wishing to claw her tongue out of her mouth as it swelled up, festering, making every thin breath so painful that she wished to fall over and let Death claim her if only to stop the ache before it grew worse.

She was back in the stables the moment her nails brushed her tongue. Relief flooded her as the dead bodies in her mind's eye disappeared, but it was short-lived as she stumbled to her knees, losing the contents of her stomach as tears wet her cheeks.

"My apologies," Solanine mocked. "I should have warned you about that. I keep forgetting that you're the new girl."

It didn't matter who this woman was; she had all Death's fright and every bit of Fate's flare packed into a single lithe body, and in her presence Blythe felt only foreboding. Like every dream she'd ever held was burning away, pointless to pursue. That everyone she'd ever loved was destined to die, so why did any of it matter? Why did *life* matter?

"Just how many of you are there?" Blythe dug her fingers into the stall door and dragged herself to her feet, struggling with every inch.

"You speak as though you're different from the rest of us." Solanine hummed as she looped a slow half-circle around Blythe, who stood with her back pressed against the stall gate and a horse bucking its protest behind her. Blythe didn't blame the creature. If she could manage to get her hands on the latch, she'd open it just to let the poor thing run as far away as it could get.

"How do you know who I am?" Blythe demanded, praying she wouldn't stammer.

"Isn't it obvious? You summoned me." Solanine sported her cruelty with a smile. "Part of my job is keeping those like us in line, and you've broken the rules, little lamb. So here I am."

"I didn't summon anyone," Blythe gritted out, wishing she could succumb to the weakness in her knees and sit. But in this woman's presence, she knew that was as good as a death sentence.

She focused instead on her palms, on the itch beneath their surface and the magic that seemed to await her summons. Whatever Solanine's plans were, Blythe had no intention of going down without a fight.

"If you believe that, then you must not understand that magic of yours." She reached forward to snatch Blythe's wrist, and when she sliced a bloodred nail against it, Blythe's skin erupted into thorns.

Solanine hissed as she yanked herself away, blood as black as tar sliding from her palm and down her wrist. Blythe, however, didn't have so much as a mark on her.

"So the new girl bites." Her blazing eyes fell to Blythe's unmarked arm, and in her mind's eye Blythe saw the stables collapsing. Saw her mother's horse with its neck twisted and the young foal on top of her, both of them crushed by the rubble. But while the stables seemed to tremble in reality, they didn't come down. A warm, placid heat stirred in Blythe's belly, and she managed to stand taller before the woman, the magic within her ready to heed her call.

Solanine took one look at the vines now winding around Blythe's heels and scoffed. "Am I meant to be threatened by a magic you clearly have no idea how to wield?"

Blythe fought not to let her fear show, but waves of sorrow

pressed upon her as the woman filled her head with thoughts of destruction. Of the beautiful world around her eradicated, turned to nothing more than dust and rubble. Blythe's magic faltered as Solanine sauntered toward her, the heels of her boots clacking against the floor.

"Such a shame," the woman whispered as she took Blythe's cheeks in her hands. "Though I suppose this body of yours is quite frail, isn't it? Let's hope your next life will be kinder."

When Solanine's nails pressed to her throat, Blythe knew that she was done for. She only hoped that someone other than Elijah would find her body. That he would be spared the most gruesome details of her death. That time would heal him and he would not be forever alone or succumb to his grief.

She shut her eyes, waiting for Death, but the reaper never came.

The moment Solanine drew blood, she dropped her hold on Blythe. Her eyes were as wide as saucers as she stared down at the trail of it upon her finger and then up at Blythe's face.

"Rima?" Never would Blythe have expected the soft crack of Solanine's voice. She lifted her finger to her lips, tongue sliding along the blood without ever dropping Blythe's gaze. "You have her blood."

It took Blythe a long moment to recognize that the name belonged to Signa's mother. "How do you know Rima?"

Solanine dropped her hand. Out of all the blasted powers she could have, Blythe would have given anything in that moment to be able to read minds. The look in the woman's eyes was indecipherable, a mix of longing and resentment. Sorrow, perhaps.

"I suppose you are the right age... you're the baby, aren't you?"

Solanine countered. A question for a question. "The one she would flaunt to anyone who gave her the time." She tilted her head, curious, but Blythe ducked away, not letting this woman get a closer look at her eyes.

Signa. She thought that Blythe was Signa. And for now, Blythe didn't think it wise to clarify.

"You didn't answer me." Blythe spoke each word slowly, leaning into her fear and giving herself an excuse to keep her eyes low. "How do you know who Rima is?"

Solanine's response was not a whisper. It held no embarrassment, no fear. Just pure stated fact as she told Blythe, "I know Rima because I'm the one who killed her."

Blythe felt that truth like a bolt of lightning down her spine. Her chest squeezed, but there was no time to process the truth of those words or that Solanine was stepping back toward the hay bales. She looked angry to do it. Like she was warring with the desire to finish what she started and choke the life out of Blythe, bringing the stables down around her. But once Solanine took a seat, she didn't get back up.

"You hardly look a thing like her." The woman scrunched her nose in distaste. "A similar mouth, perhaps. And clearly the same penchant for inspiring chaos, if you're summoning me. I should have known that Rima's child would be special. Oh, she would have died happy to discover what you became. If only she was alive to find out."

Blythe wanted to condemn how lightly Solanine spoke of Rima's death, as though it was simply something that had happened and was not part of a disaster caused by her hand. But Blythe spoke nothing of her true identity, or corrected that Rima was merely her aunt.

Something told her that this connection to Rima was the only thing keeping her alive. "I didn't summon—"

"You did." Solanine sighed, exasperated. "You have upended the world's balance, but as you are of Rima's blood, I will offer you a chance to fix your mess, just as I offered her."

Blythe hadn't the faintest clue what mess was hers to fix, and Solanine didn't seem the type to provide that information willingly. She ground her teeth. "And what happens if I fail?"

Images of fallen bodies filled her mind. She saw her father not bleeding from his throat this time, but stabbed in the stomach over and over again. Flashes of his corpse being tossed to sea, swelling in the bottom of the ocean. Thorn Grove falling to ruin from his absence, several maids forced to life on the streets after failed efforts at finding employment.

"Chaos, little lamb." Solanine's eyes gleamed. "Absolute chaos." She plucked a piece of straw from beneath her, twirling it between her fingertips. Blythe couldn't look away from the smoke that wisped up, there one second and then gone as the straw flared into a fire, then to ash.

"Best of luck to you making things right." Solanine's scorching eyes lifted to Blythe's. "I imagine I'll be seeing you again very soon."

Blythe did not linger in the stables. The moment Solanine disappeared—because of course *she* had teleportation abilities—so did Blythe, grabbing her skirts and racing back to the safety of . . .

Well, she didn't know anymore. Thorn Grove was no longer the sanctuary it had once been, nor was it the haven Blythe had built in her head. To her surprise, the longer Blythe was away from Wisteria, the more homesick she became for a place she hadn't realized felt like home.

In that moment, Blythe would have given anything to speak with Aris. Either for him to tell her just who Solanine was and what problem needed solving to be rid of her, or to fall into the comfort of his conversation and seek distraction among their bickering. She'd take either of the options, happily. But for Aris to help her, he'd have to know the truth about who Blythe really was—a secret she'd hardly accepted herself.

"Done making decisions for me already?" Blythe glared down at her left hand, waiting for the band of light to pulse. Willing it to send her back to Wisteria. But the wretched thing remained still, cold, and entirely unhelpful. If not for the faintest glow of light on her finger, she wouldn't even know it still existed.

All along, Blythe had felt like the magic was leading her closer to Aris. That it was the representation of their bond to each other, magicked to life. So why was it so still now? Had it only wanted her to uncover the truth of who she was? To learn that her connection with Aris went much deeper than she could have fathomed, just to disappear once it put her into a spiral?

"You blasted thing," she whispered at the ring and whatever magic was at play within it. "I despise you."

How much easier it would have been if Aris could learn the truth in some other way. Then she wouldn't foolishly spend hours thinking over all the possibilities of what might happen once she told him, or face his disappointment when he discovered that after centuries of searching for his wife, Blythe was who he'd been waiting for.

As much as Aris irked her, he was also magnetic. For every bit of ego he imbued, there was also charm and immense passion. Never had Blythe met someone with such an appetite for traversing the world, or with such fascinating creativity. She was drawn to it, more attracted than she cared to acknowledge.

Whether he felt the same about her, however . . .

If anything could be gathered from his reaction to their kiss, it was that Aris wanted nothing to do with her. Blythe couldn't accept that fact changing simply because he knew the truth of her identity. She had no desire for Aris to suddenly alter his opinions over memories she was only beginning to remember, or because he believed her to be someone she simply wasn't. Did she have Life's powers? Yes. And perhaps she *was* reincarnated, but that didn't mean that she and Mila would ever be the same person.

Blythe didn't want him to want Mila. She wanted him to want *her*, which was horrible and embarrassing and a truth that was consuming her thoughts. But Aris had been clear about his feelings, which meant that there was no world in which Blythe could tell him the truth. At least not yet.

For now, she needed to shift her focus to better understanding her magic and figuring out who she was and what Solanine expected her to fix.

She returned to the manor to find it far rowdier than when she'd left. Nervous murmurs echoed across the entryway, and Blythe saw that the staff had ceased their decorating and were piled near the doors to the kitchen. She hurried forward, squeezing between two of the maids to sneak a look inside.

At first, she saw nothing other than Elijah prowling, opening every cupboard in search of something.

"Father?" Blythe tried to decipher what he might be looking for. "Has something happened?" While nothing *seemed* out of place, the tension was palpable.

Elijah tensed at the sound of his daughter's voice and whipped his head to face her. "Go to your room. Keep it locked until I come up—"

"What's going on?" She gripped the edge of the door, refusing to take so much as a step until she had answers.

"You will be the death of me one day, Blythe, I swear it." He smoothed his thumb and forefinger over his brows, exasperated. "Some of the staff have reported seeing a strange figure disappear into the kitchen."

"A figure?" Blythe's heart stuttered. "What did they look like?"

It was one of the maids who answered. "They were tall," she said, just as another chimed in, "With hair as red as blood. Never seen a thing like it."

"No one got a great look," Elijah quelled. "It could be nothing, but until we know more, I'd prefer that you stay safe in your room."

The last thing Blythe wanted was to *leave,* especially knowing that Solanine's hair was as red as described. She was about to argue that she be allowed to stay near Elijah and assist his investigation when the front doors swung open behind the group and Warwick came hurtling inside. Blythe caught a glance of Mitra just outside, whinnying and bucking. William Crepsley held her tight by the bridle, trying to soothe the mare. Blythe saw them for only a second before the doors slammed shut.

"Mr. Hawthorne!" A sheen of sweat veiled Warwick's face as he pushed his way through. "Someone has broken into the stables."

Blythe's blood ran cold. "They couldn't have possibly. I was just there!"

"Then we should count our blessings that you missed them," Warwick said. "Someone tried to take Mitra. Mr. Crepsley found her running back from the moors, half saddled and looking like she'd seen a ghost."

Blythe pressed a hand to her throat, her skin clammy. She didn't like this, not one bit.

Solanine had promised chaos. And chaos, it seemed, started now.

CHAPTER TWENTY-ONE

Thoughts of Solanine plagued Blythe throughout the night. She wasn't safe even in her dreams, where she watched as everyone she loved fell, their corpses bleeding or bloated or sliced into pieces and scattered on the ground. She tossed and turned for hours, jolting awake with the lone thought that this woman was out there, waiting for something. *Wanting* for something.

The memory of her voice had Blythe's body curling in on itself, the hairs of her neck raised and alert. And if a simple memory could do that to her—to someone who knew that the paranormal was real and who apparently was one of these mythical deities herself—she feared what Solanine would do to Elijah. Blythe needed to cut the head off this snake before it could seep any more venom.

But to do that, she needed her cousin.

When the sun rose on Christmas morning, Elijah appeared at her door with a lovely silk gown of powder blue with dropped sleeves and silver tulle along the skirt that looked iridescent when twirled about. She slipped into it in the late afternoon, silent and mulling about her own thoughts as she let one of the staff help ready her for the ball. No longer unmarried, she wore her pale blond hair down and cleaned her wedding ring until it sparkled, the golden snake once again drawing her thoughts back to Aris. She knew he, too, could likely help her. But it was Signa who had saved Blythe's life once, and Signa who had been willing to give up everything and everyone she loved to save Blythe a second time. And so, more than Aris, it was her cousin's help that she sought.

At least, this was the excuse Blythe gave herself, as well as that she now knew one small truth of what had happened the night of Rima Farrow's death. Though how to break that news to Signa, she wasn't sure.

"Has my cousin arrived?" Blythe asked one of the older maids, having taken to pacing and fretting about, much to the annoyance of several of the staff who were forced to work around her, lighting the candles and finalizing last-minute decor.

"Not yet, Your Highness."

Blythe groaned and continued her pacing. It wasn't that she *wanted* to be front and center, the first person any arriving guest would see. Especially not when she knew how much fun high society would have with their musings and theorizing about her missing husband. It was the very thing she'd told Aris she despised, but she couldn't worry about her family's reputation taking the hit now. With Solanine's threat looming, Blythe needed to be there the moment Signa arrived.

Unfortunately, thirty minutes into the party and her cousin

was still nowhere to be found. Blythe stared out the frosted window, fretting at her gloves. The skin beneath them was itching something fierce, and it was only when she ripped one off that she realized why—there were no longer faint blue veins on her wrist. Roots stretched beneath Blythe's skin, slipping up her palms, where ivy was beginning to sprout.

Blythe swallowed her scream as she shoved the glove back on.

"When you see Miss Farrow, send her to me immediately!" Blythe demanded before she threw open the parlor. She slammed the door shut as she stumbled into a chair and tore off her gloves. Her arm was worsening by the second, tiny thorns piercing through her skin. They were smaller than the ones she'd produced the day prior against Solanine, but this time Blythe had no control over them.

She couldn't make sense of time or thoughts, or anything other than an overwhelming need to escape. To return to her suite, or maybe to the garden. She could bury herself there. Let her body take root and become one with the earth so that she might never have to deal with whatever was happening to her or the threat on the lives of those she loved.

Just when she thought she could bear no more, the door creaked open and a trembling voice called out, "Blythe? What's going on?"

Blythe's entire body was covered in ivy when she turned toward her cousin. Roots and vines snaked through her hair, consuming her, and Signa covered her mouth at the sight. She ran to Blythe, dropping to her knees beside her.

"Breathe!" Signa grabbed Blythe by the shoulders, wincing as the thorns drew blood that blossomed through her white gloves.

The sight of it had anxious laughter bubbling in Blythe's throat. What was it that Aris had called her? A sweetbrier, full of thorns in his side? If only he could see how right he was. Or maybe she was becoming one with the aptly named Thorn Grove.

She laughed again at the thought, doubled over and delirious.

Undeterred, Signa took Blythe by the chin. "Get a hold of yourself and breathe before you turn this place into a terrarium!"

Blythe startled when Signa squeezed, forcing her to draw a trembling breath, then a second.

"Very good," Signa soothed after several long minutes of this. She dropped her hold on Blythe's chin and instead threaded their fingers together. She held close even as ivy swept up her wrists and along her forearms, ensnaring her. "Shut your eyes and picture in your mind that you are wholly yourself," her cousin whispered, a portrait of calm. "No ivy. No flora. Just Blythe, bare skinned and at ease."

There was little to do but obey, though it was no easy feat. One second Blythe imagined herself bare skinned, only for her mind to betray her a moment later with thoughts of the garden and all the strange things that could blossom upon her skin. She was glad that her eyes were shut so she didn't have to see what wild creations she must have conjured when Signa winced and said more urgently, "Bare skinned, Blythe! Imagine that we are in the snow. Do you remember when we made snow angels all those months ago? You were in a coat, and there was nothing green as far as the eye could see. Can you picture that day?"

Blythe tried her hardest, casting out thoughts of the garden in favor of the winter. She thought not of the snow angels but of her time in Brude. Of the frosted air that hunted any spare inch of skin it could find. Of sledding with Aris and navigating the canals, worlds away from her mother's garden.

"You're doing amazing," whispered Signa after a good while. "You can open your eyes."

Blythe opened them in time to see the last of the ivy disappearing into her palms. No longer was there moss sprouting beneath her fingernails, and when she raked her hands over her head, she found only hair. Only after triple-checking herself was Blythe able to sob her relief.

"You knew." She made no effort to stop the accusation from tumbling out of her. "You knew what I was, didn't you? *Who* I was. That's what you wanted to tell me."

Signa took her by the left wrist and extended Blythe's hand so that it was before her, the band of light shimmering on her ring finger. "I'd have told you if I was able, Blythe. I swear that I tried. You saw what happened back in Fiore. I tried writing you letters after that, but the ink would disappear from the page before I could send it. I never wanted to lie to you, not again."

Blythe gritted her teeth, eyes blurring with tears as she tore her hand away from Signa. "Have you known all this time? Were you only pretending to be the one using my powers?"

"Of course not!" This was spoken with such resoluteness that Blythe had no choice but to believe her cousin. "For the longest time I truly believed it was me. I felt those powers every time you used them, and they always felt wrong. Too hot and so painful that it made me sick. I had no idea of the truth until the day you poured your blood onto that tapestry and struck a deal with Fate."

Signa was suddenly crouched before her, taking both of Blythe's hands tight in hers. "I am glad that I can speak freely now, if only to tell you that I will *always* be on your side. I tried everything I could think of to tell you, but it seems the magic had other plans."

It was too much. The magic, Aris, Solanine and her connection to Rima, the truth of who Blythe was... all of it was too much.

"There's something I need to tell you, too," Blythe whispered, her voice cracking. Signa only shook her head.

"Later," she whispered. "Perhaps when doing so will not turn your body to thorns that will impale us all."

Words about Rima sat at the top of her tongue, and though Blythe desperately wanted to say them aloud, she knew that Signa was right. It was too big of a truth, and Blythe was in no position to delicately break the news to her cousin. She fell forward, letting Signa pull her into an embrace as Blythe cried into her cousin's chest.

She had no idea how long they remained like that, crumpled on the floor with Signa smoothing a reassuring hand down Blythe's hair. Eventually, though, as the hour grew later and the volume within Thorn Grove rose, Signa whispered, "Would a gift make you feel better?"

Perhaps it was silly that those were the words that roused her, but Blythe leaned up with a tired sniffle and whispered, "It probably won't make me feel worse."

Signa smiled, rising to her feet and disappearing for a brief moment before she returned with a glittering silver box.

"Last year you gave me something that meant more to me than you probably ever realized," Signa said as she set the box upon Blythe's lap. "This year, I wanted to return the favor."

Exhausted as she was, there was always energy for presents, and Blythe desperately wanted the distraction. She wasted no time tearing into the pretty parchment. Inside glistened a mask—one made of petals both as white as the snow and as blue as a summer sky. It was unlike any she'd seen, though it wasn't the flowers that made the mask unique. It was the fact that it didn't just cover her eyes, but had gilded branches that stretched past her temples and around her head like a circlet. It was a marvelous thing, strange in its loveliness, and Blythe did not hesitate to put it on.

"It's outstanding," she whispered, holding it to her face as Signa helped fasten it.

"I think so, too. And as a bonus, no one will be able to tell that you've been crying." Signa smiled, and Blythe took a moment to finally look her over, truly seeing her cousin for the first time since she arrived.

Signa was wearing the mask that Blythe had given her for last year's masquerade, one with similar gilded branches but that curved around the right side of her face like vines, with delicately sculpted petals and ivy that spilled over the other side of her head and down past her blue eye. Again she wore red, though this time it was a deep burgundy made from satin, with golden adornments along the sleeves and bodice. She wore her hair down just as Blythe did, sporting loose waves that suited her so much better than any style she'd ever worn while living at Thorn Grove.

"Do you remember when you had to wear that awful yellow dress?" Blythe teased, laughing when Signa's nose scrunched.

"I assume you mean when I looked like a walking banana? I try very hard *not* to remember."

For the first time all day, Blythe drew an easy breath. "I'm glad you're here. There's so much we need to discuss."

"And we have all the time in the world to do it. But first, we've a ball to attend. If we wait any longer, Elijah will come looking for you." Signa took Blythe by the arm and led her out of the parlor, and in their nearness Blythe noticed she had the pallor of someone who had not seen the sun in a good while.

Blythe wanted to tell her cousin all about the danger they were in and that they in fact did *not* have all the time in the world. But at the sight of such pallor, Blythe instead cupped her free hand over Signa's and asked, "Have you still been reading those journals?"

Signa's smile thinned. "I can't seem to stop. There are only a few left."

"And have you found anything useful?"

Signa's voice wavered. "I can't say for certain... but I believe it possible that I was not the first in my family to be touched by the paranormal."

Blythe's throat tightened, but there were too many eyes monitoring them to share the truth. She wondered whether she might pull her cousin back into the parlor, but someone called out to her before Blythe had the chance.

"Miss Hawthorne!" The familiar voice was one that grated across Blythe's skin, making her neck and body curl in on itself. She and Signa both turned to find Diana Blackwater fluttering a fan. Her lips were pinched, eyes squinted in a false smile as she made her way toward them.

"My apologies. How could I forget that you're a Dryden now? I never imagined I'd be referring to you as *Your Highness*!" She spoke too loudly, laughing as she fanned herself.

"I imagine it's quite a change for you, considering you don't often have a reason to speak with anyone of prestige," Signa offered with an innocent smile. Several others had gathered nearby to listen, assessing everything from Blythe's dress to her belly, likely wondering if she was already hosting a royal heir. Each one of those eyes searched for the prince, and it took everything within Blythe to ignore the surprised gasps that sounded as she took a flute of champagne from a passing tray. She wasn't going to *drink* it. This was a Thorn Grove party, after all. Still, it would at least keep the pregnancy questions at bay.

Signa's jab seemed to have found its way between Diana's ribs. The young woman tensed, though it was Blythe who she remained fixated on, fan stilling in her hands for the briefest second before continuing anew. "Wherever is the prince? I didn't see him come in with you."

Blythe bit back the foul words cloying her tongue. She had enough on her mind as it was; the last thing she needed was for high society to involve itself.

"My husband is a busy man," she answered simply, loud enough for any eavesdroppers to hear. "It's unfortunate that business often keeps him away, though he was very kind to not want me to miss spending the holiday with my father."

Diana hummed under her breath. "I see. And did you forget to pack your belongings? I would have thought you'd be wearing something a little more . . . royal."

How grand Blythe's visions were of skewering this woman and roasting her on a spit. Her palms itched, wishing to unleash a torrent of sharpened vines. But as such things were unbecoming of a lady, she kept such grand idealizations to herself and instead used the sharpest weapon a woman of her status was trained to wield—her words.

"Mind your tongue, Diana. My father gifted me this dress."

The glare Diana flashed her upon use of her Christian name was white-hot.

"My apologies," she chided, this time with a long and dreamy sigh. "It's just that I think of how well I am treated by my dear Greggory, and I cannot help but wish the same kind of treatment for my treasured friend. He is the son of a viscount, you know. A proper man."

"How great it must have been to find success with the season," Signa quipped. "Which one was it, again? Your third? Oh, you must be so relieved."

Blythe noticed the gold engagement ring glittering on Diana's finger and said a silent prayer for the future viscount. The poor bastard.

Diana shut her fan with a snap as she glared at Signa, then once again back to Blythe.

"My father overheard yours talking about Verena at the club," she said. "He said that Mr. Hawthorne visited the palace himself during your honeymoon. One could wonder at the strangeness, don't you think? I could perhaps give you some advice if you've been unable to hold the prince's attention. Or perhaps it's that your father is simply incapable of being alone?"

Blythe did not breathe, having to still her mind from a deluge of thoughts about turning Diana into the most hideous tree. She would strike it down, chop up the wood, and feed it to her hearth. And every night she would sit and warm her toes by the most glorious fire as she watched the wood turn to ash.

The more she thought about it, however, the more a deep heat within her flared to life, her magic threatening to surface. With every passing second, the hall spun from gold and silver to red as rich as blood. Her budding rage was so palpable that Blythe could taste it. She gnashed her teeth together, trying to quell her mind from thoughts of vines tearing up through the marble and ensnaring Diana by the ankles. Of dragging her underground and burying this foul woman alive. There were so many glorious possibilities.

She could handle whatever nonsense Diana wanted to theorize about her. But her father? She would sooner stuff moss down the woman's throat than listen to one more word pass her foul lips.

Blythe drew a step forward, only for a hand much larger than Signa's to grip her shoulder from behind and halt her murderous intent.

She spun to demand that everyone mind their own business, yet the words halted at her lips when she looked upon two molten eyes that did not stare back at her, but instead bore into Diana as if burning into the depths of the woman's soul.

"Speak one more word to my wife," Aris growled, "and I will tear your tongue from your throat."

CHAPTER TWENTY-TWO

Aris's warning struck like a thunderclap. Vultures whose eyes had gleamed only moments prior scattered like mice, bowing low before fleeing the scene. All but Diana, that is, for she was too stunned to move.

Aris stood before her in a suit of rich navy, golden trim along his lapel. His mask was a bewitching creation of black-and-gold papier-mâché that cut stark angles across his face and made him appear every bit an austere prince looking down upon a ballroom full of his inferiors. He was more barbered than Blythe had seen him in a long while, his blond hair neatly coiffed and his well-tailored wardrobe making Blythe's heart stutter at the sight of him. Even in his severity—or perhaps *because* of it—Aris was utterly handsome.

He did not further scold Diana. He did not demean her with cruel names or draw any more attention to the situation. Aris was fire set ablaze in a consuming rage as his eyes devoured the girl, feasting upon her flesh and bones. His touch, however, was gentle against Blythe's skin as he took hold of her hand.

"Come," he said, fingers threading through hers. "We've no business associating with such a creature. I've known children with less abysmal manners."

Even if Blythe had wanted to, there was no point arguing. Aris burned as hot as a star as he led her past a stunned Signa and through a throng of guests who parted as they made their way to the ballroom. There was a saunter in his step that Blythe had grown accustomed to, for Aris treated every domain he entered like he was the most esteemed guest.

It had been a long while since Blythe set foot on this ballroom floor—the night of Lord Wakefield's death, specifically. It smelled of sugar and spruce trees, and had been decorated with shimmering amber candles and holly with a bow tied around every marble pillar. Thorn Grove knew how to put on the charm when it wanted to, but given its record of unsavory situations, Blythe wondered why so many people still attended these parties. She could only chalk it up to morbid curiosity, a twisted desire of the ton to not miss whatever scandal might happen next.

"You're here." Blythe didn't mean to whisper it. In fact, she hardly recognized that she had until Aris acknowledged the words with a tightened grip as he carved a path toward a dance floor bathed in the warmth of golden candlelight. Most guests hurried out of their way, someone in a fox mask making such haste that their shoulder knocked into Blythe's. With the heat of Aris's body beside her, the person felt so cold that Blythe shuddered.

"Of course I am." Aris's hand slipped around her waist, drawing Blythe into his chest as the music of a waltz swelled. "As if I'd leave you alone with such vultures."

The crowd gave the two a wide berth, and tucked there against Aris, Blythe could not help but be reminded of the memory of him and Life dancing in the forest glade. She shut her eyes as it played in her mind, not like something that happened to a stranger centuries prior, but to *her* just last week.

"I had no choice but to leave," she told him, mostly to distract herself from Life's memories as they beat against her skull. "Your temper tantrum was making Wisteria inhospitable."

The right side of Aris's jaw ticked. "I came to Thorn Grove the night you left to ensure that you were safe. But what I don't understand is how you managed to leave in the first place."

"Neither do I," she answered honestly. "It's your magic that created these ridiculous rings to begin with. Shouldn't you be the one figuring that out?"

"Enough," Aris growled low in her ear, sending a wave of shivers down her spine. "No more arguing. Five minutes alone with you and I'm already wondering why I ever thought an apology was worthwhile."

His words, callous as they were, held no bite. In fact, Blythe smiled at them, genuinely this time.

"If you've come to apologize, I won't stop you."

He leaned his head back, a war of emotion on his face. "Mila's room is not a place I visit often. It's a part of Wisteria that rarely shows itself to me, and for good reason. It's all I have left of her, and it remains well protected."

"I understand," Blythe whispered. "Had I known how much it would hurt you, I would have never touched that mirror. I shouldn't have even been in that room to begin with."

"No," he agreed, "you shouldn't have. Though how I handled the situation left much to be desired. Especially considering how the rest of our day went."

Blythe pressed closer, refusing to let him see the blush that was warming its way onto her cheeks. Despite all that was going on in her world, she'd been unable to cast aside the memory of their bodies and everything that had nearly happened between them. "I told you already that I understand, Aris. We don't have to discuss it."

"I would prefer that we did." There was an edge to his voice that Blythe mistook for anger. Though when she dared a look at him, peeking up beneath her lashes, she saw that Aris looked every bit as flustered as she felt.

"I have no expectations of you," she told him softly.

"I'm aware. I'll only say this once, Blythe, so do not ask me to repeat myself—I felt something that night that I have not felt in a very long while." His thumb skimmed her waist as Aris pulled her far closer than what was considered polite for company. "It took me by surprise, and I fear that I may not have responded as well as I should have."

It was the first time she'd heard her name upon his tongue, and Blythe nearly melted into the sound of it. Her body was a traitor, overly aware of the press of his chest against hers. Of the way his breath rose the hairs along her neck, and the way she ached to arch closer against him.

"I was taken by surprise, too" was all she could trust herself to whisper. "You know I despise you."

"And you know that I despise you," he echoed, a smile slanting his lips. "It's a conundrum, and one that I fear we will have to tend to."

"Indeed." She wished at once to have Diana's fan so that she might cool herself. Her body was on fire, the world blurring around the edges as he spun her. "For one thing, we can be sure not to put ourselves in such a compromising position again. Especially when we're not thinking clearly."

"I've had three days to get myself thinking clearly." Aris leaned in, his lips so near to her ear that she felt them grazing her neck. "And I admit that my suggestion for 'tending' to the problem is far less wholesome. Assuming, of course, that you might be willing to try at least one more compromising position."

Blythe didn't dare choke in the middle of the dance floor. Not when there were a dozen eyes dissecting her. She imagined what anyone who saw them must think, for there wasn't a single soul in attendance who could say that Aris wasn't enraptured by his new bride. Perhaps even a little *too* enraptured, if the few quiet giggles were any indicator.

This time, however, Blythe paid them no mind. If they wanted to watch, then she'd be sure to give them a show. She didn't know why—perhaps it was out of her own desires, or perhaps it was due to

Life's newly awoken memories leaking into her—but Blythe pressed onto her toes to capture Aris's lips with hers, losing herself in a kiss that set her body ablaze. Her hunger for him was more potent than ever, and she craved nothing more than his touch.

Burn was too casual a word, for Blythe did not burn for this man; she incinerated. And in that moment, she knew there would be no getting it out of her system. No satiating the hunger.

Blythe was breathless when Aris broke the kiss, stilling their bodies as the music stopped. She was on fire, more alive than ever, only her world did not cease its spinning even when he stilled them. Breathless, Blythe swayed as the crowd softened into a haze that had her smile waning. She stumbled backward, only managing to keep on her feet because of how tightly Aris clutched her hand.

"Blythe? Blythe, what's wrong?" he demanded, but the words were muddled. She tried to answer. Tried to give voice to so much as a single word, but instead her hand clasped instinctively around her throat. It felt like she was being roasted from the inside out.

Blythe's eyes flew toward the corner, searching the shadows for Death. What she saw instead was a flash of red hair and the gilded face of a fox mask as she fainted upon the ballroom floor.

CHAPTER TWENTY-THREE

When Blythe came to nearly an hour later, it was to a cacophony of familiar voices arguing over her.

"Hasn't Thorn Grove seen enough parties in its days?" Aris spat. "It's not as if any of them have turned out well."

"What would you have me do? Bar my doors and ostracize my family further? I will not be the widower who's shut away in some haunted old manor." The second voice was Elijah's, and its contempt had Blythe straining to open her eyes.

"None of that matters." Signa spoke louder than the others, a sharpness to her tone that snapped the men to silence. "We don't know that anything's happened. It's not been even a year since her recovery. Her body is still frail."

"Perhaps she would recover faster if she was to return to Thorn Grove permanently," Elijah suggested.

This was met with strident protest from her husband. "Is there something wrong with our home?"

"I've been meaning to ask you that very same question. Blythe arrived here barefoot and without so much as an escort. It's no wonder she's fainted; she could have caught her death out there!"

"She's not a porcelain doll, Elijah. Your daughter isn't going to shatter if she's not carried on a palanquin."

The room dissolved into so much bickering that Blythe couldn't make out what was said next. Every voice was fighting to be on top of the next, and all she wished was for them to cease their arguing so that she could drift back to sleep. Then Blythe heard a fourth voice. A watery one that spoke low into her ear.

"Wake up," it said, soft among the bickering. Eyes weighted by exhaustion, Blythe struggled to crack one open. Death peered down at her, his eyes as silver as the stars. For once, Blythe did not find his presence unnerving. Rather, there was a familiarity that squeezed her heart. A comfort that had not been there days ago.

How many times had Death looked at her with those eyes? Fleeting memories teased the edges of her mind. Ones of him laughing as they sat beside each other beneath the bend of a wisteria tree. Memories of him and Aris quarreling over whatever her husband felt like quarreling about that day and joking together once they'd reached a truce. Memories of the two of them sampling new liquors and of being dragged across the world whenever Aris was excited for them to see a new piece of art, or to try something they'd never before eaten.

So warmed was Blythe by the memories that there was no controlling the tear that fell down her cheek. Death startled at the sight of it until understanding dawned. The severity of his shadows lessened, growing brighter in the face of her recognition.

"Tell me it's not time?" she whispered.

His touch was tender as he brushed one gloved finger across her cheek to swipe away the tear. "It's not your time. Not yet."

Once, Blythe would have cowered beneath his presence. Now, the touch had her lips cracking into the smallest smile before she gave his hand a gentle squeeze. There was so much more she wanted to say to him—so much more to discuss—but there before Aris and her father was not the time.

"Then I suppose I should wake up." Her chest was tight as she stared at the wallpapered ceiling of her bedroom at Thorn Grove, tracing outlines of blue-and-silver whorls the same as she'd done so many times before. How many months had she lain in this spot, her body aching with exhaustion just as it was now? How many days had she filled with only her own mind for company as maids wandered the halls, whispering about the dying girl they thought too weak to hear them?

With every whorl, Blythe's heart pushed higher into her throat, threatening to suffocate her. She hadn't noticed that the voices around her had gone quiet until someone—her father, she thought—sank against the edge of her bed.

"Are you well?" he asked at the same time as Signa demanded, "What happened?"

Blythe opened her eyes to find Signa's face contorted with a familiar look. One that meant Signa had found herself another puzzle and was in desperate need of solving it. Blythe eased herself upright, trying to keep her attention pressed forward and far away from the ceiling. Even the weight of the blankets reminded her of a being trapped in a spider's web, awaiting her death as she suffocated upon a bed of silk.

"I'm fine," she managed, though the sound was ragged. "Perhaps I've exerted myself too much over the past few days."

Or perhaps it was Solanine making good on her threat.

There was tea at Blythe's bedside, the scent wafting up in tendrils of steam that made her nauseous. The walls were too close. Too cramped. The scent too familiar. And the wallpaper... God, the wallpaper. She wished the fire in Thorn Grove's library all those months ago had spread down to her room just to have burned it.

Each breath was measured, and each as desperate as the last. It wasn't until Aris stepped forward that some of the tension in her belly snapped, automatically more relaxed as he came to Elijah's side and took hold of her hands. Her fingers curled around his, desperate to escape this room and free herself of its memories. One shared look between them, and recognition sparked in Aris's eyes. Suddenly his arms were slipping beneath Blythe and lifting her from the bed.

"We're going home." He didn't take the time to sort it out as a discussion. Given that Blythe was distracted by the thundering of her own heart, she didn't hear Elijah's argument. Only saw Death take hold of Signa's hand and draw her back, and heard when Aris whispered, "Sitting in the room she almost died in will do her no good. With all due respect, I'm taking my wife home."

Home. For so long Blythe had envisioned Thorn Grove when she'd heard that word. Why was it, then, that she wished only to return to the comfort of Wisteria Gardens? The comfort of a place where she had felt like an outsider since the moment she'd arrived?

"I will check in with you tomorrow," Aris told his arguing father-in-law as he swept toward the door. "You all will be welcome to visit, should you wish that."

As much as Blythe wanted to assure the others that she was fine, she couldn't manage to get the words out. She could only turn, eyes pleading with Signa, whom she still needed desperately to speak with.

"I'll be there," Signa whispered, understanding the look. "As soon as you're well enough to have me, I'll be there. I swear it."

Blythe was too tired to nod, relief crumpling her frame. She held tightly on to Aris, shutting her eyes as she curled into his chest.

Though he made a show of bundling her into a blanket and easing her into a carriage Blythe was quite certain was not theirs, the moment they were inside with the curtains drawn, Aris pushed the carriage door open once more. Only this time it did not open to the alarmed faces of her family, but into Wisteria.

A very warm, very *festive* Wisteria.

Aris helped Blythe into the palace, which curled itself around her in greeting. It was well furnished now, not with ice and sculptures like when it had been masquerading as Verena, but as it had been the very first time Blythe had laid eyes on it, back when she attended his ball. Marble pillars stretched toward a ceiling of red, draped in ivy that was adorned with red and gold ribbons. Holly dangled from the mantel, woven around towering candles that bathed the room in a haze of amber light. Three stockings hung above the fireplace—one blue and adorned with a silver *B*, one gold and adorned with an *A*, and a final red stocking that Blythe had to squint at to see that it also had a *B*, though beside it was a small paw print with golden stitching.

"You gave the fox a stocking?" Blythe asked, incredulous.

"Why wouldn't I?" Aris's neck retracted, as if he found the question distasteful. "Beasty is a part of this family."

"*Beasty? That* is what you chose to name her?"

"I thought you'd appreciate having her named after you."

For perhaps the first time, Blythe found she had no immediate retort. From the corner of Beasty's favorite chair, curled and warming by the hearth, the fox snored so contentedly that Blythe couldn't help but laugh, bested by them both. Grasping the arm of her own chair for support, she eased herself onto the cushion and let warmth sink into her bones. No longer was the fire gasping or struggling to maintain life. It blazed, proud and powerful, as she stretched her feet toward the flames. She could understand why the fox enjoyed the spot so much.

"You're the most ridiculous man I've ever met." It was perhaps the greatest compliment she could give him, and Aris soaked it in. He settled a blanket over her shoulders and shifted into the spot beside her, moving a touch slower than his usual. Less assured.

A cup of tea appeared before them each, and Aris stirred several spoonfuls of honey into his own. Unlike the tea at Thorn Grove, this one's scent was wonderfully mild to her unnerved stomach.

"I want to know whether you're all right," he told her as he tapped his spoon against the side of the porcelain to dry it. "A true answer."

“I’d rather discuss anything else.” Leaving her tea alone for now, Blythe burrowed deeper into her blanket.

“I would rather never discuss how I’m feeling,” Aris said, “though unfortunately we are married and obligated to such conversations.”

She frowned, wishing to disappear into her cocoon. If she was to bare her soul, it would not be for free. “Then tell me something true and I’ll do the same.”

“Something true?” Aris relaxed in his seat, cup and saucer floating before him. No longer did Blythe have to squint to see the golden threads that held them up. They were so apparent that she wondered what might happen if she were to reach out to touch one.

Aris ran a hand over his jawline, one leg swung over the other as he leaned back with a casual grace that had Blythe’s chest aching with familiarity. She instantly recalled a dozen more times he had sat just like this, his neck exposed as he propped an elbow onto the top of his seat and tipped his head against his fist.

“I’ll agree to that deal,” he said. “But only if you go first.”

Blythe had been trailing her eyes down the length of him, taking in the leanness of his frame. The veins of his forearms and the delicate hollow of his throat. It took far too much effort for her to pry her attention away. She shifted in her seat as a traitorous heat stirred in her low belly.

Why in heaven’s name was she like this?

“I remained living in that room at Thorn Grove even after my recovery, but I’m beginning to wonder whether I actually despised it all along,” she began, surprised by how easily the words slipped free. “After we came here, I believed that I missed my home, but now

I realize I miss only its people. Stepping back into that room was like returning to a nightmare I've only just escaped. Lying sick in that bed, staring up at that ceiling and then at so many worried faces of people wondering whether I might die... I am glad you brought me home, Aris. I'm glad you got me out of there."

She took the cup of tea in her bare hands, clutching her fingers around the porcelain just to have something solid and warm to focus on. Something *real*.

Aris took one look at how tightly she clutched her cup, and suddenly the hearth burned stronger, its heat sinking into her tightened muscles. "I'm done trying to run you out of Wisteria. When you left this place, I was relieved. I thought I was glad to no longer have to care for you or wonder whether you'd be outside my door ready to terrorize me as soon as it opened. But to my surprise, a larger part of me felt your absence in ways I do not yet understand.

"I have made thousands of deals in my life," he continued, lifting his hand so that the band of light on his finger caught the hearth's glow, "but none of them have ever manifested themselves to such an extreme. As many fates as I have woven, I have never seen my own. But I do not believe in coincidence, Sweetbrier, and after all that has happened I am not so foolish as to believe that you aren't a part of my story. I have watched humans fight against their fates for a millennium, and I have no intention of doing the same to my own. We are bonded, you and I."

Blood rushed in Blythe's ears, making her head fuzzy. They were more than just *bonded*, but as far as Aris knew, it was Signa who'd exhibited Life's powers. Blythe was weak. She was frail and soft, and so incredibly *human*. So why would he ever expect the torrent of power that brewed heavy in her chest even then?

"I'm done running," she told him, setting her teacup aside. If she wanted answers—about who she was, and whatever it was that Solanine demanded she fix—then being at Wisteria and triggering her memories was likely her best shot. And of course there was another much larger reason that Wisteria felt more comfortable to her now than anywhere else in the world.

A smile drew across Aris's lips, and he rose to his feet. He extended his hand to her, palm up. "I'm glad to hear it. Because there's something I'd like to give you."

CHAPTER TWENTY-FOUR

Blythe supposed she should have been more frustrated by her current circumstance than she was. She certainly would have preferred to be able to walk on her own, yet she gave no protest as Aris scooped her into his arms, her skirts nearly dragging on the floor as he tucked her against the warmth of his chest.

It was, admittedly, a very good chest. It helped that he smelled nice, too. Like spiced apples and wisteria, which was the only reason she did not demand he set her down. That, and the fact that climbing the stairs all the way to the top floor seemed exhausting.

Aris spared Life's portrait a fleeting glance as they passed, his eyes darkening as they flitted toward the door to his study. The look was there and gone again within seconds as he continued onward, past the ballroom and down the left side of the hall. It was, she thought, the direction of Life's room. Though this time the hall did not don its ivory paneling or patches of clover to pave their way. Instead, it was empty but for an imposing door of white oak that had a handle of pearl.

Aris set Blythe gently onto her feet before opening the door to a room that was infinitely larger inside than she'd expected. It was brighter, too. So bright that she had to squint, for everything from the floor to the ceiling was an unblemished, iridescent white.

"I don't understand," she said, hooding her eyes from the light. "What is this place?"

He took hold of her shoulders, positioning her in the center of the room. "It's yours," Aris whispered, as if anything louder might shatter such a delicate space. He bent so that his lips were nearer to her ear, each word sending tiny pulses of electricity shooting up her spine. "I'm gifting you a room in Wisteria of your very own, of which your imagination may run free to create whatever you'd like."

He lifted his hand, and from it the stark-white ceiling split as if being torn at a seam, spreading open into a clear summer sky.

Blythe's heart leapt as she watched the sky restitch itself, shifting back to stark white seconds later. At once Blythe thought of Life's room and how strikingly impossible it was. Then she remembered the first wonderscape Aris had shown her over dinner—a midnight lake where the water touched the stars. A dream given life.

Sensing that she finally understood what was being offered to her, Aris straightened and kept but one hand upon her midback. "I realize that you and I are doing this all backward, but consider this a peace offering. I want you to feel comfortable in Wisteria. In your home." He gave her a gentle nudge forward, toward an easel and canvas that had appeared with a wide assortment of paints beside it. "Go on. Build the room of your dreams."

Slowly, Blythe took a seat before the easel and picked up the bare paintbrush. As vivid as her imagination was—and as much as she prided herself on her cleverness—in the face of so much possibility Blythe found herself with a sudden lack of foresight. She could turn this place into her own personal beach if she wanted, a place where the sun was always shining and where she could lounge to her heart's content. Or she could turn it into an identical version of what she remembered from her mother's garden, though perhaps being surrounded by the very thing that had tried to overtake her body wasn't her finest idea.

Blythe thought then of the fairy-tale books her father had gifted to her, tucked safely in her suite at Thorn Grove, and had a sudden idea of what the perfect addition to Wisteria would be.

She dipped her brush into the colors and began to paint the most fantastical library she could pull from her imagination. The moment something came to life on the canvas, the ground instantaneously trembled as Aris rolled up his sleeves and got to work on making it a reality.

"It should be warm!" she noted, clenching tight to her chair as the room split and built itself around her. "But not too bright," she noted, dulling the colors in the corner with a haze of soft lights. "Cozy and always a little dreary but with light enough to see the pages without squinting."

Again the ground shifted, manifesting the dark wood floors and the ornate scarlet-and-gold rugs she painted. Blythe and Aris fell into a rhythm, losing themselves in the creation as they crafted bookcases that stretched several stories and wove latticed bridges between the rows, adorning each with glowing lanterns and arches of ivy and wisteria. Above, the highest shelves gave way to a starry sky that Blythe took a dry brush to splatter white paint upon, inspired by the first wonderscape Aris had ever shown her. A perfect harvest moon loomed over its center, and owls with glittering silver feathers perched atop the highest shelves.

"And where are you planning to read all these books?" Aris mused when Blythe leaned back, inspecting her work thus far. "You're forgetting the furniture."

She shushed him, threatening her husband with a wag of the paintbrush before she continued. "I'm not done."

Tucked in the farthest corner was a green velvet settee placed before an arched window that displayed a false landscape of an eternally overcast garden. The cushions were deeply set with pillows that felt as plush as clouds, and flowering ivy hung from the bookshelves that surrounded her in all directions. The library smelled of salt water and tobacco. Of worn leather and musky flowers and the pages of old books—a special touch from Aris. Another one of his additions was the towering Christmas tree that stood in the room's center, strung with tiny twinkling lights and pine cones, the tips of them frosted white as if they'd just been plucked from the snow. And on the shelves sat everything she could ever want and a million different stories she never thought she needed. It was a place where time meant nothing and a person could become forever lost. She could spend the rest of her life perusing these shelves and never grow bored. For it was dreamed up by her own mind, after all.

"It's perfect," she whispered as a star shot across her inky sky, leaving a trail of gossamer that she would have never thought of painting. There was such a swelling of emotion rising within Blythe's chest that she spun to face Aris, beaming as brightly as the moon above. Despite everything on her mind and the ache in her bones, one look at Aris was all it took for a wash of calm to settle over her. It helped, too, that his eyes mirrored her delight.

"Should you want for anything else, paint it. The magic will listen." He stepped forward then, brushing his thumb down the length of her cheek. It came away blue. "Do try to get more of the paint on the canvas next time, though. You're wearing half of it."

Blythe could have blushed. She could have come up with some clever retort. But instead she reached behind her for the paint and dipped two fingers into the closest colors before dragging them quickly across Aris's chin.

"Speak for yourself, " she told him simply. "You're wearing even more than I am."

It took Aris only a second to overcome his surprise before he spun toward Blythe with a devious air. He lunged forward, reaching around her for the paints. Blythe squealed as Aris surrounded her, trying to wrangle a tube of paint from him as he managed a bright blue handprint along her dress.

"You brute!" She jumped on him, wrapping her legs around his body as she tried to wrestle the paint from his grip. "I liked this dress!"

Aris wrapped his free arm beneath her, brow quirking as he observed their positions—him with one hand up and holding a tube of paint, and the other below Blythe and propping her up as she'd pounced on him. Amusement brimming in his words, he whispered, "Take the dress off and I'll fix it for you."

The bluntness of his words surprised her. Blythe stilled as Aris backed her slowly against the nearest wall, step by languid step. He gave her plenty of time to unfold herself from him. To untangle herself and slip away from this situation. Instead, Blythe gave little thought to her actions as she pressed a kiss to his lips.

Aris froze, and at first Blythe tried to pull back, understanding what a fool she must have been to get so caught up in the moment, especially given all that had happened the last time. But before she could claw her way out of her own skin and disappear into the ether, Aris dropped the tube of paint to the floor and held her close.

Her body burned beneath his touch, new and familiar all at once. She'd tasted his lips only twice prior, yet they already felt achingly familiar, as if they'd been molded to fit hers. And though she and Aris hadn't personally taken their relationship to the level of her visions, she craved the intimacy of his phantom touch. Blythe knew what his hands would feel like against her bare skin. How he would handle her not like some fragile creature but with a fervent passion. His hand stroked the length of her hair, taking a fistful as he cupped her cheek in his palm. With every touch, Life's memories bled together with her own, urging her forward. Confirming what Blythe had already known for a long while—in every sense of the word, she wanted him.

And she knew at that moment that he felt the same. She could feel it in the press of his body against hers. In his touch as his fingers curled around her jaw, thumb brushing across her bottom lip. Desire glazed his eyes, though there was sharpness to them, too. A pinch between his brows that made her wonder whether he might once again flee.

"You are the most infuriating creature." As abrasive as he was, there was a tenderness in those words. A gentle laughter that was as soft as the bend of an owl's wing. "You have been a thorn in my side since day one. There have been times when I've wanted nothing more than to have you out of my life, and I have imagined countless ways that I might be rid of you. Countless ways that I might quiet that filthy mouth of yours. Yet since the moment I saw you stalking the halls of my home, I've also felt something stirring that I do not understand, but that I've not felt in a very long time. And this time I will not run from it."

Blythe sucked in a breath when she felt his hand slip along her thigh. "Tell me that this is all right, or tell me to leave and we can pretend that this never happened. But tell me something, Sweetbrier."

Breath tight in her throat, it was all Blythe could do to whisper, "This is more than all right." And then his lips were upon her, his hand moving farther up as the other braced her. Blythe was used to soft touches. Used to people treating her like a porcelain doll, always on the verge of breaking. What she wasn't used to was fingers that curled against her skin and tore off her stockings. A mouth that drank her in as if she was the ambrosia of the gods.

She gasped as they stumbled back into one of the bookshelves, her back arching as Aris lowered himself to his knees. Her bustle disappeared beneath his fingertips as he kissed the delicate skin of her inner thigh and then up inch by inch, until her legs buckled and he drew a sharp breath from her lips.

"It seems that I've found a way to keep you quiet, after all," he teased, taunting her with languid kisses that she could no longer take. Blythe curled her fingers in Aris's hair, eyes fluttering shut as she guided his lips higher. She bit back a cry when he willingly obliged.

None of her late night trysts or nights spent curious and alone in her room could compare to the pleasure that shot through her body as his tongue slid across her. She felt like a boat on a storming sea, riding fierce waves that threatened to topple her. Blythe let them come, one hand buried in his hair and the other gripping the shelf for balance. Her breaths grew more ragged by the minute, and while this was by no means the wisest thing to do when she was already so dizzy, it was exactly what she needed. A few minutes to tune out the world and forget about everything else but the man between her thighs. To make sense of him.

The way Aris's hands roved her body made Blythe feel like she was something to be praised. Like she was the most captivating sculpture and he was but a patron admiring every square inch of the work. He tasted her, teased her, lingering whenever he drew a moan from her lips. But never for too long.

He was drawing it out. Savoring each taste of her skin and every ounce of pleasure that he earned. She tightened her grip in his hair as the pressure within her mounted, begging for a release she found only when Aris's eyes flicked up to her, alight with an undeniable hunger that sent her over the edge. She arched into him as pleasure crashed into her with waves that left her breathless. Only when she could take it no more did Aris peel away, far too satisfied with himself as he rose to his feet. He took her chin in his hand, bending to capture her mouth in another kiss.

Seeing him so smug did things to Blythe's body that she didn't know were possible. Power thrummed through him, raw and ravenous, and she ached for more.

Aris took her hips in hand, a puff of amusement slipping through his lips when he caught her staring. "Do you like what you see, Sweetbrier?"

She turned from him, casting a tart expression at the wall. "I'm not giving you the satisfaction of an answer."

Aris's laughter flowed as freely as air. "Words are not the only form of answers, love." He bent to ensnare her lips in his, and Blythe leaned closer, pressing against the hardness of his body. Slowly, however, Aris leaned away.

"Rest, Sweetbrier," he said, peeling back with a willpower that Blythe simply did not have. "There will be opportunities for us once you're feeling back to your spitfire self."

He adjusted himself then, clearing his throat and smoothing out his clothing. It was as disheveled as she'd ever seen him, and everything about the sight set Blythe's cravings for him ablaze.

She tried to tip her head back. To cool herself. But she just couldn't stop staring even as he backed toward her door.

"Merry Christmas," he whispered, a smile tugging his lips as he opened it. "Enjoy your library."

CHAPTER TWENTY-FIVE

It wasn't a lack of comfort that kept Blythe awake late into the witching hours. On the contrary, she had nearly merged with the pillows on her chaise and was quite certain that she would be spending the majority of her nights sleeping beneath the stars in this library. The fox seemed to enjoy it, too. Blythe wasn't sure when the beastly thing had managed to sneak in, but she listened to its sleepy grunts as she stared up at the sky.

She could still feel Aris's touch burning into her skin and sank into the memory of his lips against hers. Had she felt more herself, Blythe would have kept him in her library, learning every inch of his body and giving into her most primal desires. Such wanting, however, was not the only thing keeping Blythe awake.

Her fingers tapped against the spine of a book, wishing that the past week had been a fever dream so that she could steady her mind on the pages and get lost in its story.

But Blythe couldn't stop thinking about Solanine and her

threats, or of the power that thrummed within her own blood. She tipped her head back, a weariness in her bones. For a month Life's ghost had plagued her, skirting the corners of her mind whenever Blythe least wanted her. Even now she could hear echoes of the woman's laughter reverberating through her skull.

Mila was everywhere, taunting Blythe with knowledge that she didn't have. With a history that Blythe was only beginning to recollect.

"I tire of your games," Blythe whispered, not to the room but to whatever it was that rested within her. To *Life*. "If you have business with me, then tell me why and let us be done with it."

No sooner had she spoken than she doubled over with a cry, hands flying to her temples. It was like her mind was being cracked in two as an image beat against her skull.

Blythe gritted through the pain, not wanting Aris to overhear her struggle. At once she regretted her challenge, terrified by whatever it was that seemed to be trying to escape from within her. Yet the more she second-guessed herself and tried to force Life away in a panic, the harder Life pushed back, squeezing until Blythe could take it no more.

She collapsed against her pillow, struggling for breath and too weak to fight her off. "Fine!" Blythe spat, tears prickling from the pain. "Show me, then. Show me why you're here!"

Blythe shut her eyes and let Life's thoughts fill her own.

The first thing Blythe saw was a flourishing garden and an unmistakable woman sitting with her bare feet pressed into the soil. It was the same woman Blythe had followed through the halls of Wisteria weeks ago. The same one whose portrait loomed over the heart of the palace.

Life wore a muslin gown of white, hair as pale as milk spilling over her shoulders and down to her hips as she leaned with her back against a towering wisteria tree. Cupped in her palms was a handful of dirt.

In every picture that Blythe had seen of Life, the woman's eyes had always been missing. Looking at her now, she understood why. Aris had been doing the woman a disservice when he'd said that her eyes were silver. They were as gray as storm clouds, with flecks of onyx dotted across them like constellations. The colors melted together into an impossible hue that no paintbrush could capture, and were set behind pale lashes.

To Blythe's surprise, whatever she was seeing did not feel like past memories. She did not inhabit the woman's skin, but instead crouched before her. Life's eyes blinked slowly as they stared at Blythe, and the woman reached a hand out for her. Somehow there wasn't so much as a hint of dirt marring her fair palm.

Blythe felt no hesitation to take hold of the offered hand. In fact, it seemed at that moment that nothing could feel more natural as she took a seat beside Life, who was silent as she wove her fingers through Blythe's and guided her hand to the soil.

At first Blythe grimaced, for the soil was cold and making a home for itself beneath her fingernails. Soon, though, her body relaxed into the motion of shaping the earth between her hands. Her skin warmed, a pulse of heat striking her chest when the earth between her palms began to shift, shaping itself.

Blythe nearly pulled away, startled, but Life held fast as a plump, squat figure with rounded arms and stubby legs emerged from the soil. Blythe's jaw tightened as she watched it twitch, then rise from the ground. She gasped, unmoving when the creature toddled over her ankles toward a bush full of berries beside her. She expected it to feel repulsive. Expected her body to erupt in shudders as it used her like a stepping stool. Instead, the strange creature was warm and pleasant to the touch, and Blythe found her steady breaths returning.

"It won't hurt you. Keep watching." The voice that spoke wasn't human. Never had Blythe heard a sound so soft, flowing as gracefully as water in a fountain. The voice did not seem to come from a single body, but from the trees themselves. From each and every leaf that rustled in the wind, and from each blade of grass that bowed to the weight of their bodies.

It was a voice that could not be ignored. One that had Blythe's head swiveling to watch the creature pluck two berries from the nearby bush. Small as it was, the effort nearly caused it to fall. Still, after a few more tries it managed to snap off the berries and plop them onto its face in the spot where eyes might go. As it rushed to join others with tiny twigs sprouting from their heads, or leaves draping from them like hair, Blythe realized she felt nothing but peace. The more she watched, the cuter the strange creatures became.

"They are rather cute, aren't they?" Mila parroted, as though Blythe had voiced the thought aloud. "We begin from the earth, just as we end. It's the most magnificent thing." Her toes curled into the soil, and she lifted her eyes to focus them on Blythe.

"We?" Blythe's voice felt so much smaller in comparison. So much quieter. "You mean . . . those are—"

"Souls, yes." The sun shone a little brighter with Mila's butter-soft laughter. "You're seeing them in their rawest form. When a soul has found its desire to live, I will provide it a body," Mila explained. "From there, it's given a journey to have here on this earth. Then, one day, that journey will end and its body will return to the soil while its soul carries on. That is the way of things—Life, Fate, and then Death. Every role has its part, and each of those parts is as beautiful as the next."

The strange creatures were toppling over one another, playing like children. Blythe's attention narrowed when one of them stopped suddenly. It had only a second to wave at the others before it winked out of existence in a flash of gold. Life drew her knees to her chest, resting her arms upon them.

"Onward it goes to discover its fate," she mused, joy crinkling the corners of her eyes. "I wonder what story Aris will weave for it."

Though they were allegedly meant to be one and the same, Blythe felt none of the joy that her other half seemed to. "Is that truly all there is?" she asked. "Life, Fate, and then Death?"

"Of course not." Mila's laugh was as delicate as wind chimes. "So much more goes into a life, dear self. And there are more out there, just like us. You've already met one of them."

Solanine.

The back of Blythe's neck prickled with nerves. "What does she want with me?"

The sorrow in Life's eyes was painful to behold. "It's not your fault," she soothed. "You didn't know, but now you must fix it. You've upset the balance."

"The balance of *what*?" In the back of her mind Blythe knew she was still asleep on the chaise in her library, and that reality could pluck her away from whatever dream space Life had drawn her to at any moment. She had to calm herself. To breathe deeply no matter how much her mind was churning, if only to remain there a few moments longer.

"There are rules you must learn," Mila said. "Most will come naturally, but others may not. We've all been tempted. We get too attached to humans and make foolish mistakes, but those mistakes have consequences.

"I am part of you," she continued. "Your memories will come in time, if you choose to let them, but I cannot tell you what you do not already know in your soul. You have to realize it yourself—there is but one rule to the power you wield. There is but one thing you can do that would forever upset the balance of this world. Think, Blythe. You know what it is."

Blythe wanted to argue. To demand that Mila hand her the answer and not waste any more precious time. But the deeper the question seeped into her mind, the more Blythe felt its answer searing her tongue. "The dead," she said. "That's what Solanine meant about the horse. I'm not supposed to bring anyone back from the dead."

"No matter how much you may want to. She is a distracted sort, but should such a thing ever happen, breaking that rule would only invite Chaos."

Chaos. She should have guessed that's who Solanine was.

"So what, Chaos wants me to kill the horse? To pay for the life that I gave?" Blythe snorted. "It was hardly even dead."

Mila shut her eyes, her sigh rousing a gale of wind that brushed along the trees, making the leaves sing. "I cannot say more than what you already know. Chaos reigns when the balance of nature is upset, and you, more than anyone, must respect the natural balance of this world. All who live must one day die."

Another one of the strange creatures winked out in Blythe's periphery with a golden flash, and she found her thoughts straying to Aris. Was he sitting in his study with a needle in hand, constructing the fate of the soul Life had just plucked from the earth? Would he be able to give her the answers that Mila couldn't?

"He's searching for you, you know," Blythe told the woman. "He's been searching for a very long time."

"I know." Mila reached forward to take Blythe's hand in hers once more. With the soil between them, Blythe hadn't realized just how formidable the woman was. She did not have the delicate, gentle hands of a lady. They were strong and calloused, commanding enough that a squeeze from them drew Blythe's attention to the fire that shone in the woman's eyes. "Which is why I'm glad that he's finally found us."

Mila's smile was a marvel, as dazzling as light itself and impossible to turn away from.

"I will not bother you again." Mila's words were a promise. "But that doesn't mean I am not still a part of your soul. You may rest easy knowing that I am but a small part, for you have had centuries to learn and grow from when that soul belonged only to me. The life you have lived is different from the one that I did. I am your origin, and you are my future. We are different, Blythe. But history has a way of repeating itself, and you cannot let it. You must fix what has been set in motion." There was a wateriness to her words that drew Blythe's focus. Only then did she notice that Mila was diffusing at the edges, fading with the light.

"What *history*?" Blythe demanded. "If you want me to understand, then do not give me riddles!" But it was too late. Mila could say no more, and Blythe was tossed back into the throes of reality.

CHAPTER TWENTY-SIX

Blythe could still feel the mud caked beneath her fingernails as she snapped her eyes open. She threw herself from the chaise in a panic; it felt like a hundred tiny insects were crawling inside her, buried beneath the first layer of her skin.

Her library was still just that—her library, a placid dreamscape where rain pattered against the window and a mighty hearth warred with the winter chill. Had it not been for the soil dirtying her fingertips, she might have believed that her discussion with Mila had been a dream. Truthfully, she wished it *had* been, for as pleasant as Mila had been, Blythe couldn't wrap her mind around the fact that she'd spoken with a ghost. How Signa managed to do it on the daily was beyond her understanding.

Blythe asked the room to make her a river that glinted silver beneath the moonlight, and in that river she scrubbed her hands clean before hurrying out of the library to hunt for Aris. It didn't take long to find him—he'd left the door to his study ajar.

With quiet steps Blythe approached Life's portrait. She must have passed it several hundred times, only now she felt the chill of the water against the woman's skin and had the memory of her gown being tugged by the pond. As certain as she was that she was no longer dreaming, the hum of insects irked the corners of her mind and Blythe couldn't silence what sounded like the quiet chirping of foxes and rattling bushes behind her.

When Blythe scrutinized the portrait, she recognized that Life had not been alone in it. Aris had been shading himself beneath the trees, and Blythe heard his voice teasing her from the depths of this memory. So distracted was she in her effort to make out the words that she nearly missed his true voice calling out to her in the present.

"So the dead awakens," Aris called. His voice was oddly hoarse. "Come in, Sweetbrier. I've something to show you."

His voice drew her to the present. No longer did she feel the lapping water at her waist but instead the polished marble beneath her feet. She curled her slippered toes against it, grounding herself. As quickly as it came, Life's memory slipped away like a falling star.

She forced down the weariness in her body as she crossed the threshold. And while Blythe knew better than to be surprised, she had a fleeting sense of disbelief that what she was seeing could be real. For how else was she to explain the factory that awaited behind a portrait?

Probably, she supposed, the same way that one might explain a library of stars and windows of forever-dreary skies. She doubted there would ever come a day when she would walk into one of Aris's creations and feel nothing. When she wouldn't find his mind positively magical.

Blythe followed his voice, ducking under rows of tapestries strung on moving lines. She had to weave through them, stumbling in the dim light and tripping over a corner of a rug. She threw out her arms to catch herself, only to be halted by a thousand golden threads before she could bump into one of the creations.

"Mind your step," Aris said from behind her, his words low and heavy with exhaustion. "You don't want to touch those."

Aris's shirt was looser than when she'd last seen him, the top buttons undone and his sleeves disheveled and rolled up to his arms. There was a splash of red paint on his collar that made her blush at the memory of how it'd gotten there.

"What is this place?" she asked as the threads unwound themselves from her, disappearing into a slant of light.

"It's where a soul comes to have its fate woven." He waved her forward, maneuvering through the room with the grace of someone who'd walked these floors a thousand times. Blythe tried her best to keep up, craning her neck this way and that, curious where the souls might be hiding. The room wasn't chilled as was usual when Death or a spirit was nearby, and she could see no tiny mud creatures like the one Mila had helped her build.

"I don't see any spirits," Blythe whispered, not wanting to offend them in case any could hear her. Aris only laughed.

"I didn't mean it so literally. This room is fueled by my magic. Even when I'm without a needle in hand, fates are forever being woven. It's the perk of my powers, and I suppose the powers of those like me. Regardless of where we are or what we're doing, so long as we exist then the world will continue as it should."

That, at least, answered the question of her own abilities. It stood to reason that if Fate and the others had a purpose, then Life must, too. But Blythe had existed for twenty-one years without knowing what she was capable of. She had never crafted a life in her hands, nor had she so much as glimpsed a soul until moments ago. There were a million things she didn't understand, but at least she could feel relief about this.

She glanced again to the tapestries that emerged from God only knew where. Each one that slid into view was empty at first, gaining stitches as it traveled across its line. On the opposite side, coming in from the reverse wall, were stitches that undid themselves thread by thread until they ended up bare. Where the threads *went*, however, was a curious question indeed. For while she watched them fall to the floor, they disappeared before she could blink.

She had to give Aris some credit; it was meticulously organized.

As odd a place as this self-sustained factory was, it captivated her. Though Blythe told herself to keep close to Aris, she found herself distracted by the glistening threads and wandering closer to the tapestries, desperate to understand the stories they foretold. She stretched out her finger to skim it along one's surface without any awareness of what she was doing, but Aris caught her hand before she could make contact.

"As nosy as ever," he chided without any harshness. "Fight the temptation. Should you touch those threads with your bare skin, you'll feel like you're inside someone else's body, experiencing their entire life in a matter of seconds."

"Seconds?" Blythe snatched her hand back, clutching it to her chest as though it were primed to betray her. "How is that possible?"

"In the same way that all this is possible, which is to say that I have no idea. In this room, only seconds would have passed. But you'll feel every minute of their life. Every breath, every ache, every last piece of who they are. And when you are yourself again, you'll feel lost in your own body."

Blythe clamped her teeth tight, keeping her hands tucked to her sides.

"And that's what you do each day?" Terror weakened her voice. "You disappear like that? Into another life?"

A hint of a smile cleaved Aris's face. "For the ones I weave by hand, yes. At least in a sense. I've grown to become more aware that it's not my own body or memories that I'm experiencing, but ones that I'm in control of weaving. Still, I'm sure you understand now why I prefer some variety in my stories."

She did, though Blythe could hardly stomach the idea of being trapped in such a state. She'd always known that Aris held more power than she could fathom, but to live so many lives . . . to be so many different people while still trying to stay true to himself. She wondered how he managed not to split at the seams each time he came back to himself.

They came to a desk at the back of the room. Upon it was what was probably meant to be another tapestry, though compared to the others it was an abomination, disfigured and fraying at the edges.

"Is that normal?" She bent to get a closer look at the monstrosity. Where the other tapestries started with a thread of silver and ended with one of black, this one was reversed. And if that wasn't odd enough, no other colors existed in between. There was only a starting stitch of black, and everything else that followed was silver. Even as it lay spread atop the table, new stitches wove into the tapestry. And yet, somehow, it never appeared to grow any longer.

Aris lifted the tapestry, holding it at a distance as though the thing might somehow soil him. "It certainly is not *normal,*" he scoffed, squinting as he twisted it from front to back to inspect the endless stitching. "I was looking for any signs of who might be responsible for Thorn Grove's vandalisms when I heard it calling out. This abomination even *sounds* hideous, as grating as a bow dragged across too-taut strings."

Blythe listened for the sound but heard nothing. "Who does it belong to?"

Aris's frown deepened. He pried one hand from his gloves with the help of his teeth and brushed a bare finger down the length of the silver threads. "That's the strangest part; I haven't a clue. I can touch the threads all I like, but I see nothing. I've only ever known one other like this. It was years ago, but the entire tapestry turned black before I could piece together whose it was."

If it was true that silver was meant to represent Life, then perhaps this monstrosity belonged to her. Blythe lifted her own hand to inspect it, and when Aris didn't draw away, she held her breath and gingerly tapped the threads with a finger. Her breath loosened when nothing happened. At least, she hadn't *seen* anything. But the moment she eased away from the tapestry her stomach hollowed as if someone had dug a shovel through her insides.

“I don’t see anything, either.” She pressed a hand over her mouth, which began to prickle as though she’d eaten something tart. “But good God, Aris. It’s sickening. Can you not burn the thing?”

“I already tried.” Aris tossed it back on the table and promptly wiped his hands with a handkerchief. “Even the flames want no part of it. Your tapestry and Signa’s were odd, too, though they were nothing like this.”

She heard Mila’s warning—*you must fix what has been set in motion*—as her attention fell to the tapestry once more. It had not changed in the seconds she’d looked away, yet she still had to rub her hands over her arms to ease the rising goose bumps. The longer she stared at it, the more ill she felt, as if the ground were trying to swallow her whole.

“You think it’s connected to whatever is happening at Thorn Grove.” It wasn’t a question, but Aris nodded.

“I don’t believe in coincidence.”

Looking at the tapestry, neither did she.

“Whatever it is, I will handle it,” Aris promised, the authority in his voice making Blythe realize just how terrified she must have seemed. She was still so cold. Still fighting wave after wave of goose bumps and a churning stomach since touching the tapestry. A sudden cough rattled her lungs, and her fear turned to alarm at the spray of blood on her fingertips. Aris was beside her within the second, one hand steadying Blythe as more blood spilled from her throat onto her trembling hands.

“Breathe.” It was an urgent, whispered command that Blythe had no use for. It took every ounce of her effort to draw the breaths in, her eyes watering as she collapsed against him. Her mouth tasted of iron, and she realized with horror that part of the blood had come not from her throat, but from the roof of her mouth. She pressed her tongue to the spot, letting out a cry when she felt the rough, painful patches.

Sores.

Blythe clutched her throat, praying that this was a dream. That she would wake up any minute to find that she was still lying on her library chaise.

"Aris." Blythe grabbed for his hand, heart thundering as she tried to process what was happening.

Had someone fed her something? Given her something?

For over a month she'd been so tired but had believed it a passing illness. Remnants of an old poisoning that she was still recovering from, or a lingering cold.

But as her vision filled with flashes of dirt and her skin itched as if invisible insects were crawling on her, she knew the truth of it. Her husband was right—nothing was a coincidence.

"Aris." She whispered his name again, fingers digging into his skin as she tasted belladonna on her tongue. "It's Chaos."

PART THREE

CHAPTER TWENTY-SEVEN

Aris

Elijah Hawthorne arrived before dawn. If he thought it odd that Aris opened the door of Wisteria Gardens and not a servant, he kept his opinions to himself as he followed his son-in-law through the foyer and into a warmly lit parlor where two cups of steaming tea had been set out. Neither man drank theirs, too consumed by the silence.

Elijah's hands clenched around the handle of his teacup, his knuckles so white that they were nearly colorless as Aris paced before the hearth, unable to sit. It wasn't as if he could console the man, for what was there to be said? He knew better than to lie to Elijah with sweet words—not when he couldn't read Blythe's tapestry to see whether there was any merit to them.

How much easier it would have been if he'd only ignored her from the first day she'd set foot in Wisteria. How unfortunate it was that his blood burned at the thought of her ailment, or that he wished to tear through every tapestry he'd ever woven to hunt down information about why Chaos might possibly be interested in her. Blythe was a leech on his mind, sucking him dry of all rational thoughts. From the time he awoke crafting plans for that day's adventure to when he set his head upon his pillow and let his mind replay memories of her laughter, she engrossed him, stuck in his head like an inescapable song.

Aris had fallen for someone before, and what a fool he'd been for it. For his life was infinite, and Blythe's was a short and fragile thing. It would have been better if she died now, before such feelings ensnared him. She was a parasite, one of which Aris had no idea how to free himself from.

So why was it that he so desperately wanted her to live? To watch her eyes light up when she tasted the richest chocolate, and to see her fall so heartbreakingly in love with the world he thought he'd grown numb to?

Aris has never minded the passing of time. He could go ages before he ever cared enough to glance up from his work and discover how many years had passed. But every moment with Blythe was one in which he found himself wishing that time could be infinite. This girl had dug herself a home beneath his skin, and his body burned every time he earned a smile from her lips.

He despised her for it, and yet he could not pull himself away.

Aris sat straighter when he heard the doctor clambering down the stairs, only vaguely listening as he prattled on about how Blythe was stable. He didn't wait for the doctor to finish speaking before he pushed past the man and up the stairs to Blythe's suite.

Blythe would be fine. She had to be.

Elijah was on his heels as Aris opened the door to Blythe sitting upright in a chair, dressed in a pale muslin gown. She smiled as they entered, but not even a beautiful dress and combed hair could hide the bags beneath her eyes or the way her skin clung to her bones. It didn't matter how much time she'd put into playing healthy; she couldn't hide the truth that had Elijah's eyes darkening.

Aris knew all too well what happened when Chaos struck. He knew of the plagues that befell the world, and the lives that were ruthlessly taken when balance was not kept. It had happened to Mila when Death had tried to keep her alive all those years ago, and now it was coming for Blythe.

But why?

Elijah closed the space between himself and his daughter in three long strides, but when he tried to take her hand, she waved him off.

"I'm well enough not to warrant your fussing," Blythe said, scratching absently at her cuticles. "I appreciate everyone's concern, but I have no need for coddling."

It was a lie. Two months unable to stray far from someone made it easy to learn their tells. Aris only ever needed to glance at the skin around her nails to learn Blythe's truths. "You need rest," he said. There was a strand of hair that was threatening to fall into her face. As much as his hand ached to reach out and tuck it behind her ear, he held himself back, gritting his teeth when Elijah brushed it aside instead.

"I can take you to Thorn Grove," Elijah told his daughter. "You'll be comfortable there, where we managed to remedy you once before."

"She wasn't this ill until she *went* to Thorn Grove," Aris argued. He wished with everything in him that he could bite his tongue and stay out of it. That he could let fate take its course before he grew any more attached to this woman.

It wouldn't have been the first time he'd been physically attracted to a person since Mila's death, but loathe as he was to admit it, this was more than physical attraction alone. And in the face of it, Aris stood no chance.

"She'll remain at Wisteria, where I can monitor her." Aris stepped closer, speaking in a whisper meant only for Elijah. "Try as she may to persuade us otherwise, we both know that she is unwell. There are too many people at Thorn Grove. Too many variables. And if I know your daughter at all, then I'm certain that she will not drop her guard around you, Elijah. She will not relax, because she won't want you to see her pain."

For a long while Elijah said nothing, scratching at his nail beds just the same as Blythe. The more Aris witnessed them together, the more he recognized how alike they were. Each was a firecracker concealed by flesh, just waiting for the smallest spark to ignite. The man's eyes blazed as he looked Aris over, but Aris held steady until the flames within them snuffed out.

"I don't want to leave her," he whispered, the words like a soul shattered.

Aris wasn't sure *why* he was even bothering to entertain this man. He could let his threads weave around Elijah's body and throw him out of Wisteria. He could seep his own thoughts deep into the man's psyche until he trusted Aris more than he trusted anyone.

But he'd promised Blythe that he would not touch Elijah, and even had that promise never been made, Aris still wasn't certain that he would have used his powers. As infuriating as it was, for one reason or another he found himself wanting to impress Elijah Hawthorne. Not only that, but he wanted the man to *like* him.

It was pathetic how much Aris had fallen.

He stepped closer, clasping Elijah by the arm and bowing his head low. "I will take care of your daughter, Elijah. I swear it on my life."

Oh, how he meant it. Despite all his conflicting emotions and terror at the realization of what was happening to him, Aris meant every word. He would find Chaos, and he would burn her alive if that was what it took.

Elijah, too, must have sensed that sincerity, for it was the only reason he was able to peel away.

It took another ten minutes for Elijah to say his goodbyes and ensure that Blythe was not about to keel over on the spot before he could convince himself to leave. When the door shut behind him, Blythe slumped into her seat with the deepest sigh Aris had ever known. Just as he'd expected, she all but crumpled into the pillows, the exhaustion more evident now that her father had left. Aris wondered if perhaps she was a better liar than he'd given her credit for.

"He's gone?" she asked, breathless despite her position stuffed into the sofa and masquerading as one of the cushions.

"He's gone," Aris echoed, moving to sit beside her. Small as she was, somehow she still took up the entire chaise, leaving him only a sliver of an edge to balance himself on. "You should try—"

"Tell me to get some rest again and I will rip out your tongue." The severity of the threat stalled his words. "I know what happens if I lie in bed while sick. One day I will be molded to it and will spend my days staring at the ceiling and waiting for your brother to come fetch me."

Aris's mouth soured at the thought. "That's not what I was going to say," he lied. "I was going to suggest that you tell me how you're truly feeling and how you'd like to spend your day."

Her eyes sparked, and good God did he feel it like a lightning strike to his core. He swallowed, hands balled into fists at his side to steady the emotion. How easily he had allowed himself to get wrapped up in this girl. This beautiful, deplorable wife of his.

She was meant to be the bane of his existence. A hindrance to his every waking moment. So why was it that seeing that spark in her eyes felt like it had awoken something within him? Why was it that he felt the need to earn that look over and over again and draw delight from those pretty lips?

He was meant to be looking for Mila. And yet in that moment Aris feared all the things he might do to please this woman before him. This infernal, infuriating creature.

"I need to see Signa," she told him, but Aris only shook his head.

"Give me your day," he said. "See Signa this evening if you must, but give me your day."

While Blythe looked primed to argue, something halted the words on her tongue. Aris wondered what she might be thinking. Whether she, too, felt the same conflict warring in her heart. The same draw to him as he did her. Aris knew that she did physically, at least, for she was young and curious and horrible at concealing the emotions on her face.

Whether it was beyond that physical attraction, however… Aris's throat constricted at the thought, unsure if he wanted to find out.

"Then take me somewhere," Blythe whispered. "Do not keep me locked away like some fragile heirloom, Aris. If I'm to give you my day, then take me away from here and show me something that only you can."

He did not care for the way her words sounded like a final plea. Though he had every instinct to lock her away in an effort to keep her safe, if Blythe wanted to see the world, then he would show her the world. Whether she realized it or not, he was putty between her palms. He would spend every minute plucking the stars from the sky to deliver a bouquet of constellations if that's what it took to please her.

Because the truth of it could no longer be ignored. For the second time in his life, Aris Dryden was falling in love. Only this time, he prayed that fate would be on his side.

CHAPTER TWENTY-EIGHT

ARIS BROUGHT THEM TO THE TOP OF A LUSH HILL, WHERE BLADES OF ripe grass and poppies as red as rubies scratched greetings against Blythe's calves. The sky was an impossible shade of blue so lovely that it seemed magicked from a painting and was filled with clouds so perfectly constructed that Blythe wondered how much had been painted by Aris's hand.

Balmy wind swept through her hair and kicked up her skirts, a welcome pairing to the sun that bore down on them. Blythe tipped her head back to welcome it.

They overlooked a tiny town built into the cliffside, set upon thin roads and switchbacks pocked with wildflowers. In the distance stretched endless acres of farmland—fields of crops and sprawling pens filled with animals. Blythe tried to take a step toward one of the red-roofed barns only to wobble, off-balance since their arrival. As much as she appreciated the ease of it, Blythe wasn't certain that she'd ever become adjusted to Aris's method of transportation.

As he reached for her arm to help steady her, Blythe noticed he was dressed differently than he'd been moments ago. Simpler than she'd ever seen him, his black pants casual and his white tunic loose at the collar, top buttons undone. At any moment he looked ready to pick up a shovel and begin turning the fields, and as she stared at the sculpting of his arms and the way the sunlight cast a sheen of gold across his tanned skin, Blythe thought of their prior night together and the way her body had burned for his touch.

She would speak with Signa that night. She would confide in her cousin, share all that she knew, and determine a plan to face Chaos. But in the event that she got it wrong—in the event that Chaos won—Blythe would not spend her final moments stuck alone in her bedroom suite counting the whorls in the wallpaper. This time when she faced her impending doom, she would spend it traversing the countryside with a handsome man.

"This place is as beautiful as a painting," she said, bracing herself against him as they started across a stretch of grassy plains and toward the town. Her steps were slower and her breathing a little unsteady, but at any moment Aris could whisk them back to the comfort of Wisteria if need be.

"It is," he agreed. "But we're not here for the town."

Aris slowed to a leisurely stroll to help guide her. It would have been so much easier to appear directly in the distant village, but she was glad for the view. Not to mention that trying to explain to someone how they'd arrived out of thin air didn't seem like the most fruitful way to spend the day.

Like Brude, this town was unfamiliar to her. Despite how many times she tore through her own memories, Blythe couldn't place ever seeing it depicted in any book or museum portrait. The entire town fit along one long stretch of road, and it didn't feel oppressive in the same way the giant factories and industrial buildings an hour outside of Thorn Grove did. She tried to place where they could be by the language of the townsfolk who watched them with the keen eyes of those who didn't often have visitors, but she couldn't quite place it.

"We're far north, in a town called Hateno," Aris told her, ducking under eaves as he led her through a small alleyway where grass sprouted between every sporadic stone. It seemed that at one point someone had tried to turn the streets into a cobblestone path only to give up halfway through. Blythe stepped gingerly, not wanting to trample any of the new growth.

"Have you visited this place often?" she asked as she fought to keep up with Aris, who navigated the streets with expert precision. "You seem to know it well."

They were getting deeper into the village, passing through the streets as they made their way toward the farmland. Each step had Blythe's chest growing hot and her cheeks flushing from the mildest exertion.

"I've woven the fates of all who have lived here," Aris told her, offering Blythe an arm to loop her hand around. "And thus I know these streets as well as if they were my own. I've visited once or twice in recent years, but the village is small and I haven't wanted to draw attention."

Knowing all that she did about Aris, Blythe guessed that whatever he'd brought her to see must be remarkable to hold his interest.

She squeezed his arm tighter, wishing she had the energy to hasten her steps. At this rate, though, she supposed she should have counted herself lucky to still have the energy to even be out of bed. She drew each breath slowly, trying not to let on to just how winded she was or how her ankles had swollen. Her thighs were burning with the exertion, and while she knew that staying in bed was the smarter option, she couldn't bear it. For as long as she could, she would *live*, no matter how exhausted she was.

Aris helped her over rolling hills dotted with cattle, pausing while Blythe petted each and every one and laughed as a small herd of sheep followed behind them. Soon, she and Aris came across a collection of withered old buildings, one of them a small house and another a large shed with a roof half sloped from the weather.

The world quieted as she approached, so still that it felt as though its embodiment was right there with her, bowing its head to listen as someone in that shed began to sing. It was music unlike any she'd ever known, a voice as smooth and free flowing as a summertime stream.

"What is this?" Blythe whispered as Aris maneuvered her closer, pulled toward the voice in a way she didn't understand. Blythe could spend an eternity rooted in that spot, lost to time for as long as the man inside continued to sing. She had never believed in angels until that moment, for how could a mere human ever sound so enchanting?

Aris gestured to a small hole in the shed, and Blythe pressed close to peer inside, though it was too dark to see much other than a man who shoveled hay as he sang. It seemed a few sheep had followed him, bleating happily every so often, but other than that, he was alone. For the life of her, Blythe could not understand how.

A voice like his should fill theaters and be written about in every paper throughout the world.

"This is who we came to see." Aris tucked an arm around Blythe's waist and drew her closer. She tried to ignore how her breath hitched at his touch.

"He's incredible," Blythe told him, though such a word hardly did justice to the man's talent, for he slipped effortlessly into a new song that reminded her of the summer sun upon her skin. The language was not one she knew, but there was no need for words when emotion seeped into his every breath. "He should be on a proper stage."

Aris hummed low in his throat. "He dreams of that. Some days he wonders what it might be like to sing beneath the burn of lights and capture the attention of a crowd of hundreds. He slips into his shed and imagines it's a theater filled with people who paid for the privilege of hearing him. Other nights, he wonders whether it would be worth it to turn his passion into a job and uproot his entire life and family to chase a dream. He's content in this place, with this life and these people. Who is to say what future might await him, should he decide to take the risk?"

It seemed so unfair that Blythe should get to hear this man when the rest of the world could not.

"And what will he decide?" she pressed, needing desperately to know. "Will he risk it?"

It was a long while before Aris answered, for both his attention and Blythe's were captured by the most effortless crescendo. Blythe hadn't realized her cheeks were damp until Aris brushed a thumb across her skin, soothing tears away.

"He will stay here," he said as a veil of quiet befell them. "He could have the entire world in the palm of his hand if he wanted it, but he chooses confirmed happiness rather than the gamble. Fear will stop him from taking a risk, as it does with so many."

Blythe felt each word like a blow to her gut. "But he could still change his mind, couldn't he?"

"Why should he? He will have a content life here, and you said yourself how wonderful that can be."

Her heart stuttered at the words. Because yes, that *was* wonderful, and she *had* meant it, but there was a void in her soul as the man stopped singing. He had ruined all other music for her, and she didn't understand how fear could keep such a talent from shining the way it was meant to.

She clutched Aris's hand, understanding now what he'd meant several weeks ago when he'd been so dissatisfied with one of his tapestries. How difficult it was to watch the most talented people allow fear to stop them from becoming all that they could be.

Still, she tried to tell herself that he was going to be content with his life. Always curious and wondering what could have been, perhaps, but happy all the same. And that counted for something.

Aris peeled away from the shed, pressed close enough for her to feel the rise and fall of his chest. His eyes skimmed down her body, taking in their situation before lifting to meet hers.

"I've been thinking a great deal about fear these days," he told her. "About how even I fall victim to it. Perhaps I have been rash in my judgments; from the outside, it's easy to see all the possibilities. To view someone like a chess piece, and know precisely where we might place them on our board." He lifted a tentative hand and set it against her cheek. Blythe stilled beneath his touch, not daring to breathe out of worry that it might scare him away.

"But when you *are* that piece, you see only what's in front of you. A looming king ready to call checkmate with no way to avoid the loss. For years I have felt bitterness toward every soul who bows to their fear. And yet I now find myself ruled by my own. You have bewitched me, Sweetbrier, and for that I am terrified."

Blythe wished for her feelings not to be true. Wished that she could still despise this man that her body yearned for. It would be so much easier that way, if he never learned the truth of who she was.

Blythe, too, was terrified. And yet she couldn't help but wonder what it might feel like to ignore that terror and give in to the desire to press against him. To give herself, body and soul, to a man she knew would care for it.

This time, she did not let the fear push her away. This time she acknowledged it, giving it the space and consideration it deserved without bowing to it as she lifted onto her toes to claim Aris's lips with hers.

Aris's touch was tentative at first, hesitant as his fingers splayed over the curve of her waist. Only as the kiss deepened did his hold on her tighten, those fingers eventually curling into her dress, pulling her against his body with a desperate want.

Blythe peppered soft kisses above the collar of his tunic. "You're always so put together. So polished. I like seeing you undone." Blythe gasped as he took hold of her hips, pressing her against the shed.

"Good, Sweetbrier." His voice was a raw husk, the brogue of it thicker than she'd ever heard. "I want to be undone by you."

His hand inched up the burning skin of her thigh, and suddenly they were in a room she at once knew belonged to Aris.

There were no lakes of midnight. No constellations pressed so low that she could reach out and snatch one from the sky. Instead, it looked as though they were in a shop. One gilded wall was filled with countless trinkets—strange coins, stacks of leather-bound journals, vases that appeared to be from an age long ago.... Another wall was made entirely of mosaic, bathing the room in a rainbow of diffused light as the midday sun shone through it. The bed was something out of a storybook, its back posts spiraling into a wisteria tree that canopied them. Aris set her upon it as a petal fell loose, gliding down onto the duvet.

Blythe hadn't thought his room would be so hypnotizing. But then again, Aris always did surprise her.

"I can stop," he whispered, and Blythe wondered whether he was feeling the same fear that pulsed through her. One that told her she was too thin. Too bony. That she would not compare to the wife he once had. That this was a bad idea.

But she thought of the singer—of the dream he wanted but was too afraid to chase—and buried those fears.

She wanted him. Wanted *this*. And so she took Aris's hand and slid it to the back of her gown, helping him slip it off.

For years she had avoided courting. Avoided anything more than fleeting whimsies and impulsive trysts, because no one had ever captured her attention. It had always felt like something was missing. Like a small piece of her had been carved out, and she'd been searching for a way to make it whole.

Now she understood why. All this time, she had been waiting for Aris.

He peeled off her chemise and she his tunic, layer by layer until they were bare skinned. Her breath loosened when their bodies connected, back arching as she savored his touch. The hands that roved over her body. That gripped her tight, not worried that she was some fragile thing so easily broken. The rhythm of his hips against hers, and how he lured pleasure from her lips with every motion. Golden threads ensnared her wrists, pinning her to the bed.

Thumb brushing down past her navel, to the most sensitive part of her, Aris asked, "Still despise me, Sweetbrier?"

In his ear Blythe whispered, "Don't get cocky."

His laugh was a throaty, brilliant sound that pushed her over the edge as he went deeper. There was no fear as she lost herself to him. No hesitation.

This was what had been missing. *This* was what her mind, her soul, her body, had been waiting for all this time.

With Aris, nothing had ever felt more right.

CHAPTER TWENTY-NINE

Aris

If there was one thing that Aris hated above all else, it was swallowing his pride.

He folded and unfolded his arms, unable to get comfortable as he paced the floor of his study. Signa had arrived moments ago to visit Blythe, and he could feel his brother lingering nearby.

Waiting.

Expectant.

A complete and total nuisance.

Death, too, must have known there was something wrong with Blythe, and if his persistence was any indicator, the fool likely wanted to help. Every cell in Aris's body told him to ignore his brother. Told him that he could figure this out on his own, and that Death could fall into a ditch and never emerge for all Aris cared.

But then he thought of Blythe. Of how long it had taken for her to trek through the hills of Hateno, trying and failing to mask her breathlessness and how easily her skin flushed with exertion. Her illness was becoming worse with each day. She'd been half delirious when she'd spoken of Chaos, but if it was true that the demon had somehow involved herself in Blythe's life . . .

Aris may have been arrogant, but he was no fool. Against Chaos, he stood no chance. He clenched his fists, steadying his rage as he prowled to the door and threw it open.

"Come in," he demanded, rolling his eyes as Death swept inside not a second later. His shadows leaked into the study, dimming the light so profusely that Aris sighed as his eyes readjusted.

"It's bad enough that you have to come here to drop off Signa," he grumbled. "Why haven't you left?"

"Because Blythe is sick and you need my help."

Aris's tongue burned with the threat of words he did not wish to speak aloud. Words that would have him indebted to his brother and build a bridge between them that he wasn't sure he was ready to cross. Once, Aris might have let pride make the decision for him. But with the memory of Blythe's laughter on his mind—as soft and lovely as a spring gale and plaguing his thoughts like an inescapable song—he turned to his brother and forced out the truth despite how much it pained him.

"It's Solanine," he said. "She's the reason Blythe has fallen ill."

"Solanine?" The shadows sank from Death's body, revealing hair as white as bone and a face that Aris struggled to look at. "Do we know why?"

Aris turned away, focusing his attention on the corner where the fouled tapestry lay. Its song was grating even then, causing a persistent throbbing along his temples that Aris couldn't shake.

"No," he said. "But I believe it has something to do with *that*."

Death followed his gaze and slipped over to the tapestry, bent like a crow to inspect it.

"Your quality is slipping, brother. This is hideous," Death noted without inflection. He was met by Aris's incredulous scoff.

"*I* didn't make it." Aris grabbed the tapestry from the table and grimaced at the feeling of it between his hands—like he'd spent hours digging around in the dirt and would need to scrub them clean. "I found it not long before Solanine showed up. She threatened Blythe—told her that she'd 'disturbed the balance' or some crock."

Aris had wanted to know every excruciating detail, but Blythe had been so weak when they'd spoken about it that he hadn't wanted to push.

"I've only seen one like it before, and it disappeared before I was able to uncover its origin."

Death remained unmoving as he examined the heinous black threads that forever stitched themselves but never grew. An abomination.

"The last time Solanine got involved in our lives—"

"Hundreds of millions of people died," Aris finished for his brother. "I'm aware. Which is why we have to stop it this time. So long as Blythe is breathing, we have a chance to fix what we once failed to."

Death straightened, determination hardening his resolve as he met Aris's gaze. "I suppose our thoughts are aligned?"

A war of emotion flooded through Aris, but he showed not even the barest hint of it as he nodded.

"I suppose they are," he admitted. "It's time we pay Chaos a visit."

Chaos was not an easy person to find.

She did her work swiftly, upturning nations, pitting lovers against each other, and otherwise brewing up one trouble or another before she hurried on to the next thing. She'd never been capable of settling in one place for an extended period, and typically stuck to larger cities and flashier towns where word of her destruction could be more easily spread. If there was a single truth Aris knew about her, it was that she had no appreciation for quiet work. When it came to her preferences, the louder the better.

Death, likewise, had never cared for Chaos, but had come to understand the inner workings of her mind given all his years cleaning up her messes and guiding the horrified souls whose lives she took without remorse. He had learned to decipher which deaths had been brought about by her hand, and after three attempts following Death's lead, the brothers found Chaos not lording over a looming war nor with her eyes aglow as she watched destruction unfold. To their surprise, they found her posing as a student, uniform and all, at a finishing school.

It was called Hellebore House, and they arrived not upon its grounds, but in a dimly lit room with two small beds. Solanine sat contentedly on one of them while two other girls bickered nearby.

They were walking tentatively across the floor, several books stacked atop their heads to practice their posture. Aris hadn't a clue what was going on, but his brows lifted toward the ceiling as one of the girls whipped a book off her head and spun to hurl it at the second young lady behind her.

Aris stilled time before they could notice his arrival, grimacing at the spine of the book that stopped a mere inch from the girl's face.

Solanine, who'd been leaning forward in eager anticipation, groaned at the interference. "Do you know how long I've waited for her to snap? We were finally getting to the good part!"

The moment she spoke, Aris felt his stomach plummet. It was as if someone had taken a knife and carved out all that was good within him. Any sense of hope or light disappeared as dread weighed his body down, making each step toward her feel like he was climbing the world's tallest mountain.

In the end it was Death who swept forward in his torrent of shadows. He was larger than he'd been moments prior, and Aris couldn't understand how he was able to get so close to Solanine when she was in one of her moods, bombarding everyone with despair that festered like a disease. And yet Death's voice did not waver as he asked, "What are you doing in this place?"

Solanine's smile was predatory.

"I've been inspired back here by recent events." Her voice was so light. So deceptively cheerful that the grief and pain slicing through Aris's heart felt nonsensical. "Young minds are so malleable. It's amazing how much fun it is to devastate them." Solanine tilted her head to peer around Death and observe Aris. His body stiffened at her grin.

"They're sisters," she told him. "Twins, actually, and if all goes well, then the argument should be irreparable. Would you like to stay and watch?"

"I'll pass." It took a great deal of control for his words not to sound as pained as he felt. He puffed a slow breath from between his lips. It'd been ages since he'd last seen Solanine, and still he could not look at her without instant regret for all his past self had done with her.

He and Solanine had burned hot and fast, together only a few short months. Practically seconds in human time. He had not known Life back then, nor had he learned to give thought to the fates he crafted. He did try *now*, despite what anyone wanted to believe. But back then Aris had cared solely for a good show, and if there was one thing that Solanine could be counted on to provide, it was that.

"I am not the same man I once was," he said. "I have no desire to harass the humans."

"It's not harassment, Ari." She slipped around Death, sauntering forward. "It's inspiration. Humans cannot exist in a stagnant world. They always need something to feel angry or righteous about. It's what keeps them going, and the world spinning. I'm certain this moment will fuel these girls' minds for years to come."

The thrill in her voice had Aris wondering whether Mila had ever had the misfortune of meeting this demon. He had no doubts that the two of them would have become fast enemies. Even Aris believed that the world would be a better place without Chaos, but what did he know? In the end, she believed in her job the very same as he and Death believed in theirs.

"Release your hold on them," Solanine said, her eyes sparking a devilish red. "I won't tell you twice."

Even back when Aris had known her intimately, Solanine had never been patient. She always needed to be involved in something. Always needed the dramatics, and to be in the center of flaring tempers. He should have known better than to hope that some part of her would have changed after all these centuries.

"Do whatever you wish to these girls," Aris said flatly, ignoring a sharp warning hiss from his brother. He didn't care what Death thought of him; there was but a single soul that Aris was here to protect. "I'll free them as soon as you tell me what business you have with my wife."

He realized too late the danger of his words. Realized as Solanine's spine straightened and her lips pulled into a slow grin that he'd made a grave misstep.

"Your *wife?*" How joyous she sounded as she shifted closer, moonlight shining wickedly upon her. "Well, this just keeps getting more interesting."

Aris had no plan as he matched her steps to close the space between them, fueled by his terror. But one step too close and his knees buckled. He clutched his chest as she halted his breath with images of Mila drowning in a lake. Of white hair floating around a pale face and rosy lips that were struggling for breath. In his mind's eye Aris tried to save her, but no matter how much he ran, he couldn't reach her.

"It'll be a shame when she dies. If she's anything like her mother, I'm sure she would have been one to watch."

Her *mother*?

Though Aris knew she was standing there before him at Hellebore House, Solanine's voice echoed as if she were miles away. He could see only an endless lake with towering evergreens that surrounded a clearing he'd once spent much of his time in. It was the clearing he'd brought Mila to, the one in the portrait that hung outside his study.

He hadn't been able to bring himself to it since her death, for it was at that lake on a warm summer day that Aris had realized his heart belonged to him no longer. He had watched Mila venture into the water, her dress billowing first around her ankles, then around her waist. He'd stared, struck by her beauty. By the gentle swaying of her hips and the happiness she found in every lily pad and wisp of wind against her skin.

She'd turned back to look at him from the water, and when her smile was like lightning to his heart, Aris realized for the first time that he was in love.

Now the ghost of Mila's face stared up at him from beneath the water, but she wasn't alone. Blythe was in the woods, staggering against the trees. Her fingers were pressed to her neck, unable to stall the blood that pooled down her throat and stained the collar of her white dress. Her desperate eyes caught sight of Aris, and she reached a hand for him at the same time that Mila's pale hand shot out of the water, both of them begging for his help.

But he could only choose one.

Aris knew he should run to Mila. She was the obvious choice; she was who he had waited centuries to find, if only to hold her in his arms once more.

So why couldn't he get his legs to move? Why did his eyes keep straying across the clearing, to where he prayed Blythe would not die?

He couldn't move, frozen by his indecision.

"Aris."

Aris clutched his chest, knocking his fist against it to seize control of himself and force breath into his lungs. He needed to move. Needed to hurry. He could pull Mila out and then run to Blythe. He could make it to both of them—

"Aris, get ahold of yourself."

The voice wasn't gentle but a hurricane that shook the trees and struck him square in the chest. Aris realized vaguely that it belonged to his brother.

His brother, who stood beside him in reality. Who gripped Aris tight by the shoulders until Mila's body sank below the depths and Blythe crumpled among the trees as the vision disappeared.

Whatever noise Aris made hardly sounded human as he came to, left with the image of both Mila's and Blythe's envisioned deaths plaguing his mind. He whipped his head up to face Solanine, the gold in his eyes glinting as a million threads shone around him. "Meddle with my mind again and I'll slit your throat."

Solanine remained unfazed, standing before him with her hands on her hips.

"It seems that even Fate has fears," Solanine mused as she observed his struggle. From the drumming of her fingers to the bouncing of her heels, Chaos was forever moving, unable to exist within stillness.

It took everything in Aris to resist the urge to strike, not wanting to give the monster any further reason to go after Blythe. "What will it take to get you to leave her alone?"

Solanine didn't require so much as a second to consider. "I'm afraid I can't do that. Your *wife* has upset the very balance of nature itself. She breathes only because of whose blood she carries in her veins, but that won't protect her for long. Like Rima, I am giving this girl a single chance to fix her mistakes. You best pray that she's not as foolish as her mother."

Rima? Aris slid a look at Death. Did Solanine believe that Blythe was a Farrow? If she did, he wasn't about to tell her otherwise.

Instead, he said, "Tell us what she needs to do and we'll ensure that it happens."

"I'll do no such thing." Solanine was perilous in her delight. "If she fails, then she fails on her own merits. That's part of the fun."

Aris clenched his fists. She may have believed she had given Blythe a chance, but the truth was that none of Solanine's marks had ever survived. This game she was playing with Blythe was simply another show. Another way for her to weave chaos into their lives in the form of hope.

It was Death who lashed out this time, his shadows sweeping into a large scythe he sliced down upon her. It carved clean through Solanine's body, but she only sighed as her skin pieced itself back together and blood as dark and thick as tar soiled the carpet.

"You will not harm her," Aris hissed. "Keep away from my wife, or this time I swear that I will find a way to destroy you."

"Good luck with that," she said with a gentle laugh. "People like us can't die unless we go willingly. And even then, we'll always come back."

The room shone a brilliant gold as Aris's threads snapped toward her, but Solanine was gone before a single one could wrap around her.

Murder was at the forefront of Aris's mind as he forced his bones to straighten. They'd gone weary in Solanine's presence, every muscle aching.

"That girl is the devil," he snapped. "I've no idea how you can get so close to her."

"You've been much closer to her than I have," Death said with a knowing look. His shadows encompassed the book that was still floating in midair in front of one of the student's faces, primed to strike. He pushed it to the side, ensuring it would miss its mark.

"An appreciated reminder, thank you, brother." Aris smacked invisible dirt from his clothing, despising how easily he'd been brought to his knees. "I should have known what a spectacular waste of time this would be. She's not changed one bit."

Once, long ago, Aris could have always been counted on to know what Death was thinking. Now, distracted as he was, he didn't notice that Death had not immediately agreed with him. He did not recognize the glaze over his brother's eyes as a plan took shape in his mind.

Aris may have regretted this visit, but for Death, perhaps it had not been so useless after all.

CHAPTER THIRTY

In exchange for the adventure, Blythe had allowed Aris his doting.

Her husband had not shown his care in a way that Blythe was used to, but with gifts of sweets and rooms that could change at her heart's desire. He showed it in every doctor he had taken her to earlier that afternoon, whether they relied on traditional medicine, plants and herbs, or something called hygienic medicine that she'd never heard of but required little more than a healthy diet and avoidance of overwork. He would scowl at the doctors as they led her through their tests, always looking over their shoulders and asking a million different questions without ever seeming satisfied with the answers.

No one had been able to pinpoint what was wrong with her. Blythe had her theories, of course, belladonna poisoning being the first, as she was intimately familiar with its symptoms, all of which she had. And yet the tests had shown none in her system.

Blythe sat for hours in her library, twirling the wedding ring on her finger. She hadn't felt anything from the band of light since the two of them had kissed at the Christmas masquerade, as if their being close was keeping the magic of the ring quelled and satisfied.

Aris had sneaked away to his study an hour earlier, quiet and distracted. Blythe could see in the way his expression hollowed and his touch became firmer that he had not forgotten what she'd said about Chaos.

Aris was afraid, and as much as Blythe had wished to admit the truth of who she was as she'd laid her head against his bare chest, she hadn't been able to get the words out. She needed more time, but to get that she first needed to figure out what Chaos wanted with her.

Signa arrived at the library that evening, shadows slipping from her skin and promptly disappearing. Before so much as acknowledging Blythe, Signa's head tipped to the sky, besotted as her eyes darted from one corner to the next, taking in the impossibilities of the midnight sky and the forever-dreary window. Out of all the impossibilities, it was the quiet hooting from the highest shelf that garnered the most curiosity.

"Is that an *owl?*"

"Of course," Blythe answered coyly. "Every library should have one." She hurried to her cousin, offering a quick embrace before pulling Signa to her favorite corner by the window and motioning for her to have a seat on the green velvet settee.

It was hard not to notice that Signa, too, was looking frail and haggard. She carried a bag with her, and at the top Blythe spotted one of Rima Farrow's leather-bound journals.

A thousand words sat on the tip of Blythe's tongue—pleas for help, admittances of her fears and all the truths she'd learned—but at the sight of her cousin she pushed every thought aside and asked, "Are you well?"

The question alone was enough to break Signa, who covered her face as she melted into the chaise. Blythe may not have been able to *see* her crying, but she could certainly hear it between her cousin's sniffling.

"I am the most horrible person who ever existed," Signa cried. "I'm supposed to be the one asking you that!"

Blythe slid closer to Signa, winding her arms around her cousin's shoulders and trying to goad her upright from the depths of the couch. "It seems that we have more to discuss than I imagined." Quieter, she asked, "What's wrong?"

Signa made a face that was part scowl and part grimace before she leaned around Blythe and grabbed for her bag, plucking out the notebook. She tossed it onto Blythe's lap. "Half of these pages are *ruined,* soiled by the ink or torn out entirely. I can't make any sense of it, but it's as I told you earlier. I do not believe that we are the first in this family to have run-ins with the paranormal."

Blythe's fingers curled along the spine of the journal. She worried that the books might catch fire from the way Signa's bloodshot eyes burned holes in them. "Signa—"

"I think my mother was involved with someone." She plucked the journal back from Blythe's hands and flipped the pages open, erratic. "All I can decipher is that they were fast friends. I'm not certain that my mother knew the full extent of who she was dealing with at first, and from what I've gathered it seems maybe they were in a relationship that went awry. I think my mother was afraid when she called it off, but I don't know why. Death told me there are likely other deities out there—Time, Dream...."

"Chaos," Blythe said, to which Signa nodded.

"Yes, Chaos. And perhaps more he doesn't even know exist—"

"No, Signa." Blythe reached forward to take hold of Signa's fretting hands, easing them away from the book. "It's Chaos who killed your mother."

She told her cousin everything. Told her about Solanine cornering her in the stables. Of the visions she had seen, and how Blythe had been saved only because the woman somehow recognized that Blythe shared the same blood as Rima.

"She thought I was you," Blythe told her. "I'm the right age, and have the right blood. It's what saved me from being killed that night." She thought of what Signa had said about believing her mother might have been in a relationship with the demon that was Solanine. Though she'd never voice the question aloud, she wondered just what type of person Rima Farrow must have been to be capable of being with someone like Chaos.

By the time she was through telling Signa all that she knew, her cousin was ghost white. Signa sat with her hands folded in her lap, trying to bury them within her skirts.

"I wanted to tell you the moment I found out," Blythe explained, "but with all that happened at the ball—"

"When I believed that it was me with the power to resurrect, I made the mistake of threatening to bring Elijah back should he be hanged." Signa cut her off, not meeting Blythe's eyes. "What resulted from that conversation was the first time I'd ever seen Aris and his brother agree on something—using those powers in such a way would only invite Chaos. It was a rule I was not meant to break.

"My mother was trying to save someone," Signa continued, her shoulders bowing with a great weight. "In the journals, she wrote about a friend of hers who had drowned by slipping beneath the ice of a frozen lake. By the time they got to her body, her skin was blue and she was no longer breathing. That friend's name was Amity, only I know for a fact that Amity did not die because I met her as a spirit who had perished the same night as my parents. On one page, the journal claimed that Amity had died. But on the next, my mother spoke of Amity as if nothing had happened. I read each entry three times before I noticed that there were pages missing between them. There was no sign that anyone had torn them; rather, it was like the pages had disappeared from existence. The only proof I had was that this journal had several pages fewer than the others.

"I believe that a week passed between the drowning and the next entry, where my mother wrote about someone new who had arrived at the finishing school she was attending. A woman with hair as red as flame, who she called Sol. That woman... she must have been Chaos. If my mother somehow brought Amity back to life when she was meant to die, then perhaps she summoned Chaos." Signa leaned back in her seat, rubbing a hand over weary eyes.

Blythe's stomach twisted tighter with each word, her skin clammy in a cold sweat that had her breathing harder, eyeing the nearest wastebasket in case she grew sick.

Rima Farrow had somehow summoned Chaos. Whatever might have happened between them after that, the result of that summoning was undeniable—all of Foxglove had perished.

Blythe could not afford for those around her to suffer the same fate. She rested a hand on her cousin's arm, wishing she could soothe Signa's tired eyes and fill her gaunt cheeks with life. She didn't have to think about it for long, however, because with each passing second Signa began to look better than Blythe had seen her in months. Blythe withdrew her hand swiftly, knowing better than to use untested powers on her cousin.

"It seems I have work to do." Blythe kept her voice gentle as she leaned back, drawing her feet beneath her and onto the couch.

"What *work*?" Signa spat, growing tenser as her anger rose inch by inch to the surface. "What does she want you to do, kill a *horse*? One horse hardly makes a difference in the grand scheme of the world."

Blythe scratched one finger against the journal, wearing a groove into the leather. She didn't care for the look in Signa's eyes, or for the fire in her words. Blythe agreed that this was a lot of fuss for a horse she'd accidentally brought back to life, and it pained her to think about taking away something so beautiful. But what choice did she have but to try?

"What happens if you let it live?" Signa asked. There was a dark intensity in her voice that made Blythe see the reaper within her cousin for perhaps the first time.

"Then she'll kill me. And I didn't get the impression that she's a patient sort."

Anyone who saw Signa in that moment might think her feral, a child spirited away from the woods, body hunched like a predator's. Her hair was a dark curtain around her face, shielding murderous eyes.

"You're not going to die."

Despite Signa's conviction, it was a hollow promise. "At least if I do, we know that I'll keep reincarnating."

"Do not make light of it! This woman killed my parents, and there is no world in which I could bear losing you. Nor could Elijah."

"I'm *sick*, Signa. It's just like last time—"

"Surely there must be a way to use your powers on yourself."

Perhaps if Blythe were more familiar with her abilities, that might be possible. Mila seemed to have lived a long while, after all.

Blythe wanted there to be a world in which she could promise Signa that she'd be all right. But at this rate, she'd be lucky if she had a week left in her.

Blythe could cry, of course. Part of her wished she was like an animal and could escape into the woods to die in secret, leaving everyone uncertain as to what might have happened to her. But when it came down to it, Blythe had already been given a second chance at life that had been wonderful. After all, hadn't that been what she'd wished for in her mother's garden? To have had the time to make just one more memory with someone?

In that regard, she had been lucky. Blythe had made countless new memories. She had fallen in *love*—or at least she had started to, though it would take a good while before she'd be ready to admit that aloud.

Blythe took hold of her cousin after a beat too long. "You are the girl who cannot die, and I am the girl who will always continue to live. There will be periods of our lives when we may not have each other, but you and I are destined. No matter what happens, you will never escape me for long."

Signa turned her head, and those strange eyes that hardly ever blinked fluttered a dozen times as her bottom lip wavered.

"You don't know that for certain," Signa argued. "How could you when you don't even understand the extent of what you can do? If you speak to Aris, perhaps he could help. Perhaps he could teach you—"

"And perhaps I could devastate him again when I die anyway." Blythe's smile was thin, and when Signa refused to look at her, she squeezed her cousin's arm gently. "I am not happy with these prospects, either, but I'm also not afraid. Not when I now know what's waiting for me on the other side."

For a moment Signa looked as though she wanted to pull her arm back. Instead, she put her other hand on top of Blythe's and sniffled, emotion weighing her words.

"What if you forget everything again?" she asked. "What if you forget who I am?"

"Is that what you're worried about?" Blythe laughed. "Should that happen, then you will simply have to charm me just as you have once before. That shouldn't be difficult, given how horrid our first meeting went. But that's not going to happen this time, all right? I believe I was left without my memories because of *how* I died. It was a tragedy that Life had to forget just to be able to live with herself.

That's never going to happen again. The next time I die, Death will make sure of that."

Blythe had already decided as much. He owed her, after all.

Only then did Signa draw away. "I tire of hearing you talk like this. I have saved you once, and I'll do it again if I must."

Blythe wanted to believe her. If anyone could get out of this situation, it was the two of them. But Signa did not know the terror that was Chaos, or how her bones had quaked when that woman locked eyes with her.

"Don't worry." The wonderscape stole Blythe's whisper, carrying it upon the breeze. "I'm not giving up without a fight."

"Good." Signa reached forward, squeezing Blythe's hands. "Then it's time that we return to Thorn Grove."

CHAPTER THIRTY-ONE

THEY WAITED UNTIL THE DARKEST HOURS OF THE NIGHT, AT A TIME when only ghosts wandered the snowcapped moors, to sneak into Thorn Grove's stables.

Even the horses slept, the stables eerily silent as Blythe and Signa slipped inside. Death's shadows dripped from their bodies until the reaper stood beside them, determination hardening his stare. According to him he'd been with Aris, though Death wasn't willing to share where they'd gone.

Knowing them as she did, Blythe hardly had to venture a guess.

"Did Solanine hurt either of you?" she asked him quietly.

He offered the smallest shrug. "The only thing injured was Aris's pride. We haven't long before he notices we're gone."

Blythe's jaw tightened as she steadied her emotions. She crept along the stalls, guilt making a knotted home in her chest. "I hate this."

"So do I," he whispered. "But there's only one way for nature's balance to become so misaligned, and this is how we remedy it."

Signa's sight was so well adjusted to the darkness that she took the lead, carving the path forward. "There's no other choice, Blythe."

They were right. All three of them had reached the same conclusion about what needed to happen next, but that didn't mean she had to like it. Wordlessly, Blythe followed Signa past Mitra as the mare huffed a curious greeting, and to the deepest part of the stables where the horse she'd brought back from the dead awaited them.

Even now, Blythe looked at it and saw only beauty. The silver haze that emitted from its skin. The comforting warmth of its body as her hands rested along its neck, brushing down the length of it with soothing strokes.

It was too exquisite a creature to kill, and yet this would not be the first time they brought death upon it.

"I'm sorry." Blythe spoke softly as she curled her fingers into its mane. "I am so, so sorry."

The horse did not deserve to die, yet Blythe knew no other way to protect her family from Chaos. She knew too well the story of Foxglove, and of the plague brought about by Life's demise. Blythe did not want to consent to the death of this creature, but for the sake of everyone she cared for, she would.

"Will it be painful?" she asked, to which Death responded gently.

"I promise it will not feel a thing."

He peeled off his gloves, and Blythe wondered whether it was for her benefit that he was in his human form. He didn't need to be; the more time Blythe spent in his presence, the more she relaxed, taken over by a sense of comfort that likely came from Life's nostalgia.

She fought the urge to shut her eyes as he reached a pale hand toward the horse. If she was going to lay claim on its life, then the very least she could do was witness its final moments. But when Death settled his touch against its neck, it did not fall. Instead the silver haze shone brighter as the horse nuzzled its face into Death's palm.

Blythe did not miss his quiet gasp, or the way his fingers curled against the horse's muzzle, surprised. He looked back to Blythe, a wildness in his eyes, and whispered, "I can't kill it."

Signa stepped forward to lay her hands upon the creature while Blythe remained rooted in place, unable to look away from the light that was radiating so intensely from its body. A light that no one else seemed to notice.

She had laid claim on this creature's life, and now it seemed it could not die.

Panic rose in her throat. She could offer Chaos another life, perhaps. But whose? Balwin's? Mitra's? And what if it didn't work? What if she took an innocent life and still failed to protect her own?

The idea made her queasy. Blythe stumbled backward, away from Signa's fearful eyes and Death's stunned expression, toward the same hay bales that Chaos had sat on when she'd cornered Blythe days ago. Only this time when Blythe reached out to catch herself, her vision went black. The stables faded from view as she tuned out whatever urgent words Death and Signa whispered to each other, her mind slipping into a strange place that seemed to toe the edge of dreaming. Her body was no longer near the horses, but standing barefoot atop powdered snow in her mother's garden. All her limbs were numb, quivering from a cold that made every step send shocks of electricity through her. The pain was enough to knock her to her knees, leaving her grappling in a bush of roses with thorns that tore at her skin, drawing blood that neither healed nor brought more flowers to life.

All she could see of her own body were strong hands that didn't look like her own, so caked in mud that she couldn't determine the color of them. As fast as her heart raced, her body was weighed down by a fatigue that settled deep into her bones, telling her that this snow was the perfect place to close her eyes and rest. Tempting as it was, Blythe knew in the back of her mind that she would die if she succumbed to that desire. While every step made her cry out, she dragged herself up with the help of the nearby tree, blood bubbling beneath her nail beds as she dug her fingers into the bark to keep standing.

She recognized the garden, but why was she there?

A glance over her shoulder had her stomach hollowing at the sight of her mother's gravestone. She needed to hurry and escape before she was buried beside it. Blythe stumbled toward the gate, wishing with every muddy step that she could chop off her legs and be rid of the pain that had her eyes watering. Each sob felt like a serrated blade dragging up her throat.

Several times she fell upon the snow, having to drag herself until she made it to the gate. The iron doors opened with a terrible moan and she pushed forward, onward to Thorn Grove where a bath and a hot meal awaited her.

At the tinny scraping of the garden gates, Blythe's eyes fluttered open. She lurched upright, straw in her hair, and nearly slammed her face against Signa's, who had bent to inspect her. Death, too, stood distressingly close.

She was back in the stables, looking down at her legs and nearly crying when she could feel herself wriggling her toes. She tried to stand, but the first time Blythe blinked she saw roses waiting behind her eyelids. Saw bushes of snowcapped hellebore and vines that clawed along the garden floor, and felt the unease of it all.

"Blythe?" It sounded as though she was below the surface of water and Signa was shouting at her from above, the words a hollow echo as Blythe's mind followed the path of vines. "Blythe!" She said something else, too. Something about Aris, but Blythe couldn't focus enough to understand.

This was not like the vision she'd just had in the garden; this was one of Life's.

An invisible hand guided her into its depths, far into a maze that Blythe had never seen before.

With each step, images flashed in her periphery. Pale skirts and glances of hair like wheat that disappeared the second she turned to look. A couple spinning mid-dance, or hand in hand as they darted through shelves. Blythe heard their giggles. Heard the dulcet words of lovers as they flitted by, but could never quite make out what they said.

She hurried after them, breathless by the time she came to a halt. Only then could she see Mila standing before her, swept up in Aris's embrace. Neither appeared to notice her, and as Blythe stepped forward to reach out for them, her hand skimmed through their forms like water.

"Don't do this," Aris whispered, bending to press his forehead upon the woman's. "We can save you. Let us save you."

Mila pressed to her toes, loosening her hold on her lover. "This is the way of things, Aris. You must let me go."

But Aris did not let her go. He pulled away, and Blythe was quick to follow as Aris sought his brother. Together they concocted a plan, going against Mila's wishes in order to save her. Blythe knew what happened next, but still she followed the story, watching as a plague tore through the world, ravaging life after countless life. She watched Death's guilt turn to distress. Aris's sorrow manifest into anger. Watched as Mila died all the same, made a husk by her despair and by the betrayal of those she had trusted.

Watching the memory play out reawakened a wound buried deep within her. Blythe's head throbbed, and soon the world surrounding her morphed into garden hedges. Ones that familiar blond hair swept behind, humming an all too familiar song. It was a woman in a sun hat whom Blythe had seen a hundred times before, bent at the waist and humming as she tended to the garden.

"Mother?" Blythe tried to step around her. Tried to catch a glimpse of the woman's face, though the figure turned as soon as Blythe did.

"You rascal!" her mother chided someone in the distance. A small boy with hair of harvest orange. Lillian turned to chase after the boy, her laughter rattling in Blythe's skull.

Thunder raged in Blythe's heart as she followed them. Yet no matter how many steps she took, she never ended up any closer. She was panting and breathless as she followed after the ghost, who she saw only in quick glimpses from the corner of her eye.

Blythe stumbled, clutching her chest, for it felt ready to burst through her skin. The garden had disappeared into a hallway of old portraits and the familiar mahogany floors of Thorn Grove. Outside a room just past her bedroom door, a figure skirted the edges of her vision.

Only it was no longer a woman with blond hair, laughing as Blythe chased her. It was a figure in a fox mask. One with hair as red as flame.

The pounding of her own heart warned Blythe to stay back. She braced her body against the wall, standing beside her mother's portrait as the figure took a step toward her. But before it could approach, the light of the room shifted and the masked figure jerked their head to it.

"Blythe?" It was Aris's voice, low and worried. The sound of it was all it took for the masked figure to retreat to Thorn Grove's shadows. Slowly, the hallway vanished, and Blythe's bleary eyes adjusted enough to know that she was back in her library. Back safe at Wisteria. She hadn't even felt Death move her.

"She's been like this for several minutes," her cousin whispered, voice thick with concern.

"It looks like a seizure," Death said. "Has this happened before?"

Blythe folded into her knees, ignoring the voices. If only she could manifest Thorn Grove again. Something important was within those halls, she was certain of it. But she couldn't make sense of what was up and what was down, let alone control her voice enough to tell the others that.

"Get away from her," Aris spat, lifting her from the ground. "You're scaring us, Sweetbrier. If you can hear me, I need you to let us know."

She wanted to open her eyes. Wanted to soothe him and assure the others that they had nothing to worry about. But before she could open her eyes to do that, Lillian's butter-soft laughter warmed the air. It was a sound that drowned out all else, and Blythe relaxed against it.

She no longer heard Aris calling out to her. She had no knowledge of his growing concern or where he took her, let alone of the sweat that drenched her gown.

Blythe was certain that her mother had led her to that room in Thorn Grove. She only needed to get in there to discover what was waiting for her inside.

Blythe tipped her head against Aris's chest, and from behind the darkness of her eyelids, she followed her mother toward the darkness.

CHAPTER THIRTY-TWO

Blythe knew the truth of her situation. Still, she let the others argue, too numb to admit it aloud.

"Her brother had a bout of delirium just as she did when he took belladonna," Signa said as Aris laid Blythe in the bed. "It's a common symptom."

"I know that," growled her husband. "We've had her tested for it by a dozen doctors, but there's no poison anywhere in her system. This isn't the work of belladonna, but of Chaos."

"It'll keep getting worse if we don't do something. She won't be able to hold on much longer." This voice sounded like the midnight wind, sweeping across the suite with such severity that Blythe's breath caught in her throat.

"Signa's right," Blythe managed to choke out. It didn't matter what her blood did or did not show proof of; Blythe had experienced these symptoms before. The sores, the hallucinations, the familiar taste of poison on her breath. "I may not have consumed any, but nevertheless it's how Chaos has chosen to kill me."

Every hair on her body stood on end as Death swept toward her, his cold sinking into every pore as terror seized her. He was too close.

He was too close, and she was too ill.

Aris held out his arm, halting his brother with eyes that burned a lethal gold. "Step away from my wife."

Death stilled. Behind him, even Signa looked as though she was holding her breath.

As Aris helped her to sit up, all Blythe could think was that she wished he still hated her.

He had spent centuries waiting for his wife's soul to return to him. He'd searched everywhere, tearing himself apart to find her. Should she tell him that she'd found him at last, only to die again? Aris wouldn't be able to bear it, nor would she if she was forced to watch him experience such grief.

Blythe didn't know how it was possible, yet the fact remained that she was being poisoned again. She was as weak now as she'd been in those final months, and knew in her bones that her chances of making it out alive were slim. One sideways glance at Death confirmed as much. His eyes were fathomless as he watched his brother gingerly tuck the blankets around her, and he gritted his jaw tight. Steeling herself, Blythe placed a gentle hand upon Aris's.

"Go to my father," she told him. "I need to know that he is well."

Aris set more of his weight onto the bed. "I'm not leaving you."

"Chaos has been to Thorn Grove once already. This is a game

to her, and it's one I don't want my father involved in." She gave his hand a gentle squeeze. "Please. Signa will stay with me, and she's kept me alive once before."

His tightened expression showed just how displeased he was with this idea. Even so, he gave up the battle with a quiet sigh and told Signa, "I'll be back within minutes. Call for me if she needs anything, and keep that bastard away from her."

"I'll keep her safe" came Signa's quick answer.

He held her cousin's stare for a long while before disappearing in a snap of gold. Blythe waited several seconds, confirming he was gone before she lifted her head to look Death in the eye. "This cannot end up like last time."

Signa sucked in a breath, turning away at once to hide her tears. Death, too, sank to his knees beside the bed. His hands were gloved, and although she trembled, Blythe reached to take them.

"I'm so sorry," he whispered, head bowed. "I have waited so long to tell you that, and it will never be enough. I know it won't, but I have spent every day since we lost you wishing to atone for the pain my brother and I caused. There will never be words to tell you how sorry I am."

There was a pressure within her. An emotion not of her own, but perhaps a remnant of Mila's. It tightened, a frost brewing in her chest. "You ignored her wishes," she said, too weak to stave off the feelings roiling through her. "Your selfishness made everything so much worse than it needed to be. She could have found you sooner. You could have spared millions of lives."

"I don't expect you to forgive me—"

"It's not up to me to forgive," she corrected. "I know what

happened. And to some extent it's true that I feel the pain of it. Mila's emotions are bundled somewhere deep inside of me. But they're not mine. I am not so kind a person as she was, Sylas. If I'm meant to die, then you need to let me." The sound of his name felt familiar on her tongue. For the first time, it felt *right*.

"That's not going to happen," Signa cut in, crossing to stand beside Death at the edge of the bed. She placed a hand on his shoulder. "I told you already, we're going to save you."

Blythe merely smiled, for she already knew what Signa was unwilling to admit. While Blythe wanted more than anything to live, her body was waning too quickly.

"If I die, I don't want my father to know." It was a quiet admittance, one that took a great deal out of her. Whatever resolve Blythe had felt cracked in that moment as she covered her mouth with a threatening sob. "He can't lose anyone else. He won't survive the grief. Tell him that I went to Verena. Send him letters. Have Aris give him fantastical illusions of me living my best life if you must. I don't care. Just protect him, Signa. Swear to me that you'll both protect him until I'm back."

Signa shut her eyes. "And what of Aris? Shouldn't he know the truth of who you are and all that he'll be losing?"

In that moment, Blythe made her decision. "Tell him," she said, "and I will never forgive you." She couldn't stand to hurt him. He could forget her easily, move on to searching for Life once more. And when the time came, she would find him again. That's when she would tell him, when they had a full lifetime together to look forward to.

She thought of Life's warning, of needing to fix things before history could repeat itself and Aris made a mess of the world by once again trying to save her. If he didn't know the truth of who she was, then maybe that would be enough. But that wasn't to say that Blythe was giving up yet.

There were no coincidences in this world, so it could not be one that she'd seen her mother today of all days. Signa had called it a hallucination, and perhaps she was right. But something stirred within Blythe's chest, telling her that there was more to her vision. That maybe someone was trying to steer her in the right direction.

"I haven't eaten in hours," she told Signa after a long while, leaning in to the grogginess of her voice. "Aris is usually in charge of the meals. Do you think that you could fetch me something?"

"I'd rather not leave you," Signa argued, but Blythe waved her off with a flourish of her hand.

"I appreciate your concern, but the only immediate danger I'm in is perishing of hunger. It'll only take a few minutes, I'm sure. Leave Sylas with me, if you'd like."

Blythe knew that wouldn't happen even before Signa took hold of his arm.

"Come," she told the reaper. "We'll be faster together."

Whatever Sylas said next was lost to her, for his shadows wound around himself and Signa as they, too, disappeared.

Only then did Blythe notice two amber eyes watching her from the floor. In the absence of others, the fox tentatively hopped to the edge of her bed, chittering its greeting.

"Have you decided that we're finally friends?" Blythe asked, reaching to stroke the beast behind the ears. It wasn't nearly as soft as she expected, and only seconds after she'd begun to pet it did it try to snap at her hand. Blythe yanked back just in time.

"You are a foul creature," she told it. "And if I'm to die, you are perhaps the one beast that I will not miss."

Again the fox chittered, this time as though it were laughing. And when it leapt from Blythe's bed to scurry down the hall, she pulled her sheets back and followed after it.

Knowing Signa, it wouldn't be long until she was back with biscuits or something she could grab quickly. When Blythe made it to the hall, she pressed her hand against the banister and leaned most of her weight against it as she hurried down the stairs. Her eyes flashed at once to the front door and the golden threads woven around it.

"We've only got this one shot," she told it preemptively, trying not to trip over the fox that chased circles around her heels, urging her on with its chittering. "Don't let me down."

Perhaps her mother was a mere hallucination. Perhaps she had truly lost her mind after all, and she was even sicker than anyone realized. But Blythe had to know for sure. She had to follow after this vision and see where it led.

And so she slammed her hand against the door just as she heard Signa's voice call out for her from upstairs.

"Take me to Thorn Grove," Blythe told it.

This time it did not fight back. One by one the threads unraveled, and she opened the door into her sitting room at Thorn Grove manor.

CHAPTER THIRTY-THREE

Aris

Aris Dryden knew better than to get attached to a human. Blink, and their life would pass before his eyes.

He especially knew how unwise it was to get attached to the woman he'd been forced into a marriage with. And yet his body seemed to gravitate toward her. He always knew precisely which part of the house she was in and found himself making a dozen mental notes whenever he spent time with her. She enjoyed chocolate but didn't have the taste for anything too sweet. Her brows were always a little furrowed, and her lips would pucker whenever she thought of a particularly witty quip, having to hold in her own laughter. Travel delighted her; she'd spend time anywhere, though she preferred the warmth to the cold. It couldn't be too warm, though, because then she'd become monstrous and irate, unbearable to deal with. Not that she'd ever admit it.

With each passing day, Blythe felt more and more like a sun

and Aris the earth, content to revolve around her every whim. He needed to get to the bottom of the peculiar tapestry and figure out why Chaos had her sights set on Blythe. Instead, he was standing outside of Grey's with Elijah Hawthorne because that was what she had asked of him.

Who was this person he was becoming?

"I will use all resources to get to the bottom of who's behind this," Aris told Elijah as he gingerly stepped over shattered glass. Looking around Grey's Gentleman's Club, he almost wondered whether they should somehow incorporate the shattered glass into the decor. It would certainly liven up the dark leather furniture and dreary walls that gave the place an air of what Aris could only describe as forced masculinity. It was all very stuffy and not what he would have expected from Elijah Hawthorne, who couldn't have looked less enthused to be there if he tried.

"My brother will appreciate that," Elijah said, a bitter curve to his lips. "He insists that his son should inherit the place. Were it up to me, I'd have burned it by now." He plucked a bottle of scotch from a table, saw that the back half was shattered, and tossed it aside with a grimace.

"How is my daughter?" he asked after a while, stomping over the wreckage without sorrow. If anything, Elijah looked more annoyed than he did upset, as if this entire ordeal had cost him nothing but his sanity.

Aris admired that about Elijah Hawthorne: with him, Aris needn't worry about half-truths or clever words with alternative meanings. He had never much cared for those and was glad he and

Elijah could have an honest conversation without all the forced niceties. Or at least as honest as could possibly be.

"She's why I'm here," he told the man. "Blythe is unwell, Elijah, though I promise you on everything sacred that I'm doing my best to help her."

A shadow passed over his father-in-law's face. He hadn't needed to be told of Blythe's condition; he already knew. "Do you care for my daughter, Aris?"

Aris wished it wasn't so difficult for him to answer such a question. Not because he wasn't sure of his answer, but because he could not admit the truth without betraying Mila.

"It was not always the case," he answered after a long while of mulling his words, for Elijah deserved whatever bit of the truth Aris could give. "But I care for your daughter in a way I have not cared for anyone since the death of my late wife."

The doubt that had creased Elijah's face smoothed over. "You lost a wife," he repeated, a familiar heaviness in those words. "I'm very sorry to hear it."

"I loved her more than anything in this world, as I'm sure you understand. I would have burned everyone and everything down for her. And for a long while, I believed that I would never care for anyone again. I will not delude you by claiming that my initial union with your daughter was made out of love. But it is my hope that you believe me when I tell you that I care for her now and that I want her to be healthy."

"That is all well and good," Elijah said with a quiet ferocity. "But what of Blythe? Would you burn the world for her, as well?"

It was not the question that surprised Aris, but how easily the answer came, the words spilling from his tongue before he realized what he was admitting. "I would."

Elijah responded by settling a hand upon his shoulder, and Aris had no idea what to do. He might have magicked people into pretending, but the reality was that he'd never had a father before. How strange it was to be treated like a son. And stranger still that he liked it.

"Then I'm glad that she has you," Elijah told him. "And I'm glad for the truth. My daughter tries too hard to spare my feelings, but I know there is no Verena, even though I saw it with my own eyes. It is not on any map, and I've not met a single soul who recognizes the name. When I traveled to meet you, my carriage circled the same peak three times." Aris fell still, though there was no accusation in Elijah's words. Only facts.

"Until my Lillian's death, I was never one to believe in the paranormal," he continued, fishing a key from his pocket and leading them to Grey's back office. "Even now, I wonder if it's only the mind of a sad and grieving man playing tricks on him. But that palace... you are no prince, are you?"

Aris had always known that Blythe was unnervingly clever, and it seemed she'd gotten it from her father. For whatever reason, Aris found that he did not wish to lie to the man whose phantom touch still burned his shoulder. So he answered, "No, I am not," without the barest hint of hesitation. And to his credit, Elijah nodded.

"Good," the man said, unwavering as he held Aris's stare. "Then do whatever you must to save my daughter's life."

Elijah did not look at the mess of his desk as he pushed the door open. Instead his focus remained with Aris, who took in the sight of opened ledgers and half-spilled bottles of ink that leaked slowly onto the floor.

"Items from Thorn Grove have been going missing," he told Aris. "Small things at first. Boots, a teacup...but now the ledgers from my office are gone, as well. I believe that whoever has vandalized Grey's is the same person who broke into Thorn Grove and the stables."

Elijah pulled out his leather chair. The cushion was slit through the middle, though he paid the cut no mind as he rested his head back. "Signa Farrow managed to find one of the tunnels leading into the manor within her first month of living at the manor. It stands to reason that someone else has done the same."

There was another leather armchair across from Elijah, still unscathed, and Aris took a seat. He steepled his fingers, wishing he could pluck Blythe from the situation. He could always take her somewhere far away under the guise of a vacation. He could suggest they have a proper honeymoon this time, away from everything and anyone who could possibly be trying to hurt her or her family.

Not that it would matter. Chaos would find them one way or another, and Blythe's time left on this earth was dwindling quickly.

Aris ran his hands through his hair, then down his face with a quiet sigh from somewhere deep in his chest. He had to do something, and though Blythe would likely murder him in his sleep if she were to find out, Aris had but one option. He stood, and with far more effort than he would ever admit, he allowed thousands of golden threads to encompass Elijah, effectively freezing the man just as he'd done during his and Blythe's wedding ceremony.

There were more threads in the room, of course. Millions of them woven into the very fabric of the universe, telling the story of each person who had ever set foot on this ground. One-by-one Aris inspected them, beginning near the door and working his way toward the desk. He slid a finger against one, following its trail with a scrutiny only he could manage. For it was his eyes alone that could decipher any strangeness in the threads, and while all of them were meant to be gold, tiny fibers had changed the coloring of several in particular.

They were silver, just the same as the peculiar tapestry.

Just the same as *Life*. But what did it mean?

He ran a finger over the thread before easing away with a sigh when he saw nothing. He returned to his seat and released Elijah, who stretched his legs.

"I was wrong to try to take Blythe away from Wisteria," the man said, to which Aris nodded as if he'd been listening astutely all the while. "Something is happening, and I fear she is somehow connected. Keep her away from Thorn Grove, Aris. Keep her safe."

"You have my word."

Aris had lost a wife once already, and he would not lose another. He had told Blythe that a person could not change their fate once it was written. But if this was to be his, then he would find a way around that rule.

Even if it meant rewriting fate itself.

Aris did not immediately return to Blythe's room. Instead, he made his way back to his study and to the peculiar tapestry. He had not been able to scratch its existence from his mind since the night it first appeared. Even now it wove endlessly atop his desk, the silver threads never growing longer. Once, the color would have sent him into a spiral, but there was a wrongness to the cloth. This was not Life, but something new entirely.

It was Signa who had first shown a thread of silver on her tapestry months ago, and yet it was Blythe who had captivated his thoughts so wholly.

From the moment he'd laid eyes on her, Aris had known that Blythe Hawthorne was someone special. For so long he'd tried to ignore the pull he felt toward her, only to find himself falling prey to his own impulses more times than he could count.

At first he had told himself that he needed Blythe close as a way to integrate himself into Signa's life. But somewhere along the way he'd found himself growing increasingly curious about the girl who had shoved her finger into his chest and told him precisely what she thought of him during their initial introduction. He'd even given in to those impulses on more than one occasion, going as far as to kiss her under the guise of taste-testing for poison, just so he might finally know what her lips tasted like and rid himself of the curiosity.

Signa Farrow was like water—quiet, thoughtful, clever. But Blythe held the passion of fervent flames. She was a fire, all-consuming and never satiated, and Aris could not stop himself from some compulsive need to be burned.

How long had it been since he'd felt such desire for another soul? Another body? This ignorant beast of a girl had consumed his every thought whether it be waking or dreaming, and he couldn't shake her no matter how hard he'd tried. Blythe was a sponge for the world and all its delights, and day by day Aris found himself craving her.

He wanted her. Her mind, her body, her time. He wanted *her.* But first, there was something he had to do.

Aris stood beneath Life's portrait. How many years had he worked on it, painting the canvas over and starting from scratch as he tried to capture her likeness? How long had it been since he'd begun searching for her, unwilling to say goodbye?

He pressed his palm against the canvas, smoothing his thumb down her skin and wishing that he could feel her warmth.

"I'm married again, Mila." His voice was little more than a puff of air. "I bet you never expected that."

Oh, how he had loved this woman. He had prayed to any god that might listen to let him find her, if only to see her one last time. His world had grown brighter with Mila as his light, and since the moment he'd lost her Aris had felt as if he'd been wading through the darkness.

He could not continue like this, one foot in this relationship and the other primed to flee. Blythe was the first person who Aris burned for since Mila, and Blythe deserved more. She deserved a proper husband, or at the very least a relationship with a man who wasn't chasing a ghost.

"One day, I will see you again. In another lifetime, perhaps we shall find each other." But for now, this was goodbye. The portrait slipped away beneath his touch, disappearing until he was left grasping only bare stone.

Mila was gone.

Aris didn't allow himself to linger or give way to the emotion swelling in his throat. He stalked into his study and toward the tapestry whose song grated against his ears with a new resoluteness. He took hold of a pair of shears from his desk and dragged it across the cloth, determined to see its ruin. The threads tore in half, only to begin restitching themselves seconds later, as good as new. He tried to tear it. To feed it to a fire that tossed soot back at his face. To slice it in half and *then* feed it to the fire in hopes of incinerating the fabric before it had a chance to restitch itself. At one point he thought he'd done it until he turned to see the pristine tapestry lying on his desk once more.

He groaned, knowing he'd have to get more creative if he was to best this beast. But Blythe was waiting just down the hall, and she took priority. He could tamper with the tapestry once she was asleep.

He made his way toward the study door, about to open it when he stilled. Glancing up, he saw that several of the tapestries were frosted in a thin layer of ice. The chill seeped through the room, filling Aris with such rage that he pressed forward, intent to ignore his brother.

"I have no desire to speak with you," Aris spat.

"You have no choice." There was once a time when Death's voice had not raised the hair along his neck or put a pit of hostility in Aris's stomach. There was a time when he had viewed the man behind him as no less than a brother and had filled his hours prattling on endlessly at Death's side. But now the hairs along his neck did rise, because Aris knew that, yet again, Death had his sights set on his wife. It would be Death's hand that took Blythe from this earth unless Aris did something to stop it.

"Blythe is gone," Death said, and for a moment Aris felt nothing. He did not breathe. Body numbed as the world began to fog around his vision until suddenly Signa was there. She smacked Death on the shoulder, slipping around his shadows.

"You're going to give him a heart attack," she spat before turning to Aris. "Blythe isn't dead. She's just . . . *gone*."

It was alarming the way his heart kicked back to life. The breath knocked back into him and he looked away, fisting his hands so that neither would see how they trembled.

"How can she be gone?" he demanded, relying on his anger to fuel him so that fear would not get the better of his mind.

"That's just it," Signa began, sounding winded. "I haven't the faintest clue. I thought I saw her downstairs, but when I tried to follow her through the door—"

"She left through the door?" Aris nearly lost his balance. He turned fully toward the two, gripping the edge of the nearest table to steady himself.

Signa blinked those strange eyes of hers. "Yes. But I couldn't find her anywhere outside—"

"The *front* door?" Aris clarified. "This was the front door, down near the parlor?"

"Do you have another *front* door?" Signa snapped. "When she opened it, I thought I saw—"

"Little Bird." Death's shadows slipped first around her feet, then upward to cover Signa's mouth. "Be quiet."

Death did not see the glare she cast him, for he looked only at Aris, whose knees were so close to giving out that only his brother's shadows held him upright.

He had wondered all this time how Blythe had managed to escape to Thorn Grove prior to the Christmas ball. He had wondered why the burn of their rings had calmed, for it had always felt as though they'd been trying to tell them something. To steer them toward each other.

Their rings were bound by the threads of fate. And Aris finally understood why.

At once the room of his felt impossibly small as he stumbled past the others and toward the tapestries.

It wasn't possible. For weeks prior to their marriage he'd studied Blythe's tapestry, wishing to incinerate it. To hunt down every clue and piece of information he could garner to use against her. But like the peculiar new tapestry on his desk, hers had still been weaving itself, continuing onward without any regard for him. Aris had given up on watching the tapestry once it became apparent that there was nothing to learn from it, and he hadn't looked back since. Not until now.

He focused every bit of his attention on the tapestries, listening to their songs. Sorting through them in his mind until he heard a sound unlike any other. One so lovely that it could belong to no instrument but to a choir of angels who had blessed his ears alone. Aris pushed everything aside as he hunted for it, digging through row upon row until he came toward the back. If he hadn't recognized the hideously bruised tapestry behind it as Signa Farrow's, then Aris would not have recognized whose tapestry the sound belonged to, for it did not look as it had those short months ago.

Blythe's tapestry no longer resembled the keys of a piano. It no longer swept to the floor, weaving an endless story for itself. Instead, it was like the one on his desk: a single color that had Aris dropping to his knees. He reached for it with fingers that would never be gentle enough, eyes hot as he drew it from its line.

The threads were as silver as the stars, and they drew a cry from his lips as he folded against the tapestry and hugged it to his body with great desperation.

"It cannot be," he whispered against the fabric, over and over again until he felt Death's chill against his back. "After all this time, it cannot be true."

"But it is," his brother whispered. "She is here." The words shot through Aris like a pistol.

It was rare, but sometimes when the lives of two people were so intertwined, the color of one tapestry would bleed onto the other. Now that he saw the truth laid bare before him, Aris wondered how he ever could have believed that Signa Farrow was the woman he'd been searching for. Life's tapestry was the most breathtaking that he had ever laid eyes on, and he knew without a sliver of a doubt who it belonged to.

The woman he had not stopped thinking about. The one his very skin burned for.

His wife.

His *wife*. There before him all this time.

What a fool he'd been not to see it before.

Never again would she hurt because of him. Never again would she hurt at all if he could help it. For he knew better than anyone that second chances did not come often, and Aris would sooner die than allow this one to slip by.

After all this time, Life had found him. *Blythe* had found him.

With great care he hung the tapestry, looking between it and the band of light on his ring finger. Distantly, he could feel the shape of Blythe's presence. They could not communicate in their minds like Death and Signa, but Aris wondered now whether it was her soul that he felt pulsing on the other end of the ring. That's what they were, after all—two souls infinitely bound. Only hers wasn't burning quite so hot as it once had.

"What was it that you saw, Signa?" There was a new firmness to his voice. A resolve that Aris had not felt in centuries.

"You're not going to believe it," she whispered, stepping forward. "But it looked like Thorn Grove on the other side of that door." When she reached for his hands, Aris did not pull away.

"I do believe you," he told her. "And we must hurry."

Blythe had told him on the day of their marriage that the carriage had taken her to Thorn Grove's garden. One more glance at the tapestry that had troubled his mind for weeks, and Aris understood whose song grated against him.

This time, his wife needn't die. This time, Aris knew how to save her.

PART FOUR

CHAPTER THIRTY-FOUR

Blythe felt like a thief in her own home as she pressed against the walls of her suite. It was strange how she felt the need to tiptoe so that no one would know she was there.

She had no idea of the time, only that it was dark, with no midday light filtering in through her curtains. There were candles in her nightstand, though Blythe hesitated before reaching for one as a quiet creaking down the hall rose the hairs on her neck.

Unless she was mistaken, it was coming from the precise direction in which she'd seen someone disappear in her hallucination.

A noise in itself wasn't unusual; this was a manor, after all, full of maids who sometimes kept odd hours with their tidying and the sound of wuthering along the moors. There wasn't a night that passed in which thin branches did not scrape across the panes of her window and try to claw their way inside. There'd been a point the year prior when many people, including her father, had even claimed to hear the sound of a woman crying at all hours of the night.

No sound was strange when it came to Thorn Grove; rather, it was the direction it came from that was unusual, as Blythe had been the sole person to live in this wing before moving to Wisteria.

She flattened her palms against the wall, bracing herself as two hearths swam in her vision, in a room that had only one. She curled her fingers into the wallpaper, half ready to tear it off.

God, did she despise being so tired. Just the escape through Wisteria's door and into Thorn Grove had her ready to sit down. But she had to keep going. Something had guided her here, and Blythe knew from the experience with her ring what happened when you tried to ignore magic.

If she was going to uncover the truth, then she needed to do it before the spinning in her mind became any more unbearable. She took a small step forward to press her ear to the door, listening as someone padded by, each of their steps slow and deliberate, trying hard not to be heard. Again a door creaked, and this time Blythe used the sound as a cover as she cracked open her own door and squinted her eyes through the darkness just in time to see a figure enter her mother's room.

Whoever it was, they were at least a head taller than her and appeared to be wearing a hood. Beyond that, it was too dark to make out anything more than their general shape. It was unwise, she knew, to chase creeping hooded figures through the darkness of a haunted manor. But given that she was already dying, what was the harm?

Relying on the final dregs of her energy, Blythe made a quick grab for the poker propped beside her hearth. She clenched it tight before tiptoeing out of her room and to the door beside the framed portrait of her mother.

Surely it was her own imagination that had her mind playing tricks on her—it had, after all, been a long while since she'd truly examined the portrait—but Blythe could have sworn that her mother's face was more drawn than usual. Had her mother's eyes always been pinched and sallow at the corners, staring out with such concern?

Blythe's heart could have won at the races for how swiftly it beat against her chest. She sucked in a long breath through pursed lips, then pushed it out again to steady her trembling as she said a prayer that her body would cooperate.

As she squeezed the poker, ensuring it fit well in her grasp, she felt a pulse of heat on her ring finger. It was gentle, as if Aris was searching for her. If something *did* happen, Blythe hoped that this strange bond of theirs might somehow warn him. Because she wasn't going to wait. Not when her head was swimming and her body felt ready to give out at any minute.

Before she could change her mind or allow weakness to best her, Blythe kicked the door open and let her poker swing.

To her surprise, it made almost immediate contact. She nearly screamed at the resistance on the other end of it, her chest a tight coil when a figure winced and then immediately slumped over, their body hitting the floor.

Now Blythe did squeal, glancing around the room as she tried to figure out what she was meant to do next. She hadn't expected to actually *hit* someone.

The body had its back to her, its face to the floor and head obscured by the hood. Though she might have been able to make out more in the daylight, here in the night she could see only a sliver of red hair.

Blythe pressed the end of the poker against the softest part of their neck. Whoever this was, they'd been making their way into one of the hidden tunnels behind a portrait in her mother's room. The door had been a secret to even the staff, one of the old escape routes in Thorn Grove that her mother had shown her as a child if ever they needed to flee the manor.

Men's clothing was scattered about, and Blythe realized that this person had dropped the pieces during their fall. Streaks of grime coated the walls and armoire, and a vase of dried flowers had been emptied in the corner. It sat by the window with bedsheets tied around its rim. To fetch snow, Blythe realized. It'd been used to fetch snow for drinkable water. How very clever.

Blythe glanced down, noticing then that this person—this *man*, perhaps—wore her father's boots and a suit that was a touch too wide for his lean frame.

Nerves knotted Blythe's throat. The figure was unconscious but still breathing. It seemed that luck was finally on Blythe's side to have allowed her to land such a blow. She could tie the man up and wait for help to arrive. They could interrogate him to determine what he knew about the break-ins at Grey's or whether he was involved with Solanine.

But first, she needed to see his face. Blythe could only hope that the man didn't rouse as she crouched down and dared to yank back his hood. She regretted it the next second, stumbling back with a scream as she threw herself away from the body.

Away from the face that she had once believed to know better than anyone. Because it wasn't possible.

It wasn't.

She gripped her ring finger, wishing more than ever that she could use it to send a message to Aris to come and find her *now,* because she understood then why Chaos had sought her out and why she'd been led to this room of all places.

She turned, sprinting for the door when a hand grabbed her waist and yanked her back. Another hand covered her mouth tasting of dirt and metal and smelling so foul that Blythe fought down her gagging. Thrashing in his grip, Blythe bit down on his palm with every ounce of fight left in her.

Her teeth met flesh. Rank but real, solid *flesh.* Because this was no dream. This was real. Thorns erupted through her skin and the man jerked back with a hiss of breath as one sliced through him. But he didn't release his hold.

"Calm down!" he hissed against her ear, and Blythe wanted to recoil at the sound of his voice. "I'm going to let you go, but you have to promise that you're not going to scream. Do you understand?"

Though every fiber of her being wished to bite down on his flesh and tear off his fingers one by one, she resisted the urge. He ripped the poker from her hand, tossing it to the side as tears burned hot in Blythe's eyes.

Poker or not, she would fight him. She'd turn herself into a briar patch, ensnaring every inch of him in thorns if need be. But for now, she nodded.

"Good." He eased his hold and cautiously withdrew his hands.

Even so she could still feel that he was there behind her, ready to pounce should she try anything.

She should have thrust the poker through his throat when she'd had the chance. Because *he* certainly hadn't hesitated. Not when it came to trying to kill her.

"Hello, Blythe," he whispered. "I'm glad to see you're well."

She couldn't say whether it was rage or heartbreak that tore her throat open as she turned to look upon the familiar freckled face.

"Hello, Percy."

CHAPTER THIRTY-FIVE

"This isn't possible." Surely Blythe had already died. She must have become a spirit, trapped and forced to forever roam the halls of Thorn Grove. That, at least, would have made more sense than her dead brother standing before her. "I was told that you died."

He was fairer than she remembered, and now that she'd had a good look at his eyes, Blythe could see that the color had been leached from them. Out of all the strange beings she knew, Percy looked most inhuman, and the sight of him standing before her with his shoulders hunched and his body unsteady had thorns rising to the surface of her skin once again.

"I don't remember," he whispered, drawing back toward what was once their mother's bed. There was a masquerade mask of a fox face beside it. "For weeks I've tried to piece it together, but all I remember is seeing Lillian, a man of shadows, and vines tearing up from the earth. And then there was this . . . this hound. It looked as if he'd stepped from the pits of hell."

Even amid all his grievances with Grey's and their father's refusal to let him inherit it, Blythe couldn't remember ever seeing Percy's shoulders so bowed. Never had she seen him so distraught, quaking like a sailor caught in a hurricane.

She stretched out a tentative hand, pressing it against her brother's wrist to confirm that his skin would not suddenly evaporate at the touch. He brushed his thumb against hers before she could pull away, and Blythe sucked in a breath at the sharpness of his nails against her skin.

"I'm real, B," he whispered. "At least I believe I am."

She snatched her hand back, tongue fuzzy with moss as her powers inched to the surface, ready to defend her if he came any closer. She fought them back for now, instead grabbing two sharp pins from her hair.

"You have no right to call me that," she snarled in a voice every bit as poisonous as the ivy that wanted to snake around her fingers. "What do you expect from me, Percy? A welcome parade? You tried to kill me!"

Blythe lunged forward, stabbing at him with the pins. Percy jumped back, managing to avoid one, but the other stuck into his thigh. With a hiss of breath he bent at the waist to tend to it as blood blossomed on his pants. Only, it was not red blood but black as tar. Blythe covered her mouth at the sight, stumbling toward the door.

"Let me explain!" he called after her, and blast her treacherous heart and its dreaded *feelings*. His words halted Blythe in her tracks. For months she had wondered what she'd done wrong. Wondered how she could have angered her brother to the point that he'd decided that killing her was the only option.

The safest thing Blythe could do for herself was to run and find the others. Instead she turned, and even then she could not see him as a killer. When she looked at Percy, she saw only her brother. A much more *dead* version of her brother, but nonetheless.

Percy teetered several paces closer, stiff on his feet. Blythe recognized his walk; she'd seen it earlier that day, when she'd envisioned herself trapped in her mother's garden. But perhaps it wasn't herself that she had envisioned, perhaps it had been Percy. That, at least, would explain why the garden had been torn apart last she'd seen it.

"I never should have involved you," Percy told her, his eyes seeming to scan the corners of the room with increasing paranoia. "I wasn't in my right mind. I was afraid of losing everything, and I'm sorry—"

"'Sorry' isn't enough to justify nearly killing someone." As strong as she tried to be, Blythe struggled to speak those words. After so long wishing for the chance to speak face-to-face with her brother and for him to explain why he'd betrayed her, this was all he could come up with?

A laugh tore through her, drawing tears from her eyes as she hugged her arms tightly around herself. "You put me through hell, Percy. You made every bone in my body feel as though it were on fire. You watched as I could no longer see straight. As I could no longer hold my food down or manage conversation. You left me alone in my room, staring at a ceiling I believed would be the last thing I ever saw. You witnessed all of this, and still you poisoned me."

Even then, Percy did not meet her eye. He was watching the corners, as if anticipating Death to leap from them at any moment. She should have expected as much; Percy always had been a coward.

"You killed me," she told him, withholding none of her bitterness. "And it's your fault that I'm dying again now."

Only then did his head jerk up to look at her, and so terrifying were his fathomless eyes that Blythe wished she could look away. She wouldn't, though. She didn't dare give him any advantage over her.

"I haven't done a thing to you since I've been back," he said. "I'm *glad* that you're here, Blythe. I didn't know how to stop the poisonings because I couldn't face you after knowing what I'd done. You were so sick."

"I don't want to hear it," she spat, brushing down the thorns prickling along her arms. "How long have you been living in Mother's suite?"

"Since early November, I think? I don't know the exact date."

"And who else knows you're here?"

"No one," Percy told her. "I've been in this room since I returned, drinking snow and sneaking into the kitchens through the tunnels."

"I'll have them all blocked," she swore, feeling a cruel pang of satisfaction when his jaw visibly tightened.

Good. Let him worry.

"No one but Signa and I know that you're dead, you fool. But I swear that I'll tell them. I'll tell Father everything you've done to me, and I will spare no detail. For months I've been well, and then you show up and—" She cut off as the realization struck like a knife through her gut.

She'd been well up to the night of the wedding. After that she had chalked up her symptoms to a passing cold or allergies from the poor state in which Wisteria had been kept, but as she examined the jaggedness of Percy's nails and thought back to her earlier vision, she remembered what else had happened the day of her marriage. Remembered when she'd visited her mother's garden and noticed her magic for the first time in the form of a single crimson petal.

Blythe held her stomach, noticing that Percy's fingernails were not caked with mud but blood. They were torn apart, the skin shredded and the tips frostbitten.

He had clawed his way out from the ground, and it was because of her.

A year ago, Signa had taken Percy's life. She had given the rest of his years to Blythe, to save her from the belladonna poisoning. And now Blythe had unknowingly brought him back. It was no wonder Chaos had sought her out, and all that had happened was but a taste of what was to come.

"You're not meant to be here, Percy," she whispered, feeling the weight of those words settling into her bones. Her hands ached to find more pins and sink them deep into his neck. To end him then and there, and save herself.

And yet she couldn't. Because despite all that had happened, when she looked at Percy, she saw the face of her brother staring back at her. The face of someone she had grown up with, and who she'd spent years of her life chasing through trees and sneaking late night snacks from the kitchen with.

Perhaps *he* was capable of murder, but Blythe? She would never move for the killing blow. Instead she stepped toward him, stilling when he flinched back. Silently, Blythe reached her hand forward, waiting for Percy to place his palm in hers. It was a great effort not to shudder at the harshness of his frostbitten fingers against her skin.

It didn't matter what pain he had caused her; Blythe could not bear to see her brother like this. She shut her eyes, summoning her magic to the surface. She'd never healed anyone intentionally, but that didn't stop her from picturing Percy's hands in her mind's eye, healthy and unblemished as she let her powers flow freely. It was the first time she'd knowingly summoned it this way, and the magic welcomed her with great delight, as though it'd been waiting for her all this time. Blythe leaned into its embrace, flooding herself with its warmth.

"You're the one who broke into Grey's," she said as she worked. Her words held no question, for it was the only thing that made sense. "Even after all this time, you're still angry."

"Of course I am," he spat, and in that moment Blythe saw the extent of his cruelty firsthand. "It was *mine*, Blythe. All these years, it was meant to be mine. I shouldn't have had it taken away just because our father lost his mind."

Her brother had become a fool. A heartless, callous fool.

"You have a son," she said, feeling the need to tell him. "With Eliza Wakefield. She was forced to marry Byron when you disappeared, and he's claimed the child as his own. He thinks you're dead, but he hasn't been able to confirm it."

The tremors in Percy's hand paused, if only for a moment. "A son? I hadn't even known she was pregnant." His laugh was not a joyous sound but as hollow and haunted as the halls surrounding them. "Has it truly been that long since..."

"Since you died?" she finished. "It has."

The magic was harder than she expected it to be. Lines of concentration embedded deep into her forehead as she strained to do something she had done to Signa by accident. Trying to heal Percy had her hands aching. She could barely feel her fingers, and as she drew back to reevaluate the situation Blythe had to smother her gasp. While pink, fleshy skin now coated Percy's formerly frostbitten fingers, the tips of her own were turning gray. She peeled back, smothering her hands in her skirts to avoid his notice.

It seemed the healthier his body became, the worse her own succumbed. The extent of their connection had never been clearer—if Percy was to live, she could not. It was his stolen years that Blythe had been surviving on, after all.

But how Percy even had a body left to return to was astounding. She supposed if the frogs were able to reunite their bones and reform their flesh, then she shouldn't have been so surprised that he could, too. Still, how unnatural it was to be looking upon him.

"What do you remember?" she found herself asking, gripping fistfuls of her skirts to quell her trembling. Blythe could hardly feel the fabric against the tips of her fingers.

"From when I was dead?" Percy was heedless of Blythe's scrutiny as she tried to calculate whether he'd returned taller than he'd been in the past. And had he always had so many freckles on his nose? Her brother may physically have come back, but it wasn't right. Everything she remembered about him was slightly off, a picture painted from memory rather than reference.

"It was cold," Percy continued. "I didn't realize I was suffocating at first, but my body could hardly move. All I remember is dirt around me and my lungs filling with it as I tried to force my way out. It wasn't even a proper *grave.*

"It feels like there are things inside of me, Blythe." At this, his voice began to shake. "Like worms are writhing through me. Insects scavenging my bones even now. My skin... none of this feels right."

Blythe's stomach grew cold. It didn't match at all with what she knew about death, though she also hadn't been present in the garden when Percy died. Still, why couldn't Percy have been reincarnated? Or gone to the afterlife? She needed to ask Sylas. Needed to ask him why Percy was here while her mother was still dead.

But there was no time. The adrenaline of finding Percy was wearing off, and the corners of Blythe's vision were becoming bleary as her body grew nauseous from standing, and she knew she had to make a choice quickly—Percy's life, or her own.

The truth was that Blythe knew herself and knew there was only one option. Yet before she could say it aloud there was a flash of light followed by the most intense darkness Blythe had ever known. Percy screamed, and Blythe was taken up by a thousand threads of gold encompassing her at once. Only as the darkness cleared could

Blythe see that Sylas was upon her brother, gripping a scythe that shone as silver as the moon. He drew it back, only for terror to rip through Blythe's throat.

"Don't hurt him!" she cried, noticing then that Signa was just behind them. Her cousin's face was grave, expression resolute, and she didn't once turn toward Blythe.

"Dear God," Signa whispered, unable to look away from the man before them. "Blythe, what have you done?"

CHAPTER THIRTY-SIX

Aris

Aris had never had a taste for murder. It was, he thought, too simple a method for revenge. But the moment he laid eyes on Percy Hawthorne, Aris decided it was never too late to change one's stance.

Death, however, was quicker, recognizing Percy and sweeping toward him. His shadows pinned the boy to the wall, and Percy's cry was enough to peel the skin from bones.

Before the reaper, he cowered, pressing the back of his head against the wall and trying to turn away as if inches of distance might somehow save him. Poor, foolish bastard. There would be no saving Percy; if Death didn't end his life, then Aris would.

Rage was a bitter poison festering in his veins, fueling the anger that sharpened his tongue and had him thinking through all the ways he might deliver Percy's fate.

"This is who the tapestry belongs to." With slow footsteps Aris pushed past his brother, clenching Percy's jaw between one hand. "A blight upon the world." Never had Aris blazed brighter, such a fearsome gold that Percy cried out as he slammed his eyes shut.

Good, Aris thought. *Let them burn.* He squeezed tighter, only this time it was not Percy's face that he clenched, but his throat, stealing the boy's breath until a voice came from behind him.

"Please," it said, the softest whimper. He'd thrown his threads around Blythe the moment he'd entered the room, sensing a threat, and they bound her like a cocoon. Knowing Blythe, she would have fought against them. Would have raged and screamed and demanded that he release her.

So why was it that her body lay slumped against the threads not as if they were ensnaring her but *holding* her?

"Please," she repeated, and Aris realized then that it wasn't emotion that had stolen her voice. It was pain. He could see it in her eyes, as glassy as a doll's. In her fingertips, gray and trembling as they fumbled to grasp the threads around her.

This was his wife. His lover. The missing half of his soul that he'd searched the entire world to find and had been too foolish to realize was right there before him. She was the sun to his moon. The promise of warmth after an eternal winter. All of that, he knew with certainty. Just as he knew that, without help, this was to be her last night on earth.

"Don't kill him."

The words had barely passed Blythe's lips before she slumped deeper into the threads that loosened their hold just in time for Aris to catch her.

"Blythe." Her name was ambrosia that he offered to the night, praying it would let him keep her. "Blythe, you must wake up."

The room held still, tense and waiting for someone to make a move. It was Death who stirred first, and Aris's heart sank as his brother lowered the scythe of shadows. His despair was a frigid thing, seeping through the room with such force that Aris clutched his bride closer so that she might share his warmth.

"Why are you stopping?" Signa demanded. Her voice was strong despite the tears that rolled down her face. "He's the reason she's dying!"

Aris was certain his brother understood that as well as he did. And were it up to Aris, Percy would have long been dead. Yet Blythe's plea would not stop ringing in his ears.

Don't kill him.

When Death turned toward him, Aris felt the impact strike clean through his heart. He knew what Death was thinking; his brother had always been predictable. Kind and self-righteous, and so damned respectful that Aris had hated him. He'd abused Death because of it, taking advantage of his kindness by demanding he help defy Life's wishes no matter the cost.

Once, Death had listened to him. He had been every bit as selfish as Aris, and look at where it got them.

"I will not deny her again," Death said, though the words held no bite. Not when Aris had already known they were coming.

"We can't stand here and do nothing!" Signa dipped a hand into her pocket, fishing out a handful of belladonna berries. Aris wished in that moment that he were a better man. Wished that he had the courage to stop Signa before those berries passed her lips, knowing that it was what his wife would want. But if Signa was willing to go against Blythe's wishes when Aris could not... well, he wasn't a good enough man to stop her from trying. His threads dove for her, but the attempt was half-hearted, reaching Signa only after she swallowed the belladonna.

The effect was instantaneous. She crumpled to the floor, swathed in Death's shadows. Her chest rose and fell with hastened breaths before suddenly it stilled, and he watched as her reaper form rose to its feet, dark eyed and white haired, and craving the same blood as Aris.

"Signa—" Death warned, but she paid him no heed as she stalked toward Percy. Given his state, he must have been able to see her, for the coward spread placating hands before him.

"Please," he whispered, every quivering word making Aris's lips curl with displeasure. "You don't want to do this."

Signa's laugh was a bitter thing, and Aris wondered how he had ever believed she could be Life, who valued souls too much to ever bring one's ruin.

"Oh, I certainly do," she spat, wasting no time before she lunged, grabbing hold of Percy's wrist.

But he did not fall, and Aris had to shield his eyes from the intensity of a silver light that now shone from Percy.

Death was upon Signa in the same second, and Aris believed it was to avoid Percy's retaliation before a wicked laugh reverberated across the room.

"Hello, darlings." Chaos sang her words as she bounded toward them, buzzing from the thrill. "Don't any of you know the rules?"

Death stepped forward, trying to veil Signa from view. "Do not patronize me, Chaos. I am the one responsible for all those dead or dying."

Solanine hummed under her breath as she flicked a finger toward Percy. "I hate to be the one to inform you of the obvious, but that man is neither. He has Life's blessing. Not even you can take that away."

"That girl stole from Death," Solanine said gleefully, pointing to Blythe, weak in Aris's arms. "She brought back a soul that has been in the ground rotting for a year—a soul, mind you, whose death was the only reason she was able to live.

"Her life is the sacrifice," Solanine continued. "She will pay for that boy's life with her own."

"You can have the boy," Aris demanded. Gently he laid Blythe upon the ground, carefully setting down her head before he rose to his feet and crossed toward the others. "Bringing him back was a mistake. If he's who you want, take him."

"It doesn't work like that. When Life gives her blessing, she extends someone's time on earth. They'll live out an entire lifetime without threat of being taken early."

"It was the same with the horse," Signa whispered. "That's why we couldn't kill it."

Aris hadn't a clue what horse she was referring to, but he cared little for the panic in Signa's voice or the way Solanine's eyes narrowed as she leaned to get a better view of who spoke.

Death fought her off at every turn, but Chaos was fast. She slipped around him until she was close enough to reach for Signa, her hand halted by Death's shadows a mere inch from Signa's face.

"You." Her shock was evident as she strained against Death's

shadows, scrutinizing Signa, from her peculiar eyes to the set of her determined lips. "Dear God, you're the spitting image of Rima."

It was impossible to say whether Signa felt the terror Solanine's magic could bring, but she did not waver beneath Chaos. She held her chin high, challenge in her eyes, and spat at the deity's feet.

"Get my mother's name off your filthy tongue."

Solanine reeled back, as surprised as Aris had ever known her. Yet the shock was short-lived before her head fell back with a mighty laugh.

"Oh, I like you. You've got her fire."

"I wouldn't know," Signa seethed. "I've never met her."

Solanine looked more amused than she had any right to be. "I claim no responsibility for your mother's choices, little Farrow. I was merely there to enjoy the show."

Shadows danced at Signa's feet, flickering and irate. The room was cooling so fast that Aris tensed when Blythe winced from behind him. As much as he would have loved to see whether anyone could knock Solanine on her ass, there was no time.

Aris stepped forward. "We'll find someone to give you. If not Percy, then another in his place."

Annoyed as she was to have her attention spun to him, Solanine scoffed. "I owe your wife nothing. If you want history to repeat itself, then try and save her, Aris. Put on a good show. Because that girl is not mortal, and a single human life will not be enough to exchange for hers."

Aris's nails dug into his palms as he realized it truly had all been a game to Solanine. Blythe had never stood a chance at surviving.

Dread made his feet heavy and his body hollow as he stared at the smile on Chaos's lips, wondering how it could exist when the woman he loved would soon disappear from him.

There was a quiet scraping against the ground as Blythe stirred behind him, and Aris nearly stumbled as he turned to face her. In one shaky step he was beside her, seated on the ground and pulling her against him. He balanced her head gingerly on his lap, and as he combed his fingers through her hair—more like straw by the minute—her eyes fluttered, struggling to open. In that moment, there on his knees as he cradled her body, nothing else mattered. He didn't care that they had an audience. Didn't care that Chaos had descended on them, or who was watching him lose himself as he bent to kiss her, tasting salt from the tears that dampened her skin.

Oh, how he wished to memorize the way she felt in his arms. The way the seam of her lips parted for him and how sweet she tasted.

He would have spent an eternity with her, gladly. Would have spent a lifetime exploring the world beside her.

"Even now you are a thorn in my side, Sweetbrier," he whispered, smoothing her hair away from her clammy skin. "I don't know how you expect me to exist without you again."

Aris did not care as Chaos cleared her throat. He did not care for the weight of his brother's sorrow as it pressed against him, or for the boy he wished would keel over and die so that this nightmare might come to an end. For now he cared only for Blythe, imagining that the two of them were alone beneath the wisteria tree.

"So you know the truth," she whispered with a laugh so bittersweet that Aris felt his heart shatter. "I had hoped you wouldn't figure it out."

"I know," he admitted. "But I loved you even before I did."

Love. That was what he felt for her. What fear had made him avoid for so long. How foolish he'd been to avoid something as precious and fleeting as love. It was not something to be had in secret, or to be held close to his chest and shared only in the safest depths of his mind.

If Aris could go back, he would love her abundantly. Recklessly. He would hold on tight and never let go.

But that was the thing about lessons: They were always learned too late.

Even as Blythe strained to sit up, Aris wished that he could forever embrace her. That this nightmare would diffuse into a beautiful dream where only they remained. His heart stalled when she took his hand, knowing this would be the last time he would hold her.

"I want it to be peaceful this time," she whispered. "I want you to lay me on a bed of wisteria or send me away in a river of stars, as you should have done before."

"I will." His fingers curled around her. "I promise that I will."

Her smile was a withering, feeble thing. It wouldn't be much longer now.

"Take care of my father, all right? Don't let Percy—"

"Nothing will happen to your father, Blythe." He kissed her again, hoping to steal those worries. To soothe her soul so that she might rest easy. "He will have my protection, always."

Although Blythe kept her smile, its edges drooped. "You won't have to search for me this time, Aris. One day, I promise that I will find you beneath the bend of a wisteria tree. Wait for me just a little longer."

He would wait until every last star in the sky had faded from existence. He would have told her that, too, had Aris not felt his brother encroaching from behind.

"Aris," Death warned softly, but he already knew.

Signa stepped between Death and her cousin, sinking to her knees to grab Blythe's hand. "Please don't go," she whispered, holding tight. "You can fight this, Blythe. I know you can. We can find another way."

"Silly Signa," Blythe said by way of answer, tucking Signa's hair behind her ear. "Remember what I said. You are the girl who cannot die, and I am the one who will forever be reborn. Do not think you can escape me so easily."

With Aris's assistance, Blythe used the last dregs of her energy to sit up, attention turning toward her brother. He was still cowering against the wall. The front of his pants was soiled, and Aris's body grew hot with disgust.

He was a worm. A vile, pathetic worm that Aris yearned to squash beneath his boot. He was proud when Blythe lifted her chin, so much braver, so much more powerful even while on the precipice of death.

"I do not forgive you," she told the pathetic creature who did not so much as give Blythe the proper respect until Aris demanded it, his threads winding around Percy's throat and forcing him to look her in the eye.

"You are not the brother that I once knew," she said. "You are not the one that I will mourn. You are selfish and cruel and entitled, and I'm glad that our father was a smart enough man to never give you what you wanted. I hope that the life you've stolen from me provides all that you deserve, Percy."

Aris held her as Death drew ever closer, leaving Percy to scramble toward the window. Signa nearly leapt to her feet to stop him, but hesitated at the low rattle in Blythe's throat.

"Let him go," Death commanded. "He doesn't deserve to be here."

"How long does she have left?" Aris asked, doing everything in his power not to fall apart when Death answered.

"Hours, if we're lucky."

It was a wonder that Death and Fate had ever gotten along. No matter the beauty of a soul or the brilliance of a life that Fate crafted, Death always took them in the end.

For years Aris had allowed himself to be angry with Death, even knowing that he had forced his hand. For ages he had not been able to look his brother in the eye, knowing that both his wife's tragic death and his brother's guilt were of no fault but his own. Grief had threatened to bury him, and he'd had no choice but to turn that grief into rage. To pin it on someone. But Aris knew the truth of it as well as Death did, and yet here he was once again begging his brother to come to his rescue.

"All who live must one day die," Death whispered. "You'll find her again, Aris."

"Or you can save her." It was Signa who spoke, her words hardly audible as she took hold of Aris's arm.

"You are a *deity*," she prodded. "Two birds with one stone, Aris. Do what needs to be done, and save her."

This time, Death heard her. He swept forward with a hiss of reproach. "Signa," he called, but the girl didn't meet his stare. Her eyes bore into Fate's, then flickered once, briefly, toward Chaos.

And he understood.

Aris stood, lifting Blythe with him, and set her in Death's gloved arms.

"Take her back to Wisteria." He looked his brother hard in the eye. "Watch over her, do you understand me?"

For ages they had fought, Aris masking his guilt as disdain. But in this moment, he needed his brother more than anyone, and as darkness clouded Death's eyes, Aris knew that he understood.

"Do not be a fool," Death warned, but Aris wasn't listening.

"Go, brother," he commanded. "I'll be right behind you. And should Blythe die before I return, know that I will kill you all." Aris straightened his gloves, expressionless as he strode past them toward Chaos. There was no inflection in his voice. No anger or grief. Only facts as he looked upon her.

"I will not be bested by you again," he promised as he hurried her to the window. "Of that, I swear on my very life."

CHAPTER THIRTY-SEVEN

Aris

Fifteen minutes had passed since Percy Hawthorne fled. Fifteen long minutes that stretched like an eternity when Aris knew his wife was waiting for him. He would have given anything to be with her for every second of the pain she was suffering, but for her sake, this was something he had no choice but to do.

Aris crossed through the moors beyond Thorn Grove. The Hawthorne boy had stolen a horse and disappeared into the woods bordering the estate, seeking refuge near a quaint cottage. Trailing his finger across one of the thousands of gossamer threads woven through these woods, Fate learned that the cottage had recently belonged to Charlotte Killinger, a young lady Percy once thought infatuated with him, as he'd wrongly believed about a myriad of women.

"Charlotte cannot help you," Fate whispered against the black night. There was little moonlight as he made his way into the forest, though the cottage itself was situated in a small clearing where silver light slipped through bare branches. "She no longer lives here."

A wry stallion that tried biting at Aris as he approached the cottage was all he noticed at first glance. Its reins were fastened around a tree, the knot hasty. On those frostbitten limbs of his, Percy wouldn't get far without a horse.

With each step forward, Fate ran his fingers along threads that only he could see. Threads that showed him the weaving of the world, all a place had been and all it was to become in this lifetime. He saw those who'd lived in this cottage. Felt the beating lives of the trees as he watched every soul that had traversed them. He saw Lillian and Elijah Hawthorne journeying into the forest's depths as he gifted her a garden that would become one of her greatest loves. Saw a heartbroken woman named Marjorie Hargreaves mourn the loss of her son. He turned his head and the vision changed to Signa Farrow on horseback as she rushed toward a fire, then to Blythe arm in arm with Charlotte as they took a turn about the grounds.

He saw Percy, too. Saw how often he'd crept through the shadows to steal the belladonna berries. Saw his nefariousness unravel, premeditated. Most importantly, though, Aris saw where Percy was hiding now.

Percy Hawthorne was not a boy who deserved to live. But Aris was no bringer of death, especially when his wife had bestowed a blessing, accidental or not. But death was not the only way to ensure that this monster never again showed his face to the Hawthornes.

"You cannot hide." Aris was every bit a predator as he sauntered toward a well situated on the outskirts of the property. "Not from Fate." He plucked a blueberry from a thriving bush and popped it into his mouth, sensing his wife's touch upon it.

Perfect. It was perfect.

Situating his elbows on the worn stones of the well, Aris stretched forward to peer down into its dark abyss. Percy was clutching a ladder with hands that shook so fiercely Aris wondered whether he might break it. The legs of Percy's pants and boots were in the water as he curled against the ladder, trying to make himself as small as he could against the shadows.

"Hello, Percy." With his words, every glimmer of the stars and every ounce of moonlight swept toward Aris. He consumed them, skin aglow in light that beamed down. The boy winced, ducking against the sight. "Why don't you come out of there?"

"You're not him, are you?" Why Aris sensed even the slightest hint of relief in Percy's voice was beyond his understanding. "You're not—"

"Death?" Aris finished for him. At his back a million threads wove themselves around the well. "I am much worse."

The only warning of Fate's embrace was a darkening of his molten snare before his threads stretched down the well, forming shackles around Percy's wrists and neck. He did not *yank* Percy out; that would be too easy. Too quick. Instead, Aris took his time, relaxing against the stone as he lifted the boy inch by inch in a casual expenditure of power until Percy was on his feet before him, struggling for breath that Aris barely allowed him to have.

All the while, Aris kept his eyes locked on Percy's. How unnatural they were. How hideous, just like the rest of him. "I never expected we'd have the chance to meet."

Percy's knees quaked. He let out a sound so pathetic that a better man might have taken pity on him. But Aris was no better man.

"Please." Percy's skin was as colorless as snow, the life leached from it just like his eyes. He was an abomination, and as he reached forward, Aris stepped back and brushed off his shirt before it could be fouled. "I never meant to—"

"Save your breath. I know precisely who you are and how much pain you've caused my wife." Aris closed the distance between himself and Percy, setting his gloves aside so as to not soil them before he flattened his fingertips against Percy's temples. One by one the threads surrounding him slackened, and as Aris pressed, they began to rework themselves.

If Blythe wanted her brother alive, fine. It wasn't like Aris had any choice in the matter. But Fate was not kind, and he had no intention of changing himself any time soon.

"This world will never be charitable toward you." Each word was as clear and precise as the next, not a warning but a curse. "You will not be pitied but reviled. All who see you will avert their stares and shut their doors to you. Never will you see any of the Hawthornes again, for you are to run far from this place. Run until your bones ache and your feet bleed, and then keep going. You shall never again speak with your sister or seek comfort from anyone you've ever known.

"You have no home," Aris continued, his thumb grinding into Percy's cheek as he held the boy's face upright, forcing him to maintain Aris's stare. "And you never will. You shall want for everything, yet you shall have nothing. You may not die for a lifetime more, but every day you will wish to. Every day you will ache and want to end the miserable life that you are hereby cursed to. And every night when you are thinking about those things, you will remember me. You will know that I am always there, watching you. And that, if I wanted to, I could make your life even worse."

There was no cottage. No woods surrounding them. It was as if all the light in the world was solely with Aris, who shone with such luminance that Percy screamed as threads sewed his eyes open, forcing him to look upon Fate's splendor.

"You will remember me," Aris whispered, "and with every breath you will remember all that you have done to earn such a fate."

Only then did the threads unravel, and Aris turned away to slip back into his gloves as Percy dropped unceremoniously to his knees. Aris cut a path toward the horse and had barely grasped its reins when he sensed Percy stirring behind him. Half blinded, the boy grappled for a rock that he tried to throw at Aris's head. It would have been a painful blow—lethal perhaps, had it hit a human—but Aris never turned. His magic halted the rock, sending it flying back at Percy as he mounted the horse.

"Best of luck to you, Percy," he said. "You're going to need it."

And with a snap of the reins, Aris was gone.

CHAPTER THIRTY-EIGHT

BLYTHE SPENT THE NIGHT OF HER DEATH SURROUNDED BY THOSE SHE loved.

In the haze of her vision, she'd seen her cousin fending off the reaper more than once, and though she was glad for it, Blythe knew Signa's efforts would soon be wasted.

She was not afraid. Her mother would be waiting for her, and Elijah would be well cared for. She knew deep within her weary bones that she needn't worry. Aris would keep him safe.

Still, she mourned the loss of her father and the relationship she'd only just discovered. Who knew whether she'd return with her memories, or how long they might take to be found. Who knew the type of person she might become in her next life.

"Sylas." Blythe summoned the attention of the gray-eyed reaper, who drew a cautious step closer. "Will I have any say in who I'm to become?"

His voice was a gentle caress of wind against her cheek, and it eased her body. "I haven't the faintest clue. That's your domain."

She supposed it was. Perhaps when she died she would return with all the answers and the knowledge of her power. That, at least, would be a silver lining.

"I have seen reincarnations in many forms," he continued after a beat, as if sensing her dissatisfaction with the answer. "Souls that return as a different sex. People who wish to spend their days lounging without a care in the world and end up returning as a common house cat. Everything in this world is connected by life and death. I have no doubt that you'll be able to return as whoever you wish."

Emotion swelled in her throat, and she was too weak to stop it. It was a relief when Aris arrived, appearing in a flash and taking two long strides toward her bed.

"I'm sorry," he whispered, bending to press a kiss to her forehead. "There was something that could not wait."

Blythe had been waiting for him, refusing to let the calming quiet overtake her until he'd arrived. Now that he was here, she felt as if too much weight had settled onto her body. Like she'd been tossed into the ocean and left to sink.

"It's time, Aris." She hardly had a voice left, her tongue like cotton. Head wilting to the side, her pleading eyes caught Sylas's. "I want you to take me now, before I become any worse."

Was she mistaken, or did his eyes flicker to Signa?

"You are young, Blythe. You do not deserve this." Aris's voice may have been softened for her ears, but the word slammed against her like a current.

"No one *deserves* anything, Aris. We haven't the time to—" Her argument was cut off with the swift press of his lips against hers. No matter how tired she was—no matter how much she wished to shut her eyes and fall into that endless sleep—for this she would always find the energy.

His palm was smooth against her cheek, deft fingers threading through her hair. Blythe made no move to pull away. The longer he kissed her, the more the image behind her eyelids began to shift, the silky blue petals of wisteria falling upon her like droplets of rain. She could see only those petals and a river of silver stars beneath her feet, the current dragging her in, ready to lay its claim on her.

Its beauty had her chest lightening; she could think of no better way to go.

But then the heat of Aris's lips was gone, and the river pulled her under. She floated down it, cold and lost to the world as wisteria fell. Even among its beauty, she felt the claws of panic tearing through her.

Was she gone? Was this what death looked like?

In the distance, voice watery and nearly impossible to hear, Aris spoke to someone who was not her. She looked for him but saw nothing; he seemed another world away.

"She will not die," he said as Blythe's heart sank to the bottom of that river of stars. "You will take me and let her live."

Blythe was a captive in this beautiful world that Aris had caged her within. She thrashed against its constraints, calling for him, screaming out so that he might see reason. But every attempted cry burned as the river pulled her under, singeing her throat. The wisteria had stretched its vines around her neck, holding as she clawed through the wisteria petals that obscured the water's surface so that she could look at the true world he'd hidden from her.

As much as she fought, Blythe could not keep her eyes open for long. She saw only slivers of her husband, who had dropped to his knees before Sylas.

"Balance cannot be restored with a human soul," Aris told him, not once looking away from the reaper. "But it can be restored with mine. Give her my years, brother. Give her all that I am, and save her."

Blythe tried to scream, only for the river to fill her throat, sparing her no sound. Aris had promised not to use his powers on her. He had *promised*, and yet here she was unable to escape his hold.

She hated him. Hated how much she loved this fool of a husband, far too much to let him save her.

Signa had taken notice of Blythe's silent plea for help, yet Signa's face was pinched with determination, almost as if she had expected this. As if she'd been waiting for it. Signa's jaw tightened, and she turned to avoid Blythe's gaze.

Life's heart was a fragile thing, fractured and tentatively mended by an apprentice's hand. But in that moment, it shattered beyond repair.

"This was my fault to begin with," Aris was saying. "I could tell you that I'm sorry, Sylas, but such words hold little weight. Let me prove it to you both. This will not change all the harm that I have caused, but let it be a start. Let her *live*."

She prayed that Sylas would be selfish. That he would ignore Aris's pleas, but Blythe sensed her defeat the moment Sylas's shadows slunk to the corners as if to mourn. To weep.

"I will honor your request," whispered the reaper, who lowered himself to one knee before his brother, slipping off his gloves. "But only if you swear to return to us someday."

Aris glanced once more behind him and at Blythe before answering. And when he saw that her eyes were open, he smiled. There was a glow to his skin, a quiet happiness that made him more beautiful than Blythe had ever seen him. "I do. I swear that I will find you again." He turned back to Sylas. "Both of you." Head held high, Aris reached his hand toward his brother, who clasped it in both of his own.

Every silver star melted away as the color drained from Aris's skin. Petal by petal, the wisteria disintegrated as his body slumped forward, lowered to the ground by the reaper's tender touch. Breath flooded Blythe's lungs, the very pulse of life thrumming through her with such force that the scream that'd been raging silently within her finally loosened from her throat. She threw herself upright onto shaking legs, fumbling toward Aris.

But all that was left was the shell of a man who had once burned so bright.

"What have you done?" Blythe demanded, the earth quaking with her sob. She slumped beside him, cradling Aris's head in her lap as one by one the threads around them winked out of sight. All the magic in the world seemed to disappear with his final breath, and it was as if Chaos was standing over her even then, stealing every ounce of hope and every dream that Blythe had ever had.

But as she folded over him, lost in her tears and her aching, Aris was smiling. And to him, Blythe whispered, "You foolish man. What have you done?"

CHAPTER THIRTY-NINE

THERE WAS NO PRECEDENT FOR THE DEATH OF AN IMMORTAL. There was no knowing whether Aris would ever return. Whether he'd remember her if he did, or if he'd even be himself.

Every morning Blythe stood in her late husband's study, waiting for the motionless tapestries to move. Waiting for color to spill onto the blank canvases, or for the threading of still needles. Because Aris could not truly be gone. He was too powerful. Too imposing of a soul to ever simply disappear.

And yet a day passed. Then three. A week later, and still the tapestries had not moved.

One week was but a glimmer of the time Aris had spent waiting and searching for her, and already Blythe could not fathom how he'd done it. In knowing him, her soul had filled in a way she'd not been able to fully appreciate until the palace was absent of his quips and laughter. She had fractured with his loss, and Blythe wasn't convinced she would ever be whole again.

There was no life left in Wisteria Gardens. There was no magic nor color. The manor had truly been little more than bare stone walls falsified into something grand by Aris's magic alone. He was like one of the sorcerers she'd always read about in fairy tales, seeping magic into every facet of the world around him. And now, without the grand facade, she once again saw every crack in the home's design. Every split stone and unadorned wall that appeared half ready to crumble.

His room was gone. Every piece of art and each trinket that he'd collected remained, but the rest of his bedroom was nothing but stone. A sterile museum for a man who had once burned so bright. So extravagant.

Blythe's room, too, was nothing but an armoire and chair, somehow sparser than when she'd first found it. Even the splendor of her library had vanished, and she knew in her heart that it could only mean one thing—Aris was truly gone, and he was perhaps never coming back.

For weeks after Aris had abandoned her, Blythe could not find it in herself to speak. It was as though she'd forgotten how, unwilling to relearn what it meant to live in a world that did not seep with magic. A world without Aris.

She took no company in those weeks, her windows barred by thorny briars as she relied solely on the meals left at her doorstep to sustain both her existence as well as that of the blasted fox. Day by day she tired of watching the creature paw at his bedroom door. His study. The parlor that Aris had spent so many of his nights in. Waiting for a man who would never answer.

"He's not coming back," she told her one day, nearly a month later, the words fire in her throat.

But the awful creature only inclined her head, blinking those amber eyes that so cruelly reminded Blythe of her husband. She spoke again, sharper this time.

"I said he's not coming back!" Blythe screamed the words that had plagued her all this time. "He's never going to open that door, don't you understand? Not for as long as you're alive, and maybe not ever. He is *gone*, you beast!" With each word, Blythe dissolved closer to the floor until she was on her knees, sobbing.

"He is gone."

She curled her fingers into the ground, heedless of how long she spent there. Minutes? Days? What did any of it matter when time kept moving no matter how much she begged it to stop? It wasn't until she felt the brush of a tail against her skin that she stirred, flinching when a cold nose pressed against her hand.

Blythe stared down at the fox as the animal let out the softest whimper, her ears flattening against her skull. Slowly, she crawled onto Blythe's lap, curling against Blythe's stomach with a tired sigh.

Hands shaking, Blythe stroked her fingers down Beasty's back, over and over again as she dampened the fox's fur with her tears.

"It's just you and me," she whispered, settling herself on the floor with the beast. Her skin itched with vines that seeped from her as if to root the pair in that very spot forever. Blythe made no move to stop them as she cradled the fox close. "He's really gone."

Elijah Hawthorne arrived at Wisteria's doorstep every morning without fail. Blythe never once let him inside, her briar patch growing thicker around the palace each day. Still, that did not stop him from taking residency on her doorstep. Had she not accepted the food he left for her, Blythe had no doubt he'd have broken whatever window or door necessary to ensure she was alive. As it was, Elijah did not press. He, more than anyone, would understand what she was feeling. It was the same pain that had driven him to near madness only a year prior. One that had him drowning his sorrows in liquor and trying to dull the ache with lavish parties.

Blythe's body turned to thorns that tried to bury her into the earth every time she shut her eyes. She could hardly see her own skin, too overwhelmed by her grief to find the will to draw back her powers. Each day she roused only when Elijah appeared, long enough to feed herself and Beasty before once again lying down near the door, listening to her father's updates without ever responding. He told her that Grey's was doing well again and that he was in conversation with a potential buyer, and provided updates on Thorn Grove and her nephew. Mostly, though, Elijah spoke of Blythe's mother, telling stories of their courting and the earliest days of their marriage.

"I knew I would marry Lillian the moment I laid eyes on her," he said, a smile in his voice.

Sometimes Blythe listened through her tears. Other times she'd let the moss fill her ears and the growing bramble consume her as she drowned him out.

She never gave confirmation that she heard Elijah. Never thanked him for coming or allowed him inside even when the weather was at its foulest. But she never told him to go away, either, nor had she forbade the fox from sneaking out and spending an hour getting petted and cooed at.

At first the stories of her mother brought pain, but as Elijah recounted a time that she and Blythe had gotten into the most absurd argument over Blythe's childhood penchant for making a mess of her dresses, only for Blythe to point out that the hem of Lillian's dress, too, was covered with soil, Blythe found herself smiling at the memory. And with every day that passed she tried to listen closer. Tried to slip free from the sorrow that was rooting her to that spot.

And when Blythe finally was ready to open that door, Elijah was there. He took one look at his daughter—at the thorns protruding from her skin and the ivy that was growing from her hair—and wrapped her tight in his arms.

"He is why you're still here with us, isn't he?" he asked, weeping as he held her so tight that Blythe was not convinced he'd ever let go. "He is who I have to thank."

There was no use hiding it anymore. Not when the evidence was there upon her skin and throughout all of Wisteria, its bare gray floors and walls torn apart by roots and hellebore pocking the floor every time she cried.

Elijah took it all in, but he did not flinch. He only held Blythe closer, ignoring the blood that her thorns drew and smoothing his hands over her arms until those thorns disappeared.

"You have every right to be angry," he told her. "You have every right to be sad, or to be anything in between. But you're going to be all right, Blythe." He kissed the top of her head as she fell into his chest, burying her tears in his shirt as he smoothed a hand down her hair. "I know it doesn't seem like it right now, but you're going to be all right."

By the third month, most of the bramble had receded from the palace.

Though the walls remained bare, Elijah's arrival had breathed new life into Wisteria. He'd taken to decorating, bringing paints and brushes so they could adorn the walls in color. At first Blythe had resisted, struck by the memory of her and Aris crafting her wonderscape whenever she so much as touched a brush. But after several days of watching her father tinker away at turning the kitchen walls into a lavender garden befitting the palace's name, she'd tentatively joined in.

At first she started with the parlor, following her father's lead in the kitchen and continuing the theme. Rather than stave off his memory, she let herself channel Aris's likeness as she painted her mother's garden. She let herself be extravagant and fantastical and all the things he would have loved as she lost hour after hour shading the light of the pond. Filling the buds of the roses and sneaking imaginary beasts between the stems. She carved out lily after lily until the walls were no longer bare but full of life. Full of memories that brought her more comfort than they did pain.

And then she moved on to the halls, painting them as she remembered from the first time she'd ever seen Wisteria. For weeks she worked like this, painting as her father cooked or laundered. As he set her up slowly but surely in a home that no longer solely ached with Aris's loss, but had reminders of his life at every turn.

Painting was the only thing to ease her mind, for whenever she was not lost with a brush Blythe found herself sitting in front of a hearth that no longer burned at all hours, reliving the night of Aris's death over and over again. She thought of all the ways she might have prevented it. Of everything she'd do differently.

If only she'd never gotten out of the carriage the day of their wedding. If only she'd never set foot in the garden or hadn't let herself think of Percy and how she wished he was still alive. Blythe hated herself for awakening her powers, because if she never had, then Aris would still be here.

They could have built a life together. They could have been so happy. Instead, she had only a paintbrush and a broken heart.

If only.

If only.

If only.

Sylas came to check on Blythe often in those days, even when she wished that he wouldn't.

She hadn't spoken to him or Signa since the night it happened. How could she, when he was the one who had stolen Aris away from this world, and when Signa had so pointedly turned away from Blythe's pleas?

For weeks Blythe held nothing but rage for them both, though she knew even then that it was misguided. Knew that she would have done the same if she'd been in Signa's position, and that Aris would have been inconsolable if left to suffer such a loss again.

Blythe couldn't fathom how he'd done it. He had waited centuries for her, trusting all the while that she would find him despite never seeing any signs. And here she was only months in, convinced that she was doomed to never see him again.

He had waited. He had *believed*. So what choice did she have but to do the same for him, no matter how impossible it felt?

When a chill seeped through the room and shadows stirred in the corners late one evening as her father slept soundly deeper within the palace, Blythe decided she'd had enough. This time when Sylas paid her a visit, she did not ignore him. This time, she stood and reached out her hand.

"Take me to see my cousin," she said, and without hesitation, he did.

Foxglove was tidier than the last time Blythe had visited. Brighter, too, the springtime sky a cloudless blue. Even Signa looked more put together, no longer bearing heavy shadows beneath her eyes or stains on her dress as she hurried to her feet. She held her hands clasped to her chest, forcing herself not to fret at them.

"I didn't think you'd come," her cousin hurried to say, twisting to glance behind her. "Liam, could you fetch us some tea?"

Blythe shouldn't have been surprised by the teapot that floated into view by a phantom hand that poured its contents into three porcelain cups. Nor should she have been so surprised when Sylas took hold of one, his shadows bending to form a chair beneath him.

"I didn't know you could drink tea," Blythe murmured, to which he shrugged as the shadows leached from his skin.

"Only when I'm parched. Shepherding you around all the time gets exhausting."

Blythe smiled into her cup. For a moment, his teasing had reminded her of Aris. She was glad to see Sylas shed his incorporeal form, for Blythe didn't have the space in her brain to fathom how a shadow could drink tea. How strange her life had become.

The silence stretched among the three of them, no one certain of what to say first.

"What became of Chaos?" It was Blythe who broke the silence, her lips warm from the tea's steam. The question had been weighing on her for some time now, and it seemed the easiest place to start.

Signa's fingers clenched tighter around the handle of her porcelain cup, and Sylas's eyes slid over to her before he answered. "In the game of Chaos, we were the ones who lost. We may not have played exactly as she anticipated, but I imagine the outcome was . . . satisfactory. It's likely she's already become bored with us."

Blythe set her teacup down so hard that it clattered against the saucer. "That's it, then? She's off to wreak more havoc and we're just going to let her go like none of this ever happened?" Blythe turned to her cousin, her fingernails digging into the edge of the table. "You're fine with this?"

"Of course I'm not *fine*." Signa sighed. "I've finished every journal I could find and still have no idea who Solanine truly was to my mother. Not once does she mention my father in her journals until the morning of her wedding. There are two conflicting sides of me—one that wants to see Solanine dead for all the pain she's caused and another that wants to sit her down and ask a thousand questions to make sense of this story."

"As interested as she was in you, Signa, I doubt this will be the last that we see of Solanine." Though Sylas leaned casually back in his seat, there was a hardness in his expression.

"So we just wait for her?" The plan was so ridiculous that Blythe scoffed. "We don't pursue her? Try to stop her? We just... move on?"

"What's the alternative?" he asked. "We make an enemy out of her? Let her pin her sights on Elijah or your friends? Chaos is ever moving. She craves reaction and sets her sights on the next project the moment things become too stagnant. It's not fair, but one day, when my brother returns and you and Signa both have fully mastered your abilities, we will face her again. But for now—for the sake of those we love who cannot protect themselves as we can—our safest option is to let her go."

The truth of his words was more bitter than any poison Blythe had consumed. Yet as ill as she felt, she knew that Sylas's plan was the best they had. At least for now.

"It seems ridiculous to ask how you're faring, but I cannot help myself," Signa began after another awkward silence that Blythe did not help fill. "Is there anything we can do to help you?"

Signa, of all people, should understand how impossible the question was to answer.

Blythe would never be *well.* A part of her was forever lost, and there was no mending the pain of Aris's absence. She could only rebuild herself around it, which was why she had finally deemed it time to pay her cousin a visit.

"I am becoming more myself each day," she decided finally. "Though it's a slow process, considering I no longer know who that self is."

Sylas was right; Blythe still did not understand the power coursing through her or the possibilities of what she could do. She'd tried to magic the front door and disappear elsewhere as Aris had. Tried to transport herself to another place entirely, as was possible for both brothers. But it seemed that was not a skill in Blythe's repertoire.

She had, however, learned how simple it was to breathe life into the world. For any organic matter not involving a soul, she needed only to touch it and watch the world bloom around her. Souls, however, were trickier, and Blythe had a feeling she had a long while to go before she could form them as easily as Mila had, let alone at all.

Which meant that it was time for her to get started.

Aris was gone, but with every passing day Blythe understood that the world would carry on without him, and that she needed to try, as well.

If Blythe and Aris shared a tapestry, the threads would burn red with passion. And though she loved him—or perhaps *because* she loved him—Blythe would not allow her world to stall for another day longer. She needed to believe that, one day, he would come back to her. And when he did, she didn't want him to know that she had spent her time dull and aching. She wanted infinite stories to share.

And so she leaned forward, the knot of grief in her chest loosening just a little.

“I want to learn about my powers,” she told the others. “Will you both help me?”

“We would like nothing more.” Signa wasted no time reaching out, taking hold of one of Blythe’s hands and encompassing it between both of her own. Sylas flinched, surprised when Blythe reached to take his, too, and squeezed tight.

These were her people. Her eternal family forevermore, and for the first time since Aris’s death, Blythe smiled.

EPILOGUE

AT THE EDGE OF THE WOODS SITS A HAUNTED MANOR BY THE NAME of Thorn Grove.

Stories say that the old man who owns it once had a daughter, though none could remember her name. There were rumors, though—ones that said the girl had married a handsome prince and was spirited away to a palace hidden in the mountains, where all who attempted to find her lost their way among endless hedges and mazes of briar.

Others claimed to have seen her once or twice around the manor, her skin forever plump with youth. They claimed that the girl had stopped aging somewhere in her late twenties. That her hair had turned as white as powdered snow, and her eyes as gray as storm clouds. Some thought her a witch and believed that all who slept within the walls of Thorn Grove were forever marked by the devil and made to do his bidding.

Blythe had never minded the stories; she kept a collection of them for her records, filling ledgers and laughing over the myths with her father and cousin as she built a fairy tale of her own design. What she *did* mind was that as the years passed and her face remained unchanged, too many curious minds came to Wisteria Gardens searching for her.

She'd let them at first, inspecting each new arrival for signs of the late husband she'd hoped to lure in with her tales that spread around the countryside. Twenty-seven years had passed since the death of Aris Dryden, and still Blythe wore her wedding ring. The band of light beneath it, however, had not shone since the night of his death.

Each time Blythe caught a glimpse of someone standing beneath the splendor of her wisteria tree she would rush outside, chest aching with false hope. And every time they'd break her heart, having come only to question the impossibility of an ageless girl. To see whether the rumors were true.

Once, a pious woman had come ready to maim, and Signa—who had years of experience with murderous, pious women—had urged Blythe to do the very thing she'd resisted for so long: bar access to Wisteria Gardens by making the palace as much of an impossibility as she was.

From the earth Blythe brought forth endless mazes of hedges where people dared not venture after one too many souls had lost themselves seeking validity in the tales. She rose towering oaks and splendid cherry blossoms, and built herself a briar patch with thorns to which only her father was immune. Well, him and the clever foxes who forever lived at Wisteria—Beasty's lineage was every bit as monstrous as their ancestor and made the palace as much theirs as it was Blythe's.

Every day she hoped that Aris would one day find his way around the briars. That the foxes would carve his path.

That was not to say that Blythe was alone. Signa had become the most steadfast companion, as had Sylas. Her cousin, too, had stopped aging around the very same time as Blythe, simply because she'd decided to.

Signa was happy fulfilling a small fraction of Blythe's desires to travel, though it was never the same as it was with Aris. Signa needed more breaks, her insides continuing to age despite how she looked on the surface. It became clear over the years that one day, Signa *would* die. Though given her powers, Blythe wasn't worried. Signa was something strange, just like the rest of them. Something special, bridging the space between Life and Death for any soul too anxious or unable to pass on. One day, Signa's body would perish. But she would live on at Death's side, and Blythe would have her cousin with her forevermore.

Still, there was not a day that went by in which Blythe did not wish for someone else traveling at her side, whispering secrets as they visited museums or scowling about the pretentiousness of poetry. Signa was wonderful, but she did not burn for the world or simmer with the same passion as Aris. She was far more content to curl up on a couch at Foxglove, which was fine for Blythe every so often, but she yearned to be on the move. She'd built her own stories over the years, finding favorite places that she might one day share with her late husband if she was so lucky.

It would always and forever only be *him*, because Blythe understood now why Aris hadn't been able to move on. He was part of her very soul, and there was not a person in this world who would ever be able to fill the absence that his loss had carved within her.

With every breath she thought of Aris, unable to look at art without remembering how he'd come alive while creating Verena. Unable to eat without observing how the meal would never satisfy his palate. He was in every inch of her home and hearth, and in the very fabric of the world itself. She thought of him even now, as she sat in her garden at her father's side, her bare hands caked with earth. In them she held a small mound that she molded to her will, breathing life into it until another of the strange creatures she'd become so fond of scampered off, some of them gathering bits of branches or flower petals and using them as hair. Pebbles or berries for eyes. They were always so fascinatingly creative.

Blythe could spend hours watching them, though most of the souls never remained long. They would disappear in the blink of an eye, gone to find their bodies. Others were shier, following Blythe as she worked and taking their time to leave her side.

Her father, too, had taken a liking to them. He was an older man now, his beard graying and the strength of his bones no longer what they used to be. His eyes, however, hadn't lost a hint of their sharpness.

He stayed with Blythe most days, a constant reassurance whenever she needed it. There were no secrets between her and Elijah any longer; he knew the truth of who she was and all that Signa could do, and the peace of that honesty between them was worth so much more than Blythe could ever have imagined.

Elijah sat in a chair, tea in hand as he scratched behind the ear of one of the foxes that had curled in his lap.

There were a dozen more foxes that nestled near the trees around her and observed Blythe with eyes that always seemed to understand what she was doing. They never bothered her souls. Never pestered them. Usually, they watched in silence.

Except for that day, when the small black kit in Elijah's lap stood with a sharp chittering that pulled Blythe from her focus.

Elijah leaned back, protecting his drink as the fox paced circles, its ears and tail twitching.

"What's this about?" she asked her father, who was trying to mollify the fox to no avail.

"Perhaps it's heard something."

Blythe brushed the earth from her hands, shifting her attention to the woods surrounding her. To the briar patches and the hedges, trying to sense if they'd been disturbed or whether someone was coming.

But there was no one.

"Quiet, you silly thing," Blythe whispered, soothing the goose-flesh that had prickled along her skin.

But the fox did not quiet, nor did it move closer to the trees as Blythe might have expected. Instead, its head swiveled toward the front door of Wisteria, and Elijah went still.

It was possible the young kit heard a distant sound, or that it had picked up a scent in the air. It wouldn't be unfounded; animals, after all, always sensed things that humans could not.

And yet there was a tightness in Blythe's chest that she could not ignore. She stood as the fox leapt from Elijah's lap and looped a circle around her feet before it sprinted to the front door. Blythe looked to her father, breathless. She expected to see him hesitant. Expected that the hope that burned within her was all in her head. But Elijah's hands trembled as he waved her forward, his damp eyes gleaming bright in the sun.

"Go." His laugh was a joyous, radiant sound. "What are you waiting for? Go!"

Blythe didn't hear what he said next. Her body raced forward of its own accord, following the fox toward a door she'd walked through thousands of times before.

A door that had her stomach dropping to the ground, for on it was something she had not seen in twenty-seven years:

A golden thread.

There was but a single one, so thin and gossamer that Blythe would have missed it had the sunlight not shone upon the thread at precisely the right angle. It glistened, the most beautiful beacon she'd ever seen.

Blythe did not breathe as she picked up her skirts, racing toward it. Hoping and praying and yearning with everything in her that this was not her imagination. That the thread in front of her outstretched fingertips was no cruel trick or a leftover artifact that she'd not noticed before.

But then another thread wound around the handle, and then

another, urging her on until Blythe fell against the door, clasping the handle tight in her hands.

"Take me to him," she demanded, pleading with the band of light on her finger to shine once more. To burn into her skin and forever leave its mark. "Please, take me to my husband."

Shock numbed her, but still Blythe managed to force the door open, not into the halls of her home but in to a familiar town where the tune of the accordion swelled.

On the wisteria laden streets of Brude stood a man obscured by petals that trickled around him with a languid grace, as if time itself had slowed to watch their descent. Blythe drew a step forward, squinting at a face she'd not seen before but whose skin carried the golden touch of the sun itself. There were cuts on his cheeks. His neck, his hands. From thorns, Blythe realized. From the thorns of her briar patch.

Sunlight lanced through the vines of the wisteria, tipping toward the man whose golden eyes turned to Blythe and drank her in like she was his very world.

"Tell me I'm not dreaming," she whispered as the man closed the space between them, drawing Blythe into arms that were somehow familiar. Arms in which she would spend every moment for the rest of her life content. "Tell me that it's you."

His very touch was the balm she'd waited for. The salve that she could never be sure would come as he cupped her cheek in his palm.

"Hello, Sweetbrier." He took her chin in his hand, and between her lips Aris whispered, "I've finally found you."

ACKNOWLEDGMENTS

Wisteria marks my second completed series and my first trilogy, and what an incredible experience this has been. First and foremost, this book would not have been possible without you. Thank you very much, especially if you've made it this far. I have been dying to share Blythe and Aris's story for years, and I hope that you loved them as much as I have.

I want to thank the incredible teams overseas and every translator who has adapted this series into various languages to get it into the hands of readers across the world.

For the Spanish translation, a special thanks to Leo, Mariola, Patricia, Mercedes, Facu, Joaquin, Fran, Maria, and to everyone at Umbriel for being both a phenomenal publisher and a phenomenal group of people. I greatly appreciate all that you have done for me and my books, and have loved getting to know you.

For the French translation, all my love and gratitude to Sam, Janis, Adrien, Vova, and Hélène at Éditions De Saxus. You are some of the most incredible people, and I couldn't be more thankful to have met you. Being in France was the first time it ever hit me that my childhood dreams of publishing had come true. That trip and meeting all of you truly meant the world.

For the German translation, I couldn't be more thrilled to work with the arsEdition, who have put more support behind this series than I could have ever imagined. Thank you for your faith in this book, for so much hard work, and for one of the most beautiful editions I've ever seen.

There are so many more amazing teams that I've not yet had the opportunity to get to know personally, who are wonderful and deserve all my thanks—Artemis Milenyum, Eksmo, Corint, Ikar, Yoli, Plataforma 21, Rizzoli Libri, Clube do Author, Foksal, Vivat, Ciela, Konyvmoly, and Senan. I cannot thank you enough for supporting my books and getting them into the hands of readers across the world.

As always, thank you to the incomparable team at Park & Fine: Emily Sweet and Andrea Mai, for always hunting down information and new opportunities, and for being the best at what you do. Kathryn Toolan, for opening dozens of new doors for my career, facilitating all the foreign rights listed above, and for just being awesome. Stuti Telidevara and Danielle Barthel, who I'm happy to be getting to work with more and whose work I very much appreciate. And of course, all my thanks to my agent Peter Knapp, who helped take this series from just an idea (and one that he made much better) to the completed and beautiful series it is now. Thank you for your brilliant mind, your time and patience, and for always bearing with me every time I decided I wanted to try to add a new book to the series.... I can't promise I won't do it again.

In the UK, thank you to Phoebe, Kate, Lydia, Jo, and the rest of the team at Hodder & Stoughton for all your work in bringing these books across the pond.

A very special thanks to Anissa and the FairyLoot team for connecting me to such fantastic readers. Anissa, your team has been incredible to work with, and you yourself are one of my favorite people. Thank you so much for being a massive support, and always being willing to talk about anime and love triangles with me.

To everyone at Little, Brown, it's been an absolute pleasure getting to work with such an astounding team. This series has been everything I imagined and more. It was the most fantastic group project, and I appreciate all of you.

Deirdre Jones, I'm so happy to get to work with you. You are the best editor and partner for this series that I could ask for, and I'm greatly appreciative of all that you've done for me and for this series. I can't believe that I'm writing this and that we've made it to the end of book 3!

Cheryl Lew, you are just fantastic. It feels like there are some weeks when we're emailing each other five hundred times, but it's always a joy. I very much appreciate everything you've done for these books, and I'm glad to have had the opportunity to work with you on them.

Jenny Kimura, design wizard, thank you for making these books so much more beautiful than I ever expected. Every time I see a new design, I'm constantly blown away. You are such a talent, and I am immensely lucky and very grateful that you've been able to work on this series.

Stefanie Hoffman, Emilie Polster, Savannah Kennelly, Jessica

Levine, Mara Jordan, Alvina Ling, Megan Tingley, Jackie Engel, Danielle Cantarella, Victoria Stapleton, Shawn Foster, Sasha Illingworth, Mary McCue, Rina Guo, Marisa Finkelstein, Starr Baer, Chandra Wohleber, and Jody Corbett—you have all had such an important hand in making this series what it is, and I deeply appreciate each and every one of you.

Elena Masci is to thank for the US covers, and Teagan White for the UK. Thank you both for creating covers for this series that are more beautiful than I could have hoped for.

Kristin Atherton, thank you for bringing the story to life as a brilliant audiobook narrator. I will forever listen to anything you narrate.

Marta Courtenay, thank you for all of the hard work you've put into helping me promote this series. You've been a joy to get to work with, and *Foxglove* was all such a hectic blur that I don't know how I could have gotten through that launch without you.

To the street team, who have been one of the best parts of this journey. Thank you, thank you, for being wonderful, supportive, and for keeping all the early secrets I've shared with you. Getting to know you all has been so lovely.

Mysterious Galaxy, you have been along for the ride on all of my books so far, and I appreciate all that you do. I'm so happy to have such a fantastic local indie and to be able to work with all of you. The entire staff has my deepest gratitude. You all are the best!

To the friends and family who have been there during this journey, thank you for either dealing with me taking forever to respond to texts, being stressed out 90 percent of the time, and for all of the support. And for the friends who also work in publishing, thank you for dealing with my many voice messages whenever the group chat is needed.

Rachel Griffin, thank you for being one of the best people I know. I hope the book made you cry if the acknowledgment didn't.

Haley, for always being the best first reader, and someone I would happily be locked in a room with for a year in a non-creepy way.

To Josh, who has to put up with me every day. Thank you for always being so supportive and for welcoming this strange world of publishing into your life.

To my parents, who have believed in my publishing and world domination endeavors since I was a child, and who do everything in their power to support me.

To God, for making this series everything I hoped it would be for my career.

And to my dogs, sushi, and badminton for getting me through the hard times. You're all MVPs.

Adalyn Grace

ADALYN GRACE

is the #1 *New York Times, USA Today,* and internationally bestselling author of the Belladonna series and the All the Stars and Teeth duology. Prior to becoming a writer, Adalyn studied storytelling as an intern on Nickelodeon Animation's popular series *The Legend of Korra*. Local to San Diego, she spends her nonwriting days watching too much anime and playing video games with her two dorky dogs. She invites you to visit her on Instagram @authoradalyngrace or her website, AdalynGraceAuthor.com.

THE STORY CONTINUES IN